Christopher Hart, writing here as William Napier, was born in 1965 and educated in Cheltenham, Oxford and London, where he now lives. *Julia* is his third novel. His first, *The Harvest*, was shortlisted for the James Tait Black Memorial Prize and his second, *Rescue Me*, was published to great critical acclaim in 2001.

Also by William Napier, writing as Christopher Hart

The Harvest
Rescue Me

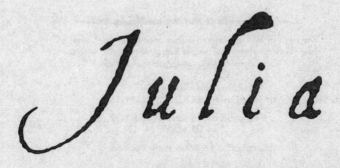

Julia

William Napier

review

Copyright © 2001 William Napier

The right of William Napier to be identified as the Author of
the Work has been asserted by him in accordance with the
Copyright, Designs and Patents Act 1988.

First published in 2001
by HEADLINE BOOK PUBLISHING

First published in paperback in 2002
by REVIEW

An imprint of Headline Book Publishing

10 9 8 7 6 5 4 3 2

The poem on page 350 is reproduced by
kind permission of Constable and Robinson Publishing Ltd,
from Helen Waddell's *Medieval Latin Lyrics*.

ISBN 0 7472 3135 4

Typeset by
Letterpart Limited, Reigate, Surrey

Maps by ML Design

Printed and bound in Great Britain by
Mackays of Chatham PLC, Chatham, Kent

HEADLINE BOOK PUBLISHING
A division of Hodder Headline
338 Euston Road
LONDON NW1 3BH

www.reviewbooks.co.uk
www.hodderheadline.com

For my parents

ACKNOWLEDGEMENTS

Many thanks to Patrick Walsh, agent extraordinaire ('Bombed!'); to Heather Holden-Brown for the original idea; to Lorraine Jerram, Jane Morpeth and all at Headline; to the staff of the Museum of London for their advice and expertise; special thanks to Jenny Hall; to the staff of the London Library, helpful as always; and to Lesley and Roy Adkins for some useful tips and an excellent reading list.

All remaining errors are, of course, mine.

INTRODUCTION

Modern-day London is a haunted city. For beneath its streets and buildings lie the ghosts of many other, far older Londons. The Romans created the new town of Londinium just before AD50. The place grew rapidly; merchants and land speculators saw its potential and the town soon became the largest in the province of Britannia, with fine public buildings and a thriving port.

While a few elements of Roman London are still visible today, other remains lie hidden from our eyes, buried beneath the compacted layers of 2,000 years of human habitation. To bring them to light, archaeologists must dig down, past Tudor and medieval London, to where Roman London lies, some six metres below present-day street level.

While archaeologists can uncover the remains of buildings and artefacts, it is the osteo-archaeologists who really bring Roman London to life by studying the skeletons that are found and comparing the people of that time with us, their modern-day counterparts.

The discovery in March 1999 in Spitalfields of a magnificent fourth-century sarcophagus and coffin containing the skeleton of a young woman aroused enormous public interest: we knew the dead girl must have been someone very special, to be afforded such an ostentatious departure to the Roman Underworld. In scenes reminiscent of the lying in state of a prominent foreign dignitary, members of the public queued for hours to file past the display in the Museum of London. The burial remains on display, along with the head reconstructed for the BBC documentary *Meet the Ancestors*, using the latest forensic techniques to give us a fascinating glimpse of a real-life Roman Londoner.

But science can't do it all. There remain numerous tantalising gaps in our profile of this anonymous noblewoman, who died in the flower of her youth. Inspired by her appearance in our lives, and using all the known facts about her and about life in the late Roman Empire, William Napier has written the exciting and poignant story of 'Julia'.

The rest, as they say, is fiction . . .

Jenny Hall
Roman Curator, Department of Early London History
and Collections, Museum of London

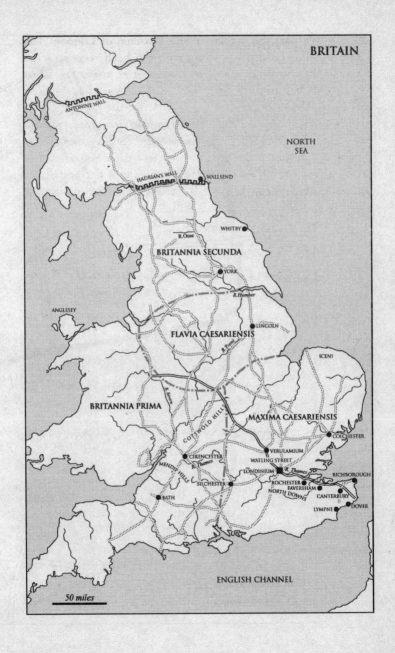

BRITAIN

NORTH
SEA

ANTONINE WALL

HADRIAN'S WALL
WALLSEND

WHITBY

R. Ouse
BRITANNIA SECUNDA

ANGLESEY

YORK

R. Humber

FLAVIA CAESARIENSIS
LINCOLN

R. Trent

ICENI

BRITANNIA PRIMA

COTSWOLD HILLS
MAXIMA CAESARIENSIS

CIRENCESTER
COLCHESTER

VERULAMIUM
MENDIP HILLS
R. Thames
WATLING STREET

LONDINIUM
R. Thames
RICHBOROUGH

SILCHESTER
ROCHESTER
FAVERSHAM

BATH
NORTH DOWNS
CANTERBURY

LYMPNE
DOVER

ENGLISH CHANNEL

50 miles

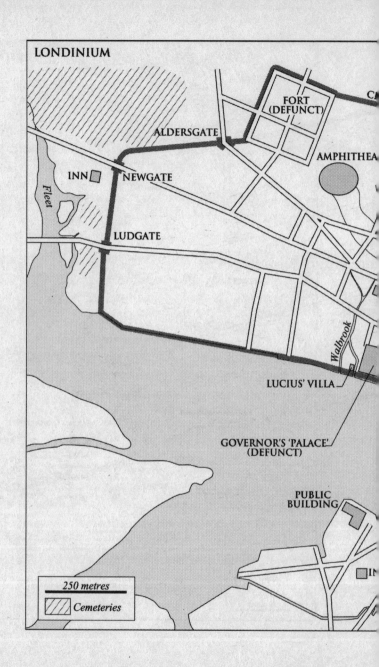

LONDINIUM

FORT
(DEFUNCT)

C

ALDERSGATE

AMPHITHEA

INN

NEWGATE

Fleet

LUDGATE

Walbrook

LUCIUS' VILLA

GOVERNOR'S 'PALACE'
(DEFUNCT)

PUBLIC
BUILDING

IN

250 metres

Cemeteries

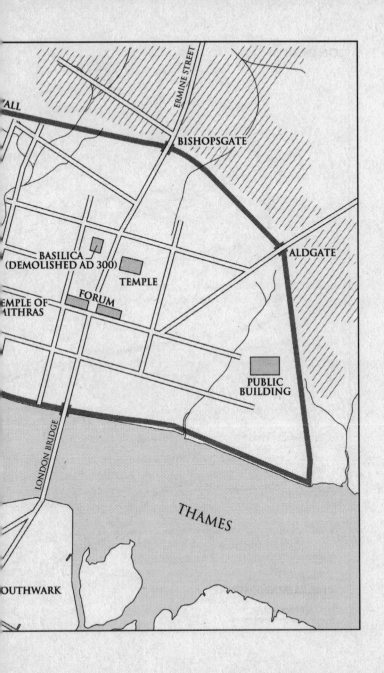

ERMINE STREET

'ALL

BISHOPSGATE

ALDGATE

BASILICA
(DEMOLISHED AD 300)

TEMPLE

EMPLE OF
MITHRAS

FORUM

PUBLIC
BUILDING

LONDON BRIDGE

THAMES

OUTHWARK

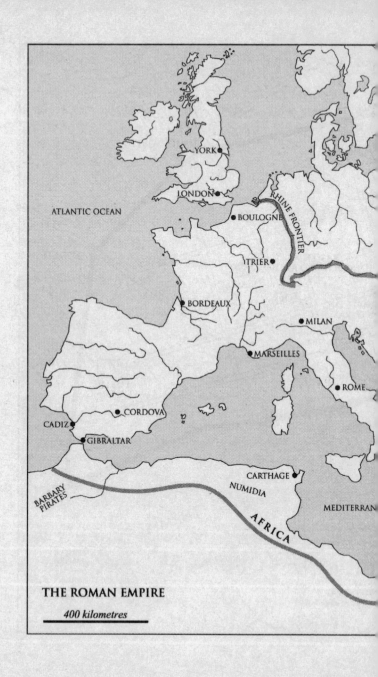

YORK

LONDON

ATLANTIC OCEAN

BOULOGNE

RHINE FRONTIER

TRIER

BORDEAUX

MILAN

MARSEILLES

ROME

CORDOVA

CADIZ

GIBRALTAR

BARBARY PIRATES

CARTHAGE

NUMIDIA

MEDITERRAN

AFRICA

THE ROMAN EMPIRE

400 kilometres

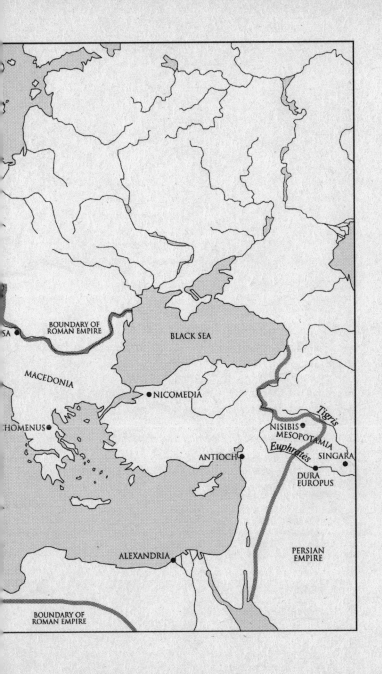

BOUNDARY OF
ROMAN EMPIRE

SA

BLACK SEA

MACEDONIA

NICOMEDIA

Tigris

HOMENUS

NISIBIS
MESOPOTAMIA
Euphrates
SINGARA

ANTIOCH

DURA
EUROPUS

ALEXANDRIA

PERSIAN
EMPIRE

BOUNDARY OF
ROMAN EMPIRE

AUTHOR'S NOTE

A novelist writing about the Ancient World has two options
with place-names: either use the originals, or the modern
equivalents. I have opted for the latter. Otherwise, instead of
'Richborough' you would have 'Rutupiae', instead of Bath you
would have 'Aquae Sulis', and instead of reading without
interruption, you would constantly be flicking to the back of
the book to look at some glossary to find out where these
places were. Personally I find this a tiresome business when
I'm reading fiction, so I have gone for the easier, if less
accurate option. But then an historical novel isn't just about
accuracy, or my characters would all be talking Latin – which
would considerably diminish its readership.

PROLOGUE

Spitalfields, London, 15 March 1999

A bright, chilly spring day. Bishopsgate – the old Roman Ermine Street that ran all the way to York – is the usual hectic blur of diesel fumes and black cabs and red buses: the number 8 running south to Victoria, the number 26 running east to Hackney Wick. The trains rumbling north out of Liverpool Street Station before veering right under Shoreditch High Street, heading for Essex and the flatlands of East Anglia. To the south lies the square mile of the City, the wealthiest square mile in the world, dedicated to London's only true and lasting religion: making lots and lots of money.

The importance of the City makes it a frequent target for terrorists, especially the IRA. Policemen in fluorescent yellow jackets are posted along Bishopsgate and all the way into the City, stopping cars for random checks. A few years ago one of London's most beautiful and historic churches, the thirteenth-century St Helen's, was devastated by a huge IRA bomb.

And so, amid the permanent background hum of pollution, anxiety and money, taxis, buses, international finance and terrorism, all of it caught on the swivelling, panoptic eye of the CCTV camera, Bishopsgate is all very modern this morning. It is all very *twentieth century*.

On the eastern side of Bishopsgate, behind tall wooden hoardings, sandwiched between the road and Spitalfields market, is a building site. Spitalfields is being redeveloped. But for the time being the site is occupied by a team of archaeologists. For in Roman times this area lay just outside the city walls. It was a cemetery. And the archaeologists of the Museum of London's Archaeology Service are hoping for some interesting finds. But nothing has prepared them for what they are about to uncover.

Partly buried in the yellow London clay is the massive stone lid of a Roman sarcophagus. No fewer than five archaeologists are risking back injury to pull it free. As soon as there is a gap, they slip steel scaffolding poles underneath to lever it off. The excitement is palpable. A sarcophagus this imposing must belong to someone very important indeed. A crowd of onlookers has gathered, executives from the development company, builders above on a gantry, even a couple of television crews, who heard only yesterday that the sarcophagus was to be opened this morning. Of course, it might contain nothing at all, or only unidentifiable remnants, brittle bones, time's rags. But then again . . .

The lid was broken in two, centuries ago. There might be nothing inside. They manage to ease off the smaller part and look down. The roar of the traffic stops, the twentieth century vanishes, time's arrow runs backwards. They are looking down at the fourth century AD. Inside the sarcophagus, perfectly preserved, untouched for seventeen centuries, lies a beautifully decorated lead coffin.

Only twice before has a Roman stone sarcophagus containing an intact lead coffin been discovered – and both were excavated in Victorian times, before the advent of painstaking scientific analysis. But the team from the Museum of London has to move fast. Work is due to begin on site, so they decide to move the sarcophagus over to the Museum in its entirety, with the unopened coffin still inside.

Hopes are running high. There is something mysterious about the burial. Around the sarcophagus in the soft clay, they have found unexpected objects: glassware, phials, objects made of jet.

It is four days before they can get the lifting gear in place and move the sarcophagus, and almost another month before they open it. On 14 April 1999, with the gentlemen of the press assembled, at precisely 7.45pm, the lid is prised off. Inside lies a perfectly preserved skeleton. It is a moment, as the museum puts it, 'both incredibly intimate and unbearably public'.

In the course of the next few days and weeks, they build up a remarkable picture of the Spitalfields find, or the 'Roman yuppie', as the newspapers have already dubbed her. Yes, a woman: wealthy, pagan, much beloved and much mourned.

She died and was buried in London. But before long, the archaeologists have made a further, astonishing discovery: she spent her childhood in southern France, Italy, or maybe Spain . . .

PART I

virginibus puerisque

CHAPTER ONE

Spain, AD 340

All the villa was silent.

In the hills round about, the heat haze shimmered on the ancient lion-coloured rocks, and in the burning blue overhead, a single, mighty Griffon vulture circled, and then cruised down and sat on its crag to watch and wait. It preened its feathers, and then took to the air again with its slow and arduous wingbeat until it caught the warm air rising, hanging there in the updraught like a ragged black T, legs dangling loose, a signal to its co-diners that there was carrion in waiting. And then circled again. In time it would be joined by others. Where one vulture is, more will follow. But for now, the lone vulture was content to circle, and watch, and wait. Down in the valley below, in the silent whitewashed villa, death was doing its steady work.

In one of the opulent marble corridors of the villa, under a heavy carved table of Spanish walnut, crouched a little girl, perhaps nine or ten years old, but small for her age. She cradled to her breast a tiny ginger kitten, so young that its eyes were still closed. The girl's eyes were wide open, charcoal-black and desperate. She watched. She waited.

In a bedchamber on the other side of the vast villa, on a high couch, a couple lay motionless. Beside the couch, a small

3

table lay on its side, as if dashed away in a fury. Bowls, and bottles of oils, and purgatives and phials of drugs and philtres lay scattered across the floor. From an upturned bowl seeped a stew of greenish bile. On the bed, stretched taut on his back, lay a man of some forty years of age, strong-featured, weather-beaten, skin hardened by the sun. His eyes were closed. Around his feet, the white sheet was tightly wrapped and tangled, as if he had tried to kick it free. By his side, a little curled up, lay a beautiful woman, her arm outstretched across his chest, her face buried in his shoulder.

Both of them were dead.

The girl peered out from under her table. The silence and emptiness made the villa feel even more enormous and lonely than normal. She shrank back against the wall, into the shadows, and hugged the kitten to her, so tightly that he mewed and struggled softly under her grasp and she relaxed her grip on his fragile bones again.

'Oh, I'm sorry, Barbus,' she whispered to him. ('Barbus' was short for Ahenobarbus, the kitten's somewhat fanciful cognomen, meaning Bronze-beard.) She leaned down and nuzzled him, and he nuzzled her in return, opened his tiny mouth to yawn, crawled in a semi-circle around in her lap, and then fell asleep again after all that effort. She gazed blurrily down at him. 'My best friend in the whole world,' she said. My only friend too, she thought. But she stifled her sobs for the kitten's sake, and let him sleep on. While he slept she made up a story about Ahenobarbus, the Fiercest Cat in the World, who protected her from all the dangerous animals of the night, from rats and mice the size of horses, and who could fly through the night sky with her on his back.

The table was richly carved with figures, little cupids and satyrs and dryads and naiads, and she talked with them for a while, and found out their names and what they were planning on doing next, but after a while that got boring.

4

She hadn't eaten for ages, and felt almost sick with hunger. Just when she thought the gnawing ache couldn't get any worse – that this was as hungry as you could possibly get – it got worse. She even wondered whether her stomach might not get so hungry that it would start to eat itself. She remembered that story about the Spartan boy that her father once told her. Some Spartan boy who had sneaked a fox cub in to dinner with him one night, hidden under his tunic, and not told anyone, because bringing a fox cub in to dinner was obviously a naughty and unacceptable thing to do, even in barbaric Sparta. And the boy had been so brave that he hadn't cried out, even when the fox cub had started to *devour his entrails*. Quite what the story was supposed to illustrate, she couldn't remember now. Something about Spartan fortitude and manliness, no doubt. She couldn't imagine Ahenobarbus devouring *her* entrails. Her mother had scolded her father for the story, saying that it would give the girl nightmares. But her father had just laughed, and ruffled her hair, and said that it would take more than that to frighten his fiery, headstrong little daughter. Her beloved parents, who now lay cold and silent in a distant corner of the villa.

Her only other hope had been her nanny, but she had fled, just like all the other slaves, when the news spread that it was the plague which her father had brought back with him from Africa. The doctors came and stood over him, as he lay there drenched in sweat, his skin as if under a sickly sheen of verdigris, and so horribly weakened that he moaned in pain. That was the most terrifying thing: to hear her father, always so brave and grown-up, moaning and whimpering like a child, curling and clutching his stomach wordlessly. The doctors stood over him, and frowned, and tutted, and then dosed him with purgatives, and bled him, and applied fresh frog skins to his boils, and slices of poisonous snakes to his forehead, 'to counter with their poison the poison that is within him'. And then they had quoted Hippocrates, and Galen, and sighed, and said that it was in the lap of the gods, and through his haze of agony, her father had begged them to go away. Which, with pompous and injured tread, they did.

When she saw the slaves fleeing at last, she ran to her parents' chamber to tell them, knocking on the door, and was astonished and dismayed when her mother would not let her in. Her voice was very weak, and she was tearful too, and it sounded as if she was kneeling on the floor, just the other side of the door.

'Oh my darling, my pet,' she whispered, 'I want so much to hold you, and I cannot . . . you cannot come in. Oh you jealous gods . . .' and she gasped, and slapped her hands down on the cold marble floor of the bedchamber in anguish that her daughter could hear. The girl had crouched close to the other side of the door, too astonished and baffled to weep, while her mother explained trembling that she could not let her in, for fear that she too should fall sick.

'How is father?'

'Oh,' said her mother, 'he is – he is much better, my darling. Yes, he is on the mend now. He still cannot speak with you – but it will not be long before we are all together again, like old times.' For a while she was silent, and then she said that she must go and tend to him now, for she, for *he* – she corrected herself – was very tired. But she told her daughter, that if anything did happen – what did she mean? – that she was to go to her Uncle Lucius: that much she remembered. But where was Uncle Lucius? She had an idea that he lived very far away – further away even than Cordova. She had an idea that it was a boat journey, even.

'Here, take this, wear it always,' she heard her mother say, and from under the door appeared the tiny amulet of Isis that normally she never removed from around her beautiful neck. 'I love you,' her mother whispered to her.

'And I love you too,' she said. And after that she heard her mother no more.

At last she had crept away, baffled and weary and sorrow-ful and full of fear, fixing the amulet of Isis awkwardly around her skinny neck. A day later she went back to the door of her parents' chamber and cried out, and knocked furiously on the door, and when there came no reply, she opened it and went in, and saw her parents lying there on their high carven couch in each other's arms, and then she had understood.

She fled away down the corridor, until she came to the place where the household gods, the *lares* and *penates*, stood in their little niches; candles still burned there, lighting the small, solemn figurines of Jupiter and Juno. Juno, 'the Patron Goddess of Nagging Wives,' her father had jokingly called her; her mother had scolded him for it, smiling despite herself. To one side was a stranger, more alien figure, in blue and green: Isis, a fist-sized bust of her, whom her mother never spoke of except with deepest reverence, and whom her father would never dare to joke about. Now it seemed to the girl that the two, god and goddess, had become her parents, or vice versa: her father, lofty, strong, victorious Jupiter. And her mother, gentle, wise and all-forgiving Isis. The girl touched the amulet hidden beneath her tunic and gave a little bow.

They had all gone now. Everyone but her. They had gone away from this dying villa, and taken her childhood with them. Her beloved parents had gone even further, into the other world beyond where she could no longer reach them. To the country beyond death. To – what was it her mother called it, that time when she was comforting her over the loss of her baby brother? 'He has gone to the land that loves silence,' said her mother. 'That is what the Egyptians call it.' She knew her mother would come back to her in time, that she would hear her voice again, at least. But not for now. For now her mother was silent. For now she felt herself to be the only person in the whole world. And she had no idea what she was going to do about it. And then, in spite of the kitten in her lap, she wept.

Some time in the heat of the mid-afternoon, she was awoken by the sound of distant hoofbeats, which clattered to a halt

7

some way beyond the villa doors, perhaps out on the road. She strained her ears to listen, and after a pause, there came a muffled thump on the courtyard doors. Just one, not the sound of a man knocking. After a further pause, she heard the clattering start up again, and elide into a fading gallop as the horseman departed.

She waited for some time, and then crawled out from under the table and looked up and down the corridor. Then she got to her feet, and set the kitten on her right shoulder, which it accepted equally enough, and made her way down the corridor and into the open courtyard. Not a soul was about. She crossed the courtyard and entered underneath the portico and came to the great oak double-doors. Stretching up, she could just reach the iron bolt of the inner door set in the greater door. She slid it back. The sunlight dazzled her eyes for some moments, and then she stepped outside into the breathless heat and gazed around. Down the long gravel pathway to the villa walls, and the black iron gates, one of them open wide; and beyond that, the vineyards, and olive groves and almond and orange groves, and in the distance, that view that never failed to make her heart leap, but now seemed to hold out some extra promise, now that the villa behind her was so very dead – beyond that, the sparkle of the far-off sea.

But how to get there? Where to go? Oh, what to do? And then something caught her eye. High in the great door over her head was planted an arrow. That was what the thump must have been. Around the shaft of the arrow she could see a piece of tightly-wrapped parchment. She could never reach it, so she went back inside and retrieved a chair. She stood first on its seat, but it was still too low, so then, more precariously, she stood up on its back (Ahenobarbus still clinging tightly to her shoulder), and stretching up, just managed to tear the parchment away from the arrow shaft, and dropped back down to the ground. She unrolled the parchment and read it.

JULIA

She had never heard the phrase 'on pain of death' before, but she understood it well enough. It meant she had to stay here, on her own, forever. In a daze, hardly knowing what she was doing, she climbed back on to the chair and neatly replaced the parchment around the arrow-shaft. Then she carried the chair back inside, closed the door behind her, and went to find a bed to sleep on. Curled up on her side with the kitten in her arms, she hoped she would never wake up until she was with her mother and father again.

She awoke in a cold sweat, trembling, out of nightmares in which foxes had been set upon her and were chasing her down endless dark corridors to kill her, because she had the plague and they all wanted her dead. As they loped along behind her, tongues lolling out of their crimson mouths, they whispered her name like a spell. She ran past an arrow that was stuck in the wall high above her head. Impaled on the arrow and stuck mewing to the wall was a tiny ginger kitten.

There was someone else in the villa. Staring wide awake and wild-eyed into the pitch blackness of the chamber, and seeing nothing, she knew that someone else was now inside, and moving silently down the corridors. They had come for her. By order of the Provincial Governor. On pain of death.

She couldn't hear their footsteps, but she could hear the sound of distant doors opening and closing, as they checked every room. As they came nearer, she heard their voice, the voice of a ghost. She thought it might be her mother come for her, but no – her mother would not have had to search for her like this. Her mother would have known instantly where she was, would have come to her, radiant, haloed in gold, standing at the foot of her couch, smiling gently, arms outstretched,

9

reaching for her. *Julia*, the voice outside called, in a dry, reedy whisper. *Julia, where are you*? They were only a room or two away now, searching behind screens and under couches, a knife, perhaps, in their hand. She rolled off her couch and slid underneath, her heart thumping painfully, the kitten aware of her blind terror and mewing in response. No sooner was she under the couch than the door opened, and she heard footsteps tread warily across the room, and that dry, reedy whisper again: 'Julia, where are you?'

It was her ancient nurse, Dorcas: not her real name, but one bestowed upon her by Julia's father, as some kind of private joke, which had stuck. Julia had never much liked her, for Dorcas was a sour-faced, sour-breathed old bird, shrivelled and humourless and much given to boasting bitterly that she had been a widow for over forty years, which meant, as Julia thought, that she must be quite unimaginably old. Her husband's early death had left her childless too, but she clearly derived no vicarious pleasure from caring for other people's children. She disliked most people, only tolerated her master and mistress, and beat Julia unmercifully whenever she was naughty – which was, as Dorcas' sinewy right arm testified, not infrequently. But now, grudging and shuffling and endlessly complaining, she had come back to this place of death for her recalcitrant charge.

Julia crawled out from underneath the couch and stood and stared at her, ready to flinch, half-expecting another blow and a curse. But it was different this time. Dorcas gazed at her with rheumy eyes and grim visage, and then whispered to her, almost tenderly, 'Come away, child. We must away.'

She didn't even object to the kitten coming too.

Dorcas had arrived in the middle of the night on a mule that looked even more ancient and misanthropic than she did. Together they mounted up, and set off – not down the valley, as Julia had vaguely expected, but up – towards the mountains. It was just one more bewilderment for the little girl: that Dorcas, her mean old nurse whom she had always thought hated her, should come back here to save her, and take her away, *on pain of death*. But she was too tired now to understand why or where . . .

As they passed out of sight of the villa for the last time, she glanced back, and her weary and defenceless mind was flooded with memories and emotions. She remembered her joy, clapping her hands above her head and running down the path to meet her father, on the day he returned from Africa, resplendent in red and gold on his magnificent Numidian stallion. And the autumn days when she and her mother went out to collect sweet chestnuts, her mother's long white woollen gown sweeping softly through the fallen leaves, like a goddess on Olympus, she had thought, and then returning arm in arm, mother and skipping daughter, to roast the chestnuts together by the fire. Or teasing Dorcas, hiding from her when it was time for her bath, playing tricks on her, and the subsequent beatings. Her father's stories of Africa, and the leopard hunt. Long, boring dinner parties, when she was confined to the kitchen with Dorcas, but also with Subo, the big fat jolly cook who always fed her titbits – and who had fled now and abandoned her, like all the rest, except only Dorcas.

She had found a crippled lizard once, whom she adopted as a pet, much to Dorcas' scorn, and nursed him back to health and strength, feeding him on flies that she laboriously collected from spiders' webs around the villa. Likewise she had discovered Ahenobarbus, not so many days ago, curled up in a corner of the kitchens, mewing plaintively. She remembered the long, lonely afternoons, when she wished for a brother or sister to play with, and had to make do with her imaginary friends, for all the other children round about, as her mother said, were peasants and slaves. When her father was away, her mother too was lonely, silent and sad, praying before the little shrine of Isis in her private rooms. Her dimmest and most distant memories of all were of the years before they came to Spain, when they had lived in Rome itself, and she remembered vast and roaring crowds, and streets, and deafening noise and the clatter of carts and horses and smells; and the great villa on the Esquiline Hill, whose rooms blurred and merged with this villa in the hills of Spain. This villa, her parents entombed within, to which she was now saying good-bye . . .

And then they rode beyond a line of cypresses, and lost all sight of the villa, and that childhood and that childhood's toys and dreams were gone forever.

CHAPTER TWO

It was a night in the high Spanish summer, and the moon and stars were out, the great summer triangle of Lyra over their heads, and Vega the loveliest star in the sky, a chill sapphire, and the mountain paths were clear enough before them. To the gentle amble of the mule, Julia leaned her head forward against Dorcas' bony back and slept.

Half-asleep, she saw or dreamed that a sleek genet trotted across their path, almost serpentine in its movements, delicate nose to the ground, looking neither to right nor to left, before disappearing into the brush again. Half asleep, she was aware at one point of the mule stopping, and Dorcas half-turning to wrap a thin woollen blanket around her shoulders, for the night was clear and they were high in the mountains now and it was the chill before dawn. She felt her legs scrape on thorns and scrub as they passed by, but she was too tired to react. Perhaps she deserved it. Perhaps it was all her fault that her parents were lost to her, perhaps it was just punishment. There must be some reason to such things.

Otherwise the silence lay undisturbed across the land, the only sound the rhythmic clopping of the mule's hooves in the still vast night.

She awoke from troubled dreams when the mule stumbled beneath them, and asked the question that had been the subject of her dreaming. 'Nurse – am I an orphan now?'

'That you are, my pet,' answered the nurse. She had never

called her 'my pet' before. 'But then,' she added, by way of grim consolation, turning a little and speaking over her shoulder, 'so am I, if you think of it.' She turned back. 'We are all orphans in the end.'

The sky was turning dove-grey in the east when the girl next opened her eyes, to find that they were wending their way down to a wide valley, still lush and fertile despite the high summer. It was the smell that had awoken her: the sharp green unmistakable sting of the sea. Her first fumbling thought was that they were approaching Rome – but that was impossible. Rome was far away. Still, this was a big, noisy and baffling city ahead of her, swarming along the coast. She vaguely took in the long dusty streets, packed with mules and donkeys laden high with crates and sacks and amphorae, the street markets and squares, the criers and hucksters, and then finally a great harbour, enclosed by a long wall against the south-westerly winds, to leeward the water as flat-calm as glass. All along the harbour wall, merchant ships were tethered and waiting, as patiently as donkeys. There were noises and shouts in many languages of which she understood none, and men so black that they must come from the very heart of Africa, where the sun burned everything as black as tar, even the earth and the trees and all the animals were black, so they said.

There was a fierce argument between her old nurse and a narrow-eyed, bow-legged, snaggle-toothed sea captain who wore gold rings in his ears and wiped his nose on his sleeve and whose hands were salt-dried and like claws. There was mention of an outbreak of plague recently up in the hills. 'News travels fast,' sneered the captain, 'faster even than those fleeing from an outbreak of plague.' He asked what they wanted to travel to Britain for. At the mention of Britain, the girl flinched and gawped at Dorcas. *Britain*? Britain was on the other side of the world, up in the great grey northern sea, fogbound and rainy and miserable, where all the natives had red hair, and no olive trees grew because it was too cold, and up on the Northern Wall built by the Emperor Hadrian to keep out the fierce tribes beyond, so her father had told her, soldiers wore three pairs of woollen socks in the winter because it was so cold. They even wore woollen socks on their *ears*. Though she hadn't quite believed her father when her told her that, and suspected he might be pulling her leg.

She stood at Dorcas' side now and plucked at her sleeve, murmuring plaintively that she didn't want to go to Britain, she wanted to stay in Spain. Dorcas' newfound tenderness towards her seemed to have evaporated already, for she rounded on her and cuffed her ear, snapping that she would go where she was ruddy well told and be grateful for it too, because there was no one else in the world who was going to look after her.

'Your Uncle Lucius is your only hope – *if* he wants you,' she spat.

Julia let her hand fall. *Lucius* – that was the name that her mother had whispered to her under the door. And London. 'Fly to London, to my brother Lucius . . . if anything happens to us, you must sail to London . . .'

Finally there was an exchange of money, and the mule was led away by a grubby little boy. There were further words between Dorcas and the captain, and a minute later the boy came back and handed Dorcas a water-bottle, a loaf of bread and a bag of dried figs, and Dorcas turned and gripped Julia's hand and led her towards a squat little merchant ship with a great lateen sail and a smaller jibsail, both once red but now much faded by wind and the salt sea.

Their 'quarters' for the voyage consisted of a dark, evil-smelling space under the deck in the prow of the ship, the boards above rotting away and covered with tattered sailcloth to keep out the rain and the sea-spray. 'In the lap of the gods now,' muttered Dorcas, crawling under a blanket and closing her eyes. 'To think at my age I should be going on a sea-voyage to god knows where. If we live, it will be a miracle.'

Julia left her and sat cross-legged in the prow of the boat with her arms around her knees and Ahenobarbus hiding down in her lap, and stared out to sea. The wind whipped and cracked through the ropes above her head, and beyond the harbour wall, the surface of the sea was already tipped with white horses and raked with cats' claws. But she did not feel afraid. She felt numb. Let anything happen, she thought. I don't care any more.

She felt a confused mixture of guilt, grief and exhilaration, as they edged out of the harbour. Then to the captain's harsh crowlike cries, the sailors shimmied up the mainmast and loosened the ropes and let down the great faded red sail. They tacked carefully first out to sea, and then turned slightly and loosened off the mainsail some way because of the strength of the southwest wind. Even so, a billowing gust caught the sail and it cracked out like a stretched bow and the whole boat seemed to creak under the force of it as it tilted to starboard. The boat took speed and within a few moments was bucketing up and down across the waves heading northwest and out past the Pillars of Hercules and into the great Atlantic Ocean.

The salt spray stung Julia's cheeks and when she laughed out loud the wind chilled her teeth even and she had to close her mouth again to keep them warm, and Ahenobarbus burrowed down ever deeper into her lap. From down below, Julia thought she could occasionally hear a groan from her ancient nurse, but she ignored it. It had been good of Dorcas to come back, she had to admit. But she couldn't think why – surely she hated her? Or was that all just grumbling and pretence? Why should the old slave be dutiful, now that her master and mistress both lay dead? Grown-ups were such difficult people to comprehend.

And then she thought of her parents. It was terrible how easy it was to forget about them, from one moment to the next. That she should be sitting here, laughing into the burly, bagging sea wind, her hair flying, her blood pumping, exhilarated and tingling to her fingertips, when her parents had both died not one week ago! She must be a very bad person. Yet at other times, she knew, she would sink back into helpless grief and not be able to move for it. At other times, she could almost believe that when she got to Britain, to the great port of London, her parents would be waiting for her there at the harbourside, her mother with her arms outstretched towards her, and her father standing a little behind and to one side, fists on his hips, legs set apart and firmly on the earth, broadly smiling. And all those memories of groans and greenish pallor, of sickness and death would turn out to be a dreadful dream. Because however hard she tried, she could not believe that her parents were really dead, and that she would never ever see them again.

She reached down inside her tunic and touched the little figure of Isis and wondered if it would all be all right.

One morning when she came up on deck at dawn, shaking sleepiness from her hair and yawning and taking in gulps of sea air, she looked around and saw that the deck was coated with fine white sand. She stared at it, puzzled, and then trotted over to where one of the sailors leaned on the taffrail: a big black sailor called Victor, whom she had given a fig to the other day, because he was the only one who didn't ignore her or treat her as a particularly vexatious article of mobile freight.

'Victor please,' she said, 'what's all this sand doing here?'

Victor looked solemnly down at her, then knelt at her feet and scraped together a little ridge of sand between his great hands and scooped it up into his palm. He raised his hand and tossed the sand up and down in front of her face. 'Africa,' he said, slowly and almost dreamily. 'This sand comes all the way from Africa, little mistress.' He turned to look over his shoulder – at Africa – and pointed in that direction with his thumb. She stared after him, and wondered if she would ever go there. If she would ever go anywhere, except miserable, rain-sodden, fog-bound, red-haired *Britain*.

But then again, she suddenly had the happy thought that if everyone there is red-haired, including the cats, at least

Ahenobarbus would fit in very nicely.

Suddenly Victor gave a gasp of pain and leaped to his feet. Looking round, Julia saw that the captain was standing right beside him, narrow-eyed, a thick vinewood knout raised over his head ready to strike Victor again.

'What the fuck are you doin', sailor? I don't see you working.'

And in a trice, Victor was gone. 'As for you, you little wretch,' added the captain, his eyes bulging down at her, 'you can piss off down below with your nanny. I don't want you around here, talking to my men and wasting their precious time. You're a pain in the arse enough as it is.'

Needing no second bidding, her face flushing with anger and resentment, Julia went for'ard and down below to find her kitten.

He was curled up on Dorcas' chest. Dorcas herself was fast asleep, which seemed unusual at this time of day. Julia bent down and carefully lifted the kitten off her chest and cradled him in her arms. 'Nurse?' she whispered. Dorcas stirred and champed her mouth and then opened her eyes and stared at her. Julia was shocked to see how yellow her eyes were. Then the old woman raised her right arm, very slowly, the effort sending a shiver through her whole body, and gave a pitiful croak from deep in her throat. Suddenly, Julia was very scared indeed. She knew what it meant. 'Nurse!' she cried again, more desperately this time, and dropping the kitten to the ground, she threw herself upon her, wanting to hug her close as she never had done before.

The old woman's breath was foul, like the stench of rotting meat, and she turned her head away from the girl and tried with her frail arms to push her away from her. 'No, child, no,' she pleaded, a look of terror as well as anguish in her eyes. 'Stay on deck, I tell you.' But the little girl clung to her like some climbing plant, wrapped around her limbs in a way that the old woman had never felt before. Despite her sickness, she found the strength to jab the girl sharply in the ribs. The girl sprang back. 'No, girl, I say,' she rasped. 'Stay away from me. On deck.' Exhausted with the effort of this, she let her head fall to one side and breathed stertorously, a rattle deep in her throat.

Hardly able to see through her blur of tears, Julia knelt and swept her hands about until she found Ahenobarbus. She snatched him up and raced up the ladder to the deck and sat cross-legged in her usual pose in the prow, in the slight shade of the jibsail, rising and falling with the sea swell, salt cheeks, eyes fixed and unseeing on the far horizon.

Around noon, the sun at its white burning height, she heard the captain's rasping call behind her but did not turn. He said something about her brain frying like an egg in the heat of the sun and didn't she have some head covering? She ignored him. His voice sounded again, closer this time. 'And where's your dear old nanny? Why's she not up here enjoying the sun warming her old bones? Eh?' For it was indeed the first day that the old nurse hadn't appeared on deck. Suddenly the captain's voice turned harsh and he was striding over towards her. 'Don't you ignore me, you little tyke! When you're on my ship, you fucking well answer me or I'll give you a belting, you understand?' He was standing over her now, leaning his whiskery, snaggle-toothed face close to hers. Julia turned at last and looked at him, his face only inches from hers, and said nothing. Then she looked back out to sea. She felt both stubborn and terrified at the same time.

'Well, you're a bold little tart and no mistake, aren't you?' The captain strode over to the hatchway and called down to Dorcas. 'Nursey! Nanny dear! I do hope you're not sickening for something down there, nursey nursey! 'Cos we don't much care for sickness on a boat like ours! Has this terrible habit of getting around, if you know what I mean?'

Absolute silence from down below. The captain hesitated, evidently pondering whether he could be bothered to get down the ladder and investigate, or whether the dried-up, knackered old crone was just having a sleep. He decided it was the latter.

He gave another ferocious glare and snort in Julia's direction, then he stumped back aft and began to beat the new deaf and dumb lad with his vinewood knout. It amused him, to some extent, because the lad couldn't squeal out in pain.

The sun was setting across the Bay of Biscay and the temperature was dropping. The crew had given a collective sigh of relief, for it meant that they had now sailed beyond the range of the hated Barbary pirates. Night fell quickly, and far to the east, as Victor pointed out to her in a soft whisper when he passed her by to let out the jibsail, there was a faint light on the horizon.

'You shouldn't be talking to me,' hissed Julia. 'Your captain will beat you again.'

'Not likely. He's down below, with his mistress in his arms.' Julia looked so puzzled, even horrified, at this – that any man as repulsive as the captain should have a mistress! – that Victor gave a low, fruity laugh. 'Though she looks suspiciously like an empty wine-jar to some!' he added. Then he nodded over to the east again. 'That's the town of Bordeaux,' he told her. 'In Gaul. Stopped there many a time – fine wine they have, too. Far too good for the likes of some.' And he winked at her.

Julia stared for a moment, then scrambled to her feet, her legs numb from sitting for so long, and went down below to tell her nurse that the captain was not only horrid, but also drunk, and she hated him very much; and that they were passing the town of Bordeaux, famous for its wine, though far too good for the likes of some.

But Dorcas was in no state to take an interest in the wines of Bordeaux. The air in the cabin was rank and fetid, and her breath worse, her face slick with sweat, her lips more shrivelled than ever, eyes closed, mouth open, blanket pushed back off her frail body, and her head tossing from side to side and finding no rest. Julia whispered to her, told her things she never dreamed she would say to her, pleaded with her . . . and got no answer. The old woman was beyond hearing. But she seemed to be mumbling something. Julia leaned closer to hear her, and this time, instead of pushing her away for her own good, Julia was jolted forward against the old woman's chest, a claw-like hand gripping the back of her head. The sudden strength of the desperate and dying. Hugging the girl to her withered dugs as if for bitter and wormwood succour. Spittle bubbling on her pale lips, Dorcas whispered about her visions of the future: the last gasp of the all-seeing soul in this world, the unopposable prophecies of the dying. Julia writhed terrified under her grip, as her kitten writhed in hers, but could not break free. And she heard her nurse babble of temples burning and walls crumbling; of rivers of fire washing away whole cities, and great ships stranded on mountain tops. Reversals of nature, and unnatural births. Of a white bird in a dark sky; and of a much greater, darker bird, flying low over a forlorn and desolate country, stooping on some terrified creature, and then caught outstretched in a thorn tree, barbed there, wings outstretched, like a criminal. Like the Christians' own crucified god . . .

'Beneath the surface of the sea,' she whispered, 'great shapes moving, a green shroud, the true Prince of this World, the Sower of the Stars, the Maker . . . moving shapes beneath the water, and burning fires, not extinguished . . . night-time cries, but not of any beast . . .' Julia squirmed under her bony grip, desperate to get away, but could not. 'Child,' the old woman whispered at last, her breath the breath of a body already entombed, 'child, do not go north. Save yourself.'

At last the girl broke free. Sobbing, she stumbled up on deck and found a windless corner to curl up in, and to wonder without answer about the true nature of the Prince of this World, the Maker . . . An orphan under the cold indifferent stars, a small girl huddled under a square of sailcloth shivering with a ginger kitten huddled into her for its own comfort.

She slept fitfully, her fist bunched tightly around her amulet of Isis, dreaming of great shapes moving underwater, and a green shroud, and temples burning, and walls crumbling, and a great bird caught wings outstretched in a thorn tree . . . And in the dead heart of the night she heard a muffled splash, and deep cries out of the ocean's depths, not of any beast.

In the morning, she awoke and crept downstairs to see her nurse . . .

'What have you done with her?' she screamed.

'What have you done with her?' she screamed again, more furious now, racing to the back of the boat and finding the captain. 'What have you done with my nurse?'

The captain, turning towards her from where he had been staring aft, sucking an orange, wiped his sleeve across his mouth and adopted an expression of extravagant puzzlement.

'Why, who, my dear?'

'My nurse!'

'Ah, your dear old nanny,' said the captain sweetly. 'And she *was* an old dear, wasn't she? But alas, you know, your poor old nanny took sick, she did – and maybe you were even a little bit naughty about it, weren't you? You knew that she was a bit sick in her head and her tummy, and didn't tell us anything about it, did you, because you knew we wouldn't like it? We run a tight ship and can't afford to have sick old nannies on board, now can we?' He stopped and stared at her, then said abruptly, 'Stick your tongue out.'

She did as she was told.

The captain stared at it narrow-eyed, grunted, and told her to put it away again. Then he suddenly snapped forward and hissed into her ear. 'Your nanny's gone overboard.' He stood up again and smiled. 'She was dead already, of course. Jupiter's arsehole, we wouldn't do nothing so *barbaric* as tip her over the side when she still had breath in her body, now would we, lads?' He looked around for applause. Some of the sailors laughed with him.

Julia glanced up and saw Victor, turning away and gazing out to the far horizon, and also the tow-haired, deaf and dumb boy, his face a mass of bruises, skulking around behind a stack of barrels.

'Of course we wouldn't,' resumed the captain. 'We gave her a nice, holy burial – wearing hankies over our faces so we didn't catch her fever ourselves, obviously – with a few sacred and sensitive words about committing her soul into the lap of the gods and all that stuff. And then,' he bawled triumphantly, '*we tipped the stinky old bitch into the wawtah!*' And he laughed uproariously.

He continued to laugh as his eyes followed the girl's small figure fleeing back down the ship to the prow, silenced good and proper, so he hoped. His laughter subsided, settled into a strong grin. He'd net a tidy enough profit from this trip anyhow, with the boatload of Spanish fish-sauce, olive oil and wine; and the return journey, with good British timber and maybe some Baltic amber, would do well too. But best of all, he was already feeling the heavy weight of an extra gold solidus or two in his purse, for doing *fuck all*. It would just fall into his lap. Because a pretty little Hispanic girl could fetch a very good price in the slave markets of London.

At dusk she sat in her usual place in the prow of the boat, left well alone by all the sailors on board, even by Victor who she thought had befriended her. There was something about her, they all felt it: it wasn't just the risk of attracting their captain's enmity that made them shun her. There hovered some aura about her, neither good nor evil exactly: almost an aura of power. And at nightfall she slept there in the prow alone, under a heap of sailcloth, shivering, unable to make herself return down below to that place of death.

In the night she awoke – it must have been the middle of the night, and through her sleepy eyes she saw the starstudded sky and the moon already lying on the western horizon and falling. Its light came to her across the waves: to *her*, her only, a broad path of silver on the water, beckoning her, taking her into the sky, there to join hands . . . And she heard a voice, as pure as silver, coming through the night air to her from the stars, and it was her mother's voice, singing the old lullaby that she used to sing to her.

> *A lark falls only for you*
> *Sings only for you*
> *My love my love my love*
>
> *I am waiting for you*
> *For only to adore you*
> *My heart is for you*
> *My love my love my love*
>
> *For only you the sunbeams*
> *The birds sing only*
> *My love my love my love*
>
> *Soon these tears will have cried*
> *All loneliness have died*
> *My love my love my love*
>
> *I will have you with me*
> *In my arms only*
> *For you are only*
> *My love my love my love*

Then there was a flurry of shooting stars far down on the southern horizon, and one brighter than all the rest, and she thought that it was her mother, passing over her, watching over her, and felt safe.

She laid her head down again and dreamed of stepping out over the side of the boat, not sinking and drowning in the dark waves, but stepping out lightly upon the surface of the sea, and walking that wide track across the waters to the silvered rim of the world. There on the far shore the spirits would be gathered, reaching out to take her hand in theirs, and lead her to her mother, her father, her baby brother even, who must have grown up now and be old enough for them to play together. And all her toys would be there too, all her lost toys, left abandoned in the dying villa in Spain. And they would live forever, as the priests taught, in the sunlit fields of heaven.

CHAPTER THREE

Julia awoke feeling cold, and longed for the warm sunshine of the Spanish summer that they had now left far behind. In a great curve, the boat was easing from northerly to north-westerly and then due east, catching the blustering sou'-westerlies full in its lateen mainsail and tilting hard to port all the way. The colour of the sea changed too, from the deep blue of the Mediterranean behind them, to the vast green of the Atlantic, to something greyer here, with less light in it. This was the great channel that separated Gaul from Britain. She strained her eyes; at times she fancied she could see the Gaulish shoreline far to the south, but she could not be sure. Of the fog-shrouded coasts of Britain, there was as yet no sign.

In spite of all the terrors of the past days, and her dislike, already strongly established, of this miserable little northern island to which she felt banished by circumstances, she began to look forward to arriving there and finding the home of her Uncle Lucius. Who he was she had no idea, she had never met him. She pictured him to be very like her father, brown and weather-beaten and crinkly-eyed and with big strong hands to lift her and whirl her around. Then she remembered vaguely that he wasn't a soldier, like her father, but something impor-tant in the provincial administration, and she wasn't so sure that provincial administrators, no matter how important, had hands as big and strong and brown as soldiers did. But she still hoped that he had a very big house indeed, with hot baths, and slaves, and clean clothes, and maybe a pet lizard or two about the place. She couldn't remember if he had a wife or children or not. 'Uncle Lucius: London' was all she knew. Would he know her? He probably had no idea she was coming. It would all be very exciting. She began to describe it all, very vividly and very luxuriously, to Ahenobarbus, who stared at her blue-eyed as she chattered, and looked rather sceptical about whether their destined accommodation would *really* have a pet bear cub in the courtyard for them to play with, and whether they would each have a hundred slaves, to attend to their every whim.

That evening, Ahenobarbus got stuck inside a barrel of anchovies, mewing pitifully, and came out smelling very unpleasant indeed. Fortunately, none of the sailors, nor the captain had seen him there, or his fate might have been grim indeed.

Towards late afternoon on the following day, Julia suffered a crushing disappointment. Glancing up from behind a bulwark where she crouched, talking to her adoring Ahenobarbus, she saw to her astonishment that there was a coastline not far to the north, perhaps only five miles distant, which must be Britain. And there was not a wisp of fog to be seen! Far from being fog-bound, rain-sodden, bleak and barbaric in aspect, it looked positively pleasant. Julia was deeply disappointed. She had expected vast black looming cliffs swept with monstrous waves, and swirls of sea-mist and the cries of forlorn sea-birds, and perhaps the odd blue-painted, red-haired native Briton leaping about in the mist on a cliff-top, shaking his spear at them and yelling some appalling curse ... but far from it. Britain looked positively civilised. A green land, much greener than Spain, thickly forested in parts, and less mountainous. There were rolling hills, and a pale blue sky dotted with white clouds, and once in a wide mild valley she saw an opulent whitewashed villa. Sometime further on, she saw a great lighthouse on a cliff top above the white chalk cliffs, and little figures on top were just firing the beacon for dusk.

Then they rounded the headland and veered north and north west, hugging the coast which was flat and marshy now. They edged between the land on their left, and a great flat island of mud and reeds on their right, which now that she saw it, brought back to her the long hours spent poring over her father's maps in the library. She thought it might be the island of Tanatus, and this the Wantsum channel, that passed north and then turned them into the mouth of the great River Thames, on which the city of London stood. To her left stood a new fort, where the old Arch of Richborough had once so triumphally stood. This was the arch through which all the soldiers of Britain passed as they marched onward to the wild frontiers. Marble-clad, towering forty feet into the sky, seen from far off, it was an unanswerable symbol of Roman strength and military muscle. But then the soldiers had started stripping the arch for building materials to reinforce the walls and fortresses of the Saxon shore, and finally it was demolished to make way for a more practical, if less impressive, army fort.

The estuary was vast and still untamed, the shores on either side far distant and uncertain and mud-strewn, the foreshore was a wide expanse of mudflats and reedbeds. She saw all kinds of birds, a marsh harrier razing low in the setting sun and skimming the tops of the reeds that arched in the gentle wind, and a great ungainly spoonbill that stood on the edge of the water and raked through the mud with its wide, odd bill. She saw a grey heron standing patient and motionless in the shallows spearing fish, and then taking to the air when they passed by, beating its wings with dreamlike slowness. There were flocks of dunlin, and pairs of oystercatchers, a single lonely curlew. To the south, she could see hills arising, in the thickening darkness, and much of that high downland country was still densely forested. To the west, upstream, she strained her eyes to see the city of London, glowing in the gathering darkness with a million lights, like the lights of Rome. Then she remembered that London was nothing like the size of Rome; it was only a small frontier town on a far-flung river, and there would probably be little to see in the darkness. Besides, the west wind was getting up now, and the boat was having to tack laboriously across stream and back to reach its destination. She wondered how much longer they would be. And when the captain came stumping down the deck to the prow to stare out ahead, and roar abuse at another boat crowding in front of them, she plucked up courage and asked him if they would arrive in London before nightfall.

The captain turned and stared at her, with such coldness in his eyes that she shivered under them.

'Never you worry, my lady,' he said. 'We'll get you there just in time for the market at dawn tomorrow.'

'But I don't want to go to the market,' said Julia, puzzled. 'I haven't any money to spend anyway.'

The captain chortled. 'Jupiter's arse, *what* a little lady.' Then he glanced aft and shouted out for someone to bring him a piece of rope. One of the crew brought a length of coarse hemp, and before Julia knew what was happening, the captain had wrenched her arms behind her back and ordered the sailor to bind her wrists as tightly as he could. 'Nothing but trouble, this one, I just know it,' he growled. 'Best have her tied up till we offload her for good.'

Julia kicked and screamed and spat, and got in one good bite on the sailor's bulging upper arm, which clearly startled him, and threatened to tell her Uncle Lucius, who would have them all crucified all the way along the road to London. At which the captain roared with laughter, and repeated the words 'Uncle Lucius' in a girlish lisp, and ordered the sailor to bind her wrists even more tightly. When he had finished, the captain lifted Julia bodily and pushed her against the foremast, so that the ropes around her wrists snagged on one of the rope-hooks there and she was held fast, her arms twisted at an unnatural angle and aching abominably.

'Curse you!' she whispered at the captain, as he turned to leave her.

He stopped, theatrically, slowly turned, and came close to her again, leaning down. 'What did you say?'

She said no more.

The last thing Julia saw, before she fell into shallow and pained sleep, hanging there on the mast half-suspended by her wrists, was a small ginger kitten slipping inside a barrel of anchovies.

At dawn the captain came down the deck to the foresail to taunt the girl some more, and also to toss a bucket of cold water over her, by way of making her nice and clean and presentable for the slave market. All he found was a tangle of rope on a hook, a little bloodstained and chewed. But what had broken it was a clean knife-cut that had slit it in pieces with a single thrust or two.

The captain flinched at the sinking feeling in his heart, and even worse, the empty feeling in his pocket. She'd have fetched at least a solidus, maybe two. He leaned heavily on the taffrail and stared out across the river to the gravel islands to the south. Still, he reflected: there was no way a skinny little tyke like that would have made it to the shore. She must have drowned. And somewhat cheered by that thought, he made his way back aft, where he found Victor crouching over a little block of wood, whittling it with his knife, and gave him a violent blow across his back with his vinewood knout. Just in case. Victor paused, froze, did not look round. And then, when the pain had subsided a little, he continued with his work.

The captain stomped away.

In the distance upstream they could see the long stretch of the bridge across the unbanked river, half a mile long and a ten-minute walk with an ox-cart. The river was on the ebb-tide which made it harder to come into the river's edge, but safer once there, because at least the currents wouldn't carry you back and dash you on the bridge's great stone piers through which the dark waters rushed. To their right arose the city of London, on a modest two hills, unlike the seven hills of Rome, but an impressive little provincial capital nonetheless.

The sea-going ship was too deep-draughted for mooring. The captain himself navigated the ship into midstream, skilfully wielding the twin steering oars at the back, and ordered the anchor to be let down. Then he let the ship drift back and the anchor lodged fast. Small boats were lowered, loaded up and rowed out to the dockside, which was buffered with timbers and great canvas sacks stuffed with wool. As the boats bumped to a halt, the crew jumped ashore and tied up, one rope fore and one aft. Then they began to unload onto the dockside, while the captain haggled with a local official over which wharf they should be using. There seemed to be some mix-up. Soon enough, however, a plump merchant, a Greek called Diogenes, came waddling down in person and after a cursory inspection of the goods, nodded to his steward and declared that all was in order. They were to unload into wharf number five. Then off came the amphorae of oil, and anchovies, and garum – the fish sauce used in cookery all over the Empire. The steward ticked each item off on his tablet, and finally agreed that the tally, at least, was satisfactory. The plump merchant, however, demanded a look at the goods at random, and indicated a barrel of anchovies. One of the crew came forward and prised off the lid of a barrel with an iron wrench . . .

It was hard to say who was more surprised when a small girl stood up out of the barrel, a kitten clinging to her breast. Before any of them could do anything about it, she vaulted over the side and dashed for the end of the dockside, just beneath the bridge, where she stopped and looked back.

'You little bitch,' growled the captain, furious at having been tricked. 'You come back here to your master, or by

Jupiter I'll have you beaten half to death for a runaway slave.'

'I'm not a slave,' she shouted back at him. 'I'm not a slave, I don't belong to you, I don't belong to *anyone*.'

Backing away, she held her finger out towards the captain who, having grabbed the iron wrench off one of his crew, was making towards her. She held her skinny forefinger out and pointed straight at him, as a crowd gathered to watch this exciting bit of street theatre.

The little girl looked up at him from under her tousled, salt-tangled hair, and fixed her huge dark eyes on him. He saw that she was quite unafraid of him. He also saw the little amulet of Isis hanging free around her throat. 'Curse you,' she said softly, unhurriedly. 'If you come any closer to me, I will tear your eyes out. And if you kill me, my spirit will haunt you and your children and your children's children for all eternity.'

The captain stopped. He couldn't move.

The girl turned and ran, up the slope to the foot of the bridge and then right, into the babbling, teeming heart of the city. The captain watched her go, a small, dark-haired figure, fierce and vehement like him, but not yet embittered and parched in her soul, not yet twisted as he was into the same shape as the twisted and fallen world. He envied her, hated her. He wanted to forget her. She was too much like what he had once been.

After a while she stopped running and looked back. No one was following her. The city was large and populous, and she felt safe now. No one would look twice at a filthy little girl with a ginger kitten (very sleepy now, on account of having gorged himself, for the second night running, on far too many anchovies.) She touched a small stone phallus at a street-corner, one of Rome's universal good luck symbols, and wandered north.

She heard so many strange voices among the dockers and merchants and lightermen, a Babel of Greek and Latin and Celtic and the occasional Saxon and even a snatch of Syrian, she guessed: both throaty and nasal. But as she passed into the city proper, all she heard soon enough was Latin, spoken more slowly here than in her native Spain, and with a peculiar lilting tone that sounded very strange to her.

She was making her way up a narrow street between tall houses, sloping upwards to the forum, under striped awnings where shops were selling their wares, when she felt a plucking at her sleeve. She looked round and at the sight of him, her fists flew and she punched him hard on his startled, retreating chin. It was the tow-haired deaf and dumb boy from the ship – so they were still in pursuit of her after all! She turned away from him to run, and felt again his pull, his bunched fist holding the edge of her tunic. She whipped back on him.

'Let me go you little louse!' she yelled. 'Have you any idea who I am? Just wait till my Uncle Lucius hears about this, he'll whip the skin off your back! He'll have you crucified – upside down – and then set on fire!' She was just getting into her stride, thinking up further tortures for the boy, not one of which, of course, he could hear, when it occurred to her that perhaps all was not as it seemed. Why would they send this useless boy after her? Where were the others? And what on earth did that gesturing mean?

The boy was pointing to himself with his left hand, his right still clinging to her tunic – and then pointing at her, and then twining his middle and forefingers closely together and nodding vigorously and smiling. Finally she understood. He wasn't trying to capture her and take her back. He wanted to go with her.

She detached herself from his grasp and sighed, in what sounded to her a pleasingly grown-up, world-weary, just slightly cynical sort of way. Then she took him by the arm and dragged him into an even narrower, darker side street and crouched down beside him. 'Look – I'm very glad you escaped from that pig of a captain and all that, but you can't go with me. I'm going to see my Uncle Lucius who's very rich and lives in the biggest house in Britain with over a thousand slaves and a pet bear cub in the courtyard, and he just won't want you as well, because, well frankly, you smell rather, and you're deaf and dumb and really not much good to anyone. But I wish you well, Isis protect you and all that. Now, you go that way' – she pointed vaguely west – 'and I'm going this way. Best of luck.'

She turned and made her way up the hill towards the broad light of the forum. Glancing back she saw that the boy was trotting obediently after her like a little puppy. 'Oh, will you go *away*!' she yelled at him, before realising that it was no good shouting. A shout was much like a whisper to a deaf boy: just another shade of silence. She sighed again, more crossly this time. 'Oh, do what you want,' she said. 'But Uncle Lucius will have no use for you, I warn you. He's got more than a thousand slaves as it is, *including* deaf ones, blind ones, ones with no arms and legs, ones that can juggle with their noses, blue ones with red hair who are Ancient Britons, one with a head like a fish, and another one who is woolly all over like a ram's skin, and . . . and . . .' Even Julia's powers of invention defeated her at this point, so she concluded, 'Well, he just won't want you, that's all.'

And so the boy followed her up the paved street, dodging the wagons and mules and cursing draymen, until they came to a broad thoroughfare running east to west. On the other side of the street was a long portico, and going through the gates, they found themselves in the forum.

It was all so overpoweringly strange and rich to her, such an assault on the senses that she was bewildered and couldn't have said whether she was enjoying her adventure or not. The straw in the streets, the stink of dung, the soldiers and sailors, hawkers and beggars, the pigs and goats and horses . . . Certainly she quite forgot to ask anyone about where Lucius might live. For now she quite forgot even her own name, she was just her five senses, feeling her way around the new city, her senses alert, as nameless and wild as an animal. The boy was always a few paces behind her as she made her way down out of the forum again and towards the far gate that led out to

Ermine Street and the road to the north.

The two children stopped among the tombs along the road.

It was dusk, and a quartermoon was already rising in the sky. Julia felt suddenly, irresistibly tired. The ancient yews, black now in the dusk, stood around the tombs like silent watchers or mourners, evergreen for eternal life but black now in the gathering dusk. Feeling strangely consoled by their presence, their mutual mourning for her lost parents, under the gaze of those motionless sentinels, she crawled up on to the broad limestone slab of a great tomb and settled herself down to sleep, curled up like an animal. Beneath her, the deaf and dumb boy sat on the grass with his back against the tomb and crossed his hands tightly over his knees. He leaned his head back against the hard stone and gazed up patiently at the moon over the yews, the pale white light whose name he didn't even know. People, when they talked of it, pursed their lips into an O, *luna*, and now he did the same, whistling up at the moon, unable to hear the sound he made, but feeling the susurrus of air between his lips and the magic in it. And as he blew out, a rag of cloud passed across the face of the moon and ebbed away again, and it seemed to the boy that his breath had blown it far and free; as if, for so long powerless and beaten in the world, he had some power after all, if only to move rags of cloud on moonlit nights with a feather of his breath; and he was comforted. For once he felt no ache of nameless longing. He had found what he had always wanted, the girl asleep beside him, the moon-girl.

It was in the heart of the night that the girl awoke with her teeth chattering, unable to believe that it could be this cold in summer. So this was Britain. Only a few days ago, she had been in Spain. It was incredible. But it was also very cold.

Thin clouds had come over since dusk, not enough to rain, but enough to obscure the moon and stars and leave the world as dark as the deepest cave in the mountains of Spain. But there were two lights which she could see, flaring out of the night, and at the sight of them she felt a sudden surge of warmth and even affection for this new city of London which so far had impressed her only as being much smaller and less beautiful than Cordova. For looking southward down the road to the massive walls of London, she could see through the yews the flicker of the two braziers atop the twin towers of North Gate. The orange flames somehow spoke of the warmth and fires and torchlight and homes that lay clustered safely within. And so she slipped off the top of the tomb and brushed herself down and picked up the kitten and made her way across the grass of the cemetery for the road back to London. Behind her followed another – she glanced back in a flash of fright before seeing that it was the deaf and dumb boy, still dogging her every footstep. When she reached the road, she turned right and headed for the great closed gates.

Hammering on the gate with her fists, no matter how hard, attracted no attention whatsoever, and after a while, feeling desperate now and tired and cold and cross, Julia searched around until she found a brickbat in a ditch. She returned and began to bang it against the closed gates with all her might. In seconds an angry voice roared out from the tower above her, 'Who goes there?'

She stepped back and craned up to see, but all she could make out was a shadowy soldier-like figure blacked out by the flaring brazier behind him.

'Me,' she said.

He snorted, perhaps with amusement. 'Well, Me,' he called down, 'you'll have to bugger off home. The gates closed at sundown, four hours ago.'

'But I don't have a home out here. Or anywhere,' she shouted back. 'And I want to get in.' No answer. 'To see my Uncle Lucius,' she added. 'He's very important and has ten thousand slaves or more.' Still an unimpressed silence. 'Hello?' she called up. But evidently the guard had gone back into the towerhouse to warm his hands at the brazier and pass the nightwatch as all soldiers do: in grumbling with his comrades.

Sensing that she was getting nowhere, and suddenly

angered by this obduracy, Julia strode back to the gates with the brickbat clutched between her hands, and rained down a volley of blows on the unperturbed British oak, continuing for a few more blows even after she heard the guard's infuriated voice bellow out again. She stopped and took an expectant step backwards.

'One more sound out of you,' began the guard, 'and I'll . . .' but he got no further before Julia leaned forward and thumped the gates one more calculated time before dropping the brick and dusting off her hands.

'Now,' she said, turning back to her deaf and dumb devotee. 'Get ready.'

And sure enough, as she had anticipated, after a few moments the enraged guard came scrambling down the steps to the gates. The smaller door in the larger two was flung open and there he stood, a grizzled veteran, eyes bulging and bloodshot, hand already raised to deliver a stinging clout to the ear. In a trice Julia had hopped over the threshold and past the guard, dragging the boy with her, and then stood behind him, hands firmly on her hips. He spun round, speechless with astonishment at the sheer cheek of it. There stood the little vixen, asking the way to the house of some Lucius, her uncle, 'high up in the government or something'.

'Lucius,' he repeated with great sarcasm. 'Well, there might just be more than one Lucius in London.'

'But not with the same name as my mother, obviously,' explained Julia with great patience. 'Fabia. He's Lucius Fabius. And then his cognomen is Quintilianus. Their father was also Lucius Fabius Quintilianus. The Elder, obviously.'

It wasn't obvious to the guard at all, and he continued to scowl down at her. Why did these patrician families keep going with this antiquated triple-named system? It was all a joke nowadays anyway. Some of the really nouveau types in Rome, he'd heard, now affected four or even five names, in a pathetic attempt to appear posher than their neighbours, with all kinds of barbarian imports, like 'Lucius Flavianus Aufidius Zenobius

Arbogastes'. It was ridiculous. A double-barrelled name used to mean a nob. Now it could mean anything.

The little girl before him raised her chin with pride – unmistakably ancient, patrician pride – and resumed: 'Quintilian. Like the celebrated rhetorician and orator, author of the *De Institutione Oratoria*, and consul in the reign of the Emperor Domitian, Marcus Fabius Quintilianus. From whom I am in fact descended, on my mother's side. My father, on the other hand, is . . . was,' she faltered momentarily, 'Marcus Julius Valerius, one of the finest soldiers and horsemen in the Roman army, and a descendant of the Julian family itself.'

Grizzled veteran he may have been, but the soldier on duty on the gate that night had never, in all his years of campaigning on the Northern Wall, or on the Rhine, or in Pannonia, experienced such a fierce onslaught of literary and family history as this. His morale vanished.

'You mean Lucius the Praepositus – the Director of the Treasury?' he muttered, staring wide-eyed at the grimy urchin before him, and her even grimier companion. 'He's your uncle?'

'That must be the one,' said the girl confidently. 'Would you take us to him, please? He has over a thousand slaves waiting for our arrival. Probably.'

The guard lowered a bulging eye on her. 'Don't push it.' Then he called up the stone steps to the guardhouse. 'Escorting a . . . a . . .' he hesitated, 'a *person* into the city, to the house of Fabius Quintilianus!' His comrades grunted back their acknowledgements. He turned to the gate one last time, and poked his head out through the door for one last look along the lonely road, to make sure that there were no more diminutive descendants of celebrated rhetoricians out there, expecting admittance at this ungodly time of night. Then he secured the door firmly again. 'Follow me,' he growled.

Now that she felt at last that she was heading in the right direction, and bound for a home of some sort, Julia's tiredness suddenly came over her, and she was only hazily aware of standing with the guard at a small wooden door at the rear of a long town villa, waiting for a slave to come and open up. There were muttered exchanges, and the slave within, clutching a torch, peered doubtfully down at the two filthy street urchins before him: a fair-haired, sottish-looking boy, and a skinny little girl, her hair tangled in elf-knots from the weeks of salt wind, hollow-cheeked and huge-eyed from a starvation diet of bread and water, tiny, and yet strong and wilful somehow, with an element of wildness about her that was both alarming and enchanting. The ginger kitten on her shoulder only added to the impression.

At last, with a noncommittal grunt, the slave allowed both children in and shut the door behind them. He led them down a corridor and pointed towards a back kitchen where embers still glowed in a fireplace, and indicated that they should sleep there.

Julia lay down and was asleep almost immediately, deep and dreamless sleep, sensing a security that she had not felt since long ago in Spain. Beside her, the deaf and dumb boy curled up close to her, ready to protect her against any danger that should come.

CHAPTER FOUR

Julia awoke fuzzily to the feeling of a hand gently shaking her shoulder. 'Child,' said a woman's voice. 'Julia – is that you?'

'Yes,' she mumbled, sitting up and rubbing her eyes and staring around, trying to remember where she was. A dumpy, snub-nosed, shiny-faced woman of forty or so was smiling down at her with motherly concern.

'Well,' said the woman, planting her plump, chapped hands on her ample hips, 'you do look a state, I must say, and you the master's niece and all. Whoever would have thought it? And what have you done with your own nurse?'

'She died,' said Julia with childish bluntness. 'She died and they tipped her over the side. But I think they tipped her over the side *before* she died. They were very wicked men, mostly. The captain was especially horrid, and his teeth were black and pointy like the teeth a woodsaw. And he smelt. And *he's* deaf and dumb,' she went on, getting into her stride now, and pointing across at the boy who was groggily awakening in the corner of the kitchen, 'and no use to anybody, and I told him not to come but he did anyway, even though I stamped my foot at him which often works. And I cursed the captain, and he hit a black sailor called Victor who was nice to me, and there was sand all the way from Africa on the deck one morning, but it tasted just the same as sand from anywhere else when I licked it later when the captain wasn't looking, and we slept outside the walls a bit last night and then met a grumpy soldier. And we passed Bordeaux in the boat too, which is famous for its wines, though far too good for the likes of some.'

The nurse didn't know what to make of this garbled stream of consciousness, and so decided to make nothing of it at all. Instead she tutted and shook her head and said she would have to get her cleaned up in time for her to see the master.

'Did Uncle Lucius know I was coming?'

'Well,' she hesitated, 'in a manner of speaking. Before your dear father passed on, he . . . he sent a letter to Lucius, begging him to take you in if need should arise, and saying that he would entrust you to the care of your old nurse to get you here, if . . . well, if need should arise. But that was a while ago.' She brightened with effort. 'But now here you are! Somewhat travel-stained, it has to be said, but safe and sound, thank the Lord Jesus.' She frowned suddenly. 'What did you say his name was?' she asked again, indicating the deaf and dumb boy.

'I've no idea,' said Julia, 'I don't suppose he has a name. He's deaf and dumb, like I said.'

'Well, you'd best stay here,' said the nurse, waggling her finger at the boy, 'and wait and see what the master wants to do with you, though I doubt he'll want to keep you, he doesn't like too many slaves about the place.'

'Doesn't he have thousands and thousands?' asked Julia, dismayed.

The nurse smiled. 'You don't know the master very well yet, young miss. He's not exactly one for mere ostentation, if you get my meaning.'

Julia nodded sagely, wondering what on earth 'mere ostentation' might look like. And then she scurried along after the disappearing form of the nurse, who could accelerate away with surprising speed, considering her breadth of beam.

'And what's your name, nurse?' she called after her.

'Bricca.'

'Are you . . . that is to say, are you a *Briton*?'

'That I am, young miss,' she said with unmistakable pride, 'as British as Caractacus, I like to say. Although proud to be a Roman too, of course.'

Julia was full of wonderment as they bustled along a corridor to the bedchambers. Her very first Briton! But, try as she might, with many a surreptitious sidelong glance, examining the neck, arms, and even ankles of the amiable Bricca, she couldn't detect *a trace of blue paint on her*.

The villa was not as vast as the one in which she had spent her childhood in Spain, but nevertheless, it was richly decorated and furnished, and entirely new to her, and consequently bewildering. After walking for ages, it seemed, Bricca at last stopped before a door in a secluded corner and opened it. There inside was a small bedchamber, with sheepskin rugs on the tessellated floor, and a modest bed, piled high with soft woollen coverlets.

'The entire villa is centrally heated,' Bricca informed her, raising her nose by several degrees into the air, 'although it is not needed in the summer months, of course. But it *is* one of less than twenty private residences in the entire capital that can boast such a civilised amenity. I sometimes wonder,' she added, in a rather less elevated tone of voice, 'if the master himself really likes the idea of central heating. He often asks for the fires under his own rooms not to be lit, even on the coldest nights. But then, that's the master for you. Now then,' she said, turning back to the doorway, 'I think the first priority is to get you into the baths, isn't it? We'll scrub half a dozen layers of dirt off you in no time, I'll wager.'

There was no reply, and glancing back, Bricca saw that the little girl, fully clothed and filthy as she was, had already crawled under the bedclothes and was fast asleep. Bricca didn't have the heart to wake her. 'Well, you sleep on for now, my poor little orphan miss,' she murmured. 'Time enough to wash away your tears and the sands of Africa when you awake. But for now, little bird, sleep on.' She shut the door gently behind her and departed.

Towards dusk Julia awoke feeling ravenous, just as the kindly nurse knocked on her door and came in with a bowl of steaming porridge. She devoured it in greedy gulps, despite Bricca's warnings about getting a burned mouth. Then she lay back down, licked her lips like a fox-cub, and slept again.

Julia slept for another twenty-four hours. She slept deeply all through that long summer day, and then more dozingly through the evening, when she could hear the bustle of slaves around the courtyard, and the sound of the fountain in the far atrium. At one point there was a clatter of horses' hooves, signalling the arrival of some visitor, or perhaps even the master himself. And still she slept on, waking just long enough to remember where she was, and to luxuriate in the clean sheets and the sudden warmth and security that she thought, only a few days ago, had forsaken her forever. After the traumas and the horrors, the sickness and death of the villa, her parents' departure for that mysterious otherworld without even saying a proper goodbye, after the groans and omens and nightmares of the boat journey, and the captain's evil smile, it seemed to her that at last she had escaped from all that, and here was the haven she had been longing for.

The following morning she awoke and slipped out of bed and stepped softly out into the courtyard. The sky overhead was a clear pale blue, different in hue from the sky of Spain but pleasantly warm nevertheless. She perched on the edge of the pool in the centre of the atrium, the *impluvium* where the rainwater collected, and dabbled her filthy feet in it. She had been told that it always rained in Britain, and so far she hadn't seen *any*. Nor any blue-painted natives. It was all very disappointing. Still, she thought Britain was all right so far. There was mildness in the air, and the people, even the gruff soldier on the gate, seemed good-humoured underneath it all.

Suddenly, she felt a scolding presence at her side. It was Bricca, snatching her by the hand and dragging her off without further ado to the baths.

'There's a lot more of you that needs washing than just your paws, my girl,' she said. 'Now you sit and steam in there for a while and then take a cold plunge, and you'll be several shades whiter by the time you've finished.'

Duly impressed that her uncle's villa had a full complement of baths, Julia sat in the tiny, steaming-hot caldarium for a while, dangling her feet over the side of the bench, and then jumped in and out of the cold pool very quickly. Just as she was about to pull her old tunic back on, Bricca appeared with a fresh one of whitest linen and bundled it on over her head. Then she considered her hair.

'We're going to have to go at that with some clippers, for a start,' she said. Julia protested violently, but to no avail. The nurse cut away the worst, most knotted clumps, and then combed the short thatch that remained until it looked almost presentable. She stood back and sighed, and then dressed it with a little olive oil. Then she told her to say 'Ah', tilted her head back, and gave her teeth a good clean, using a little ball of sponge soaked in vinegar and impaled on the end of a hazel twig. Then she had her rinse her mouth out with some mysterious decoction of mint, aniseed and gum mastic, 'so your breath will smell as sweet as a dove's'. Julia, uncertain as to the sweetness or otherwise of the average dove's breath, was obliged to believe her. Bricca then took her cheeks between her brawny red hands and turned her face towards the light of the atrium, and declared that she was 'almost presentable now'. Then she took her to the kitchens and sat her down for breakfast.

And there, crouched in the corner, filthy as ever, was the deaf and dumb boy, watching her patient and wide-eyed. Julia turned to her nurse, as she set a bowl of fresh bread and some apples and a jug of water before her.

'Nurse, has he eaten anything yet?'

Bricca sighed. 'I don't know about him, I really don't. Of course, Our Lord said to take in the hungry and homeless and treat them as your neighbour, which is all very well, but we can't feed all the waifs and strays of London now, can we? Oh, I gave him an apple, but we'll have to see what the master makes of it. I don't know, I'm sure. Feed a beggar and breed a fever, is what my old grandma used to say.'

Julia pondered these words of wisdom, and decided she couldn't make head or tail of them. So instead she asked, 'And when is the master, I mean my uncle, going to see me?'

'Why, when he returns from Colchester I suppose,' said Bricca, briskly wiping down the table all around her with a damp cloth. 'There's no money to pay the troops up there, and what money there is these days, as you know, is just a handful of copper and no use to anyone. The soldiers want pay in gold, and I don't blame them, and what is your uncle supposed to do about it, if the treasury chests are as empty as a beggar's belly in November, I should like to know? He can't conjure gold out of thin air, now can he?' Bricca shook her head. 'We are in difficult times, little miss, and no mistake. Then he was to ride down to visit the Count of the Saxon Shore, and see the fortifications on the coast of Kent, for you know all about the raids of those heathen, begging your pardon miss, but heathen Sea Wolves and piratical plunderers with their horrible great swords and their long blond pigtails, well I ask you, is that any way for a grown man to wear his hair? Yearly more bold they're becoming, and do you know, you can hear their language, all those ridiculous lisps and grunts, in the streets of London more and more every day. There's a fellow who keeps a cornershop near the forum now who's a Saxon or an Angle or some such nonsense, as bold as brass, says he's a citizen of Rome as much as anyone else, sells amber jewellery and little carved figures of lindenwood and whatnot. And there are a whole lot more, whole families of them, that live out on the islands of the River Lea, catching our fish and our eels, and I don't know about it at all. These people are all very well, but you don't want to feel *swamped*, do you now? As for the prices he charges in that shop! Twice the price of amber in the market, let me tell you! And if you do ever do any business with them, you be sure to check your change, that's my advice to you. No, those people may be all very well in ones or twos, and I'm sure they make very good soldiers when they're fighting on *our* side, but we can't have too many of them, now can we? My husband,' she chuckled, 'he says, if it keeps on like this, in a few more years we'll be living not in Britain but in Angle-land! Can you imagine it!'

And still chuckling to herself, Bricca wrung out her dish-cloth and waddled off, leaving Julia to ponder the problem of inflation in Late Imperial Rome, the future of an ethnically and culturally diverse province of Britannia, but most of all, whereabouts in the kitchen Bricca might keep the milk.

Soon enough, she found some fresh goat's milk in a pottery jug and poured herself a bowl, just as Bricca reappeared. Bricca beamed indulgently and then produced a dish from the cold room with a yellow shiny block on it.

'What on earth's that?' asked Julia.

'Why, butter, girl, to go on your bread!' cried Bricca. 'Don't tell me you've never seen butter before.'

Julia, a girl from the land of olive oil, shook her head. So Bricca, almost speechless for once at the strangeness of the world and of foreign lands where there was *no butter* – wait till she told her husband about it, when he came back from the master's farm in a few days' time after the harvest – showed the poor lamb how to spread it on her bread. At first Julia wasn't so sure about butter, but as it melted over her tongue she realised how delicious it was, and ate a great deal more. At last, pleasantly sated on butter, bread, milk and two and a half apples, she turned and gave the last half to the boy crouched behind her.

'Poor dear,' murmured Bricca. 'And to think he hasn't even

got a name. Surdus, we'll call him: Deaf Boy.'

'Surdus, Surdo,' mused Julia. 'Hm.'

The boy seemed to be able to tell what they were saying, and scrabbling at the thin belt around his middle, he beckoned them over to show them a little iron tag hanging there. Julia jumped up immediately and went to inspect it. 'How odd,' she said, turning back to the nurse. 'It says *Cennla*. What a strange word. Do you think that could be his name?'

'Well I never did,' said the nurse, 'the boy is a Celt after all. Well, there's nothing wrong with the name Cennla, 'tis a fine Celtic name and not unknown among my own people even.'

'Who's that?'

'Why, the Dumnonii,' said Bricca, proudly, 'down beyond Exeter way. There are Cennlas down there too, I recall.'

They both stared at the boy. 'Well, Surdo or Cennla or whatever we're going to call you,' said Bricca at last, 'you stay there and mind how you behave, because I'm showing this young lady round the master's villa, and you'd best not be up to any mischief or I'll lambast you from here to the white cliffs of Dover.' And with that, Bricca took Julia by the hand and led her on a guided tour of the whole villa: to be exact, the Residence of the Imperial Praepositus of the Diocese of Maxima Caesariensis in the Province of Britannia.

First of all, there was a big black mosaic dog on the wall outside the villa to the left of the main door, which they had missed on their night-time arrival. Beneath it, the lettering spelled out – Julia told Bricca, who could not read – '*Cave Canem*. Beware of the Dog.'

'Well I never did,' said Bricca. 'I always thought it was just the name of the house.'

Then, stepping inside, they entered the atrium, with its multicoloured tile floor, and the impluvium in the centre to catch the rain. At one end sat a great iron-bound oak strongbox with an elaborate lock on it, and at the other end arose stairs. These were particularly new to Julia, for the villa in Spain had all been on the ground floor, but here in the walled city of London, where space was more at a premium, the south side of the villa was built up to the first floor, consisting of a narrow corridor and a row of small bedrooms, each containing a single or double bed. Below, so Bricca told her, were the stables and storerooms. They then descended the stairs and passed a modest-sized triclinium or dining-room, and on to the back of the villa where the slaves' quarters ranged along the chilly north side of the villa, beside the kitchens.

Beyond the kitchens was a wooden door, ajar. Julia followed Bricca out into a charming kitchen garden with a flower garden and an orchard beyond. It seemed a lot of space to have in the centre of the city.

'Is my uncle very rich, Bricca?' she asked.

Bricca laughed. 'I don't think anyone knows, least of all him.' She was serious again. 'But I think not so rich, no, for he gives much away. And spends far more on books than seems sensible to me. Well you can only read one at a time, can't you? But of course, as Praepositus, that is to say both tax-collector and paymaster, he controls a great deal of money, which any lesser man would pilfer for his own gain. But not the master. As honest as a jackdaw isn't, the master. But he does have a fine house and gardens, that I'll grant you. Though you know,' she sighed, 'in late years, more and more land within the city walls has turned to waste, or else become a common yard for pigs or donkeys. Your uncle bought up this patch of ground for a kitchen garden and the orchard beyond for less than a tinker's curse. You should see the flower garden in the height of summer, past its best now alas, though you can still see the foxgloves and scabious here and there. In the spring there are daffodils and primroses and bluebells, and in the summer we have windflowers and bellflowers and cowslips and pasque flowers and marguerites. I've even seen the master himself, down on his hands and knees, pulling up the weeds!

'And though the formal garden within the villa is all very well,' she smiled, 'it's out here, among his vegetables and the flowers, and beyond in the orchard among the cherry trees and the mulberry trees, or sitting under that old walnut tree there, that you'll most likely find him of a summer's evening, sitting quite on his own and thinking heaven knows what sad thoughts.'

Julia gazed around the neat vegetable garden, and the flower garden, and the orchard beyond, and thought that it was probably the place where she would choose to come with her sad thoughts, too.

They went back inside the villa, passed through the kitchens and then turned off again and entered the last and most magnificent room in the villa: a roofed public hall. Whereas in warmer climates, the open atrium often served as the main reception room, here something a little more substantial was necessary. It was a magnificent, long room, the floor decorated with the most colourful mosaics, the walls covered with delicate frescoes of mythological subjects; it was heated underground by hypocausts, and all around the sides were ranged long couches and elegant low tables of oak and shale.

Bricca pointed out the double doors in the far wall, which opened, she explained, into the private apartments and the great library and accounting office of the master himself. No one could go in there without express permission.

And finally, returning to the centre of the villa, alongside the atrium was the great peristyle or open courtyard and garden, the heart of the villa in summer, with its columns grown with climbing roses, and borders and fountains, and sundials, and statuary. There were box hedges and little pathways that delighted Julia as she ran back and forth along them, giggling and hiding from Bricca behind pediments and statuary. On the walls beneath the peristyle were frescoes of gods and goddesses, heroic scenes and comical scenes, and at one end, a picture of a very old man with a huge willy being chased by a pelican, which amused Julia greatly.

'I don't know, I'm sure,' tutted Bricca. 'What would the *Bishop* say . . . Still, the paintings here are not nearly so bad as those that adorn the walls of the Vicarius' Palace, so I have heard.' And she shook her head.

Julia stopped running for a moment, breathless. 'So you are a . . . Christian, then, Bricca?'

'That I am, little miss,' said Bricca, firmly, 'like the Emperor himself.'

Julia frowned. 'It's all very confusing nowadays, isn't it?' she said. 'My grandpa remembered when the Emperor was burning Christians in their own churches in Cordova. But that was another Emperor, long ago, wasn't it?'

'Aye, my child,' said Bricca, crossing herself lightly. 'That was in the wicked days of the Emperor Diocletian, cursed be his soul. But those times are past, or so I hope. Let's not talk about such things. Live and let live, I say.'

'Uncle is not a Christian though, is he?'

'Good heavens no, child!' cried Bricca with amusement. 'Not for him a religion of slaves and humble folk such as ourselves, even if it is good enough for the Emperor! No, your uncle's only religion, I believe, is his books, and the service of Rome. Philosopholy, or whatever he calls it. All those Greeks . . .' Her voice tailed off vaguely. 'I can't make head nor tail of it all myself. Well, never mind. I'm sure it's all for the best.

'Now then,' she went on, 'you amuse yourself hereabout, because I have work to do, not least washing the linen. And don't you get into any mischief. We'll just have to wait until the master gets back before we know what to do with you.' And tutting to herself again, she waddled off.

And so Julia began to play in the great formal garden, filled with curious statues of naked boys astride leaping dolphins, and grotesque satyrs peeping out from amid the ivy, and a gentle fountain that trickled beneath the shade of a small holm-oak. She made up stories for herself, of gods and goddesses, heroes and maidens, and imaginary friends, who would keep her company for years to come.

It was late in the afternoon. She had spent half an hour being a woodland dryad and flitting mysteriously between the trees in the Vale of Tempe, and then a while being Helen of Troy, but that got boring quite quickly, because Helen of Troy never actually seemed to *do* very much, did she? Except sit and stare out of the window and sigh a great deal, and send a lot of men to early (although awfully heroic) deaths. And then she had spent at least another two hours being Queen Cleopatra of Egypt, on her golden barge sailing down the Nile, with thousands of slavegirls to wait on her hand and foot, and bring whatever food she asked for, and lots of dresses, a different-coloured one for every day of the week – no, every day of the *month* – and yet all her slavegirls loved her very much because she was so nice and kind to them, unlike most queens who were cruel and imperious. Sometimes she even gave away some of her old cast-off dresses (here represented by the leaves of a chestnut tree) to any slave-girls who particularly pleased her. It was all very regal and satisfying, and time flew by.

At last, however, she tired and grew a little sad and lonely, feeling that the statues in the garden, even if they were silently obedient to her every whim, were somehow not as much fun as real friends would be. And then she thought back to her lost parents, and her home in Spain, and the woods of sweet chestnut where the nuts would soon be ripening. Soon the slaves would be sent out to gather them, to bake them in the kitchen ranges and then grind them into rich flour. But the slaves were all gone, and her parents dead, and the sweet chestnuts would never be gathered.

It was through bleary, tear-filled eyes that her gaze gradually focused on the great grey statue of Jupiter that stood at the end of the garden beneath the covered walkway. She got up and walked towards it and stared up at it: the noble, impassive face, the mighty torso and the arm raised aloft, the Father of the Gods, the Father of Rome, and she thought of him as her own father now, the god and the man somehow blurred into each other. Beyond the statue was a small bust of a goddess on a pediment, Demeter perhaps, she couldn't be sure, carved out of finest Parian marble, with a gentle face and enigmatic smile. And that was her mother. So she trotted back into the garden to pick some flowers to lay before the statues so that they would know she hadn't forgotten them and wasn't playing and just having fun without them but actually missing them dreadfully.

She found some roses, the last of the summer, deep red ones and some smaller creamy white ones, with many tight petals, and had just picked a bunch of them when she stood and turned, and bumped straight into a very tall man in a long white tunic.

'And just what do you think you are doing?' he asked.

Julia held her breath and gazed up at him. The sun setting behind him made it difficult to see his features at first, and cast his face into shadow which made him all the more sinister. He had dark hair, greying at the temples, cropped very close in a rather old-fashioned and ascetic style. His eyes were large and dark but there were heavy lines around them. His nose was fine, but he had further deep lines, deep grooves running down his cheeks, and a wide, thin mouth down-turned in an arc of grim-set pessimism. He towered over the little girl, very tall, almost six feet perhaps. His frame was lean and rigidly held, and he gestured with his arm in the direction of the rose borders as he spoke, with a great rigidity and deliberateness. On the little finger of his left hand he wore a fine silver signet ring. Although she found him rather frightening, Julia could not imagine him ever shouting or raising his voice. She thought he was the saddest man she had ever seen.

And she guessed he was her uncle.

'I'm . . . I was just picking some flowers to put by my – '

'And are they your flowers to pick?'

His even, steady voice, like his gaze, made her feel acutely uncomfortable, and her eyes began to fill with tears. 'I don't know,' she stammered, 'I don't know if this is . . . I mean, no, I suppose not. They – '

'And so why are you picking them? Is this the way to behave in a house in which you are a guest? Is this how you repay hospitality? I cannot believe that these are the manners which your parents taught you.'

'They are *for* my parents!' she cried out fiercely, stamping her foot, her eyes flowing freely with tears now. 'I mean, I was going to lay them at the feet of those statues, over there.' She pointed.

He didn't look round at where she was pointing, but continued to gaze fixedly down at her. 'Which statues?' he asked, his voice suddenly, strangely gentler, more hesitant.

'Jupiter the Father,' she said, 'and the other one, just behind him, the goddess . . .'

'Ah,' he said. He clamped his mouth even more tightly shut than usual, and there was an awkward silence. Julia thought that he was not so angry with her now. At last he said, 'And so you must be my late sister's girl. Julia.'

She nodded. 'My parents died in Spain,' she said, before realising that he must already know that. She wiped her eyes and sniffed. 'And are you,' she hesitated with shyness, for it was already hard to think of this grim and imposing man as her uncle, 'are you . . . Lucius?'

'I am,' he said quietly, already beginning to turn away. 'You may lay the roses before the statues of the gods, as you were intending. Later, before your evening meal, you will come to visit me in the library.' And he went away without another word, already damning himself inwardly for his own insensitivity and stupidity. For Lucius was the kind of man who, no matter how severe he was on the world, was many times more severe on himself.

As he reached the doors leading to his own apartments along the western side of the villa, he paused and turned back, concealed from view behind a column. He saw before him a serious, solitary little girl, kneeling reverently before the great statue of Jupiter, laying red roses down in the sand at his feet, and then rising to do the same before the goddess Minerva: white roses for her, laid at the foot of the pediment, the little girl's large black eyes wounded, her mouth strong, her hands steady as she held them out before her, palms upturned, to petition the gods in prayer for a little girl's dreams.

When she came back into the kitchen, she found Bricca busily packing up some apples and a hunk of bread in a cloth bag, and Cennla, looking more filthy and miserable than ever, huddled silently in the corner. Bricca turned when Julia burst in, and tried to hide what she was doing – but too late.

'What's that?' demanded the girl. 'What are you doing?'

'Oh nothing,' mumbled Bricca, 'just a little something . . . nothing much, miss, just something for the poor lad, you wouldn't object now, would you?'

'What do you mean, for the poor lad? What poor lad?'

'Why, this poor deaf and dumb creature,' said Bricca, waving her hand towards the corner, 'Cennla, to keep on his journey.'

Cennla – Deaf Boy – could hear nothing of these exchanges, but he understood everything. With his eyes he saw everything and was very afraid.

'Why, where's he going?'

Bricca sighed. 'The Lord knows where. Out of the house, is the master's only orders. We really have no place for him here.'

'You *can't*,' cried Julia, with a sudden ferocity that impressed Bricca despite herself. 'You can't just turn him out of the house like that, I won't let you!' And to emphasise the point, she ran across to the nurse and snatched the pitiful little cloth bag out of her hands. 'He's deaf and dumb and no use to anyone, and what will become of him?'

'It's the master's orders, miss. You know there's nothing else to be done.'

'Lucius would never do such a thing, he can't mean it!' And still clutching the cloth bag in her bunched fist, Julia ran out of the kitchen and across the gardens to the west wing and her uncle's private, sacrosanct apartments.

She ran down the covered way and flung open one door, but found nothing inside but a large desk and walls covered in shelves filled with the dullest and dustiest looking scrolls. The next door along was a double-door, of British oak, heavily inlaid with bronze depicting a fight between an eagle and a serpent, and this too she flung open. Before her lay a magnificent room, the walls painted a dark, solemn terracotta and decorated with frescoed panels of gods and goddesses, birds and beasts and fishes, with a great west window of pale green glass at the end, and a beautiful mosaic floor decorated with every kind of creature of myth and legend. In the centre of the room stood a low, shale-topped table, polished a beautiful, lustrous charcoal grey.

It was Lucius' library.

And in the softly filtered light of the west window, haloed by the gold of the setting sun and the millions of dancing dust-motes that it picked up, in a meditative cloud of stoical philosophy, was Lucius himself, standing at a plain wooden lectern. Julia noticed to her surprise that there was not a single chair in the room; her uncle obviously did his reading in this rather ascetic position. The inner walls of the room were lined with shelves of polished wood, filled with many hundreds of scrolls, and even a few of those new-fangled *books*, their pages bound together down one side; though they were few in number, and Lucius privately regarded them as rather clumsy and barbaric. They would certainly, he believed, never fully replace the scroll, in elegance as well as utility.

Lucius raised his head, very slowly, and gazed at the dishevelled, panting figure of his niece standing in the doorway, clutching a tatty cloth bag in her bunched fist.

'Do you not think that it might have been more polite had you knocked and waited for an answer before bursting so peremptorily into my private chambers?'

'Oh, but Uncle!' cried Julia, not even pausing to wonder what 'peremptorily' might mean, 'you can't send him away, not just like that, with just this miserable little bag of apples to go with him, he's completely useless to anyone, deaf and dumb like he is – I mean Surdo, that is to say, Cennla – a Celt you know, like Bricca from down beyond Exeter way, and he's no good to anyone, as deaf as a dumpling, so Bricca says, and as mute as a milking-stool – doesn't she put things oddly? But anyway, you've got to keep him or else there's no knowing where he'll end up, dead in a ditch, or under the wheels of a wagon because he didn't hear it coming, or crushed to death and all mangled up by a herd of stampeding bulls, or maybe carried off by a great eagle or a serpent – well, all right, maybe not a serpent, but anyway a very sticky end somewhere, or else he'll end up back on that ship with the horrid captain who will beat him with his vinewood stick just because it amuses him, oh Uncle, please!'

Lucius felt quite overwhelmed by this torrent of ill-considered verbiage. He also felt a very unpleasant confusion of emotions in his own breast, which he struggled to master. The passions: those demons and traitors in the soul, forever seeking to undermine and overthrow the sovereignty of Reason. He felt annoyance at the girl's interruption, in the midst of his daily reading of Seneca; further annoyance at her presuming to influence his government of an orderly household; but annoyed most of all because he could already feel himself being swayed by her entreaties. And on top of all that, he felt something quite different at the way she addressed him so familiarly as 'Uncle.' Never in his life had anyone been so familiar with him, not since he was a boy. This bewilderment of feelings gave a sharp edge to his tongue.

'Did your parents educate you in any way whatsoever?' he asked, his voice still quiet and even.

'Well, of course they did!' replied Julia with indignation. 'My father told me all about Africa, where he went often you know, and the beautiful horses of Numidia – he had a Numidian stallion himself which was the fastest horse in all the Western Empire – and also the leopards and lions and things, and then my mother taught me Greek, well a little bit anyway, though I didn't like it very much, all those funny squiggly letters you had to learn, and I don't think she enjoyed it much either honestly, and often we'd just get bored and after a while we'd run away and sneak out of the house and go up into the chestnut woods or down to the meadows and pick flowers in the springtime . . .' The girl's voice trailed off and her eyes fell away from him and he thought he could see her lips trembling.

This was all so very difficult. Lucius was used to reprimanding his slaves and his clerks and his accounts secretaries, he could make grown men blanch without even raising his voice. But reprimanding a little girl like this . . . it was quite beyond his experience, especially a little girl who was his niece, whose parents had recently died, and who reminded him so peculiarly of her mother, his sister, when she was a little girl, and they had played together on their father's estate in the beautiful Sabine valley south of Rome. Every time he tried to scold her, now, it all became so difficult, and confused . . .

Obviously it was very wrong of him to try to criticise her parents for bringing her up badly, especially at this time. *De mortuis nihil nisi bonum,* he scolded himself. Say nothing of the dead except good. His sister had always been very different from him, impetuous, passionate, laughing – and, he feared, his brother-in-law was much the same, although a fine soldier, it was well-known. But Lucius did not suppose that they had raised their daughter – well, as *he* would expect to raise a child.

Awkwardly, he left his lectern and crossed over to the table where he picked up a small scroll.

'This, ah,' he coughed awkwardly, 'this was delivered to me yesterday by a messenger of the Imperial *cursus*. 'I wanted to see you about it, ah . . . I shall read it.' This was so very, so damnably difficult. He took a deep breath, and began to read.

To Lucius Fabius Quintilianus, at London, greetings. To contain a possible outbreak of plague in our province, it was necessary to reduce by fire the house of your brother-in-law, near Cordova, with all its effects. There were no survivors. We pray for the souls of the deceased.

Cornelius Symmichus, Governor

Lucius laid the scroll down again. 'It is . . . deeply to be regretted,' he said at last.

There was a long silence. Julia ached to be held, hugged, but her mother was gone away, and there was no such comfort to be had here. For a passing moment she thought she hated her uncle. He was like a corpse. And somehow he was to blame for what had happened to the villa in Spain, her childhood home that lay 'reduced by fire', a smoking field of ash and cinders, with her toys and her dolls and her childhood lying blackened and burned among them. And her parents, still lying in state upon their bed, she imagined, white and pristine and untouched among the ruins.

'But,' she suddenly blurted out, 'but who will pay the ferryman?'

Lucius smiled, despite himself, and turned away to hide it. Indeed, his sister and brother-in-law had gone to the other-world with no one having laid a coin in their mouths for Charon, the ferryman, to take them across the River Styx to Hades. He found himself thinking rapidly, inventing, *lying* . . . what would Plato have called it? The Noble Lie. The tale told to still a childish heart. He turned back to the girl.

'Those that die together,' he said cautiously, 'that is to say – a married couple – do not have to pay the ferryman. He will take them across the Styx for nothing, on account of the love that they bear one another.'

'Is that true?'

Lucius nodded.

'And no mourning?' said Julia. 'What will happen to them, without a proper funeral?' For she had seen rich people after death, mourned in the greatest style, anointed with costly oils and unguents, laid out on a bier draped with golden cloths and bewailed by hired mourners, before a magnificent funeral dinner, and then a slow procession by torchlight to a cemetery beyond the villa or the town walls, with musicians and dancers and mourners and the grieving family following after. And she had seen how poor people died, too: tipped into

JULIA

a common grave, earth raked over, nameless and forgotten as dead flowers.

'Ah,' said Lucius, 'but what need have they of mourning now? Your parents are together, in the fields of heaven. Why should we be mourning?'

Julia frowned with thought. 'But is Hades the same as the Fields of Heaven? It never sounds like it. It always confuses me.'

'Child,' said Lucius, hearing a gentleness in his own voice that unsteadied him, 'all we know is that the good in this life will go to a good place after. Do we not?'

She nodded, still deep in thought, and turned away to the door. As she went, Lucius said after her, 'Oh, and Julia,' – it was the first time he had used her name directly, how strange it sounded – 'the boy, the boy in the kitchen . . .'

She turned back. 'You mean Cennla?'

'Cennla, yes. He can stay. Tell Bricca. He can help her in the kitchens. Sweeping up or whatever,' he added vaguely. 'Attending to the fires . . . I don't imagine – '

But whatever it was that Lucius didn't imagine was never made known, for he was interrupted by a small, fast-moving body which jumped up at him and flung its arms around his neck and kissed him on his flinching cheek and cried out, 'Oh thank you, Uncle!' before detaching itself and racing out of the room.

Lucius Fabius Quintilianus had not been kissed since the reign of the Emperor Diocletian, when he was four. And that was by one of his father's slave-girls, a pretty blonde German, who was sold to another owner soon afterwards on account of her proclivity for also kissing Lucius' older brother, who was fourteen, and perhaps not quite so innocent a recipient of a pretty slave-girl's affections.

Lucius turned once more to his lectern, touching the back of his hand gently to his cheek, and then dropped it down and began to run his finger over the opening lines of Seneca's *De Tranquillitate Animi*, Upon the Tranquillity of the Soul, but with

59

a very untranquil soul indeed. For his eyes could take nothing in, and all he could ponder on was the nature of truth and lies, and the Noble Lie, and stories as ways of comforting the sorrowful, and perhaps even – though it seemed a dangerous thought – to ascertain the more mysterious truths of our existence, which lay beyond the reach of Reason. Could that be?

He also pondered what on earth he was going to do about this small bundle of vehemence and noise and laughter and sudden tears and unconsidered, spontaneous affection that was his late sister's only child.

He would have to look into getting her a pedagogue.

CHAPTER FIVE

It had been a long and dramatic day, and after her supper of scrambled eggs and bread and butter and honeycakes, Julia was ready to crawl into bed.

'What'll I do tomorrow, Bricca? Will I be able to go out into the town and explore?'

'Not on your own, certainly not,' said Bricca, 'but I suppose the master wouldn't mind you coming with me to the market. He's said something about getting you a pedagogue sooner or later, apparently.'

Julia pulled a face. 'Yuck. Some smelly old Greek.'

'Now don't you be so rude, or Queen Boody will be after you.'

Julia frowned at her nurse. 'Queen who?'

Bricca smiled. 'Don't you know who Queen Boody was?' Julia shook her head, wide-eyed. 'Well, a fierce old queen was she, with long red hair, and she did very many terrible things, although to be fair many terrible things were done to her and her kind first of all. But she comes in the night,' – she leaned forward and tickled Julia till she squealed, – 'to put the frightening spiders on naughty little girls!'

Julia wriggled out of her nurse's clutches, and said again, 'But who *was* she? Oh, do tell me, Bricca!'

'I thought you said you were tired.'

'Not any more I'm not, honest. Oh, I do love stories, Mummy used to tell me such wonderful stories . . .'

Bricca looked down at the little girl, and pondered. 'Well, it's hardly a story for one as young as yourself, but I suppose . . .'

Julia knew then that she had won, and settled herself back in bed and waited for Bricca to begin.

'Well,' said Bricca, 'this was a long time ago, way back when the first Roman soldiers came to Britain, many generations ago. All of Britain was under the tribes then, as now only the far western and northern country is.' She gave a shudder. 'And terrible some of those northern tribes are, so I have heard tell. God save we never have to meet them on a rainy night.'

Julia giggled at this, but Bricca looked stern. 'Well, as I was saying, Queen Boody, or to give her her real name, Queen Boudica, which means Victory in the Old Language – Queen Boudica was Queen of the eastern country, the wide fenlands and the horse runs and the cornlands to the north and the east of here, looking out over the great North Sea. It is a flat country and very rich in corn and pasture, and famous for its horses, which in those days were held as sacred, as they still are in some parts. Boudica's people were called the Iceni. Now the Romans had conquered Britain, and made the Iceni their allies, and all seemed well enough at that.

'Then one day Boudica's husband, King Prasutagus, took sick and died, or was killed in battle or an accident, it doesn't matter much either way. Whichever, he was as cold stone dead as a slate before you could curse a cockroach. Now the Romans never did understand or much *try* to understand the ways of the Celts, and especially they never did understand how the women of the Celts could be as strong in respect and rule as the men. So Boudica became Queen over her people, now her husband was dead, but to the Romans, it seemed as if they had no ruler at all.

'So, one terrible day, they came to the palace of Queen Boudica in the heart of Iceni country, and demanded that they should all bow to Rome and from now on admit that they were no better than slaves. Well, the Iceni were, still are really, a proud, stiff-necked people, all horse-people are if you notice, a wild and proud people of the plains, not like my people of the western woodlands and moors, who are more likely to slip away and hide at trouble – and come back and hock your horses in the night! But not the Iceni, who wouldn't bow or be slaves to anyone, no, not the Emperor of Great Rome himself, who went by the name of Nero in those days. Now nothing enrages Rome more than that: not to be recognised. And so the soldiers did a terrible and stupid thing. They took Boudica herself and tied her up to a cart, before all her people, and stripped her naked, and whipped her until she bled – which is a terrible thing to do to anyone, but to a *Queen*! Can you imagine the disgrace? The Iceni felt as if their whole nation had been whipped and disgraced. Furthermore, the soldiers took Boudica's two daughters, her two lovely daughters, both with the long red hair, just like their mother, and again in front of the people, and their own mother, they . . .' Bricca bit her lip. 'Well, they disgraced them too, and dirtied them, in an even more terrible way, which you shall hear of one day but not till you're a deal older. No!' insisted Bricca, raising her hand firmly at Julia's complaints. 'The world is a worse place than you can imagine in your pretty little head, my sweet, and should not be all known to you yet.

'Well, the soldiers marched away from the palace at the end of that dreadful day, wiping their hands clean and thinking they had done a good job and they would hear no more from *that* quarter. They had no idea what they had done. Better to have gone weaponless into a she-wolf's lair, and slain her cubs before her eyes, than commit those crimes that they did before God that day.

'Back in Colchester, and St Albans, and London, the soldiers and the citizens settled down to a peaceful old life, not knowing that all the demons of hell had broken loose in that wide horse-country of the Iceni. One day, the people of London looked out, it must have been on the hills to the north of the town where the people went for the pannage of their pigs, beside the first springs and ponds of the Fleet River that flows out finally into the Thames beside the Western Gate – you shall see it all soon enough, my pet – and anyhow, one day, certain people of London were up on the low hills there, and looking over towards Colchester way, so they said, it seemed as if the horizon was on fire.

'Which it was.

'For Queen Boudica in her vengeful fury had called all her people together, men, women and children, and with them the whole tribe of the Trinovantes too, their neighbours, and seizing whatever weapons they could find, axes and knives and mattocks and hayforks, they marched out of the fastnesses of their horse-country and fell on Colchester.'

Bricca paused. Julia, wide-eyed, breathless, urged her to go on.

'The slaughter was terrible,' said Bricca slowly. 'All the town of Colchester, the greatest in the kingdom at that time, was put to the sword. Everyone, every age, every sex. Many sought refuge in the temple, but the Iceni just barred the doors and burned the whole thing down, with all the people and the sacred bust of the Emperor inside it. Any that escaped, they slew in the streets, until they slithered and slipped in the blood of the slain. And some they did not kill, not straight away, but took captive, and led away to the sacred oak groves of the black goddess, Andraste, that they used to worship in the ancient druid times. There the Iceni, mostly the Iceni women, ochone! took their revenge on their hated captive women, with a revenge that was too terrible for words . . .'

Again Bricca paused.

'You will read of it all one day, when you are older, I suppose,' she said at last. 'They were terrible times, and I pray to God that we never see their like again.

'But Boudica was not done yet; her thirst for vengeance was still unslaked. The people of London waited for the Roman soldiers to return to save them, but it was hopeless. The Commander of the Army, called Suetonius, was in the far west, doing battle on the island of Mona off the coast of Wales, which was the very seat of the druids and their power. And so the citizens of London shut their flimsy gates and prayed – for in those days, there were no great stone walls and watchtowers around the city, as now; it was more like a trading-post on the riverbank. And in time,' – Bricca sighed – 'over the horizon came the war-party of the Iceni, many thousands strong, and at their head, the terrible figure of Boudica herself in her chariot, with her eye-paint of green malachite, and her red hair down to her waist, and a thick torc of twisted gold about her neck, and further gold bands about her arms. And thumping against the sides of her chariot as she rode, were the severed and bloody heads of her victims, hanging there as trophies.

'Well, the same fate befell the people of London as the people of Colchester. All of them who had refused to be evacuated with the cavalry. The earth of the town was turned to red ash and laid utterly waste.

'Finally, the Roman General, Suetonius, having heard of the slaughter, hurried back from Wales. With his much smaller army, he met the great war-party of the Iceni people beside the North Road, in the midland country. Boudica released a hare from under her cloak – for the hare was ever the animal of the witch and the sorceress, you know – and took heart from the direction the hare ran in. She saw it as a sign that they should have victory that day, and then all her people raised a great warlike shout and threw their spears in the air. And then – so much for hares and witchery – they hurled themselves across the battlefield and clashed against the iron wall of the legions, and nearly all of the Iceni were slaughtered.'

'What happened to Queen Boudica?'

Bricca shook her head. 'They say she fled back to her own country when she saw the battle was lost, and refusing to be taken captive, swallowed poison instead, and died there. But none knows her place of burial, and some say she lives on as a demon – to frighten little girls!' Bricca tried to laugh, but the mood of the tale had been too dark for that.

'What about her daughters?'

'No one knows, my child, but their fate was not kind. It can be a cruel world, and nothing is certain under the sun.' Bricca sighed. 'There, now I've frightened you good and proper,' she lamented, 'and you'll never get to sleep.'

'Yes I will,' said Julia, 'I'm not frightened.' Well, she thought to herself, as she buried herself down under the bedclothes, not *that* frightened. Then she sat up again and asked Bricca to bring her Ahenobarbus for company. Once he was installed – the Fiercest Cat in the World – she felt a lot safer from the haunting of Queen Boody.

But still her dreams were filled with visions of red-haired Celts, and strange terrors, and dark rites in the sacred oak groves of the druids. And she knew that of all the territories conquered by Rome, the Province of Britain was the only one that had not been wholly conquered from shore to shore, but that in the mountain wildernesses of the far west and north, the tribal peoples of old still held sway, and beyond the Wall that the Emperor Hadrian had built more than two hundred years ago – she shivered with terrified delight at the thought – still lived ferocious, nameless, uncivilised people who rode chariots, and worshipped demon-gods. They spoke a language that none understood, and knew nothing of the art of writing, and covered their naked bodies in blue tattoos so that the soldiers called them *Picts* or Painted People. And she wondered if she would ever see such things in real life.

CHAPTER SIX

It was a clear and sunny day when Julia awoke. Bricca was knocking on her door and telling her to hurry, for she was going into town and had permission from the master to take his niece with her.

Julia was up and dressed in seconds, and soon driving Bricca to distraction by getting in her way in the kitchen, hopping from one foot to another in her excitement.

At last the nurse was ready. Bearing a huge withy-basket over her arm, and tightening her purse-belt around her ample girth, she headed out of the kitchen backdoor with Julia eagerly following.

It seemed strange, having been in the heart of this great town for two days and nights now, and still to have hardly seen it. The mad flight from the ship down by the dockside, and the race through the city with Cennla in tow, seemed days ago now. At that time she had barely registered her surroundings, she had been so tired. But now, she had all the time in the world to look around with the greedy curious eyes of a child, and she saw everything.

She saw what a magnificent position Lucius' house actually occupied: right upon the Thames riverbank, with the orchards and gardens stretching away to the west. And to the east, beside the main entrance, the Walbrook Stream, which ran through the heart of London and down to the Thames. Just the other side of the Walbrook rose the magnificent pile of the Vicarius' Residence, 'where they have a fountain and a pond that is more than a hundred feet long,' said Bricca, pointing it out, 'and staterooms and banqueting halls the like of which you never saw.' So, thought Julia, the Vicarius and my uncle are next-door neighbours. And she felt very proud of him.

They hurried up beside the Walbrook and then crossed over it on a little, arched wooden bridge. Julia hung on tightly to her nurse's hand as they plunged ever deeper into the narrow streets of the town, heading for the forum and the marketplace, the crowds thickening around them.

'Of course,' said Bricca, 'it's not as busy as it usually is. Lots of people are out on the local farms getting the harvest in.'

As they negotiated their way between a gooseherd and his gaggle of geese, and a rumbling cart piled high with last night's straw and nightsoil, Julia wondered what on earth it was like when it was *really* crowded.

Approaching the marketplace, other sights, sounds and smells assaulted her senses: the sharp reek of charcoal furnaces, where the coppersmiths were working in their little shops; the rich, sweet odour of cattle; the cries of stallholders, booksellers, cheesemakers, water-carriers offering their services. The oaths of lightermen, wheeling goods up on wooden wheelbarrows from the docksides: amphorae of oil and wine and bundles of cloth, silver-firwood barrels, red Gaulish pottery, Rhenish glassware, Italian bronzeware, and dates and figs all the way from Palestine, where that Jew called Joshua, or 'Jesus' in Greek, had been put to death on a cross as a common criminal, and whom her nurse now worshipped as God.

It was all very strange.

A brazen whistle made Julia glance up, and she saw a couple of leery-eyed workmen up on some wooden scaffolding, grinning down at Bricca. 'Plenty to get hold of there, my darling!' one of them called out.

'Pity your girl can't say the same of you!' snapped back Bricca, wiggling her little finger at the workman, whose jaw dropped in astonishment. 'Come along,' she said, seizing Julia's hand and dragging her away. 'Loutish workmen, always wolf-whistling at us, a right earache they are.'

They hurried on.

A local official from the town council was remonstrating with a pork butcher about the state of his stall. 'Orders are orders,' said the official, 'and these new orders regarding the right conduct of the market in London have come all the way from the Praetorian Prefect himself, in Trier.'

The pork butcher was redfaced and furious. 'And why should we take any notice of what some bloody pen-pusher in Belgica tells us!' he yelled.

'Quite right too,' Bricca called out. 'Bloody foreigners, poking their noses in.'

Julia saw flaxen-headed women with their hair plaited and piled up on their heads. 'The way tarts used to dress, with their blonde wigs,' muttered Bricca, 'but now blonde wigs are all the rage for any respectable matron.' And for good luck against the forces of moral laxity and disorder, at the corner of the street, she reached out and touched a little painted Herm's outsize phallus.

'Bricca,' said Julia, puzzled, 'Christians don't worship – I mean, in Cordova, the Christians smashed all the Herms one night and the Vicarius forbade anyone from setting them up ever again. I mean, Christians only worship their own god, that Jew who died, don't they?'

'And rose again,' added Bricca, 'and conquered death for all of us. Well, yes,' she went on, sounding a little confused, 'of course we only believe in the Lord Jesus. But – well, it doesn't do any harm trying for a little good luck as well, now does it?'

And before Julia's brow could become any more corrugated with theological puzzlement, Bricca pulled her onward.

Julia's attention was somewhat distracted anyway by an enormous shoe, almost as big as her, hanging out over a shop doorway.

'What's that?' she asked.

'Why, a cobbler's, of course,' said her nurse. 'Come *along*, child.'

Suddenly they erupted into the forum: a great wide space of light and babble, honking geese and braying donkeys and human cries, and the furious exchange of goods and money.

'But where's your Basilica?' asked Julia, surprised that the forum of London had no great town hall like other cities.

Bricca looked wary. 'Ah, well, that's a long story. The finest Basilica north of the Alps, was the Basilica of London in its day. But now . . .' She gestured towards the north side of the forum. 'They reduced it to rubble, and now even that's gone to repair the walls and the towers.'

'Why on earth did they do that?'

Bricca sighed. 'There was a revolt, before I was born, when my parents were still young. A man called Carausius revolted against the Emperor, and had the support of London. This city always was a turbulent, fiery place. The revolt was put down, and then just to remind the city not to do it again, they pulled down the Basilica as well. Razed it in a couple of days. You see there that fine church at the eastern end? That was just the apse of the old Basilica.'

Julia gasped. The building must have been huge, magnificent.

'But there,' said Bricca, 'enough of that. Now then,' ticking off her fingers, 'things to remember: opium, henbane and mandrake from the apothecary, fresh mint if we can get it, some Whitstable oysters if they look lively enough, dried fruit, arrange a delivery of flax oil and another of olive oil, a couple more clay lamps, perhaps a bronze one if they've got any nice ones – Cennla managed to knock one off the table and break it yesterday, the clumsy dolt – hairpins, both bone and bronze, a new tunic or two for you, perhaps a nice little woollen byrrus – the famous British cloak, you know? You'll be needing it soon enough when the days shorten. And I must pay the master's bill at the bookseller's. There is such a lot to do.'

It was in a daze that Julia followed Bricca through her morning tasks, the nurse's withy-basket filling rapidly. Julia had to interrupt her constantly to ask about the Mysteries of London. She saw some children playing hopscotch, and wanted to know if children in Britain played leapfrog too, and Bricca said yes of course they did, children all over the world played leapfrog. Julia worried about the donkey going round and round the cornmill with a great wooden yoke across its withers, and wanted to know if it would have a rest for lunch, and Bricca lied shamelessly and said yes of course it would stop for lunch, it would have a magnificent lunch of fresh carrots and apples and honeycakes, and then spend the afternoon out in the fields playing with his friends.

Julia was especially fascinated by a great gilded statue of a stocky, rather ugly man with a big nose and a cleft chin that stood at the end of the forum.

'Why, that's the Emperor Constantine himself,' said Bricca, crossing herself.

'What, *our* Emperor?' asked Julia.

'No, you daft duck, the *Great* Emperor, the one who was proclaimed Emperor here in Britain, at York, and later turned Christian, God rest his soul. Our Emperor now is his youngest son, Constans. His other son, Constantius, is Emperor in the East. They're the *sons* of Constantine, remember?'

'It's all so confusing,' said Julia. 'Wasn't there another Constantine?'

'That was the oldest of the three sons,' said Bricca, 'defeated by his younger brother Constans in battle, just three years ago.'

'Why couldn't the Emperor – the Great Emperor, I mean – have called his sons something a bit different? They'd be a lot easier to work out.'

Bricca chuckled. 'These Emperors like their names to be remembered. Constantine renamed half the cities in the east after himself, it seems, or else after his mother, Helena, and moved the capital of the Empire to Constantinople. But slaves and children like us don't concern ourselves with such things, now do we?'

So Julia gave up and just let herself float, through the smells of fresh-baked bread, roasting meat and spilled wine, and the sounds of money changers rattling coins on wooden table-tops, and the coppersmiths beating out copper plate with their neat little mallets, and the cries of beggars, and one-legged soldiers, bandaged sailors, country people selling eggs, hams, herbs, and – she shuddered at this – scrawny, unattractive schoolmasters bawling out their talents for hire, sometimes both in Latin and Greek.

She particularly liked the cries of the quack doctors, who ranged all along the eastern side of the forum and affected a particular style of dress: colourful, extravagant, long-sleeved, supposed to suggest a learned and Oriental origin.

'Good People of London,' cried one such entrepreneur, who sported a small, dapper, richly oiled beard and, Julia was fascinated to see, gold-embroidered and ludicrously pointed boots of purple leather. 'Good People, I give you the Universal, Omnipotent and Plenipotentiary Panacea' – the word 'Plenipotentiary' alone caught the admiring attention of several poor gulls – 'of the most Erudite, Majestical and Hippocratical *Augurius of Athens*, whose magical and life-giving elixir I have here in my hand, transported by merchant-ship all the way from the eastern Mediterranean. A Sovereign Remedy for all kinds of Aches, Pains, Chancres, Boils, Clysters, Fluxes, Blockages, Stoppages, Discharges, Cramps, Wens, Pustules, Baldness and General Lassitude. I have only a limited number of ampoules in stock, so do not delay, Good People, but roll up and buy. It may be your only chance!'

The quack by now had a number of people hanging upon his every word, half-amused but also hypnotised by his rhetorical skills and his evidently tremendous learning.

'How much?' called out one interested party.

'My dear man,' cried the quack, 'I am practically giving it away! I have a wife and seven children to keep, and yet they languish and starve on account of my ridiculous generosity! Each day I return home, weary and footsore, to my good lady wife and my starveling babes, and my dear wife – face like a boar's behind but a heart of purest gold – asks me how my trade has gone, and how heavy is my purse, and when she sees how little money I have, she weeps, and berates me and beats me and calls me a fool and a good-for-nothing! And yet I am happy, and count myself blessed. And for why? Because each morning, I take a draught of this most marvellous Panacea of the Learned Augurius, and so enjoy perfect health! And when one has one's health, even though one's wife has a face like a boar's behind, what more can one desire?'

'A heavy purse!' called out another more sceptical listener. But the majority of the crowd, swayed by both the quack's eloquence and comical performance, began to dig into their pockets and purses.

Julia could have watched him for ages, but Bricca decided that they had had enough, and pulled her away. 'The man's a charlatan anyway,' she said. 'He couldn't heal a broken eyelash.'

'My mother could heal,' said Julia. 'I saw her once lay her hands on a slave of ours, who was close to death, all the doctors said he was finished, and he opened his eyes very wide and stared at her when she touched him, and broke out into a terrible sweat, and the next day he was cured. My mother,' she added confidentially, 'revered Isis, and Demeter, and Venus too sometimes. She said they were really all the same goddess known by different names, and it was she, the Mother Goddess, who really healed. She said I had the gift of healing too.' She sighed. 'But she could not heal Father or herself.'

Bricca looked down at Julia and said nothing. The gift of healing should surely be only a gift of those who followed the Lord. And yet she had seen healers, true healers, not like this garrulous quack in his purple boots, and they were not Christians but still faithful to the old religion. She wondered at it all but said nothing and walked on.

They had finished all that they had to do, including buying Julia a neat little byrrus of soft red wool, which she would have worn straight away if it hadn't been so hot. Then Bricca led them back round the north of the forum to show her the Temple of Jupiter that lay behind. It was much the grandest of the temples in the city, or had been. But it had about it now a distinct aura of decay, and even vandalism. It was faced with Purbeck marble while most of the other temples were simple buildings of brick and red tiling, little different to a casual observer from the houses and shops around them. People were streaming in and out of the temples all the time, leaving gifts and candles and curses, taking hopes and blessings and dreams of a better day. They saw the smaller temples of Mars, and Minerva, and Mercury; and Bricca's own temple, or church, the church of the Christians. Then Julia spotted a small Temple of Isis. She pulled away from her nurse and ascended the steps.

'Child?'

'Just a while,' said the girl, not looking back.

Inside, the temple was a simple rectangular shape, with a statue of the goddess at the back on a stone altar. Candles were lit before her, and flowers had been left on the flagstones around her. The girl knelt and closed her eyes and prayed for a while to her mother, her Mother. And then she arose and went out again, and took her nurse's hand, and they said nothing more, but walked on.

They now came to the north-west of the city, and here arose great battlemented walls of flint-hard Kentish ragstone

JULIA

and rubble-concrete, seamed with redbrick, as massive and daunting as the city walls themselves.

'This was once London Fort,' said Bricca, 'a city within a city, with its own four gates to the four winds and its own watchtowers and bastions. Nearly twelve acres of it, the home of the soldiers stationed here. Now they're stationed over on the Southwark side, which is a mercy most of the time, except when they're running amuck and getting drunk in the town, God save us all.' And she spat on her fingertips and pressed them to her forehead for good luck.

Julia gazed up in awe at the mighty walls and found them rather terrifying. Beneath the fortress walls was a low, squalid row of houses, more like huts, with rude wooden signs outside the doors, but all the shutters were still closed, despite it being past noon now.

'Why aren't *those* people out of bed yet?' she asked. 'They must be very lazy.'

'Hush, child,' said Bricca, hurrying her on. 'Those are the still – the women's quarters, for when the troops come over . . .' She tailed off. 'They're not allowed to open till the ninth hour, when respectable women will be home again.'

'Oh, I see!' cried Julia, looking back over her shoulder at the row of huts. 'You mean that's the soldiers' *brothel.*'

'Really, child, I do declare . . .' And Bricca spat on her fingertips again, and hurried on.

They then turned back down the little street beside Walbrook Stream. There were many wells and springs in this part of the town, feeding the stream, and people had thrown all sorts of offerings into the wells and fountains: coins, jewellery, spearheads, horse-and-rider brooches, little mugs of pewter, gemstones, jugs, miniature oars of bronze . . . and here there were numerous small shrines to the spirits of the waters, and the Celtic triple-goddess – virgin, mother and crone – and also to Cybele, and to Isis, and Venus, and Bacchus and Sebazios, and sometimes all of them mixed up together. Street hawkers squatted on woollen rugs in doorways and sold little ready-made clay figurines of the goddess for devotees to purchase and then toss into the muddy waters of the Walbrook with a wish and a prayer. Julia would have liked to do the same, but she had no money, and she did not think her Christian nurse would be too happy to subsidise her on this occasion. Just then, however, Bricca paused and, fumbling in her purse, drew out a copper coin and tossed it in a stream.

'Bricca,' asked Julia, very politely, when she saw this, 'could I have a coin as well?'

Bricca glanced around, as if fearing that the jealous God of the Jews might be spying on her from round a corner or an upper window, and then slipped the girl a tiny copper token. Julia folded her fingers around it and began to look for a suitable well to honour with the gift. Bricca closed her eyes and began to say a prayer to send after her votive offering.

Against the side of some of the shrines were pinned an array of curse tablets. Julia had always liked reading the curse tablets back in Spain when they visited a temple, although some of them made her shiver with a delicious frisson of terror. They could be so ferocious. Now she read:

I curse Tretia Maria, her life and mind and memory and liver and lungs all mixed up together, her words and thoughts and every foul bit of her, may the gods never give her health or happiness more

O Goddess, may they never have health till they have returned to me my stolen pig, whoever took it, and if they have already ate it, may they have the stink and the look of a pig all their lives

May Livilla be accursed for stealing my beloved from me, may she suffer agony of bowels and be wrung empty, stopped up and fetid, may the goddess dry up her organs of increase and may she never come to know motherhood but remain dry and barren forever with sagging dugs like an old bitch-hound

Julia also liked the graffiti on the walls behind. There was the usual stuff about *'Up the Greens!'* and then these words crossed out, and the words *'The Greens Fuck Their Own Mothers!'* and *'Up the Blues'* over-written. Across the Empire, the fanaticism with which people followed their chosen chariot-racing team was the same; when their teams won, their supporters would get atrociously drunk and spill out of the taverns into the streets to sing raucous and repetitive two-line songs all night in praise of their heroes.

Julia could not imagine her Uncle Lucius having much enthusiasm for the sport of chariot-racing.

Another graffito amused her too. *'The phallus of Marcus Septimius,'* someone had carefully inscribed upon the wall – not Marcus Septimius himself, she guessed – for the words were directly below a carefully-drawn image of an extremely diminutive penis indeed. Julia giggled. Why were men so obsessed with their willies all the time?

Bricca, stirring from her prayers to whatever strange and unorthodox amalgam of the Lord Jesus and some ancient Celtic goddess of the springs that she had conjured, saw what Julia was looking at, and chortled.

'Hm,' she said. 'I can well believe it.'

Then Julia saw another tablet pinned up on the wall, a wooden plaque with these words carved on to it in large letters:

> *You shall have no other gods before me, saith the Lord God of Israel, for the Lord your God is a jealous God. Oh Lord, cast down these temples and shrines of these whore-goddesses, as King Josiah cast down and utterly destroyed the groves of Ashtaroth of the Zidonians, and as the prophet Elijah slew the priests of Baal upon Mount Carmel. And cleanse this city by the sacrificial blood of your son Jesus Christ Our Saviour.*

When Julia read the horrible word 'whore-goddesses', she flinched visibly and stepped forward, raising her hands to tear the plaque from the wall and hurl it into the stream. Bricca saw what she was about to do and stepped forward and took hold of her hand and lowered it.

'It is best not,' she murmured. It wouldn't do to antagonise the more belligerent Christians of the city, who had on their side many of the soldiers and chief citizens and the Vicarius, quite apart from the Emperor himself.

Julia wrenched her arm from Bricca's grasp and looked up at her with angry, tear-filled eyes. 'How dare they call her a whore-goddess! My father would kill them, whoever wrote this, if he was alive now!'

Bricca stared down at the angry little girl, bewildered, trying to piece together why her *father*... until gradually it dawned on her what a mother-goddess might mean to a girl who had lost a beloved mother so recently and so traumatically.

Surely, there were many mysteries under the sun, and the longer she lived, the less she felt she understood. But she did feel that she should do now as the Lord Jesus – *her* Lord Jesus, not the Lord Jesus of these hateful, self-regarding fanatics – would do. She took Julia's hand again, more gently this time, and turned her away from the wall. She did not think it was much in her fiery little charge's temperament to turn the other cheek; but in this instance, it would be much the most pragmatic as well as the most Christian policy.

As they made their way down beside the Walbrook and back over the bridge to Lucius' villa, they passed one last, small, moss-grown and neglected water-shrine. Here, with silent defiance, Julia stopped and slipped into the dark, still water the token that she had been clutching in her tight, bunched fist, and said another prayer for the soul of her mother. Her mother replied, easily and swiftly, that she was not to worry on her account, all was well, but begged her daughter to hurry home for now, because there would be trouble later that day. Julia was surprised – the town seemed such a jolly, bustling place, at least until they had encountered that horrible notice on the wall – but she took her mother at her word, and reached for Bricca.

'Aye, child,' agreed Bricca, 'time we were within doors. And besides, your pedagogue was to be there by the sixth hour, I was told.'

Julia looked at her, aghast.

CHAPTER SEVEN

As soon as they entered the atrium, Julia's heart sank. For there, sitting on the strong-box at the far end of the room, was a crookbacked little man whom she knew immediately was her pedagogue.

His legs were so short that they didn't reach the ground, but swung in mid-air in a ridiculous sort of fashion. And when he jumped to his feet, on seeing them enter, she saw that his legs were so bandy that he looked like he'd spent most of his life sitting on a barrel. He came bumbling over to them, and on closer acquaintance, Julia saw that he not only had bandy legs, but also watery eyes, a snub nose, dirty fingernails, and a very black, straggly beard of the kind that collects fragments of its owner's dinners from the last five or six mealtimes. Certainly this was the case with the particular beard before her.

'Good afternoon, ladies,' he snuffled, and bowed very low. 'I am the new pedagogue hired for the young lady of the house, who goes by the name of Julia Valeria, I believe, daughter of the late and sadly lamented Marcus Julius Valerius and the similarly late . . . well, ahem, yes, his wife, Aelia – herself, I believe, the sister of Lucius Fabius Quintilianus, the master of this house, and, as his cognomen suggests, a proud descendant of no less a personage than –'

'Thank you, sir,' interrupted Julia at last, appalled by this stream of verbiage. Mustering the haughtiest tone which any nine-year-old girl could manage – which was, indeed, strikingly haughty – she told him, 'I am fully aware of my ancestors' names and achievements.'

'Well, yes, quite,' said the pedagogue. 'Doubtless you are, as any well-born and well-educated young person would be. My own name, howsomever, is Hermogenes of Orchomenus, that being the Orchomenus situate in Boeotia, and called by the Divine Bard, that is to say Homer, or in the Greek tongue, *Minyan Orchomenus*, and not the lesser-known and inferior township of Orchomenus in Arcadia, though that does have a mention in the *Metamorphoses* of Publius Ovidius Naso, does it not? And yet I trust,' he added humorously, 'that I am not personally quite so guilty of that leaden-footed *dullness of wit* for which my Boeotian countrymen are proverbial in song and story.'

God bless us and save us, thought Bricca, the man's mad.

This is terrible, thought Julia. I need to talk to Ahenobarbus at once. 'Indeed,' she said very politely, 'I am sure that you are only too educated.'

'Thank you, my lady,' said Hermogenes. 'I fancy that there are few books of any worth that are unknown to me.'

There was an awkward silence, until Julia finally blurted out, 'I must go and see my cat!' And with those words she fled, leaving her open-mouthed nurse to deal with Hermogenes the Pedagogue, of Minyan Orchomenus.

Having found Ahenobarbus, she poured out her heart to him regarding the strange and wonderful city of London – the whistling workmen, her new woollen byrrus, the quack doctor with his purple boots, the curse tablets, the sacred shrines beside the Walbrook Stream – at which marvels Ahenobarbus' eyes grew rounder and rounder in amazement. Julia then felt starving hungry and set off for the kitchens to find something to eat.

She found Cennla, hard at work, and scouring the iron pots clean with a pumice-stone and a great deal of elbow grease.

Julia barely noticed him as she sat at the table swinging her legs and feeding herself and Ahenobarbus alternately with titbits. She knew the names of all the slaves in the household now, for there weren't that many.

There was Bricca, of course, who seemed to have appointed herself Julia's nurse, since it was no doing of Lucius'. There was the beastly, beardy new pedagogue, Hermogenes, although at least he would not be sleeping under the same roof, but living in some cheap lodging house the other side of the city. There was Lucius' faithful secretary and steward, Valentinus, who oversaw the smooth running of the household and was, unlike Bricca, the soul of discretion. There was Bonosius, the lazy, jolly cook, Sannio, the stable-lad and Silvanus the gardener. Last and least, there was a giggling slave-girl, Vertissa, and another little slave-girl of only six years old, called Grata. Sometimes, Julia thought she might deign to play with her, but she was very young.

For a villa of such a size, it was a very modest household indeed.

And then of course there was the new kitchen-boy, Cennla. But for the most part, he was as invisible to Julia as all the other slaves. And to him, she was the sun and the moon in the sky.

Julia was just beginning to feel pleasantly full, and sleepily wondering how long supper might be, when she heard a distant roar, like a crowd of racing fans when their team has won. But there had been no chariot-racing today at the arena, surely? She hadn't seen any posters.

There followed another tremendous roar, and in the muffled distance, the sound of some great hubbub that both scared and electrified her. Swallowing the last of her milk, she dashed into the atrium, just in time to see Valentinus standing, panting, talking rapidly to her uncle, who had appeared from his private chambers. Lucius listened for a few seconds, then

turned on his heel and made for the door at the end leading to
the stables.

'Inform the Vicarius too,' he called over his shoulder.

'The Vicarius is already there, sir,' said Valentinus respectfully.

Lucius looked back slowly. 'Doing – nothing to stop it, I
suppose?'

Valentinus shook his head.

Even from the other side of the courtyard, Julia could see
her uncle struggling to keep down his anger. Then he walked
on, shouting ahead of himself, 'Sannio – my horse!'

Julia raced over to the steward. 'Valentinus – what's
happening?'

The steward gazed down at her, his lean face set hard.
'Rioting, my lady,' he said. 'The Christians. A good thing you
returned when you did.'

So that was what her mother had been warning her about.
The many-headed monster of the London mob was out on the
streets, devouring everything in its path. And all in the name of
that crucified Jew.

As soon as the bridle was fitted on his white mare, without
even benefit of a saddlecloth, Lucius stepped up on the block
and mounted, impatient to be off. Sannio stood back. Lucius
kicked hard and galloped out into the cobbled street, turned
left, and headed up Walbrook towards the temples of his
ancestors. Already he could see smoke arising from the north
of the city.

A little way up the stream, on its east bank, stood the small
and secretive temple of Mithras. Here, soldiers, merchants,
and patricians such as Lucius came to worship the dying and
rising god that had come from Persia. Initiates were baptised
in the blood of a sacrificial bull, and thereafter swore to live a
life of such strict morality and honesty that most citizens
abjured Mithraism altogether, preferring to stick to the old,

muddled hodge-podge of Roman religion than have such high demands made upon them.

Unfortunately for the followers of Mithras – of whom Lucius was one – their religion seemed in many respects a very close copy of that of the Christians, although the reverse was the truth. It ante-dated Christianity by centuries. Throughout the Empire, however, it was the temples of Mithras that were the most frequent target of the wrath of the Christians whenever they went on the rampage.

As Lucius rounded the corner, he saw the temple of his own religion going up in flames. A baying mob stood round about, hurling loose stones, bricks, anything they could lay their hands on, at the crumbling walls. To one side stood a colleague of his from the temple, keeping discreetly in the background and watching the flames in helpless silence. When he saw Lucius he beckoned him over.

'It is too late to save the building,' he murmured, 'but Sicilius saved the heads of Our Lord Mithras, and also Serapis. He buried them beneath the floor before the mob could discover them. They have smashed many of the statues in the temple of Jupiter and Mars.'

Lucius bunched his fist tightly into his horse's mane. His contempt for the baying mob at the doors of his temple knew no bounds. Had he a sword at this moment, he would have ridden down upon them with furious . . .

But no. That was not the way.

The smoke gradually began to clear with a shift in the wind, and then Lucius saw, mounted on horseback like him, the big, stocky figure of Decimus Clodius Albinus – the Vicarius himself. It was as Valentinus had said. He sat on his horse, impassive, regarding the surging mob, doing nothing. Albinus, the career Christian. Albinus, the hard professional soldier, self-made millionaire, and Vicarius of all Britain, out in the streets of a riotous London without even a single bodyguard. No one would dare to touch him.

Lucius kicked his horse's flanks and approached him.

'Ah, Quintilianus,' said the Vicarius evenly, regarding him without blinking through the acrid smoke. His cognomen suited him: Albinus. Pale-haired, massive-shouldered, with expressionless blue eyes and eyebrows so pale as to be almost invisible. His face was boyishly round and yet brutal. His forearms were as meaty as hams. They said that when he had served on the German frontier, he had killed men with his bare hands. He still would, if any stood in his way. And this was the man who now professed the religion of meekness and servility and turning the other cheek.

Albinus, for his part, quite openly despised the Provincial Praepositus for his lack of ambition, his modesty, and his refusal to enrich himself and his friends by dipping into the treasury chests to which he had such easy access. He must be some kind of *eunuch* to be so honest.

'Sir,' said Lucius. 'I must protest. This is wanton destruction.'

'The troops are on their way,' said Albinus.

'A little too late, don't you think?'

Albinus heard the testiness in the Praepositus' voice, and disliked it. 'Do you question my competence, Quintilianus?'

'I question – the willingness of the authorities to protect the religious sites of any but the Christians.'

'You mean the temples of false gods and blasphemous mockeries? You mean these . . . decadent houses of idols?'

'The gods that our ancestors, both yours and mine, have honoured for generations!' cried Lucius, at last moved to anger. 'The gods that guided Rome to be Mistress of the World! You dishonour your own father and mother, Albinus, if you –'

'Enough!' roared the Vicarius with a sudden, bullying violence. His face, hitherto as pale as his hair, flushed red and angry. '*We* do not burn the heathen in their temples, *we* do not rejoice at the odour of burning flesh, as the heathen did at the slaughter of Christians under Diocletian, in *your lifetime*, Praepositus. If it pleases the Emperor – and it *does* – to see false religion cast down and the True Cross elevated, then who are we to gainsay it?' He became abruptly impassive again. 'The troops, as I say, are on their way. You have no more business here, Quintilianus. Go and look to your own.' He turned his horse away, then called back over his shoulder, with the beefy contempt of the soldier for the desk-man down the ages. 'Your job is to balance the accounts. Mine is to keep order.'

What order? thought Lucius. The order of the mob. The order of popular prejudice and vulgar superstition. This pseudo-order, while the lights are going out across the Empire.

He wheeled his horse savagely, glanced back one last time at the now smoking ruin of the Temple of Mithras, and then returned home.

The villa weltered in a sour and angry atmosphere that evening, compounded by the late summer odours of the city and the turbid stench of the marketplace drifting down the valley of Walbrook Stream between the narrow houses. Bricca said they needed rain, 'to cool things down and clean things up'. Julia felt that this city of London was a noisy and furious place.

'There's plenty of vim and vigour here, that's for sure,' affirmed Bricca with a certain pride. 'Londoners are a cantankerous lot, and they won't be pushed around. But when they're at each other's throats, as nowadays, they're like ferrets in a sack, quarrelling over every temple and every dedication on a wall.' She shook her head. 'One day, though, who knows, perhaps London will be a city as great as Rome. Greater, even!'

Julia laughed at the absurd idea.

The following morning, straight after breakfast, Julia's lessons with Hermogenes began.

Valentinus ushered them into one of the smaller rooms in

the west wing, adjacent to the library, and they sat on stools side by side at a bare table, with a wax tablet and stylus, and a scruffy little scroll that Hermogenes produced from the ragged folds of his brown cloak.

'I thought that it would be amusing,' he snuffled, 'if we began by looking at a text by your own ancestor, the most illustrious Quintilian.'

Hilarious, thought Julia in quiet despair.

'Now then,' began Hermogenes, reading squint-eyed from the scroll under his nose. 'Thus says the learned orator: *"Nowadays, as soon as our children are born, we hand them over to some silly Greek maidservant, who fills their impressionable ears with all sorts of ridiculous legends . . ."'*

'Bricca didn't,' interrupted Julia immediately. 'She told me all about Queen Boody, Boudica that is, which means Victory, and she had long red hair and painted her eyes green with malachite, and rode down on London in vengeance and fire and killed everybody after what they did to her and her two beautiful daughters, who also had long red hair, and each of them had a kitten too, called, um, Lug and Log, and they used to . . .'

Hermogenes gazed straight ahead, twirling his fingers in his beard. When Julia finally finished her monologue, with the triumphant words, 'And that's not some silly legend, that's history, that is!' he took a deep breath.

'And what is history?' he asked.

'What really happened.'

'And what is a story?'

'Something made up.'

'And what is their common etymology?'

Julia shook her head.

Hermogenes, who had absolutely no sense of what a nine-year-old could and could not be expected to know (which in some ways made him an unpredictably good teacher), explained. 'The Greek word, *istoria*, gave us the words for both "history" and "story".'

Julia frowned. She had already forgotten how boring she had expected her pedagogue to be, and was puzzled into a vague sort of interest. 'So history is made up too?'

'Herodotus the Greek,' said Hermogenes, 'is commonly called the Father of History. But have you read his books? They are full of the most ludicrous legends and nonsense. Call him the Father of Lies, more like.'

Julia was out of her depth. 'I like stories,' she said at last, and very firmly.

'All very well,' said Hermogenes. 'But first we must learn to walk before we can run. Remember Icarus. Now let us begin by parsing this sentence here: which is the subject and which is the object?'

Julia sighed and began to parse.

Meanwhile, in his library, Lucius had taken delivery of a whole batch of fresh books which he had ordered from his bookseller, and which Valentinus had collected for him at dawn that morning.

For the Praepositus had decided to swallow his pride, and embark upon a serious investigation of this wretched and hysterical new religion that was now – Jove save us! – the official creed of the Empire.

Of course, he understood the basics already. The Jew, Joshua, who had been crucified in Palestine during the reign of the Emperor Tiberius, was believed to have risen again from the dead three days later, and by his death and sacrifice, appeased the savage God of the Jews, who would now forgive Joshua's followers their sins, and admit them into his paradise after death. It was a primitive and fearful religion, of course, with no nobility in it, and its central idea of the blood sacrifice of the dying and rising god was taken straight from Mithraism and other eastern religions. But this was by the by. All religions, unlike philosophy, were more or less primitive, rooted in blood and bone rather than in the more elevated regions of the mind.

What counted so much against the Christians, as Lucius had always maintained, was how they behaved. Hysterical, screaming, bickering. Wrangling over the minutiae of whether their god was of a similar substance with God Himself, *homoiousion*, or of the same substance, *homoousion*. A fine distinction, you might think; but one over which the Christians were quite prepared to beat each other to death in the streets.

And while they found plenty of time for such puerilities, they had absolutely no time for public service or the Empire that nurtured and protected them. And why? *Because the Empire was coming to an end*, they said, and all the world with it. With an unmistakably sadistic glee, they had proclaimed that the End of Days was nigh, when all would be consumed – except for those who believed in Joshua, the Christ.

Laboriously, Lucius worked his way through the Jewish Holy Books on which the new religion was based.

He found a story about the whole world being flooded; about a sea being parted down the middle, and people walking across its dry floor unharmed; about a woman being turned into a pillar of salt; about a talking ass. It was all the most preposterous farrago of childish nonsense, such as Ovid might have turned into elegantly entertaining tales for the delectation of an educated readership in the literary salons of Rome; but that anyone should actually believe all this!

With great solemnity, Lucius then turned to the ancient books of the law. In a book called Leviticus, he read that it was against the wishes of the Deity for his Chosen People to eat a seagull, ostrich, or rock-badger. It was also against His wishes for anyone to carry any part of a dead owl, hoopoe or bat about their person. If anyone did – by accident or oversight, presumably – they must wash all their clothes and be pronounced unclean until evening.

Lucius wondered if the Emperor knew about this. He thought he should be told.

Then there was Joshua himself: the Christ, the Messiah. Lucius' first obstacle was the terrible, clodhopping Greek in which these later books were written. He had read the traditional Jewish books in Latin translation, and they had a certain austere simplicity which was not displeasing. But the books about Joshua the Christ were written in a dismally plebeian Greek vernacular, *Koine*, which made Lucius wince. He gritted his teeth and read on.

This Joshua: a kind man, in his way, perhaps; sympathetic to the troubles of the oppressed, although not immune from outbursts of temper. And, like his followers, the Christians themselves, his most passionate hatred was reserved for his co-religionists, the 'scribes and pharisees', whom he called snakes, and compared to rotten sepulchres painted white.

Much of his teaching was lamentably unedifying. A philosophy of slaves. 'Do not fight,' he seemed to teach. 'Do not bother. There is nothing in this world worth fighting for. It will all end shortly, before any of you standing here see death' (he had been wrong there, clearly). 'The world is wicked and corrupt. Turn away from it. Close your eyes. Blessed are the meek. My kingdom is not of this world.'

And then more miracles: walking on water, or turning it into wine, or cursing a fig-tree because it had no fruit on it. Childish stuff.

The commentators on the Holy Books, the Fathers of the Church, were worse, if anything: as savage in their hatred of each other as of the world. And *only they were in the right*. Everyone who disagreed with what they personally believed, was wrong, and doomed to hell.

If only they could decide on what it was they *did* believe. They kept changing their minds.

And, time and again, there was the Christians' hatred of the world to contend with. 'Our existence is on earth, but our citizenship is in heaven,' wrote one. The self-righteousness. The ingratitude!

If they were so contemptuous of the protection and safety

they enjoyed in the bosom of the Empire, in the warm and civilised Mediterranean light, then let them take themselves and their wretched religion, and cross the Rhine or the Danube into the dark forests of the north, and take up residence among the German or the Sarmatian tribesmen, among the flayed and hanging corpses and the shrunken heads – and see how long their religion lasted there.

Lucius laid the scrolls aside with a sigh. It was no good.

Christianity was no religion for a servant of the Empire; for a true Roman. It was no religion for a man of intelligence and reason. Indeed, it was no religion for a grown man at all: this eternal dream of a mummy or a daddy waiting in Heaven for their children to come home to them. It might be all very well for a child, for a little girl like Julia, for instance – but not for an adult. He believed life was all about growing up, and attaining what wisdom you could. Most especially, such was the bittersweet irony of life, the wisdom to know how to die. But this Christian version of reality, like so many of the new, ecstatic eastern mystery cults and religions that had flooded into the Empire – this version did not have enough *pessimism* in it. He smiled despite himself, recognising for a moment his own fleeting reflection, there in the mirror of his mind. Very well, then: not pessimism. Reality. This religion of the Christians was but a dream of a religion. And a dream dreamed in the teeth of what a man knows is true.

Parents die. Gods are metaphors. And the world rolls onward.

As I shall be fully prepared to explain, he thought wryly, when I get to the Jewish Hell.

And so a pattern of life was established, and within a few weeks of her arrival in the strange, outlandish province of the Empire called Britannia, Julia began to feel almost at home. She thought often of her parents still, and the Spanish sunshine, and the tinkling of goat-bells in the hills and the scent of wild mountain thyme; but she realised that she could now think of them without weeping.

Instead, she had Bricca as her nurse, and Hermogenes as her tutor. Valentinus, the household steward, was aloof but kindly. And, behind him, was the stern, difficult, unsmiling figure of her uncle, whom she gradually grew to love, and missed when he was away. She was never more delighted than when she could make him smile. It was a rare event, and one to be treasured.

In the mornings she studied grammar with Hermogenes in the bare little room in the west wing, and then later on, she would often accompany Bricca out to the market. When her uncle was at home, she dined with him, and loved him for the effort that he clearly put into trying to be entertaining and conversational with a nine-year-old girl. (He failed utterly.) When he was away, she dined in the kitchens with Bricca and the other slaves, somewhat to Lucius' disapproval. But it seemed to be doing the child no harm. In time, she must start to dine only with her social equals.

Julia herself felt comfortable, secure, sometimes in a kind of dream or pleasant limbo, and didn't dislike the feeling. Sometimes she wished she had friends of her own age to play with, but there were so few of her class in the town, and none were of her age. But she had Ahenobarbus to talk to, and his conversation, from that uniquely feline perspective, was always interesting.

Late summer drifted into autumn, and then came the first days of winter and a flurry of snow. Julia shivered in the depths of her chequered byrrus and couldn't believe how cold it had grown. It could be cold in the mountains of Spain, but that had been a searing, dry, bracing cold. Here it was a chill of damp tentacles, mist rising off the great river and wrapping itself around her limbs and sucking away her warmth like some malevolent spirit.

One day, Bricca found her looking particularly moody and self-pitying in the orchard, squashing plums beneath her hobnailed winter sandals with considerable malice. After some coaxing, Bricca found out the reason for Julia's mood. Today was her birthday. She was ten.

Bricca gave her some extra honey on bread as a treat, and did her best to cheer her up. And Julia half-believed that she *was* cheered up, although she couldn't quite tell.

She was definitely cheered up the next morning, however, when Sannio the stable-lad came to pay his respects, and told her that her mount was ready to ride out. There, before her astonished eyes, standing plumply in the corner of the stables munching hay, was a short white pony even rounder in the girth than Bricca. Julia raced back into the villa to find her uncle and cover him with kisses of thanks. In doing so, she spilt a bottle of ink right across the page of tax accounts that he had been working on. Bafflingly, he found that he didn't mind. Indeed, he immediately concealed the ink-stained page beneath another, so that she wouldn't see what she had done.

Julia insisted on riding her present to market that afternoon, having christened the pony Bucephalus, after the famous war-horse of Alexander the Great.

It was a good birthday.

CHAPTER EIGHT

In that bitter winter of AD 342-343, like wolves driven to scavenging new territories by the cruelty of the weather, the Picts broke over the border.

Lucius received the news by messenger from the Vicarius' Residence. 'No doubt I am the last to be informed,' he observed. 'Afterthought that I am these days.' He paced the room. 'And we know why, don't we, Valentinus?' he said to his steward.

Valentinus maintained a diplomatic silence.

Lucius told the messenger to leave. When he had gone, he added, 'But enough of that. More to the point, we also know why the Picts are making such headway, don't we?'

'Sir?'

'Money, Valentinus. There isn't enough cash to pay the troops up on the Wall, and they're drifting away in droves. And what use is a Wall with no troops to man it?' He shook his head. 'We raised sufficient taxes this summer – just about. But I have doubts that the paychests were still full by the time they got to York.' He settled his chin on his knuckles in great gloom. 'If only the Emperor inspired as much loyalty as men feel nowadays towards gold.'

A few days later, there was even worse news.

'The Emperor himself is coming to Britain, sir, to deal with the Picts.'

Lucius looked up from his desk. 'Don't be ridiculous,

Valentinus. He wouldn't risk a winter crossing of the Channel just to confront a few Painted Tribesmen on the rampage up north.'

'I'm certain it's true, sir,' said Valentinus stubbornly. 'I heard it from one of the Vicarius' notaries at the baths.'

'Oh, at the *baths*,' repeated Lucius, leaning back and tossing his pen down. 'Well of course, if you heard it at the *baths*, it *must* be true.' Valentinus smiled. Lucius did not. 'And if it is – just what we need, isn't it? At a time when the coffers are empty. It'll cost us thousands: an Imperial Visit, with full retinue.'

'Not forgetting his pretty German boys,' added Valentinus.

Lucius nodded, his expression quite unreadable. 'Quite.'

The rumour turned out to be true. The Boy-Emperor had already sailed from Boulogne, through the churning grey winter seas of the Channel, bound for the port of Richborough. He would be in London in three days' time, weather permitting.

'But why is he coming, Uncle?' asked Julia in high excitement. 'Do you think he wants a ride on Bucephalus?'

The second question was so far beyond Lucius's comprehension – *how? what?* – that he could only ignore it. As to the why . . .

'The Emperor in his wisdom believes that by leading his legionaries against the Picts and roundly defeating them, he will win himself great martial glory,' he explained. Valentinus smiled to himself. How he enjoyed hearing his master in sarcastic mode.

'And he is a great soldier, isn't he, Uncle?' said his niece.

'Indeed he is, Julia Valeria,' replied Lucius solemnly. 'Why, not three years ago, he slew his own brother in battle, and tossed his corpse into a river, like a dead rat! And now, thanks be to Jove, he has come over to Britain, through treacherous seas, to save us, by his own personal valour and feats of arms, from the terrors of the Painted People.'

'And he is Emperor of the West?' Lucius nodded. 'And his other brother, the one he didn't kill, is still Emperor in the East? Constantine?'

'Con*stantius*,' corrected Lucius.

Julia sighed. 'It's all so confusing.'

'There are times,' said Lucius, 'when I have to agree with you.'

During the next three frenetic days, Lucius did his best to replenish the government coffers, stationing troops at the entrance to the market-place and levying a snap ten per cent tax on each day's takings. He was also in charge of acquiring supplies, requisitioning the choicest hams, cheeses and venison that could be found; and he was down at the docks, with a heavy military presence, selecting amphorae of the best Italian wine and Spanish olive oil to be despatched forthwith to the kitchens of the Vicarius' Palace.

There was a great deal of grumbling, naturally. Paying tax is never an enjoyable experience. But as he rode around, Lucius also let it be known, in the most subtle and undemonstrative manner, that the reason for this extra levy was that the Emperor Constans himself was visiting the province.

The news spread like some highly contagious and hectic fever. Londoners, sharp tradesmen as ever, began to reckon up the pros and cons, and calculated that, despite the short-term surrender of that painful ten per cent, it would soon come back to them, with interest, when the Imperial retinue came rolling into town. For if there was one thing that any Imperial retinue worth the name liked doing, it was shopping.

That taste for expensive knick-knacks was very much in evidence when the Emperor arrived in town.

'My God,' breathed Lucius. 'He's worse than his father.'

Constans and his vast retinue – including his pretty blond German youths – had sailed from Boulogne on a morning tide, a blustery sou'wester had borne them rapidly and queasily to Richborough in less than four hours. From there they had processed with great ceremony and braying of trumpets through the crumbling and badly neglected Arch of Richborough, and then headed west through the vineyards of east Kent to Canterbury. There, the new Bishop had received them with much fluttering anxiety, and bestowed upon His Imperial Magnificence so many gifts that the Boy-Emperor was almost satisfied. Furthermore, the Bishop had advised him to follow the valley of the Great Stour south-west out of Canterbury and up onto the North Downs, and proceed to London that way, rather than continue directly onwards to the Medway and Rochester, for the marshy land of the Swaleside north Kent shore was badly waterlogged at this time of year, 'and the road, Your Highness, is not so well-maintained as it used to be in your father's time. That is to say,' the Bishop bumbled on, 'not so well-maintained as it ought to be, which is royally maintained indeed, such as would befit so noble a traveller such as Your Majesty, who like unto a mighty Ship of State, borne upon its broad stone back as upon a Noble Sea-Way, weighted down with all the cares and dignities such as ought to befit so noble, ah, so noble . . .' at which point the poor Bishop ground to a halt, weighed down with far too many subordinate clauses to continue.

The Boy-Emperor eyed him coldly, and then declared that he certainly *would* proceed directly to the Medway, for he wished to visit the great ironworks of Faversham, where he was expecting a new helmet to be made and fitted for his Imperial head, none of the other three dozen or so of the helmets in his possession being quite comfortable.

'And since We shall soon be doing battle in person with the barbarian tribesmen of the north, who have so insolently dared to invade Our Empire, We think it only proper that the Imperial head should be properly protected. Do We not?'

'Oh, we do indeed, Your Imperial Sacredness,' agreed the Bishop. 'We do indeed.'

Unfortunately, the Bishop's anxieties proved only too well-founded. After a lengthy visit to the Faversham ironworks, where Constans had a new helmet made, plus two spares just for safety's sake, and a couple of suits of armour, the Emperor and his retinue proceeded onwards to the Medway, where they found the road ahead of them virtually washed away and a stretch of invading marshland before them. The Emperor urged his men ahead of Him courageously, only to see an entire baggage wagon – the one bearing his own arms and his three new helmets – slither to a halt and begin to sink into the mud, dragging its terrified drove-horses with it. The Emperor shouted and berated his men, commanding them to retrieve the wagon on pain of death, but there was nothing to be done. At last they abandoned the struggle, cut the spume-flecked horses free from their traces, and let the wagon sink below the waters with barely a sigh.

His Imperial Majesty was reduced to tears at the sight, and wept and shook his fist heavenwards and cursed the gods, before recalling that there was only one true God, so instead he prayed to Him that the wagon should be spewed forth again from the mud. After half an hour, his prayer had still not been answered. And so, lamenting his lot with head bowed, the Emperor turned and led his men back the way they had come, and then up onto the high road across the Downs to London.

They stopped overnight in Southwark, his men setting up the vast Imperial tent in drenching rain while the Emperor sat by on his horse in a monumental sulk, rainwater trickling down the back of his neck, and wondered what had ever possessed him to come to this miserable little bloody island. The one thing that cheered him up was the thought that he would be twenty soon, and surely get a lot of presents.

It would certainly take a lot more than a little white pony to satisfy him.

At last his tent was set up and the charcoal braziers lit inside. He dismounted and went on in, taking with him his two favourite German friends, Hedwig and Herman, and announcing very firmly, 'We do not wish to be disturbed until tomorrow.'

The next day was one of pale blue skies and scintillating sunshine, and the Emperor was soon in much better spirits. How fine he would look, crossing London Bridge, with this steely northern sunlight glancing off his armour! Or, even better, perhaps he should wear his new gold embroidered dalmatic, with a string of pearls, and that lovely hennaed wig . . .?

This was the sight that now met Lucius' appalled gaze, as he stood with Valentinus on the terrace of the Vicarius' Palace, gazing out across the river to London Bridge, and observing the great Imperial entrance to the city.

Julia had begged to be allowed to accompany her uncle to the Palace for such a fine view, but Lucius had declared that it was quite impossible, she would have to take her place with Bricca among the rest of the crowds lining the streets up to the forum.

'Has the Emperor already won his victory?' whispered Valentinus to his master.

Lucius smiled dryly. For it did indeed look like an Imperial Victory already, with all the men in rich gold apparel, carrying spears tipped with fluttering silken dragons, their shields with golden bosses, every piece of their armour polished to a dazzling brightness. The Emperor himself was robed in a gleaming Byzantine dalmatic, riding in an open carriage drawn by a pair of nodding white mules, themselves caparisoned in crimson and gold, their bridles inlaid with precious stones. The Emperor sat very upright and hieratic, enthroned a loving god, among heaps of white cushions, a glittering diadem resting upon his hennaed wig, looking neither to right nor left, unsmiling, unwaving, as he had many times seen his father do. Utterly removed from the world of ordinary mortals.

The crowds loved it.

When Lucius came home that afternoon, Julia wanted to chatter to him about the sights and sounds she had seen and heard, but Lucius was in no mood for it.

'In the old days, the Emperors used to dress like plain soldiers,' he said, 'eat plain soldiers' food on campaigns. Caesar himself rode as hard and fast as his men. Even when he *did* wear a laurel wreath of victory, his soldiers teased him that he only wore it to cover his receding hair line.' Lucius scowled, ferociously unamused. 'How his men adored him. Now our Emperor dresses like an Oriental despot, and imagine what the troops must say about him behind his back! No wonder they are endlessly deposing those whom they deem . . .' Lucius bit his lip. Julia looked curiously at him. 'Enough,' he resumed. 'At least you have seen an Emperor in his full regalia. I hope it pleased you.'

And he left her standing puzzled and silent, wondering how complicated the world must be, and how bad-tempered her uncle was.

One of the reasons for Lucius' bad temper was the unavoidable dinner that night at the Vicarius' Palace. For a man who regarded any form of social engagement as an ordeal, this was bad enough. But to have to dine with such inflated, unsavoury characters as the Emperor and his colleagues . . .

The dinner was mercifully brief, however, for Constans was keen to be up with the lark the next morning and on the road north to the Pictish battlegrounds. He ate sparingly, with great ostentation, as a hardened soldier on campaign. They had all been forbidden to make any mention whatsoever of his older brother Constantius, the Emperor in the East, whose ....tial prowess was renowned and genuine.

'When We return from Our wars,' declared the Emperor, 'then there will be some feasting!'

God save us, thought Lucius.

The next day the Boy-Emperor rode north, with a fresh set of armour specially made for him in London from hammered scales of bronze and finest Wealden iron. He rode out with a detachment of five hundred of his crack cavalry troops, proud Illyrians in light scale-armour, who had been billeted without notice on randomly-chosen households in the long-suffering city of London. At York they picked up a further two cohorts from the depleted and demoralised Sixth Legion *Victrix*. The legionaries were inspired, however, by the sight of the cavalry, and further impressed to find themselves suddenly under the direct command of the Emperor himself – even if, as they commented among themselves, he did look like a *complete nancy*.

They harried the invading war-parties of Pictish tribesman wherever they found them, the cavalry riding out to round them up, and if possible drive them against the killing steel wall of the legionary lines. They fought across the wintry wastes of Northumbria, and over the Wall, and on across the Cheviot Hills, cutting the Painted Men down without mercy, and leaving the occasional, selected victim flayed and hanging from a tree or post, as a sign for others to remember.

And so, thanks to the magnificent courage of His Highness the Emperor, and perhaps also, in some measure, to the flair of his cavalry and the doughty spirit of his foot-sloggers, a great victory was won, and the Painted People were utterly routed.

Then there was a great victory in London, before the Imperial retinue sailed back to Gaul. There was feasting, and carousing, and love-making, and shopping too. The Emperor gathered gifts prodigally wherever he went, and the government coffers were quite emptied again, and the soldiers who had fought with him just recently across the wastelands of the

North and into Caledonia, still wondered what had happened to their six months' back-pay.

Another great dinner took place at the Vicarius' Palace, which Lucius was again unable to avoid. This one was even more of an ordeal than the last, for there were over fifty courses, and each course was punctuated by a panegyric from one of the court poets to the Emperor's martial brilliance, each more cloying than the last. One poet even felt moved to praise 'Our Lord the Emperor's golden thighs, astride his great war steed.' This was accounted a very fine line indeed by all present, except Lucius, who felt slightly queasy.

Of course, this may have had more to do with the richness of the food. The cooks had excelled themselves in taste and ingenuity. There were roast pigeons that turned out to be made of sugar, and glazed peaches and pears that turned out to be made of mincemeat. A pair of roast peacocks were brought in aflame on great silver serving dishes. There were sows' nipples and vulvas in tuna brine, a ragout of nightingales' brains, and a pâté of fattened cranes' livers; the birds' eyes were put out when they were still alive, because blinding was well-known to fatten them better. There were fowl drowned to death in wine, geese force-fed to death with figs, and a range of the finest *garum* fish sauces from Bithynia, Carthage and Cadiz.

Naturally there were frequent visits to the *vomitarium,* so that the assembled guests could fit in more of the delicious food. As Lucius' beloved Seneca said of the art of dining, *vomunt ut edant, edunt ut vomant*: they vomit in order to eat, they eat in order to vomit.

The Emperor himself reclined at the head of the room on a little raised daïs so that all could see him feasting. He was flanked by his two close German friends, Hedwig and Herman, whom he caressed in between mouthfuls of wine, occasionally popping succulent titbits into their mouths.

Lucius found himself reclining next to Sulpicius, the younger brother of Albinus, the Vicarius. Sulpicius was of a slighter build than his brother, but of the same colouring. Even paler, if anything. He compressed his lips together frequently as if disapproving of much of what went on around him, and shimmied his sloping shoulders, staring around with his watery blue and slightly protuberant eyes. He ate very little. At last he struck up conversation with the Praepositus.

'So, Quintilianus,' he said, 'I hear that you have a young niece staying with you nowadays.'

'The daughter of my late sister,' nodded Lucius, 'and Marcus Julius Valerius, a fine soldier.'

'How did they die?' asked Sulpicius.

'Plague.'

Sulpicius licked his slender fingertips. 'Was it a quick death?'

Lucius frowned. 'I have no idea. No one was present.' There was an awkward silence.

Sulpicius resumed. 'I saw an old woman die of the plague once. Blood burst out of her nostrils in a fine mist, covered the lower half of her face. She looked like a baboon.' He reached for a roasted ram's testicle, bit into it. 'So – is she betrothed yet?'

'She's ten.'

'So?'

'No, she is not betrothed yet.'

'Do you have a suitable husband in mind?'

'One or two, perhaps.'

'Because you know, I am looking for a wife myself now.'

'You don't say?' he replied. He sipped his wine which he drank well-watered. It would not do to let one's concentration or conversation slip one iota in this poisonous company. 'Well, it will be several years yet before –'

'Surely only a year or two,' interrupted Sulpicius. 'And an orphaned soldier's daughter could do a lot worse than marry the brother of the Vicarius of Britain.'

Lucius realised at this point that Albinus, lying on the other side of the table from them, had been listening to their every word, his face expressionless as ever. And at Sulpicius' next question, Lucius knew he was in deep.

'I take it you are raising her a Christian, even though you yourself still worship the old gods?'

'I worship the gods of Rome,' replied Lucius evenly. 'I honour the Emperor, I make my sacrifices, and I believe in the truths of philosophy. I see no reason –'

'But you cannot persuade yourself of the truths of Christianity?'

Lucius shook his head. He had a sudden image of himself, barefoot, picking his way across a forest floor rippling with scorpions. 'It may come in time, Sulpicius, it may. As for my niece, I am overseeing her education in the best Roman tradition, and when she comes of age, I trust she will choose her own religion of her own volition and inclination. If that religion be the new religion of the Empire – well, I shall be as happy as any.'

'There have been riots, we hear,' said a voice from the end of the room. It was Constans himself. 'Riots between Christians and Unbelievers, in London. We do not like riots within our Empire. We will have no more.'

And with that simple solution to the world's complexities, the Emperor turned away again and resumed his gentle palping of Hedwig's smooth inner arm.

Lucius caught Albinus' gaze across the table. How he ached and longed for some glimmer of recognition, some conspiratorial wink. For surely they were all in this together, all on the same side, all struggling equally to keep order in a disordered state; and the petty tribalisms of Christians versus Mithraists versus God knows what, were irrelevant to the great and arduous labour of civilisation.

But Albinus stared back without a trace of any such recognition on his broad, bland, fish-cold face.

Lucius took another sip of wine, struggled to swallow it. He was deeply, uneasily aware of his own unease. Like the unease of the Empire to which he was so wedded.

That unease was settling and abiding, across the wheat-rich

province of Britain, and the golden mountains of Spain, the pine-dark forested frontiers of the Rhine and the Danube, the warm vine-lands of Cisalpine Gaul and the many-islanded Adriatic shores of Illyrica, and the baked coasts of Africa, Numidia and Mauretania. It was settling like the desert sands upon the ancient unblinking statuary of Egypt, and over the eastern provinces of Syria and Palestine, and the Seven Churches and the Christian heartlands of Asia. Across the vast Empire an unease was settling, not passing in the ordinary ebb and flow of human fortunes, but an abiding unease that would not pass away. Settling like soft and poisonous dust over the old bright brazen confidence of Eternal Rome, her great bossed shield of confidence tarnished now with melancholy and mistrust and intimations from other worlds, of better and worse truths than those hard, cropped, proud, pragmatical heads of the Roman Senate and People could ever have imagined.

CHAPTER NINE

The Emperor out-stayed his welcome and drained London dry. He finally went back with baggage wagons heavy-laden and groaning with presents – arms made of Wealden iron, Mendip silver and Welsh gold, jewellery of Whitby jet, Scottish bearskins, a dozen Irish wolfhounds, and an entire wardrobe of the softest British woollen cloaks.

London heaved a sigh of relief, swore a few colourful oaths at his departing train, and then went back to what London has always loved most: its one true and enduring religion, the sacred business of making money.

On a bright day the following spring, having spent the morning under the tuition of Hermogenes, Julia was racing out into the orchard to look for Ahenobarbus when she ran head first into a strange boy.

She scowled at him ferociously. 'Who are you?'

'Who are *you*?' he said.

'I asked first.'

He scraped a sandalled foot against his other shin, looked down, considered, looked up again, and finally muttered, 'Marcus.'

'Well what are you doing in my orchard? And where's Ahenobarbus?'

'It's not *your* orchard, it's the orchard of the Praepositus,

Quintilianus. Who's Ahenobarbus?'

'That still doesn't answer what you're doing here. I want to play and you're in the way.'

'Tough. I'm living here from now on.'

'No you're not.'

'Yes I am.'

'No you're not.'

The boy sighed. 'I'm bored already,' he said.

Julia bit her lip. This was so evidently a superior thing to say, and he was more than a head taller than she was, and had a scowl almost as ferocious as hers. She feared she was losing this one.

'My uncle doesn't need any more slaves.'

'Very funny. Do I look like a slave?'

'Yes. And you smell like one too.'

'You have the manners of one yourself. No, I'm a ward of Quintilianus' now.'

'What do you mean, a "ward"?'

'He's my guardian.'

'Where are your parents?'

'Dead.'

'Oh.' Julia wandered away for a bit, knelt and picked a handful of daisies. She called back, 'Why are they dead?'

'My mother died giving birth to me.' The boy reached up and began to swing from the branch of a cherry tree. 'My father died just recently. He was a friend of Quintilianus'.'

'Why did he die?'

'He died of his wounds.'

Julia stood and stared.

The boy dropped to the ground again. His voice sounded funny. 'He was a military tribune in the Sixth Legion at York. He would have been made Legate of the Legion soon. Only he rode out with the Emperor this winter to fight the Picts, and took an arrow in his thigh. No one thought much of it at the time. He was a brave man.' The boy paused, straightened his shoulders, commanded his breathing again until it settled. 'But the wound festered and the camp doctor couldn't cure him. He died – last month. Same day as Caesar.' Julia looked puzzled. 'The Ides of March,' added the boy.

Julia thought about this for a while, and then came over and offered him her handful of daisies. He looked down at them, took them, scrunched them up and dropped them in the grass. 'What do I want with your stupid daisies?' he spat. And turned and sped away into the orchard.

Julia went to look for Ahenobarbus.

That evening, Lucius called Julia into his library and told her that there was to be a new addition to the household. 'His name is Marcus Flavius Aquila,' he said.

'I've already met him,' said Julia.

Lucius went on, 'His father Publius and I became great friends when we were in Rome, and I promised to look after his youngest son if any harm should come to him. Which, alas, it has.' Lucius began to unseal a letter on his desk. 'Marcus has two older brothers, quite old enough to care for themselves, and both serving with the Fourth Legion *Scythica*, out on the Eastern Frontier. Marcus will join the army too, in time, I have no doubt. At the moment he is only,' Lucius frowned, 'twelve, I think. Twelve or thirteen, something like that. So for a few years he will be living here with us, and taking tuition from Hermogenes, like yourself.'

'Hmph,' said Julia.

Her uncle regarded her with something approaching amusement.

'I trust you will get on well enough,' he said. 'Now, off you go to supper.'

After she had gone, Lucius settled down to read his letter. It was from another old friend, Vidalius, who had written some seven weeks ago, the letter taking that long to reach him from where Vidalius lived, down on the coast near Naples.

His letters were always amusing, sarcastic, and sometimes downright dangerous. Vidalius was a scathing critic of the Christian religion, and always referred to their churches as 'charnel-houses'. Such jests could land a man in very serious trouble indeed, but Vidalius flourished on antagonism, and with his network of powerful friends in Rome and Milan, he seemed immune from punishment.

The letter recalled to Lucius' mind the long summers the two used to spend, years ago, far away from the heat and stench of Rome, at Vidalius' villa, high on the cliffs above the Bay of Naples. There they would engage in the equivalent, so they liked to think, of Cicero's *Tusculan Disputations*: all *otium cum dignitate*, fine wine, and witty philosophising. It was a selfish, self-indulgent life, but very pleasant while it lasted.

They would sit and watch the sunset over the sea beyond Capri, and Vidalius would reminisce about the reign of the wicked Tiberius. It was a conceit of Vidalius always to talk as if he remembered those from the past, personally: three hundred years ago was as yesterday to him.

'All those wicked games he used to play,' said Vidalius, chuckling, 'with his *spintriae*, and his little boys whom he called his minnows, swimming underwater and nibbling him between his legs.' Vidalius relished nuggets of human vice and wickedness almost as much as he relished human stupidity: like an epicure with a truffle.

Lucius and Vidalius were opposites by temperament – apart perhaps from their historical pessimism, and even that expressed itself in diametrically opposite ways. As the world went down in flames, Vidalius chortled gleefully and warmed his hands over the blaze. Lucius turned away in sadness.

He always felt he could never trust Vidalius, although he enjoyed the stimulus of his company and conversation. He would leave that great whitewashed villa on the cliffs above the sparkling bay, feeling as a plebeian must, coming away from a gory afternoon at the arena: exhilarated, superior, and rather unclean.

Vidalius had popular entertainment analysed. 'Give the people what they want,' he drawled, 'and soon enough they'll want what they're given: vulgarity, sex and violence. Orgies, copulation, torture with a mullet ... the usual Suetonian fodder. And to think – the mob believes that any rich man who panders to them with bread and circuses does so because he *loves* them. It's pathetic, in a puppyish sort of way. Obviously, to offer the plebs such offal only shows how much you secretly despise them. But we must pretend, must we not, *vox populi, vox dei*? And in the plebs resides power, alas. You can despise the mob all you like, but don't let it show. Remember poor Coriolanus.

'And now: about these corpse-worshippers ... or Christians, as I believe we are supposed to call them.'

'Like our Sacred Emperor, you mean,' said Lucius.

'Ah yes,' said Vidalius, positively brimming over with chuckles. 'Our Sacred and Sainted Emperor, who had that miraculous vision before the Battle of the Milvian Bridge, in which the God of the Jews appeared to him, and said, "Here, pal, clobber them with the Cross and you'll win outright." Or *In hoc signo vinces*, to report the Deity's advice verbatim. "Twas a Holy Miracle, Sir! Honest to God it was!" ' And he dissolved in giggles.

A little Vidalius went a long way, Lucius usually felt. There was plenty of cleverness here, but no wisdom. Which was what mattered, in the end.

He remembered talking to his friend once about self-examination: the scrutinising of the murkiest depths of one's own conscience, daily, and the strange and vile creatures that one often found living there. The very idea was anathema to Vidalius.

'Self-examination!' he cried with horror. 'The only kind of self-examination I go in for, my dear Quintilianus, is the matutinal scrutiny of my own, ineffably noble and handsome features in the looking-glass at the barber's!'

'But you remember that saying of Terentius',' persisted Lucius, refusing to lapse into mere badinage this time. *'All I know of human nature, I learned from me.'*

'It's a revolting suggestion,' Vidalius snapped. 'The idea that I should resemble in any way the common herd! To quote another, far more beautiful scribbler, *Odi profanum vulgus et arceo.* How could I possibly learn anything of humanity, by examining my own, infinitely superior self? Really, Quintilianus. Sometimes you sound almost like a Christian yourself, with all their preposterous notions of *universal brotherhood* and *communality of goods* – which latter doctrine is anyway, so I've heard, only an excuse for them to sleep with each other's wives.' He popped another plump red grape into his plump red mouth and smiled his plump, round smile. With his mouth full he added, 'Oh, don't look so gloomy, my dear Quint. It's all merely a jest. Life is a farce, like a play by Plautus – only rather less well-constructed.'

Lucius wished he could believe him. If only life *were* just a play, an unimportant farce. A passing show, in which nobody really suffers, and, if there is no real nobility, then at least there is no real tragedy either. All's a jest. And the play ends with the knaves and fools briskly punished, the young and beautiful and good happily married, and the wily, string-pulling slave rounding off the proceedings with a neat and knowing epilogue.

If only life were really that shallow – as shallow as one of Vidalius' epigrams. Then we could all be happy.

And here, at the end of his latest letter, was just one such epigram. After the usual, shockingly entertaining mix of scurrility, gossip, and philosophy, he signed off with the observation, *'I have realised, as I enter my sixth decade, that it is not enough for me to succeed. My friends must fail.'*

Chuckling guiltily to himself, Lucius refolded the letter and stowed it away in a desk drawer.

☆ ☆ ☆

Supper in the kitchen was a battlefield of extraordinary tensions, alliances and secret pacts. Bricca bustled about in charge. Marcus sat sullenly, secretly wishing this fierce little girl who was Quintilianus' niece would be nice to him, and regretting that he had so wantonly destroyed her stupid daisies. But he was too proud to say anything, or to try to ingratiate himself with her. Julia studiously ignored him, and instead took particular care to be kind and friendly to Cennla. Cennla in return adored Julia in his usual silence, but Julia never noticed. She was too concerned with the impression she might be making on Marcus.

At their lessons the next day, there was more competition. Hermogenes set Marcus to translate a passage of Homer into Latin – his Greek was already quite advanced – whereas he gave Julia only a tedious passage from a *Handbook for Little Mistresses of the Household*, about the Three Great Female Graces, and the Twelve Great Female Virtues. The last of which was 'silence'.

'*Silence*!' cried Julia. 'Why is silence such a good thing? Cennla is silent, but that's because he's dumb, and nobody says that's a good thing.'

Marcus looked up and glared at her: the diligent, interrupted student.

'Julia, please,' remonstrated Hermogenes. 'Do try to *study* in silence, at least.'

'But it's so *boring*,' she wailed. 'Why can't *I* read Homer? I've read lots of him in Latin translations, all about Odysseus' visit to the Underworld, and Hector's plumes nodding in the wind and frightening his baby, and the gods squabbling on Olympus, and the death of Patroclus, and Agamemnon was so upset that he killed two dogs and four horses and twelve Trojan boys and threw them all on the fire too, and people are always getting stabbed and purple gore streaming all over the ground . . . oh *why* can't I read Homer, instead of this stupid book all about *sewing* and *knitting*?'

112

'But, my dear girl,' said Hermogenes, chuckling to himself, 'your great duty in life is to learn a woman's tasks, and to serve your husband and your household well. Why, it will only be two or three years off now, and you will give up book-learning altogether, and study simply to be a good wife and needle-woman. What need have you of reading Greek?'

'If you did read too many books,' put in Marcus helpfully, 'you'd end up like one of those horrible, "educated" women in Juvenal, *"with unflinching face and dried-up breasts, arguing about politics or military matters."* And who'd want to marry you then?'

This was the last straw for Julia. Flinging down her wretched *Handbook for Little Mistresses of the Household*, and with the child's eternal cry of 'It's not fair!' she jumped to her feet and ran off to find her uncle.

Bursting into his study, she found him bent over his desk, with Valentinus standing at his side, scrutinising lists of figures. They both looked up in surprise at this unannounced interruption.

'Oh Uncle, it's not fair!' she cried again. 'Why do I have to read about the Twelve Virtues and stupid stuff like that, when just because he's a boy, Marcus gets to read all about beautiful goddesses, and Zeus turning into all sorts of animals, and battles, and shipwrecks, and, and . . .'

Lucius was on his feet, his face white with suppressed anger. 'How *dare* you come bursting into my private quarters in this insolent fashion, when I am in the midst of work.' He spoke quietly, which made his anger all the more impressive. 'You will go back to your lessons and do exactly as Hermogenes tells you. Do you understand?'

Julia quailed and backed away.

'DO YOU UNDERSTAND?'

'Yes, Uncle,' whispered Julia, and turned and fled back to her tutor.

Unfortunately for Lucius' equanimity, it was only the next day that another interruption came. Although at least this time she bothered to knock first before entering.

Lucius laid down his pen, a little wearily. 'Yes, what is it now?'

She sat down opposite him without asking permission.

'It's a passage in Quintilianus, our ancestor, that I've just found,' she said, speaking at a tremendous rate. 'I was just reading it with Hermogenes, and look what it says. Quintilianus says that girls should be as highly educated as boys, so that they can teach *their* children when they become mothers, and he says, look, *"We are told that the eloquence of the Gracchi owed much to their mother Cornelia, whose letters even today testify to the cultivation of her style. Laelia, the daughter of Gaius Laelius, is said to have reproduced the elegance of her father's language in her own speech, while the oration delivered before the triumvirs by Hortensia ..."'*

Lucius held up his hand for silence.

He could not believe that, after his severity of yesterday, she was back again, arguing again, fighting again, albeit with a little more subtlety this time. He was accustomed to having grown men tremble before his gaze. And now here was his little niece – unafraid of him. Instead of feeling anger, he felt something quite unexpected: pride.

He gazed at the girl. She gazed back. Blood met blood. It seemed to him that sparks of energy were flying from her dark, elf-tangled hair. Did her nurse never brush it?

He rested back in his chair, closed his eyes, turned his face ceilingwards. He steepled his fingers under his chin, and sighed. At last he opened his eyes again, and his ageless gaze rested on his niece: pertly perched on the edge of her seat, her hands under her thighs, leaning eagerly towards him, so young, so eager, so hungry for the world. His niece: his clever, beautiful, beloved niece.

'It seems to me that I have two options,' he said at last. 'Either you drive me to an early grave with your incessant nagging. Or – I let you loose in my library.'

He considered these two options, then he arose and beckoned her to follow him. She hurried to keep up as he strode down the corridor to the workroom and flung open the door.

Hermogenes squinted short-sightedly and then both he and Marcus stood respectfully to their feet. Julia slipped into the room under Lucius' arm.

'From henceforth,' said Lucius simply, 'they read what they want to read.' He gazed levelly down at Julia, who had already taken her seat at the table. Unsmiling, he nodded almost imperceptibly to himself. 'The library is theirs.'

Then he stepped back and closed the door behind him.

Within a month, Julia had not only mastered the Greek alphabet completely – she had previously loathed it as a set of stupid-looking squiggles – but also the rudiments of Greek grammar. Within three months, she was translating passages of Plutarch. And within six months, she was reading Homer in the original.

And more fluently than Marcus.

The competitive spirit not only accelerated Julia's education. It also, finally, ironically, broke down the barriers of mutual mistrust between her and Marcus.

Spring was in the air, and lounging out in the orchard, under the cherry trees, the two children began boasting about what they knew of the great world beyond.

'In Spain, where I was born,' said Julia, 'they don't have cherry trees, but they do have walnut trees and olive trees and almond trees, and almond blossom is even prettier than cherry blossom. They also have cork oaks, and once every few years they strip the bark off to make corks with, and load so much of it onto a donkey's back that you can hardly see the donkey at all. But it's all right, because it doesn't really weigh much, and donkeys are very strong. Though not as strong as my father was.'

'My father killed dozens of men,' said Marcus. 'He was with the Fourth *Scythica*, out in Antioch, like my brothers are now, and he fought in the Persian Wars against Shapur. And up on Hadrian's Wall, he often fought hand-to-hand with the

Painted Men and always killed them. At least, until he got his arrow wound.'

'What's it like in the north?' asked Julia.

'Cold,' said Marcus. 'Cold and grey. The sky is grey and in winter the days are very short, only a few hours. Though in summer sometimes when you're out riding across the moors there after a boar or a wolf, it's good.'

'Have you killed a wolf?'

'Of course,' said Marcus, 'lots of times.' He hoped Julia didn't go repeating this to Lucius. 'There is a lot of space up there. The mountains are huge.'

At the thought of that vast, undiscovered country lying so many leagues away, they both lay back in the grass and sighed and stared up into the big blue overhead, and lost themselves in dreams. Exciting as it was to live in London, sometimes they wished for the wide open spaces that they had both known, in different countries, before.

'I wish we could get out more,' said Marcus. 'Not just with Bricca or Hermogenes: he lectures me the whole time we're out, about the statues, the temples, the drains, even the sewers. There must be so much more to see. Britain is still half-wild, they say.'

Suddenly, Julia sat up. 'We should escape,' she said excitedly.

Marcus remained recumbent, eyes closed. 'What are you talking about?'

'Run away,' said Julia. 'Sneak out one night, when everyone else in the villa is sound asleep, and make no noise, and escape into the city, and explore, and have adventures. Maybe even go beyond the city walls,' she added vaguely, 'down to the sea or something.'

Marcus sat up very quickly. 'Are you serious?'

'Definitely. It gets so *boring*, doesn't it? Just day after day doing our lessons with Hermogenes, and going to the market, and riding out on Bucephalus. It's all right for you, you'll be old enough to have adventures anyway soon.'

'Not that soon,' said Marcus. 'Years away yet.' He folded his hands across his knees, squinted up at the sun. Then he looked at Julia. 'We'd have to take plenty of food. Supplies and stuff.'

'Apples and pears,' said Julia. 'And lots of cheese.'

'My hunting knife,' said Marcus. 'And a rope. Just in case.'

Suddenly all rivalry between them was gone. They both sat bolt upright like startled hares, eyes glittering, thrilled with the sudden prospects opening before them.

'Tonight,' said Julia. 'I'll stay awake until I hear everyone has gone to bed. I'll splash water on my face to stay awake, and then when the coast is clear, I'll come and tap on your door, three times. We can get out over the roof of the stables and down to the street that way. No one will ever know.'

She was so eager to get to bed that night that Bricca was quite anxious.

'I hope you're not sickening for something,' she said, laying her palm across the girl's forehead. 'Going to bed is usually the last thing you want to do.'

'Just tired,' murmured Julia, snuggling down into her blankets and yawning so hugely that she almost convinced herself. Her eyes watered as she yawned and she squeezed them tight shut.

'Well then, we'll see you in the morning,' said Bricca. She stood and snuffed out the tiny flame of the oil-lamp and went outside.

Julia's eyes flew open in the darkness. She lay and thought of how it felt to be about to set off on such a great pilgrimage. Who knew where they would end up? Beside the grey Northern sea? On a boat to Gaul? (She shivered with delicious terror at the thought of meeting the captain again. Marcus would have to tie him up with his rope.) Perhaps even to great Rome itself, or the Bay of Naples; or into the green valleys of Arcadia. Or lying in the shade of the date-palms of Palmyra, watching the Saracen caravans go by . . .

And thinking such thoughts, of course she fell asleep.

She awoke again at the sound of a door shutting down in the atrium below. She had no idea what time it was. She reached out and scooped some water from the basin beside her bed and splashed her eyes.

After a few moments, she slid out of bed and pulled open her door. It was black outside: well into the night, she thought. She turned back to slip into her sandals and lace them on, and settle her cloak around her shoulders, and then she crept out along the open gallery that ran the length of the first storey of the villa, to the door at the end where Marcus was waiting for her.

'Where have you *been*?' he hissed.

'Just being careful,' she whispered back. 'Come on.'

Marcus stood up and looped his leather sack over his shoulder, and followed her.

Out in the gallery again, she stopped halfway along, leaned out over the balcony and, twisting her head, looked up at the roof-tiles hanging over their heads.

'Should be all right,' she said.

'Are you sure?' said Marcus.

'Don't be such a girl,' said Julia. In a trice she had hopped onto the balcony and turned and gripped the eaves of the roof above and was hauling herself up.

'Give me a push, then!' she hissed down.

And with a final heave from Marcus, she was up. He followed her example, and being so much taller, managed the feat without a bunk-up. Soon they were both crawling carefully up the incline of the roof to the ridge, where they arrived breathless and exhilarated, sitting astride the roof-ridge like triumphant generals astride a great steed. They felt the almost irresistible urge to laugh out loud.

Marcus kicked his legs with glee, and in doing so dislodged

a loose tile which began to grate down the roof towards the edge. They watched in horror, frozen, unable to move. Finally the tile slithered to the eaves and dropped over. A moment later, there came a great *crash* from the courtyard. Almost immediately, the torches were lit and Valentinus was out in the atrium, shouting for the slaves to rouse themselves and check the whole villa for intruders.

'And take your weapons,' he called after them. 'You can't be too careful in these distempered times.'

From two floors down, Julia heard a snicker from Bucephalus, sensing something was happening that shouldn't be at this time of night, and she pictured him down there in the darkness of the stables, shifting anxiously from one neat hoof to another, nodding his head with disquiet.

'Quickly,' hissed Julia, 'let's get away.'

Slithering on their bottoms with careless haste, they slid down to the far side of the roof and peered over. It was a good ten-foot drop to the ground, but the alley below was muddy and looked like a reasonably soft landing.

Besides, there was no time for doubt or delay. Lanterns and torches were being lit all over the place down below, and soon the slaves would be out and scouring the outside of the villa too. Julia took a deep breath and dropped. She landed in a welt of clotted mud which splashed back up her legs and dirtied her tunic instantly, but otherwise there was no harm done.

'Come on,' she called up to Marcus. 'And remember to bend at the knees.'

He followed her immediately, his greater weight giving him a harder landing which he absorbed well enough by rolling sideways as he hit.

Scrambling to his feet, his eyes met hers. Their faces shone with inexpressible excitement. They were out!

And without another word, two of the filthiest (but best-educated) children in London set off on their great nocturnal adventure.

☆ ☆ ☆

The city at night was a different place.

They felt it was dangerous, and Marcus gripped his dagger tightly under his cloak. They passed groups of drunks, some of them soldiers from the fort on the Southwark side, who staggered blearily towards them and then away, shouting out foully but without anger. One of them veered so sharply left that he toppled straight into the Walbrook. His companions pressed on regardless, leaving him to his watery fate, floundering in a rising mist of wine fumes.

Julia couldn't believe how dark it was. But for the occasional flare of a torch as a late-night reveller passed them by, the city was plunged in complete blackness. Overhead there was starlight, and a scrim of cloud half-covered a gibbous moon, but the great buildings and the narrow streets of the city seemed to absorb what pale light the night sky gave, and left all its citizens in a far inkier darkness than their country cousins.

It only added to the excitement. Both children were in a permanent cold sweat, their outstretched hands trembling as they felt their way down dark alleys and along damp, rusticated walls.

Finally they emerged into the forum, and what sights met their eyes! For it was nowhere near as late as they had believed, and the night time revels were in full swing.

Nearly everybody seemed to be drunk. In the shadowy entrances of wine shops, hardened drinkers sat cradling large tankards of cheap red wine in their laps and cracking nuts between their teeth. There were fire-eaters standing on barrels, their faces shiny in the orange lights. There was a 'magician' performing tricks with an almond under three wooden beakers. Time and again his besotted audience tossed copper coins in his upturned cap, betting with assurance on which beaker hid the nut. And time and again, they got it wrong, and the magician, with an expression of great surprise on his face, found that he had amassed another handful of money.

They saw a large number of young and not so young ladies, out on the town without any escorts, richly made-up with green eyelids and carmine lips, their tunics worn rather too short for respectability, and wearing over-sized flaxen wigs. One of them even approached Marcus with the offer of 'a bit of fun, darling', which rendered the boy speechless and scarlet with embarrassment, until another of the ladies grabbed her friend's hand and dragged her away with many a squawk of mirth. Julia simultaneously grabbed Marcus' hand and dragged him away, entirely unamused.

They saw a group of musicians standing on a street corner, jigging up and down in the smoky darkness, while the most extraordinary and haunting music swirled and skirled around them. They played a weird combination of bladderskin pipes, coarse gut-stringed zithers, and hide-covered drums, which they hefted under their arms and beat with little wooden clubs or even animal bones. The sounds they made were barbaric and bewitching, and Julia stood very still for a long time, open-mouthed.

'They're Celts,' whispered Marcus, his voice a strange blend of disapproval and excitement.

At that word, Julia whipped round and stared at him, and then returned her gaze to the ragged musicians, more entranced than ever. They wore their hair long and extravagantly matted with coloured ribbons, and their faces, as she now saw in the dim light, were indeed decorated with lines and whorls and stipples of blue ink. She was also fascinated by their loud plaid trousers.

Julia looked back at Marcus, and saw that he too was entranced. Their eyes met and sparked, and they both knew the other's thoughts and needed to say nothing. *Real Celts — barbarians from the far west or the north, from the desolate moors and the mountains, the lands of the bears and druids, where they eat babies and spear their enemies' heads on stakes!* They shivered with fear and strange anticipation. *One day they would . . . One day . . .* And then they seized each other by the hand, at the same unnameable, inexpressible instant, and together raced off down a nearby street, whooping with laughter and wordless glee.

Eventually they found themselves down by the dockside. And here, perched side by side on the timbered edge of the riverbank, just downstream from the bridge, swinging their legs and staring out across the great black slow-moving river to the low gravel islands of the Southwark side, they unpacked the food they had brought for their Great Journey. By now they were both starving hungry, and they sat in companionable silence, sighing, munching, dreaming, and feeling very pleased with themselves indeed.

Seeing all the ships and boats again reminded Julia of the terrifying crossing from Spain, and the death of her nurse, and the horrible sea captain, and in a sudden burst, she told Marcus all about it. He listened and nodded, said nothing, looked out over the river, and wished that he had had such adventures to match.

Still, she was all right, this one. For a girl.

The river was on the ebbtide, and the sound of the water passing through the massive stone piers of the bridge was soothing. Overhead, the sky was now quite clear of cloud, and the stars were bright and near. Julia stared up until she was stiff-necked, thinking of how the stars shone down everywhere, all over the earth, just the same: on her and Marcus, on Lucius and on Ahenobarbus, out in the orchard now perhaps, hunting mice like the terrible predator he was; and on Bucephalus standing sleeping in his stable, and on Rome and the Emperor himself. And even on her parents lying out there in Spain.

For her heart had now, quite necessarily, erased any memory of the villa being burned to the ground on the Vicarius' orders. Instead she had settled upon a fixed image – of that pristine white villa in the hills, eternally, as pure and white as marble, silent as a temple, and in a chamber in the very centre of the villa, red roses strewn about the floor.

122

Hidden away behind white veils, a handsome man and a beautiful woman lay sleeping side by side on a white marble bier. Nobody could touch them, nobody come near; but everyone knew they were there.

And the same stars shone down on them as well.

Her reverie was interrupted by the sound of someone coming down to the dockside nearby.

They watched with interest as a little rat-like man came scurrying out between two warehouses, a leather satchel on his back. The man paused on the edge of the dockside and peered around, evidently in some trepidation, but he failed to notice the two children, sitting quietly as they were in the shadows of the bridge.

'What's he doing?' whispered Julia.

'Sssh,' said Marcus, crossing both forefingers across his lips. 'I think I can guess.'

They watched in silence as the little man, having decided that he was alone, hopped out onto one of the great flat-bottomed river barges that lay moored up beside the docks. As soon as he was in, he let the sack fall from his shoulder and upended it. In the still black night, the children could hear the patter and the high-pitched squeal of . . .

'Rats,' whispered Marcus. 'He's a ratcatcher.'

'But what's he doing letting them all go again?' asked Julia. 'Why isn't he catching them?'

Marcus grinned, his teeth a seam of quartz in the night. 'Precisely,' he said. 'He'll catch them all again tomorrow, for a few bronze pennies apiece. And the day after, and the day after that . . .' He turned round to see the ratcatcher hop back onto the dockside.

'Good evening, sir!' he called out.

It was hard to say who was more startled, the ratcatcher or Julia. She seized Marcus' arm, terrified that the man would come over and hit them, or set his rats on them or something.

She couldn't believe Marcus had just given them away like this.

The ratcatcher, however, having swallowed his panic, came sidling over to them when he saw that they were only children.

'Well, hello, my kiddywinks,' he said softly. 'And what are you doing out on a dark night like tonight?' He didn't wait for an answer to that one, already fumbling in his purse. 'And it *is* a dark night, isn't it? Too dark for you to see what's going on at the end of your nose, heh? Especially if your eyes are dazzled at the time, with, say, a fine copper coin like – oh I say! Just like this one here, that's dropped from my hand and straight into your lap!'

Marcus stared down at it, then up at the ratcatcher again. 'It might take two such coins – ' he suggested. 'One for each eye?' Think of it, he thought sourly to himself, as an extra payment for referring to us as *kiddywinks*.

The ratcatcher smiled a horrible false smile and dropped a second coin into his lap. 'There, now,' he said. 'And what do you say to that?'

'Quite extraordinary,' agreed Marcus. 'Blinding, in fact.'

The ratcatcher chuckled with relief, and tapped the side of his nose, then turned and hurried off between the warehouses to get some sleep, before another busy day's work tomorrow.

'Hmph,' said Julia with pretended disapproval, wishing she didn't feel quite such intense admiration for Marcus just at this moment. 'And where did you learn a trick like that?'

'You learn a lot being brought up in an army camp on the Wall,' said Marcus with great insouciance, flipping a coin high in the air and catching it again, apparently without having to look. 'You've got to stay sharp in the big city, you know. Come on – let's go and buy some more grub, I'm starving.'

They each ate a rissole of minced beef topped with fried onions and squashed between two halves of a bread roll, which they bought from a stall in the marketplace. It tasted delicious.

'My uncle doesn't like me eating in the street,' mumbled Julia, her mouth very full. 'He says it's vulgar and plebeian.'

'It is,' agreed Marcus, his mouth even fuller. 'Great, isn't it?'

After that, they began to get anxious that it must by now be growing very late – although the town was still thronged with people. Perhaps it was almost dawn, though the sky showed no grey light in the east. In fact, their Great Adventure had taken them no more than an hour and a half. It was not yet midnight. But, feeling very pleased with their adventure, and resolving to have another one as soon as possible, they set off for home.

Chattering away in great excitement as they were, they failed to notice a litter being carried past them by two slaves. They could not help but notice, however, when they heard the sound of Lucius' voice.

'What a surprise to find you two out so late,' he said coldly. 'And what exactly are you doing, may I ask?'

It was hard to tell if he was really cross or not, so Julia started to explain that they had only sneaked out a little earlier, actually they hadn't realised it was that late, and they hadn't done much really, only –

Lucius silenced her with a single stare. Then he said, 'Walk home ahead of me. When you get home, you will go straight to bed. You will come to see me at dawn tomorrow with a full account of your misdeeds.' He clicked his fingers and his slaves walked forwards again, with the two children forming a crestfallen vanguard.

They slept badly that night.

CHAPTER TEN

It was late spring now, and dawn was horribly early. The two children stood yawning and blinking sleepily, waiting for Lucius' summons to enter. When at last he gave it, they realised immediately that he was very angry.

He lectured them on the duties of obedient children, the penalties of disobedience, and his own duties *in loco parentis*. Finally he asked, 'So, whose idea was this ridiculous escapade?'

Julia and Marcus looked at each other, locked eyes, and then looked back at Lucius.

'Mine,' they both said simultaneously.

Lucius – the Stoic with the terrible temper – was instantly enraged.

'So you are both liars as well as everything else!' he roared. 'And I suppose you are foolish enough to believe that there is something *noble* in sharing the blame for your misdeeds? Then those who share the blame shall also share the punishment.'

He took an eelskin strap from a desk drawer, and grasping each of them by the left wrist, first Julia, then Marcus, he lashed them fiercely, six times, on the tender underside of the forearm.

They stood back afterwards, their arms clenched across their chests, hugged to themselves like wounded animals, trying not to whimper.

'Now go to your lessons,' said Lucius, sitting down behind his desk and not looking up again. 'I have work to do.'

It was hard to study when your arm felt like it had been parboiled. Intermittently they would show each other their forearms, as the rosy welts appeared across their white flesh. Odd, thought Julia, how something that hurt so much could make you so proud of yourself.

Lucius found it hard to work too.

He was doing a set of complicated calculations on the correct level of taxation for the great lead mines at Charterhouse in the Mendips. Normally he would expect the mines to hand over a straight fifty per cent of their net profits to the treasury, but this time it was fearfully convoluted, as always when you were dealing with an industry that was partly state-owned, and partly in private hands.

It was even more complicated when you had your conscience distracting you, buzzing like a hornet inside your skull.

He had been in a bad mood anyway last night. It always enraged him, having to spend a tiresome evening dining at the Vicarius' Palace with his peers, faking his every smile or expression of interest, trapped for hours in the company of mediocre minds. The news from the Empire was bad – as usual these days. There was no money, no communication, and Constans, as they managed to conclude without sounding treasonous, was a mincing incompetent who was fast losing the support of the one group that really mattered: the military.

It was a depressing catalogue of decay, followed not by any constructive ideas, but instead by a wallowing in more wine and bitchy gossip. Sulpicius, especially, excelled at this. And so Lucius had to lie there and listen to Vicarius' brother boring on about his affairs, and the Emperor's affairs, and anyone else's affairs he could think of, real or imagined. And all this time,

Lucius thought, he could have been at home in his library, in the company not of Sulpicius, but of Seneca, Plutarch, or Cicero. Such was the magic of the written word. Although too long spent in the company of the great master-spirits of philosophy and literature did have this obvious disadvantage (he smiled a wintry smile): it made one even more impatient of the conversation of mediocrities like Sulpicius.

Was it for this – here came the hornet's buzz – that he had so soundly beaten his wards? Had he made them pay, to some extent, for his own loathing of Sulpicius?

And why had he been so angry at the way they had protected each other, both claiming equal responsibility? That was a noble thing to do, and he knew it. Had he anticipated it? Had it frustrated him, to find them half-disobedient, half-noble, so that he could not easily dismiss them as merely naughty children? How mixed-up and confused everything was – including his own motives!

And had he not known that by punishing them both like that, equally, he would only drive them closer together? Imposing almost a blood-bond on them?

Yes, he had known it. So why . . .? Perhaps because he knew at a deeper level that it was fated. Beneath his anger, he had felt it was right that they should suffer together. Perhaps his punishing them had been a way of driving them towards each other, and away from him: this sour, crabby old man who was not their real father.

Another wintry smile, in the mirror of his mind.

The punishment must fit the crime – and this time, he had failed. After all, it was a crime of youthful high spirits, of thoughtless disobedience. It was not so terrible. Tomorrow he would try to be gentle with them. His children, his orphans.

And – *obiter dicta* – how stupid, truly *stupid* Vidalius was, regarding this ceaseless, miraculous labour of self-discovery. It was the only kind of progress worthy of the name: the progress of the soul towards self-knowledge. The famous maxims of the

Seven Sages of Greece were, he had always thought, of an uneven quality. *Avoid responsibility for others' debts*, for instance, struck him as crushingly banal. The wisdom of a miser rather than a sage. But there was no arguing with the supreme saying of all: *Know thyself*. (Lucius had always taken a certain grim pleasure, too, in another of the sages' maxims, so quintessentially Greek: *Most men are bad*.)

One day, the sages of the future would plumb the depths of the ocean itself. One day they would build a tower so tall that it reached out among the stars, and they would walk upon the moon (and plant it with an SPQR and a *labarum*, and claim it for the Emperor, no doubt.) But they would never fully excavate the deeps of the human heart. *All that I know of human nature, I learned from me . . .*

Lucius was a man who had learned much, painfully, by gazing unblinking into himself for long hours and years. He rarely liked what he found at those lower, sedimentary levels of swamp and selfishness. The highest-seeming motives of altruism and duty, he discovered, were often founded on the most selfish and warped impulses.

Now, in unforgiving self-examination, he found that he was jealous of Marcus and Julia. He was jealous of their youth and irresponsibility. He was afraid that they would not love him, he was afraid of lonely old age. He was disgusted to find that some of the anger he had unleashed upon them, was indeed mere peevishness at a wasted evening, spent dining with fools and boors. How weak and childish even men of his age could be. How petulant! How self-pitying! For all their philosophy.

When Cennla first saw what the master had done to Julia, his eyes misted over with rage. He even went over to the hooks on the wall and began to choose which knife to use, to avenge this terrible assault. The meat-cleaver? The serrated fruit-knife, drawn slowly across his forearm? See how he would like that?

Cennla had believed that the days of beating were over and done, left behind with the wicked captain and his vinewood knout on the boat. But now, the wickedness had followed them, and his own beloved was suffering at the hands of the unsmiling master. But he, Cennla, would avenge her, no matter what the cost.

Then he saw that she did not seem to mind the punishment, somehow. Instead she compared her weals to those of the boy, Marcus, and they laughed and put their heads together.

His fists seized up, the skin over the knuckles drum-tight. He gasped, swallowed. No one would ever . . . no one but he . . . Some nights he dreamed that demons out of hell had come for her. But he, Cennla, lay across the doorway, and they could not pass.

That night he dreamed of killing the master. Of breaking into Lucius' room and in the darkness cutting his startled face into red ribbons. When he awoke he was ashamed of himself, and to seal his secret compact with her whom he served, before first light he crouched in the stables, whipping himself, bloody backed, to share her pain.

In the morning, Julia came into the kitchens to find Cennla bending over a bucket of water, and then crooking his arm to touch a wet cloth to his back. It was covered in weals.

'Who beat you?' she asked.

He straightened up.

It must have been her uncle, she supposed. Well, it was only right that a master should beat his slaves sometimes. But it didn't seem like Lucius . . .

She reached out and touched the red wounds, skimmed her palm over the boy's skinny back. 'I'm sorry,' she said.

Then turned away to get her breakfast.

By the evening, Cennla knew that his wounds had healed. At night he got up and lit a candle and twisted and looked over his shoulder to see his back reflected in the bottom of a copper pan hanging from the wall. It was completely clear.

He never told anyone, made no sign. He was afraid.

☆ ☆ ☆

For a while the two children were good.

And then, just as the itch to be bad was becoming almost intolerable – and Lucius could sense it, all too well – he abruptly announced that they would be leaving the next day, to spend the summer in the Cotswolds.

'The what?' said Julia, after Lucius had left the room.

'The Cotswolds,' said Marcus, infuriatingly knowing. 'The hills around Cirencester. It's where all the rich London types have their country retreats, which they visit for about two weeks a year. The locals hate them.'

'How do you know? Have you ever been there?'

'Well, no,' he admitted, 'but my father told me all about it. He hated the Cotswolds too. He said that after the north, staying in the Cotswolds was like eating too much honey. It's very pretty there, though. You'll probably love it.'

'No I won't,' said Julia.

It took them five days to get there. They had ridden out at dawn, Julia nearly driving everybody mad with running around and skipping from one foot to another and only being able to keep silent by clamping her lips tightly together so the words couldn't get out. How big are the Cotswolds? she wanted to ask. Are there bears? Are the people painted blue there? Is it cold up there? Will it snow? And what will we do for lunch?

She sat in the front of the wagon wide-eyed, and saw and remembered everything, as they rode out of Newgate, and crossed the Fleet River, with Lucius riding up front on a chestnut mare, and Marcus just behind him on a skewbald pony. Behind the wagon came the entire household, apart from Silvanus and the slave-girls. Finally, bringing up the rear on a long tether, and holding up the entire train on account of his brevity of limb, breadth of girth, and absolute refusal to accelerate beyond a sedate walking pace, was

Bucephalus. Julia had insisted that he should come. Lucius had insisted that he shouldn't. Julia had insisted again that he should. And Lucius, against his better judgement, had given in.

They rode on through the water meadows beyond the Fleet, and heard the water-wheels clacking away in the streams, saw the orchards of plumtrees and peartrees, and the saffron fields, and then they came to the crossroads with Watling Street, heading north up to St Albans. They carried straight on over, taking the Silchester road, and reached Staines by evening, where they rested for the night. At dawn the next day they crossed the Thames. Julia, craning round the side of the wagon to watch a cormorant flying upstream, nearly fell right out of the wagon and into the river.

'Wouldn't have mattered that much if you had fallen in,' said Marcus cheerfully, riding alongside her after they were off the bridge. 'You could have swum all the way up the Thames to the Cotswolds then. That's where it rises, you know?'

Julia was unimpressed. '*Pig, pig, your mouth's too big . . .*' she began to chant at him.

But Marcus just tutted, in a very adult fashion, and murmured '*So* childish,' then rode back to join Lucius.

Julia sulked for five hours.

The road was busy with travellers and tinkers, and small detachments of troops marching from Silchester, whom Lucius would often stop and question.

The second night they slept in Silchester, and set off late the next day, because Lucius had made them all wait while he rode out to inspect the tile-kilns to the south of the town, and order up a batch for the rebuilt barracks in Southwark.

The third night they stopped in the middle of nowhere, billeting themselves on a bewildered shepherd and his family, high on the Marlborough Downs. In the morning, they had bites all over their arms and legs, to testify to the simple rusticity of their night's lodgings.

On the fourth night they arrived in Cirencester, with its magnificent baths and glittering shopping arcades. Here they had a grand and spacious town residence to stay in: the house of Lucianus Septimius, the provincial governor of Cirencester and the sub-province of Britannia Prima which he governed. Septimius, an easy-going hedonist, was spending the summer at his villa in the Cotswolds, not far from his house in town.

The next day they came to their villa. It was an enchanted summer. Julia found herself falling instantly in love with that country. The broad green sheep-country, and the dense beech-woods, and the dozens of little hidden valleys, unfolding one after another, which the Celtic locals called *coombes*. And the whole swathe of rich countryside bright and blossoming under May sunshine.

Lucius often dined over at the villa of Septimius, in the neighbouring valley, and, on the whole, neglected the care of his wards quite shamefully. Away from the poisonous politics and intrigues of London, he relaxed and smiled and enjoyed even the company of Septimius, no great intellect but quite without malice or guile as well.

Marcus and Julia were out all day and every day, lying in a boat on the small and lazy river, trailing their hands in the water, gazing over the side watching the flickering trout, for hours, saying nothing. Watching the flash of a kingfisher scissoring a minnow out of the river in a shower of sparks. The heron's harsh cry and the distant and lonelier cries of buzzards and red kites circling overhead. An otter on the riverbank, devouring a pike almost its own size. Lying low watching the sunset through the feathered reeds, the orange light like bars of molten copper on the river.

They played with Cennla too, as if the normal ordinances separating citizen and slave were temporarily suspended. Marcus and Cennla showed off endlessly to Julia. They wrestled with each other – Cennla won. They competed at archery – Marcus won. They caught hares and shot pigeons and cooked their catches over open fires at the edge of the woods and ate them with relish, despite being half-charcoal and wood-ash.

And when they finally packed up at the end of the summer and began the journey back to London, they were sad, autumn was upon them, and its near and brilliant forerunner, that enchanted summer, only made the autumn seem more melancholy, as all enchanted summers must.

The days shortened again, and the children returned to their studies, Marcus dutifully, Julia with real eagerness.

After their studies were over each day, she still wanted to read more – to Marcus' annoyance. In the late afternoons, with the sky already darkening and the hanging oil lamps lit, she would curl up on the great red couch in the corner of the library and read by the golden light her Virgil, and Ovid, and Livy, and Apuleius, and Apollonius Rhodius ... such stories. But most of all, she read Virgil. She read of the deaths of Euryalus and Nisus, cut down like summer flowers; and of Dido, and her hopeless love for pious Aeneas. She saw her funeral pyre high upon the cliffs of Carthage, could hear her grief sounding across the waves to her unbending lover.

It was during the following spring that their dangerous taste for adventure was renewed.

There was the time when Marcus boasted that he could swim the Thames, and Julia told him to prove it. So by moonlight they stood down by the bridge, and Marcus stripped off and plunged in. He only got as far as the first pier before the massive force of the water on the ebb bowled him hard against the stone piers, and he returned gasping and spluttering and shamefaced, admitting that, well, all right, he couldn't swim the Thames *yet*, but he would one day . . . when he was in the army, and in full armour too. Like the Batavian legionaries who could swim across the Danube even in its spring torrent.

There was the time they saw that the north wall of the church, once a part of the old Basilica, was covered in wooden scaffolding, ready for replastering. So that night, they sneaked out and climbed up the scaffolding, higher and higher, and eventually arrived breathless on the roof, and sat on the very summit of the ridge like conquering mountaineers, gasping at the view of the city that lay spread out below them, and the river and the dark wooded countryside beyond.

There was the time they stowed away on a river barge which took them all the way down the Thames before they were discovered: they only escaped a beating by vanishing over the side of the boat and making the long and arduous walk back across the marshes to the city.

More ambitious plans, to break into the Vicarius' Palace, for instance, or scale the walls of the old London Fort, were mercifully abandoned as being too dangerous. Nevertheless, the day came when they went just too far, and were caught again.

The pair were standing outside the public bath-houses down by the Thames, not far from home, waiting for Hermogenes to return from a scribe's with a fresh copy of an ancient and battered *Letters of Pliny*. To pass the time, Julia was re-enacting a scene from Euripides, for Marcus' benefit. With a cry of *euoi! euoi!*, and flinging her arms wide in a gesture of hysterical grief, she had the misfortune to connect violently with the midriff of a passer-by, who doubled over in breathless agony. When at last he stood upright again, they saw that he was very angry.

The man was lean and stringy, with sloping shoulders and

pale eyebrows and pale blue watery eyes. His tunic was a rather garish mustard-yellow. With him was a big, brutish-looking slave. He glared at the children ferociously, and let out such a stream of abuse that they were both shocked.

'I'm sorry, but it *was* an accident,' put in Julia.

In a trice, the man had grabbed her by the hair and shaken her so violently that her feet left the ground. Then he dropped her just as suddenly and turned and dashed on into the baths.

Julia crouched on the ground, cradling her head.

'Are you all right?' asked Marcus awkwardly, kneeling down next to her.

'Well, of course I'm not all right,' she spat at him, her eyes tearful with pain. 'That *beast*. Who does he think he is?'

Marcus shook his head. And then after a few moments, he said, 'You know what we should do?'

'*What* should we do?'

'Pay a visit to the baths ourselves.'

'What for?'

'Revenge.'

Normally the public-baths operated a system of women and girls in the morning, and men and boys in the afternoon. But some of the cheaper and more dubious bath-houses – such as this one – were more lax about such divisions. As long as you could pay the attendant a small fee, you were in.

It was odd, now Marcus thought about it, that their assailant should have been here at all. Vile-tempered he may have been, but he also looked wealthy and respectable. Why should he come to a bath-house like this? But Marcus was old enough by now to have a vague idea of what might be the attraction . . .

The attendant merely stared at them, unable to rouse himself as far as speech, dropped their coins into a wooden tray, and then paused on the threshold of the changing rooms.

Or changing room: there was only a single, grubby room for everybody. Round the walls were a series of stone niches where bathers left their shoes and sandals and, if they could afford it, a slave to stand guard over them. There were four slaves there now, standing around and gossiping.

Marcus thought fast.

'I'll go on in,' he said to Julia. 'Come round the corner in a while, be all excited and tell us there's another riot on in the streets outside, the Christians are upset again or something. I'll do the rest.'

He went in and began to change slowly. There in the far corner, behind the big, brutish-looking slave with the bald head and simian brow, he could clearly see a mustard-yellow tunic folded up neatly and laid in one of the stone niches.

Suddenly there was an excitable, high-pitched voice in the entrance-hall. Everyone looked up.

'Yes,' came the voice, 'an escaped leopard, really. It's already eaten two people, and someone has tied a firebrand to its tail, I saw it running down the street just now, setting fire to everything as it ran, and even the temples and churches are burned, so they say, and there's an elephant on the loose too now, and, and –'

The attendant slaves, even the brute, were out in the entrance-hall in a trice, peering into the street to look for the burning leopard and the elephant – and Marcus was dressed and on his feet and snatching the yellow tunic from its niche, bundling it up under his own clothes and heading for the door.

'I think you must have made some kind of unfortunate mistake,' said a cold voice behind him. 'That's *my* tunic you're making off with.'

Marcus froze. *Run,* he thought to himself, *just run*. But he couldn't move. There was some serpentine quality in that voice that utterly immobilised him.

And then there was the big slave up ahead, and behind him he could see Julia, bobbing up and down trying to see whether her unlikely tale had been effective.

'Grab her too!' yelled the voice behind Marcus, and with surprising dexterity, the big slave spun round and pounced on the girl, dragging her back into the changing room.

The man behind Marcus held him tightly by the scruff of his tunic, and he had to twist round to face him: the baleful pale blue eyes, the pale eyebrows. The breath of cold fury. Marcus swallowed.

Suddenly the man's hand snaked out and dealt first Marcus and then Julia a stinging blow across the face. Julia twisted and bit the slave on his arm. He roared and flung her to the ground. Marcus jumped onto his back, and was promptly torn off and held at arm's length by the slave. The pale-eyed man, meanwhile, crouched down on the floor beside Julia and, with one hand clamped around the nape of her neck, pressing her face into the hard stone floor, he began to beat her viciously with the other. Julia screamed furiously and tried to twist around to bite or scratch him, but she couldn't escape from his iron clasp.

'Oh, but I will master you, my little one,' he murmured quietly, so that only she could hear him. 'My little darling, oh but I will.'

Marcus struggled desperately, until at last the slave grew tired of holding him and dealt him a colossal blow to the side of his head that sent him sprawling semi-conscious to the floor. Turning his head groggily, Marcus saw that the pale-eyed man was still giving Julia a furious beating, although it seemed with less anger now. Indeed, though Marcus' head was spinning and he couldn't be sure of anything very much, it seemed to him that the man was giggling as he beat the girl, giggling and chuckling to himself, a tensed, toothy grin on his face . . .

The rest of the slaves and some of the men from the baths were standing around now too, cheering him on and clapping and laughing, clearly finding the whole scene immensely entertaining.

'Escaped leopard, indeed,' snorted one of the slaves. 'They're nothing but a couple of common thieves, the two of them.'

And then another voice sounded from behind the crowd. 'Stop that immediately.'

The pale-eyed man looked up in surprise. He saw a funny, dwarfish little runt in front of him, with a snub nose and a big beard.

'Well, well,' he said, 'it's Socrates himself, come to pay us a visit.' His voice turned harsh again. 'I'll beat whoever I want if I catch them stealing my clothes. These little urchins –'

'These little urchins are the wards of the Imperial Praepositus, Lucius Fabius Quintilianus,' said Hermogenes. 'And he will not be pleased at the treatment they have received at your hands.'

'And I am Sulpicius, the brother of Albinus, the Vicarius, and *I* am not pleased at my treatment at *their* hands!' roared the pale-eyed man.

Hermogenes flinched, but did not back away. Trembling, Julia was getting to her feet and trying to coax Marcus into doing likewise.

'Then take your complaint to Quintilianus,' said Hermogenes. 'I'm taking these two home.'

As the battered pair stumbled out of the bath-house, one on each arm of their tutor, Sulpicius called after them, 'Perhaps Quintilianus should give me his niece's hand in marriage, to make amends. I'm sure I could tame the little vixen!' The bath-house resounded with loud and hearty laughter.

Lucius remained supremely, Stoically expressionless when he saw the condition of the children.

'What happened to these two?'

Hermogenes told him.

Lucius nodded. 'Take yourselves off to Bricca and get washed. Ask her to put oil and vinegar on the cuts and bruises.' As they stumbled away, he called after them, 'You will give me a full account of your misbehaviour later today.'

He looked back at Hermogenes. 'So – they deserved the beating they got?'

'They deserved a beating,' admitted Hermogenes. 'But . . .' He hesitated. 'But not the beating they got. *No* child deserves the kind of beating they got. It was not . . .' He rubbed his beard. 'It was not a punishment administered justly and rationally. It was a punishment administered – with too much pleasure.'

Lucius looked down. Was there some point at which expressionless, passionless Stoicism blurred into mere cowardice? It was a question that had troubled him many times before. He had a mental image, as sharp as pain, of Sulpicius, a man from the waist up but a serpent below, slithering on his belly through the vast marble corridors of the Vicarius' Palace, leaving behind him a trail of slime and sickness and illimitable corruption.

Lucius looked up. 'Follow me,' he said.

The central courtyard of the Palace was degenerately ornate, a pathetic aping of Constantinople, with its elaborate many-coloured mosaics, frescoes, and the vulgar excess of gold leaf, enough to have paid a legion for a month. A great, overbearing statue of the Emperor stood on a plinth in the eastern apse, looking out blank-eyed over all that went on in the Palace. It was well that Albinus made such a strong public statement of his loyalties, thought Lucius. From some of his conversation, after a few glasses of wine, you might think – mistakenly, of course – that he was rather less respectful of the Divine Constans. You might even think that Albinus had Imperial ambitions himself.

'The Vicarius is not to be disturbed,' a hare-eyed steward told them as they made their way across the courtyard. 'He is on important business.'

'So am I,' said Lucius, and walked on.

Albinus was seated behind his great desk in a relaxed fashion when they walked in. He settled his inscrutable blue eyes upon them.

'Ah, Quintilianus,' he said. 'And this is your wards' tutor, I presume?'

'My wards have behaved disgracefully,' said Lucius, ignoring the question. 'But they have also been subjected to an equally disgraceful assault in the bath-houses, by your brother Sulpicius. I cannot –'

'I have already heard,' interrupted Albinus.

Lucius was taken aback, but did not show it. News travelled fast.

'Were you at the scene yourself?' asked Albinus.

'No, I heard the account of it from Hermogenes here, a slave-born but, I assure you, an entirely trustworthy –'

'I heard the account of it directly from my own brother,' said Albinus. 'He suspected that you would be here soon enough. He understands you well.' Albinus smiled briefly. 'He tells me that what he meted out was a wholly justified chastisement to two apparently quite undisciplined little urchins who tried to steal his clothing. Are you telling me that I should prefer the account of a Greek slave to that of my own brother?'

'If you are asking me whom I should judge to be the more reliable witness, then I would choose the man beside me every time.'

Albinus raised one pale eyebrow. 'You go too far, Quintilianus,' he said, without anger. He stood and walked slowly across the room to the curtained divide. When he reached it, he looked back.

'We both of us know, Praepositus, that the Empire is suffering from a degree of confusion, of indiscipline and insubordination. And these major diseases in the body politic begin with minor ailments, such as disobedient children. I am surprised, therefore, that someone such as you, so famed for your sternness, quite the match of old Cato himself, should come running to me in this – if I may say so – rather undignified way, to defend the behaviour of your unruly wards.'

'I have not defended them,' said Lucius. 'I have acknowledged their bad behaviour without hesitation. But I cannot condone your brother's wanton cruelty. And, although confusion and insubordination are certainly to be condemned, I had rather thought, Vicarius, that it was the indulgence of anger, cruelty, and worse vices, which is gnawing at the heart of our beloved Empire.'

At last Albinus was stung. He snapped his gaze round and glared at Lucius. But all he could think to say was, again, 'You go too far, Quintilianus.' And with that, he snatched back the curtains and disappeared beyond them.

Lucius turned and left the Palace. He said to Hermogenes, 'News of this visit goes no further.' He did not want his wards to think that there was anything that could exonerate their behaviour.

Later that evening, walking in the walled gardens beside the villa, Lucius was calmer again. He walked slowly, head down, Valentinus at his side.

'What was Sulpicius doing in such a bath-house anyway?' he wondered. 'The kind that you enter with dirty skin and leave with a dirty soul.'

'Well,' said Valentinus, 'he likes to be one of the boys.'

Lucius nodded. He even permitted himself a bleak smile. 'He likes to keep his finger on the pulse.'

'He likes to keep a hand in,' added Valentinus.

They laughed low. They made such filthy puns not for their humour, but for their significance. Policy was made in courts and palaces. But treachery in wine-shops and baths.

Lucius did not laugh when he summoned his wards for

inspection before bedtime. Freshly scrubbed, their wounds soothed with oil and their bruises with vinegar, they were still a sorry sight. Clean, though, thought Lucius. For all their disobedience, clean-souled. Not like those who go clad in the richest garments, their blemishes all on the inside.

'You know how angry I am with you,' he said. 'Theft is theft, and always disgraceful.'

'But uncle, it started in the street, when –'

'I am not interested,' said Lucius.

He picked up the eelskin strap from his desk, grasped them by the hand in turn and thwacked their forearms twice each. He had been intending to strike them six times, as usual, but he could see, he could *feel* the expression in their eyes and he felt his own eyes prickling, and so delivered a curtailed punishment and then quickly turned away.

He could feel their eyes on him. Looks that spoke of betrayal.

'You may go now,' he said, seating himself behind his desk and not looking up.

They went to bed. Lucius wished he could go to bed too, so early. He was very tired. But there was work to be done. Never-ending labour. Almost a palindrome, he thought: Never-ending labour for the Empire, that Empire now labouring to its end.

'I *hate* Uncle Lucius, I *hate* him.' Julia was fairly sizzling with rage as they followed Bricca up to their first floor bedrooms. 'He's such a *coward*. He should have gone straight over to the palace and challenged the Vicarius himself. And instead all he does is go and hide in his library, with his stupid books – '

'Well, you know what trouble that could get him into,' said Marcus, trying to sound reasonable and adult, 'You must put your career first. It wouldn't do to go barging in and start slagging off the Vicarius' brother now, would it? See it from his point of view.'

Julia scowled. 'He didn't even ask what happened, he didn't even want to know.'

'He didn't feel he had to. And we must bow to the *paterfamilias*.'

Julia made a noise that sounded like the guttural grunting of an angry boar. Bricca looked round in astonishment. 'Now come on, you, that's quite enough for one day,' she scolded. 'Growl like a boar and you'll smell like a boar.'

'Is that really a proverb, Bricca?'

'Never you mind and into bed with you,' said Bricca, rather pleased with herself for having just made it up like that.

Three days later, a letter arrived from the Vicarius' Palace: a carefully calculated response. Like the snake, thought Lucius, turning and biting the man who stepped on it thirty years before.

To Lucius Fabius Quintilianus, greetings.

Be assured, my dear Lucius, that there remains no ill feeling between your house and ours, despite your intemperate outburst the other day in my brother the Vicarius' audience chamber. Such eruptions are only to be expected from a man of passion such as yourself! However, it seems advisable to us that some outward sign or emblem of this freshly reborn harmony between our houses should be made. You know how the plebs do like to gossip about scandal among the ruling classes, and no scandal attracts more attention from prying eyes and wagging tongues than one involving petty squabbles amongst ourselves.

In view of this, therefore, our attention turns in all seriousness to your niece. It is clear that she is now approaching nubile age, and we would be prepared to take her hand in marriage if that is agreeable to you. There is hardly a wealth of suitors to choose from in a town as small and remote as this, we know. Therefore we await your reply with some confidence, though not in entire happiness; for, as Cicero says in one of his noble letters, Quam sint morosi, qui amant – how morose are those who love!

Sulpicius

Lucius might have deigned to pen a curt reply – but for that revolting last line. The idea that a viper like Sulpicius should pretend to *love* his niece was too laughable. He suspected that he meant it as some kind of tasteless joke. He folded the letter neatly in two, tore it into strips, and dropped it in the fire.

It was true, however, that the girl was approaching 'nubile age', in Sulpicius' charming phrase. Lucius could hardly bear to think of it. He flinched and physically turned away at the thought, as if it stood directly in front of him, squatting on his path ahead, garish-mouthed, like some evil demon. Soon some other man would take her, though not Sulpicius – not till the Nile ceased to flood and the sun turned black – and she would be gone from this silent marriageless household, with her tears and tantrums and laughter, and her kitten long since grown into a sleek fat cat, and the shadowy corners of the sad winter rooms would no longer be fitfully illuminated by the flash of her hair and her eyes, but settle back into their old accustomed bachelordom and dust.

It seemed like only yesterday that he had come from his chambers one morning at dawn to find Bricca hovering about on the threshold of the kitchens, fingers entwined, like a supplicant at a shrine of uncertain temperament. She had started to gabble to him gooselike about a girl who had turned up on the doorstep late last night, filthy, hungry and tired. And it had taken him some moments to connect this mysterious arrival with the heartbreaking letter from his sister in Spain.

Julia. His niece. His beloved, spirited, clever, disobedient little niece. Yesterday a bright-eyed girl, tomorrow a woman. And he who had never had a child, felt now, most painfully and unfairly, as if he was about to lose a child. (Though any complaint of the world's unfairness was not to be heard on the lips of a true philosopher.) That childhood was going fast, and would soon be gone forever. It was not the world's fault, but his own, he thought. It was as if he had been given some rare and wonderful and quite unexpected gift, two years ago, and not appreciating it fully, he had stowed it away on a shelf and forgotten about it. And now, going to find it again, he found it . . . not corrupted, not that: not moth-eaten or withered away, but changed into something other, and no longer that original rare and wonderful thing. That gift that would never come back to him again.

Eheu fugaces, Postume, Postume, labuntur anni . . . One of Horace's most beautiful odes: 'Alas, O Postumus, Postumus, the years glide swiftly away . . .' For *tempus edax rerum*: Time is the devourer of all things. Time beating its slow but steady wings, like a heron over the Southwark marshes, or over the haunted fields of Caecubus in Latium, on the Gulf of Amyclae, where he used to go fowling as a boy to escape from Rome, a hunk of bread in his wallet and a bow and quiver over his skinny shoulder. So long ago now, so long ago and far away. He was an old man of fifty now – half a century! – and each year he could feel ever more keenly the ebb of time: a flowing river, the course of the sun. Each year he could hear its wingbeats ever more loudly: a great and irresistible bird in its slow but steady flight into the twilight.

Why Marcus did what he did next, nobody quite knew. Least of all himself. Sometimes our own motives are as clear to us as the backs of our heads.

It was something to do with trying to impress Julia; and wanting to believe that Lucius was far more tyrannical than he really was, and that therefore they must make their escape, he and Julia, by night and forever, in a desperate and heroic fashion. At darker levels, Lucius' melancholy brought out a horrible sadism in Marcus, as melancholy can. The inveterately, pachydermatously happy are often briskly contemptuous of the unhappy, and their contempt can blur into cruelty with ease. No doubt there were other motives too, as tangled together and inextricable as ancient ivy round a tree.

He spied on Lucius, to see where his guardian kept the key to the strongbox in the atrium. He sneaked into Lucius' chambers in the cold dead of night when everyone slept. He stole the key, opened the strongbox, and pulled out three silver bars with their blunt capital letters stating their provenance, EX OFF CVRMISSI, for *ex officina Curmissi:* From the workshop of Curmissus.

At a dubious moneychanger's shop behind the forum, Marcus managed to get twenty gold solidi for them, minus an extortionate twenty per cent commission, leaving him with sixteen solidi. He took the coins home in his leather purse and showed them to a round-eyed Julia. 'Tonight,' he said, 'we run away forever.'

The plan might have worked, if it weren't for the fact that Lucius, scrupulous as ever, chose that very afternoon to assess the contents of the strongbox, and found them wanting. Having observed a certain unsteady glitter in his ward's eyes earlier that day, it was with a sinking heart that he ordered Valentinus up to Marcus' room to search for his purse. 'Try under the bed,' he said.

Valentinus returned with a tatty but bulging leather purse in his hand. Contents: sixteen shiny gold solidi.

The boy, at least, had the guts to acknowledge it. Julia was even more furious with him than her uncle. She treated him with utter contempt. To *steal*, from your own guardian!

The whipping that followed was terrible. Marcus lay in bed on his belly for forty-eight hours while Bricca sponged his wounds. When he was summoned to Lucius' rooms again, late in the evening, he rose from his bed and his back was so scabbed that it cracked.

'You are sixteen years old in a fortnight, is that correct?' asked Lucius.

'Yes, sir.'

His guardian shuffled some papers on his desk. 'No doubt you will regard this as some kind of reward, but I assure you that you will come to think differently very soon.' Lucius looked up and fixed him in the eye. 'You will report to the gatehouse of the camp in Southwark on your sixteenth birthday, and will be signed into the army. You are younger than average – eighteen is still the usual age of admittance, as I am sure you know. But special provisions can be made, and you have the sufficient height. You will be signed in as a common foot-soldier. Apart from anything else, the spoiled young sons of rich men who get signed straight in at officer class earn nothing but hatred from their men.' He could see by the look in the boy's eyes that he had already stopped listening. 'Virtue grows in adversity, vice withers. Either way it will do you good.' He might as well have been addressing a statue. Nevertheless he added, 'And you'll find plenty of adversity in the army.'

Marcus relayed this last comment to Julia with what he fancied was a cool, off-hand kind of ruggedness. They were sitting in the orchard. Marcus chewed on a grass-stalk and nodded. 'Yeah, it's gonna be tough.'

Julia sat cross-legged and stared at the ground, saying nothing. She couldn't bring herself to speak to him. She couldn't believe he was leaving her like this. She felt like her world was coming to an end. In a few days' time he would turn sixteen and then be gone. Everything would be over. She wanted to stop the course of the sun so they would never grow older and nothing would ever change. Marcus would hover forever one day short of sixteen, and they would remain like this always, here, now. Dreaming.

But instead, what was to become of her? Once he was gone her life would stop dead. After that, there would just be daily, grey existence.

Bricca saw how upset the girl was and tried to comfort her, saying that she was sure she would make other friends soon enough. Girls, perhaps. And there was always Grata, the slave-girl only a few years Julia's junior. At which Julia

148

seethed – '∂*amn* Grata!' – and gave her nurse such a tongue-lashing that Bricca shrunk under it and for a moment looked almost thin.

It was worse when Julia had to dine with Marcus and Lucius. The two of them had now reached some stage of male understanding or complicity. Lucius had decreed a stern punishment, and Marcus had accepted it with manly fortitude. Now everything was clear between them. Julia hated it.

Lucius also saw how upset she was but was wise enough not to try and cheer her up. Instead he and Marcus talked in low, solemn voices about the state of the Empire, and the re-organisation of the army, and other tedious stuff. Then Julia heard Lucius' voice ring out more clearly, and knew he was talking to her.

'The only thing that endures is change,' he said. She looked up and their eyes met. She had never seen an expression so mixed, so complicated. Then he reached out and took a fresh bread roll and broke it in two.

All was change.

A few days later, Julia awoke to feel the little amulet of Isis burning against her skin. She arose and left her room, to find that little Grata, the youngest slave-girl in the household whom Julia used to play with but nowadays rather despised, had awoken racked with a terrible fever, already sunken-cheeked and hollow-eyed from dehydration. Julia was panic-stricken for a time, thinking back to her outburst of 'damn Grata!' But no one had that kind of power. There was true religion and there was superstition. No one really had the power to bring harm to another merely by wishing it, surely?

Lucius ordered the doctor to attend immediately, but when the doctor heard it was only a slave-girl, he took his time, and went to attend the rather more lucrative ingrown toenails of a wealthy wine importer in the eastern quarter of the city. By the time he got to the Praepositus' house, the girl was comatose. By dusk she was dead.

The following evening, Julia was walking in the orchard, feeling rather sad for Grata. She was only a slave, it was true, but there had been a time when she had liked her, all the same. Under the walnut tree in the far corner of the orchard, she found a freshly-dug grave, and a neat little tombstone at its head. She ran back to the kitchens immediately.

'Bricca, has Grata been buried in the orchard? I thought it wasn't allowed to bury anyone inside the city walls?'

She felt suddenly guilty and callous when her nurse looked up, red-eyed and puffy-cheeked.

'Well,' said Bricca, trying to steady her voice, 'the poor little mite always did love that old walnut tree, climbing in it when she should have been working and suchlike.' She smiled, felt her tears coming again, swallowed them down. 'The master knew as much – he knows more about his slaves than any master I ever knew. So he ordered her to be buried there, and no more to be said about it.'

'And did my uncle have the tombstone made too? Just for a slave?'

Bricca nodded, and tried to speak again but couldn't. She nodded.

Julia wandered slowly back out to the orchard and stood and stared at the fresh grave and the little tombstone for a long time. On the slab of stone were carved the neat and perfect words:

> *Rest lightly on her, earth and dew;*
> *She put so little weight on you.*

Then Julia wept. Wept and thought that, although she might hate her uncle sometimes – all the same, what a remarkable and unpredictable man he was.

The day before Marcus was due to depart, Julia came to Bricca at dawn in tears because she thought she was going the same way as Grata, and dying. *That'll* show them, she thought. On her sheets was a smudge of blood. Bricca looked and laughed. 'You're not dying,' she said. 'Quite the opposite, chick. You're coming into womanhood. You'll be able to have babies, give life.' She stripped the covers from the girl's bed. 'Blood can mean life as well as death,' she said. 'Think of the mystery of Our Lord.'

Julia was suddenly thinking more about babies than Our Lord. She didn't want babies. Not ever. Bricca laughed again, patted the girl on her belly. 'All in good time, though,' she said. 'We'll need to get you married first. Then you'll swell up like an apple on a tree.'

Yuck, thought Julia. *Never.*

Bricca took the sheets and burned them, then scraped the ashes carefully into a little clay pot and stoppered it up. Early the next morning, when she went down to the market, she took a diversion south to the foreshore of the Thames, and she stood and said a prayer to the Lady of the River, to receive the first blood of her mistress Julia, and send her long life and fertility and make her as fertile as a Kentish orchard or a field of Norfolk corn. Such a prayer might not be strictly biblical, she knew, but you had to do something to mark the great event, now didn't you?

And then she tossed the little pot underarm and it arced out over the river and fell with barely a splash, floating for a few moments before it sank and was seen no more.

Marcus left at dawn with his possessions in a leather satchel on his back, which was still itching furiously with healing scabs. Lucius had already gone to the law sessions at the court-house in his capacity as magistrate, so only Bricca, Cennla and Julia were there to see him off.

'You will write to me, won't you?' said Julia. 'In between leave?'

'Well, I don't know if I'll have that much time, what with

weapons training and all that,' said Marcus airily. 'And of course we might get posted back to York at any time. Or even up to the Wall.'

Bricca wept softly into her apron. Cennla stood and stared. Julia scowled. 'Yes, well, we'll be busy too, of course,' she said. Busy *sewing*, she thought. And having *babies*.

'Right,' said Marcus at last. 'I must be off.'

'Oh, do take care, young master,' Bricca blurted out.

'Don't worry about me,' he said, turning towards the door. 'I'll be fine.' He caught Julia's eye at the last moment. 'I will try to write when I can.'

She scowled at him still. He smiled. Her scowl was worth a thousand words. She really *was* cross to see him go, he thought delightedly.

Then he swung out of the door and was gone.

And so two childhoods came to an end. Marcus and Julia were separated, and each into adulthood, into a new world of burdens, responsibilities, competitiveness and complexity. The price they paid was the loss of numberless imaginary worlds.

For far gone now and forever were the worlds of their games – of blood-thirsty pirates, and green-eyed sibyls living in underground caverns, and lion tamers and gladiators, and Scythian princesses in golden gowns and panther-drawn chariots, and runaway Celtic musicians . . .

From now on there was only one world, the real world, which did not mould itself like soft mud to fit a child's fancy, but was haughty, and hard-edged, and hurt like hell when you knocked your heart against it.

PART II

arma virumque

CHAPTER ELEVEN

Milo was a soldier. That was all.

Most people are defined by more than simply their profession. But soldiering wasn't Milo's profession, it was his very existence. More than just a soldier, Milo was a centurion of the Sixth Legion *Victrix*, having worked his way up through the ranks. He was one of the few.

He had reached this elevated station by killing Picts and Scots, Germans and Sarmatians, Goths, and Dacians, and Marcomanns, and for every man he had killed he had taken a wound. His flesh was cross-hatched like an old chopping board. His eyes glittered like two shield bosses. His arms were like hams. In a recent tavern brawl, a big, bearded drunk had punched him on the jaw. The drunk had broken three knuckles. Milo hadn't moved. And then he broke the drunk's arm for him. He'd had half a mind to slot him.

Milo would be thirty-five next year. In five years' time he would retire and marry some pretty British girl of child-bearing age and with good round hips, and they'd have kids, and run a good farm. He could have settled on the Rhine, or in the rich vinelands of the Danube, but he liked Britain. The food was shit but the farmland was good.

Till then, there were five more years of hard soldiering to be done. This was not a chore for Milo.

It was probable that his soldiering days would be worked out in the province, either at Southwark or else back at York, the old proud seat of the Sixth *Victrix*. Or maybe shivering his balls off back at Vindolanda on the Wall. He didn't much care. But you never knew nowadays. The old army structure had changed, and 'mobility' was the new buzzword – which was a front, as every soldier knew, for the fact that there weren't enough decent soldiers to go round nowadays to man the frontiers properly. Instead you had to depend on a load of poxy auxiliaries who couldn't march in time to save their own mothers' lives. That was no way to run an Empire.

Like all Roman soldiers, Milo looked back with nostalgia to the days of the great soldier-emperors: Septimius Severus – apart from his decision to allow soldiers to marry, a fucking disgrace – and the Antonines, and greatest of all, Trajan himself. Nowadays all you seemed to have was a whole load of confusion. Two Emperors, for a start. Constantius in the east seemed to have done OK up to now, but Constans in the west was a waste of space. Nor did Milo think much of this bright idea of having frontier troops and then a separate mobile field army: it was crass from the start. In the old days it was so much simpler. In Britain you had three permanently-stationed legions: at York, the Sixth *Victrix*, with detachments manning the Wall; at Chester, the Twentieth *Valeria*; and at Caerleon, the Second *Augusta*, ready to piss on any uppity Welshmen if they should so much as poke their noses over the border. Nowadays you had the tattered remnants of those three, no longer fielding a magnificent six thousand men per legion (plus those poxy auxiliaries), but sometimes no more than a thousand. The rest had been whittled away by the Emperor for his mobile army of *comitatenses*, who rode around the Empire supposedly plugging any gaps in the frontiers and mopping up stray barbarians who got in the way. Time would tell if this strategy was working. But two things were for certain: the Sixth *Victrix* wasn't what it used to be. And you never knew where you might be posted next.

Milo himself had served on the Rhine, and in Dacia,

precisely because his cohort had been dispatched at various times to fight with the field army in a particular campaign. It had been OK at the time, but he hoped it didn't happen again. London and York and the Wall were the territories he knew best. The nasty rumours from the east now were that Constantius was getting seven different kinds of shit kicked out of him by that hard nut, Shapur of Persia, and soon he'd be asking his little brother for the loan of a few thousand crack veterans. Considering the brothers had been virtually at war with each other on previous occasions, this didn't seem too likely. But you never knew with Emperors.

Of course, Milo's daily oath of allegiance was to the Emperor. Oh, of *course* it was. All those oaths and acts of worship and sacrifices of firstborn white bullocks were to that distant deity called Constans . . .

Bollocks they were. What did soldiering have to do with some perfumed ponce in Rome, or Milan, or Ravenna, or Trier, or Spalato, or wherever Constans was holed up at the moment? That simpering twat in make-up and a hairpiece, with his shiftless roving scented court, that heart of corruption? Rome was a madman's dream, and its courtiers moved like ghosts through its vast halls of gold and mosaic, utterly unreal . . .

No. Milo's first allegiance was to his men and his legion. And his second allegiance? Milo didn't have a second allegiance.

Milo was a soldier. That was all.

Most days he liked the job. But there were times when he did wonder . . .

Times like now, when just after breakfast he was suddenly faced with beardless wheyfaced fucking schoolboys who came here at sixteen, *sixteen* in the Name of Light, two years before they were any good even for latrine duty, just because their daddy or guardian or whoever was some pen-pushing tax-gathering Provincial fucking Praepositus. (And what had happened to his men's September pay, that was what he wanted to know.)

Marcus, this kid's name was. Or to give him his full tri-nomen (being so posh, don't you know, and nobly born), Marcus Flavius Aquila.

And boy, was he going to find army life one tough bitch.

'Right, you're signing up as a Boot, yes?' barked Milo.

'Boot?' said Marcus.

'Boot what?' Milo thwacked him on the right shoulder with his vinestick.

'Boot . . . sir?'

Another thwack. 'Sir, my granny's arse! What's my rank, soldier?'

'Centurion, sir.'

'Then you fucking call me "centurion"! And when I say come you come and when I say go you go!'

'Yes, Centurion.'

'And when I say get down on your knees and yap like an ickle-wickle puppy dog, what do you do?'

'I get down on my knees and yap like an ickle-wickle puppy dog, Centurion.'

'You learn fast, soldier. Now then, you are – take my word for it – a Boot. You're one of the honoured *caligatae* now, lad – the Boots. The ordinary fucking footsloggers, the squaddies, the poor bloody infantry, the javelin jumpers, the iron line, Marius' mules. A Boot. You're a Boot.'

'Yes, Centurion.'

'You're the scum. You're the dregs. You are the absolute lowest of the low. But it's out of such scum like you that we make the kind of fighting soldiers who stand in a line and beat the shit out of a bunch of hairy barbarians ten times their number. Yes?'

'Yes, Centurion.'

'And that's called training, and it's a very simple business. It consists of Doing Whatever You Are Fucking Well Told.'

'Yes, Centurion.'

'And if You Do What You Are Fucking Well Told for long

enough, and don't get your head hacked off by a kraut with an axe in a German forest, or skinned alive and rolled in salt by some Pictish war-party out for a bit of fun, then who knows – you might even get promoted to the dizzy rank of optio in about a hundred years' time.'

'Yes, Centurion.'

Milo stared down at the paper in front of him. 'So why didn't you come in as a Cornelius?'

'A Cornelius, Centurion?'

Milo sighed. 'An officer, lad.'

'Why . . . excuse me, Centurion, but why is an officer called a Cornelius?'

'BECAUSE IT'S A PONCY FUCKING NAME, THAT'S WHY!' Milo sighed. 'You're either a useless rich cunt, in which case you're a Cornelius, or you're a useless poor cunt, in which case you're a Boot. The only exceptions are inbetween: the NCOs, like me, who really run this fucking army. And we don't have any stupid piss-taking nicknames either, so you better remember it.'

'Yes, Centurion.'

'So, if we may return to the original question: why weren't you commissioned as a Cornelius? Your family's rich, isn't it?'

'My guardian, the Praepositus, Quintilianus, wanted me to come in as an ordinary foot-sol . . . that is to say, a Boot, Centurion. To work my way up from the ranks and not expect any special privileges.'

Milo smiled. 'Rest assured, my lad. You won't be getting any.'

Next stop after signing in was equipment. The fat, greasy quartermaster eyed Marcus suspiciously.

'I know, I know,' said Milo from behind him, 'only last week he was still sucking on his mother's tit. But orders are orders, Quartermaster, and this one is now officially a Boot.'

The quartermaster snorted and began to find Marcus his stuff.

'Get your kit off, soldier,' said Milo.

Marcus stripped.

'What's with the stripes on your back?'

Marcus glanced over his shoulder at Milo. 'My own fault, Centurion.'

'I don't doubt it, soldier. And the fault was . . .?'

Marcus whispered, utterly abject, 'I stole something.'

There was a pause, and then Milo leaned close to the boy's ear. 'You know what happens to thieves and deserters in this army, don't you, lad?' He paused. 'They get taken out onto the parade ground and beaten to death by their own comrades. Remember that.'

Marcus nodded and hung his head in misery.

The quartermaster slung him a pair of woollen breeches, a faded and grubby red woollen tunic, and a leather jerkin. Marcus pulled them on. The wool itched abominably and he knew it must be crawling with lice. Then he was handed a pair of hobnailed leather sandals and a grey cloak thickly impregnated with goosefat.

'Put that on too,' ordered Milo.

'Hold your arms out,' ordered the quartermaster.

Marcus was then laden with a saw, a basket, a handaxe, a billhook, a leather belt and chain, and a mess-tin.

'Load 'em up in the basket and follow me,' ordered Milo.

The basket weighed a ton. Arms and armour were still to come.

The armoury was dark and smoky from the charcoal fires, and the air had a sickly metallic tang. From beyond came the ring of hammer on anvil. The armourer stared at him, and then shuffled off and came back with a helmet and a jerkin of scale armour stitched onto a base of linen and leather. The helmet, made of iron and almost black, had clearly seen better days. Milo ordered him to don both helmet and armour.

'Pretty as a picture,' he said. Your mummy would weep with pride.'

'Are there any – any weapons, Centurion?' Marcus asked

tentatively. The iron helmet was already making his head ache, his throat was dry and he felt terribly nervous about everything. But if he had a sword at his side, at least it might all seem worthwhile.

'Weapons?' repeated Milo with slow sarcasm. 'Strap that basket on your back and follow me, soldier.'

Marcus followed him out onto the square. Milo glanced across to the barracks on the other side. It was built on two floors, and had a wooden staircase running up the outside.

'Right,' said Milo. 'Run over to those barracks, and then run up and down that staircase twenty times. Then report back to me.'

Marcus set off.

By the tenth ascent he was dripping with sweat. Towards the end he knew that he might faint at any minute. His legs were on fire. His head throbbed as if it had been kicked by an angry mule.

Finally he stood in front of Milo, trembling uncontrollably, blind with sweat, on the verge of collapse.

'Now then,' said Milo pleasantly. 'What was that you were saying about wanting to carry weapons as well?'

Marcus opened his mouth to explain or retract, but emitted only asthmatic gasps.

'You haven't got enough meat on you to lift a wooden fucking spoon, boy!' roared Milo. 'Now get to your barracks, take a pallet in Block Four, and report back to me at the double. You've got work to do.'

He watched the boy stagger away across the square.

Jupiter's arsehole, did he have work to do.

Marcus was back within two minutes. His first job was latrine duty.

'You swab down the seats, you wash the sponges, you lick any officer's arse that you find in there, and then you flush the whole place through with a good session at the pump. And if you don't clean the place out so well that it shines like the gods' own private shit-house on Mount Olympus, I'll have you back in there till midnight cleaning it with your tongue. Now get to work.'

Marcus comforted himself on the job with thoughts of Hercules and the Augean Stables. At least this wasn't *that* bad.

Next up was polishing armour: not his, Milo's. 'You can polish *your* armour in your own fucking time.'

Later in the morning, there was drill on the main square. This wasn't too bad, and it was a relief to lose himself among ranks of four hundred and eighty other men. Marcus switched off and acted like a mule. Like one of Marius' mules. Like a Boot.

The midday meal was a slop of thick lentil soup in his mess-tin and a hunk of coarse brown bread, and then only minutes later, Milo was barking out orders for his century, the first century of the Second Cohort, to tog up in full armour and get to the North Gate for afternoon exercises.

Marcus never knew how he managed to stand the pace. In full armour they had a fast march over London Bridge and then up to the hills of Hampstead. He grudgingly acknowledged that Milo outpaced all of them, and in full armour too. No officer's horse for him. Once there, they had to march straight across one of the Hampstead ponds without pausing. The water only came up to Marcus' waist, but his feet sank deep into the glutinous mud below, and he nearly lost his hobnailed sandals.

As soon as the men were out of the water, they had to break into a jog trot and keep it up for the full five miles east across the fields to the muddy shores of the River Lea. Here they had to build a pontoon across one of the creeks on the west bank, using only ash poles and bladders of animal skin. Marcus helped to inflate the animal skins, and nearly passed out with hyperventilation, much to the amusement of his colleagues. Finally they were ordered on a fast march back to camp, Milo roaring tirelessly all the way and thumping any slackers across the shoulders with his vinestick.

Marcus was so tired that he could barely eat that evening, ravenous though he was for the mutton stew the texture of shoe-leather, more lentil soup, and more coarse bread. Earlier that day he had given his straw pallet a brief try. It was so lumpy that it felt like it was stuffed with tree roots. He wondered how on earth he would ever get to sleep on it.

He needn't have wondered. He was asleep before his head hit the straw.

It seemed like the trumpet for reveille sounded about ten seconds later.

Apart from being tired, teased, bruised, bug-bitten, hungry, and constantly broke because pay was always late, life in the army wasn't so bad. His ears rang from Milo's bellowing, but he could already tell that, while the centurion was as hard as nails and hated anyone not pulling their weight, he was no out-and-out sadist. He had the respect and even admiration of his men.

Marcus' colleagues slowly got used to him too. Initially they had nothing but contempt for him, but gradually this merged into constant teasing, sometimes gruffly affectionate, sometimes more hostile. He could have done without the freshly-laid turd he found under his blankets one evening. But Boots' humour was never exactly subtle. He made no fuss and cleared it up himself. It never happened again.

It was Mus who first started talking to him as if he were a fellow soldier rather than a standing joke or a child. His real name was Muso, a hulking Rhinelander with rounded ox-like shoulders and a spade-beard, but 'Mus' was his comrades' joke-name for him: Mouse. Anyone less timorously mouse-like was hard to imagine. When he fought against the Teutonic tribes in his own home territory, he liked to 'lose' his one-handed sword or *spatha*, which he regarded as a weapon fit only for women, and acquire one of his enemies' monstrous two-handed axes, which he then proceeded to swing around his head, performing decapitations and dismemberments with tremendous satisfaction. 'Fuckin' Teutons,' he would philosophise. 'Fuckin' *barbarians*, they are.'

One night, sitting on a neighbouring pallet picking his toenails, Mus saw that Marcus was covered in bite marks when he pulled off his tunic and crawled into bed. 'You want to get your shit seen to,' he rumbled.

'Shit?'

'Your stuff,' explained Mus. 'Your gear. Your clobber. Your kit, mate. You can't walk around with half a hundredweight of lice on you. Weighs you down something terrible. And with your kit off you look like a fuckin' leper. The tarts will soon kick you out of bed. Worst of all, *your* lice will soon be *my* lice if you go on like that. And if that happens, Mus will *not* be a happy Boot.'

Marcus shrugged helplessly. 'What can I do?'

Mus eased himself onto one shield-sized buttock and let forth a cavernous fart. He settled back again with a contented sigh. 'Tomorrow,' he said mysteriously, 'we will enlist the help of the ants.' And he tapped his nose with his forefinger.

The next day, when they paused for a breather during their exercises up on the hills to the north of the city, Mus beckoned Marcus over to the edge of the woods.

'Here,' he said. 'Anthills. You lay your stuff over them for an hour or two, only keep your linen on, please. Don't want you flashing your meat and two veg in my face – that's not the sort of thing we boys come up here on the Heath for, I assure you. You give your underwear a good boil tonight. Tomorrow we're due to give the pallets a smoke and that'll bring out the little fuckers like Welshmen from a wood.'

'What about the ants?'

'Watch and learn,' growled Mus.

So Marcus took off his woollen cloak and woollen tunic, and laid them each over an anthill, and watched. Within a minute, ants were streaming out of their nest and crawling all over his clothes: burrowing among the fibres, into the hems, searching for the succulent young larvae of the lice. Marcus was both impressed and horrified.

'Works every time,' said Mus. 'And don't you forget it.'

Marcus nodded. He was learning fast.

He was even learning to get a taste for mutton stew.

Once it was seen that Mus was talking to the new Boot, the other soldiers grudgingly did likewise. They were hardened, leatherfaced veterans to a man. There was Britus, appropriately enough a Briton, squat, stocky and unsmiling, and Crito, a lean, silent, dark-skinned soldier who, so Mus told Marcus, was the offspring of a Gaulish mother and a Moorish father. It was not the kind of thing Crito would tell you himself. Caelius was their rather bumptious 'optio' or lieutenant and the head of their mess, who claimed to be descended from the Julian clan of Rome itself. No one believed him, so he kept repeating it *ad nauseam*. And there was Thales, a Cretan, who had somehow got into a British legion but wasn't going to explain how. 'Wily Odysseus,' the other soldiers called him sarcastically. But it was as well to stay in with Thales. He always knew where to obtain 'extra' supplies and rations. For a small fee, of course.

Just as the skies began to grey and the weather to turn colder with the onset of winter, the entire cohort was ordered one drizzling afternoon to form up in the main square, and then told that they were marching for York tomorrow. Marcus thought he could hear a silent groan go up from the men, their bones already aching with the thought of the northern cold. 'But don't look too miserable about it, ladies!' roared Milo cheerfully. 'Some of you will then be detached for a winter posting on the Wall. Now won't that be luvverly?' He looked grim again. 'OK. Get your kit sorted. We depart at the first hour tomorrow.'

A dawn march. And twenty miles to cover every day, with each soldier carrying a pack of sixty pounds or more. It was going to be quite a journey. For Marcus, however, it would also be a kind of pilgrimage. For beyond the Wall was where his father had received his fatal wound.

Marcus couldn't believe how heavy his pack was, and he still hadn't been issued with shield, sword or javelin. He was glad of the training they had had in the few weeks since he had joined, but he still worried about the march to York. It would be too shameful if he collapsed from exhaustion along the way. It was over two hundred miles to York. And they were doing it in ten days.

Mus saw him struggling with his pack. 'I got room in my pack still,' he rumbled. 'For your axe or somethin'.'

Marcus steadied himself under the weight on his back, and shook his head. 'Thanks, but I'm fine.'

Mus grinned. 'Fine you may be now, sunshine. But give me another report tonight, eh?'

It was magnificent, all the same, to march out of the East Gate of the camp and along the Southwark side and then across London Bridge in a column of four hundred and eighty men, heading north through the city to Bishopsgate, and Ermine Street, and the great north road to York. As they marched out of the gates of the fort, the blaring of trumpets was accompanied by high-pitched yowls from a horde of rather grimy-looking women who lined the street.

'Ah,' murmured Mus affectionately, 'my whores, my whores.' He turned to Marcus at his side. 'We never did get you to go and see the ladies, now did we? A real shame, that is. We'll have to give you a thorough baptism up north, eh?' He grimaced. 'Right dogs they are up there an' all, I can tell you. Bunch of hairy little bitches. But they're a fuck sight cheaper than the London whores.' He beamed and waved at the yowling women to their left, singling out one in particular who was wearing a monstrous wig of cascading, once-blonde girls. 'My darling Lollia, my only true love!' he cried out. 'I'll be back before the first snow falls, and marry you, my dear!'

'Yeah,' Lollia squawked back at him, making a very rude gesture with her bunched left fist, 'and I'm the bleedin' Goddess Diana!'

'Anyhow,' shouted Mus, 'you'll have a whole lot of the Second *Augusta* down here by this evening. And you know what *they're* like!' He guffawed, and caught the apple that Lollia threw him. He bit into it deeply, murmuring through mouthfuls of juicy apple, 'Yeah, we know *just* what those bleedin' Welshmen are like. Dicks the size of toothpicks!' And he guffawed to himself again.

Marcus had noticed that there was a great deal of conversation centred around penis size.

It was clearly a soldier thing.

They marched out of Bishopsgate and along Ermine Street, due north, following the west bank of the Lea Valley. The first night they camped just beyond Hertford, outside Youngsbury, in unprotected tents amid the ancient barrows there, humped like dark, sleeping animals. The soldiers muttered uneasily about the choice of location among the dead – the only people more superstitious than soldiers are sailors – but the centurions cheerfully ignored them.

Marcus lay awake with his calves screaming, burning, his tendons taut as hawsers. In the night he had the worst cramp of his life. He almost wept. In the morning, it was at least five miles into the march before he could talk at the same time as walk, for the pain his leg muscles gave him.

'Mus,' he said cautiously, 'why haven't we got the Eagle?'

Mus looked at him as if he was the stupidest person he'd ever met. 'The Eagle stays in camp,' he said, 'which for this legion is York. It stays there until the very last man in the legion leaves the camp. In London we're only a contingent, remember.'

'How many more of the Sixth are at York?'

'Just one other cohort – things not being what they used to be. But that's the First Cohort, five centuries of a hundred and sixty men each. We're the Second Cohort, six centuries of eighty men each. Making twelve hundred and eighty men in all.' Mus smiled with pride at his mathematical prowess. 'Plus auxiliaries, who you don't count. Twelve hundred and eighty men to defend the whole of the north. Not much, is it? But then we're not just any twelve hundred and eighty men, are we? We're the best. We're the dog's bollocks. We're Roman legionaries. We could take on ten thousand, *a hundred thousand* hairy bleedin' Celts and beat them shitless. Eh?'

'Too right,' said Marcus. *Yeah.*

They marched on.

They marched on, and the road steadily worsened. Marcus was shocked. There were potholes in the streets of London, and one or two houses here and there which were uninhabited and collapsing, used as pighouses, or else just free lodgings for bats and owls. But once away from the relative prosperity of London, things were much worse. There were places where the road to York – Ermine Street itself! – had been completely washed away by recent rain, and nothing done to repair it. To get the heavy wagons through the mud, at times, they had to lay down corduroys of wooden poles, and then heave together with the exhausted oxen to get the baggage through. It was ridiculous.

Maybe, Marcus thought, Lucius' endless pessimism, which had always made him and Julia snigger as children, wasn't so misguided after all. Things really were falling apart.

They marched on.

They marched on through the flatlands of Cambridgeshire, and a hard east wind came up across the vast miles of undrained fenland on their right, cut through their thick woollen cloaks and chilled them to the bone. Frozen, red-eyed, numbed into speechlessness, they crossed the Cam and came to Godmanchester. They marched on to Water Newton, and Stamford, and Ancaster, and Marcus began to see villa after villa deserted and grassgrown, fields fallow or unharvested, and more and more huddled travellers on the road, beggars and lepers and shivering, unhoused vagabonds.

'Where are they all coming from?' he asked.

Mus shrugged. 'Don't know where they're going to neither,' he said. 'There's no gold over the rainbow.'

Finally they came to the legionary fortress at Lincoln, and were allowed a half day of rest. Marcus salved the blisters on his feet, and the sores on his shoulders where the straps of his pack had cut cruelly into his flesh. He ached all over and the ache would not dissipate, he well knew, in just half a day. But he had never been more grateful to sit in a hot bath and steam his bones back to life.

He impressed his messmates that evening by putting away no less than eight bowls of lentil soup, and nearly three pounds of bread.

'Well well,' said Mus. 'Keep that up and you might put some meat on your sparrow's bones after all.'

They marched north out of Lincoln, and then turned west and crossed the Trent into Nottinghamshire, and then on to Doncaster, which they reached long after nightfall, in heavy rain: nearly thirty miles, a killing day's march. But Milo was relentless. He wanted them in York the day after tomorrow. The next night they camped at Castleford, and finally, at dusk on the tenth day, raising their leaden arms above their heads and giving themselves a weary but heartfelt cheer, they marched through the great gates of the legionary fortress of York, station of the Sixth for nearly three hundred years, and were home.

Milo came round that evening to inspect their kit, which had to be cleaned before lights out. He scrutinised the new Boot's stuff: *Marcus Flavius Aquila* indeed. But he liked what he saw. The boy looked like death, but his kit was spotless. And now that the wheyfaced, rabbit fear had gone from the boy's face, Milo saw an expression of set determination in his mouth and his jaw, which he liked too. He also saw the steel gleam of ambition. This one would make a good soldier. Maybe even a general, with his contacts. Though with that steel gleam of ambition in his eye, perhaps the boy might be going for a full-scale coup and the Imperial purple himself one day. Milo snorted.

Some time up on the Wall might do him good.

The next day there was a more general settling in, and checking of stores and equipment, followed by the dedication and sacrifice of a white bullock to the Divine Emperor, and a renewal of oaths of allegiance. That night, half the men were given leave to go out on the town and get roaring drunk.

The people of York, on the whole, were delighted to have the legion back in town again, spending money, and they turned a tolerant eye towards bad Boot behaviour. Marcus went with Mus, Britus and Thales to a cheap, evil-smelling tavern, where they played dice and drank vinegary wine mixed with water at first, and then later they drank it neat. Thales was the only one who didn't seem to get drunk; he entertained them all with tall tales of his brave feats around the Empire. He had killed lions in Arabia, fought bandits in Crete, slaughtered Scythians on the Danube frontier. And Mus' response to each outrageous tale was the same.

'Balls.'

Finally Mus stood up, rocking back and forth in his huge boots, and smiled benignly around. 'Right,' he said. 'I need a poke. Who's in?' Britus was, Thales wasn't. Marcus had no choice. He felt Mus' huge paw at the scruff of his neck, and he was dragged off, protesting feebly, to the nearest riverside brothel.

It was not a happy experience. He had been dreading a closer encounter with the 'hairy little bitches' so vividly described by Mus previously, and he was very drunk. The woman, old enough to be his mother, crouched on all fours and waited for him to get on with it. But when she turned to look at him, she saw that he was about to retch.

'Oi,' she shrieked, 'not in 'ere you don't you little tyke! If you want to puke you go outside. This is a clean household, this is!'

So he went outside and retched up several pints of wine vinegar, and took several lungfuls of bracing Yorkshire air, and then made his way carefully back to the fort for the night.

Phew, he thought.

The next day, weak, parched and trembling with his first ever hangover, Marcus was issued with his weapons.

First came the javelin: an ash pole of four or five feet, topped by a long iron head that was barbed at the end. The shield was a flat oval, big enough to conceal him if he crouched behind it, and made of layers of plywood glued together, each layer grained at right angles to the next, and then bound round the circumference with an iron band. Finally, his sword: not the stubby old *gladius* that had served the legions so well for centuries, but the longer, more elegant *spatha*, rather sneered at by old-timers, but just as effective in battle. There were only two rules regarding the art of swordsmanship for the Roman Boot, and they weren't hard to learn. They were: Get In Close, and Stab, Don't Slash. You could say that the entire Empire, comprising more than a hundred million people, had been built on those two rules.

Marcus was also issued with a scabbard, a sword belt and a shield belt. He was glad he'd been carrying all that weight to York. It made the extra weight of his weapons and shield less of a shock. Marius' mules indeed.

And then it was time to learn how to use them.

Marcus' throwing arm was still shamefully weak when it came to the javelin, and Milo bellowed at him unmercifully. On the other hand, he covered the ground fast, even with the burden of shield and sword, and when he came up to engage the 'enemy' – a line of straw-stuffed sacks suspended from a crossbeam – he kept his head down, bullock-like, and drove his sword into the sacks with such repeated ferocity that Milo thought he might make a good despatcher of barbarians yet. He didn't tell the lad as much, though. Couldn't let him get big ideas.

Marcus wrote home to London regularly at first. Dog-tired on his pallet at night, he tried to write at least once a week, detailing his exploits and trying to sound amusing and soldierly at the same time. He also requested them to send him some extra pairs of woollen socks.

After a while, however, he found himself writing less often. There seemed to be less to report, and anyway – *this* was his family now. That's how it felt. His old family in London: they would have to learn to live without him, as he lived without them.

Secretly, too, he thought Julia might miss him more if he wrote less.

One day he found himself writing what was to be his last letter for a long time.

To Lucius Fabius Quintilianus, at London, greetings.

I write to tell you, dear father, that we have received orders for our cohort to proceed on to the Wall the day after tomorrow, to replace the contingent that is being withdrawn from there for the winter. I do not know that I shall be able to write so often from there, as we shall be very busy.

I gather also that there is unrest again among the tribes beyond the Wall, and it is quite likely that we will be called upon to ride out on sorties and enforce order among them. Certainly, a taste of some real action would be welcome.

Greetings to all the household in London. I trust Julia's wool-working skills are coming on apace?

Your obedient Marcus

CHAPTER TWELVE

The fort on the Wall was the same as any other military fort in the Empire. You could travel from this far, bleak northern land to the very borders of Persia, and find the same stern, square walls, the same immense defensive ditches and battlements, and inside, the same grid-pattern of baths and blockhouses of such quintessentially Roman regularity and neatness.

What was slightly different, however, was the weather. Marcus had thought that the flatlands of Cambridge in an east wind were cold. But then, he thought ruefully, he hadn't known about life on the Wall in winter.

His face and hands dried out like leather, his lips cracked and bled as if they had been baked. Icicles dripped from the eaves of the barracks all day long, and froze again at night. The horses pawed pitifully at the ground and scraped back snow for the smallest clump of stiff moorland grass to eat. They went through their winter fodder with alarming appetites. The earth was frozen so iron-hard that the poor beasts broke their legs over the smallest jumps. The very cattle died in the hills of cold. It snowed, and then it grew too cold for snow, and the vast bare unforested country glittered as hard and unyielding and beautiful as diamond.

With the cold came the raiding parties from the north.

Around the Wall were various tribes of various persuasions, and Marcus had tried and failed utterly to get them all sorted out in his head. There were the Picts, the Painted

People – but he found out that this was just a Roman name for all of them, and signified little. They consisted of the Caledonians, who gave their name to the country, but they themselves were subdivided into many, mostly warring tribes. Then there were the Dalriads, further to the West, and beyond them the Scotti, from Ireland; and an associated tribe, the Attacotti,* supposedly the fiercest and most barbaric of all.

Mus looked genuinely puzzled at Marcus' puzzlement. He scratched behind his ear with his drawn sword. 'Don't know why you're even askin', he grumbled. 'They're all fuckin' barbarians, and the only language they understand is the business end of one of these. Who gives a tinker's toss what they're called?'

The one thing the tribes seemed to have in common was that they were all happy to call themselves 'client peoples' of the Romans so long as it benefited them, and to get down on bended knee and swear undying allegiance to the unknown Divine Emperor, if it pleased the Iron Hats. After the oath, the tribesmen could always go back to their priests and have it washed away from them anyway. And then again, they were equally happy, if it should benefit them more, to turn around one bloody midnight and slit the throats of the Iron Hats in their sleep.

A tribesman's only loyalty was to his chieftain, and his kin. The rest was lies and trickery. And the cattle of another tribe were always fair game, especially in winter, when bellies moaned with hunger like the wind moaning in an empty cave.

One day, one of these client chieftains came to the fort, accompanied by his finest spearmen: tall, raw-boned, fair or red-haired, magnificent men in their way. The chieftain spoke to the camp commandant, a rather feeble-minded man of equestrian rank who smiled too much and gave orders with pathetic hesitancy. After the chieftain had departed, the commandant summoned Milo and told him to get together a mounted war-party and be ready to ride out in half an hour. A rival tribe had stolen some cattle, and this chieftain had asked them to get them back.

'You will have the chap over there,' said the commandant, indicating vaguely, 'as your guide. He's worked as an Arcanus for us before. Ah, the only thing is, ah . . .' The commandant lapsed into a prolonged hesitation, and at last Milo could stand no more waiting. He saluted briskly, turned and walked out.

In the square stood a tall, leanly-muscled tribesman in dyed green breeches and a leather waistcoat. He must have been absurdly cold, but he didn't seem to feel it. He wore his blond hair short for a tribesman, and had very pale blue eyes. His nose looked like it had been broken at regular intervals throughout his life, and then re-set by a particularly incompetent doctor.

Milo stopped in front of him. 'Your name, tribesman?'

'Arcanus.'

'I know you're a Frontier Scout. What's your *name*?'

The tribesman said nothing. He simply stared straight back at Milo with his pale blue eyes, unflinching, expressionless. At last Milo sighed and turned away. *Barbarian bloody bogtrotting painted bastards*, he thought.

But he would have to do.

They rode out through the great oak gates of the fort, along the old straight track of Dere Street, with few enough hours of daylight left to them. A war-party of forty Roman legionaries on shaggy moorland ponies, coarse cloths for saddles and no stirrups, riding in a column two abreast. Milo rode at their head and Marcus not far behind. His centurion guessed that the lad would be a fair rider. Posh kids always were. They were bought their own little ponies for their sixth birthday or something.

Marcus did ride well, right hand loosely but firmly on the reins at the base of the pony's mane, the horsehair coarse and oily to the touch, curiously comforting. Shield over his left shoulder, javelin held inside it. And under his left arm, the cold reassuring steel of his sword.

Just behind Milo rode the Arcanus, the Frontier Scout. They rode for ten or twelve miles across the rolling white moorland before they picked up the trail, running parallel to the road. The Arcanus didn't even dismount to check the trail signs. One glance down from his pony, a grunt of recognition, and he jerked his battered, bony nose north-east in the direction the cattle had been driven.

'They'll be heading for Bran's Cauldron,' he said.

'Speak sense, man,' growled Milo.

'Up in those hills,' said the Arcanus, speaking more softly than ever. 'A great hollow where you can hide a hundred cattle or more. They'll not ride at night.'

Milo squinted at the frozen cloudless sky, the moon already up, and looked puzzled.

'Oh, there'll be moonlight enough,' agreed the Arcanus. 'But they'll not ride at night.'

'Not fighters either, then?'

The Arcanus smiled and shook his head. 'Not that lot,' he said with faint but stinging contempt. 'They have the hands of thieving children, and the stomachs of women. No, if we find them, they'll not fight.'

Milo nodded and chopped his right hand forwards through the icy air and the little column rode on after him.

They left the road far behind them now, the old road north, that once ran smooth and cambered from Corbridge up into the Cheviots, and down through Lauderdale to the very Firth of Forth itself, and that frontier beyond all frontiers, the turf-and-boulder wall of Antoninus. But it had been abandoned long ago, and the frontier set with the Wall of Hadrian. They were beyond it now, and into the tribal lands where the rule of Roman law meant nothing, and power kept company only with hard steel.

They rode on into the foothills, and the harsh treeless country of Rooken Edge and Ravens Knowe, Black Rig, and

Grindstone Law. The sky above them birdless, not a crow, not even a lone hawk scouring the land for carrion. Not a curlew's cry for comfort, but only the waul of the wind. The earth harder, wind colder with every step, the ponies hanging their heads low as if in prophetic sorrow for the horror to come. As if with their soft hurtless nostrils they snuffed up the odour of blood ahead and went on only in stoical obedience to something older even than the odour of slain blood.

Stones skittered under their hooves as they traversed the scaur and crested the lip of the great hollow in the hills that the Arcanus called Bran's Cauldron. Milo held up his hand and they came to a halt. One or two ponies flinched and shivered, their nostrils flared, heads bowed. The men sat still and silent.

It seemed to Marcus as if the low slanting sun had caught the edge of the whole world and dyed it with its red dying light. But it was all wrong: too red, too red. And broken with dark, uneven shapes like scattered boulders.

Milo rode on down into the hollow. They were not boulders. They were a mix of cattle and men, women and children, twisted and thrawn in their death-throes. The cattle had been spancelled and slain, poleaxed or beheaded, and from the tracks that led north out of the hollow, some more had been driven off. But the people had been cut down as they ran. Mostly beheaded, their heads mysteriously missing. Some cut down from behind, lying face down, backs bloody and bare. Some were further mutilated, limbs severed, intestines ripped out and draped around the necks of the dead like evil stoles. Genitals cut off and stuffed into gaping, gagging mouths. As a kind of joke – or perhaps it was some depraved religious rite – some of the beheaded humans had had the heads of cattle set upon their shoulders, so that they appeared like monstrous births, cauled in their own blood. Slain minotaurs in the snow.

Some of the slain men, at least, had fought back.

'Here,' said the Arcanus, appearing beside Milo and pointing at pony tracks in the thick snow. 'Here is some good.'

Milo stared at the deep tracks. 'Explain.'

'This pony carried two men,' said the Arcanus. 'One rider, one slain. It is good. Some of the attackers were slain too.'

'*Who*?' asked Milo.

'Who?' repeated the Arcanus, gazing distantly around. And then he seemed to glimpse something lying in the snow a few feet away, and he sighed, a soft 'Ah', and Milo heard in it a note of deep sadness. Of defeat, even. 'Perhaps it is not so good,' he said.

He slipped from his pony and walked a little way and retrieved something from the snow and came back and held it up to Milo. It was a long feather, perhaps the white tailfeather of a ptarmigan, but dyed deep red. 'Dyed in blood,' said the Arcanus. 'This is the work of the Attacotti.' He looked steadily at the grim leader of the Iron Hats and saw that he still did not understand. 'The Attacotti,' he said, his voice almost a whisper so that the blasphemy of what he said should not assault the ears of Heaven, 'the Attacotti eat other men.' He gestured back over his shoulder. 'The pony carrying two. Perhaps it was an Attacot and ... a human child. Tender meat.'

Now Milo was sickened. Until now, he had been consoling himself, albeit sourly, with the thought that you might see sights as atrocious as this in the arena. But *cannibalism* ...

'How many were they?'

The Arcanus shrugged. 'Sixty, maybe eighty. Good horses.'

'How long ago?'

The Arcanus glanced back at the trail disappearing away over the ridge. 'Two hours' hard riding, no more.'

Milo stared again across the snowfield of corpses.

'If we burn them, the Attacotti will see and come,' said the Arcanus.

'Let them come,' drawled Milo. 'But no, we can't spare the tinder. The hawks and the foxes will have to ...' He tailed off. Then he wheeled his pony and rode back to his men. 'We go on,' he said.

They moved through the gathering dusk, heading north,

the light thickening around them and the moonlight catching their frosted breath as thick as smoke.

As they rode, Milo questioned the Arcanus more.

'So who were the cattle-thieves, those who were slain?'

'Not my tribe.' He shrugged. 'Just a *creaght* – a band of nomads, men, women and children, who live by stealing others' cattle. Our cattle, in this case. My people's. But they were thieves, not fighters.'

'And the Attacotti who did this?'

'Not my tribe either,' said the Arcanus stubbornly.

Milo sighed. He was accustomed to the world-view of these northern Celts: my tribe, and then everybody else. It was the only distinction. Still, for all his stubbornness, and his name-lessness for that matter, Milo was getting to like this one. Broken Nose or whatever he was called. He was all right.

'My tribe,' added the Arcanus, 'do not do these things. But by their names you shall know them. They have such names as Black Ven and Sky-in-Tatters, Snakeskin and Pebbletooth, Half Ear, Bloody Midnight and Hawk in the Rain. These are not the names of human beings.'

'Where do the Attacotti come from?'

'From the Western Islands. Before that, perhaps, from beyond the sea.'

'You mean Hibernia?'

The Arcanus smiled a grim smile. 'No,' he said. 'I mean from the Islands of Demons. I mean from Hell itself.'

They had ridden only a few miles further when the Arca-nus stopped in his tracks beside Milo.

'What is it?' Milo stared around at the ground, but the Arcanus was staring straight ahead. Then he smiled.

'They are having a feast.'

'Who? Where? Stop talking in riddles, man.'

'The Attacotti,' said the Arcanus softly. 'Over there.' He pointed with his squat little dirk towards a small hill across the valley to their west. Milo squinted into the night. The hill was the site of an old Roman marching camp, long since abandoned. Its summit, less than a quarter of an acre, was still surrounded by wooden palisades. Whether it was still effectively ditched, Milo couldn't tell for the snow. But the sky above the camp – the Arcanus was right – was illumined, just discernibly, with the orange glow of firelight. And in the still night air, Milo thought he could hear the sound of . . . baboons, yikkering.

The sound, no doubt, of an Attacotti party.

He turned and gave the hand signal for total silence. They rode down into the valley in the muffling snow and up the other side towards the camp. The shrieks of celebration came to them clearly now – and also a clear view of the marching camp, recently refortified, it seemed, its wooden walls solid and unbroken. There was a single gate to the south.

Milo ordered his men to dismount.

'You, and you,' he chose two legionaries, 'take your ponies, and get that gate open. Silent as possible now.' He turned to the rest of the men. 'Dismount,' he said. 'Discard javelins. Draw swords. This one is going to be close quarters.'

Trembling with fear and excitement, Marcus slithered from his pony and drove his javelin into the ground along with all the others. He dropped his pony's reins over the butt of the javelin, shouldered his shield on his left arm, wiped his sweating right hand down his side, and drew his sword. It felt a good weight. He was comforted, too, by the hulking presence of Mus beside him. He might have preferred to be at the back, in this, his first ever fight, instead of only two ranks from the front. But he couldn't die. He knew that much, at least. Not at his age. No one could die at his age. He was Achilles without his heel. He was only sixteen. He couldn't die.

He remarked to Mus with a facetiousness he didn't feel, 'Well, like the man said, *Dulce et decorum est pro patria mori.*'

Mus glanced down at him with a jaundiced eye. '*Dulce et decorum est to keep your fuckin' head on,* more like,' he growled.

Anyway, this was no time for poetry. Let Horace keep to his verses up in his Sabine Hills. Here there was a simpler poetry to bear in mind. It went: Get in Close. Knock 'Em Down with Your Shield. And Stab, Don't Slash.

Milo stamped impatiently. The two legionaries at the gates were still trying to get the curved grappling hooks, which were roped to the ponies, into the gap between gates and posts. Then Milo snapped.

'OK,' he said. 'A shield wall once inside, and sweep forward. No prisoners.' He started walking. Two to one, he thought. Easy job.

He strode ahead of his men with his eyes set on the gates. They were still refusing to budge but he didn't slow down. Marcus watched him go and felt almost like giggling hysterically. Within seconds, Milo was going to walk straight into the wood and bloody his nose. What was he thinking of?

The noise inside the camp was a deafening, horrifying mix of drums, wails, exultant shrieks and despairing screams. Sparks from a roaring fire within spiralled into the black night sky. The animals in there would hear nothing.

Not five yards away, Milo roared, 'Get that fucking gate open NOW!'

Then it all happened at once. Marcus would never forget the sight. There was something insanely assured, magnificent about it. That, he thought afterwards, is soldiering.

An instant before it looked like Milo was going to walk head first into the gates, the two sappers managed to bang a hook of the grappling iron fast into the lower hinge. They retreated, panicking, more terrified of their centurion in a rage than any number of Attacotti, and lashed out at the rumps of the ponies with nailed sticks. Startled into action, the two stout ponies reared up against the ropes, trying desperately to get away from the unkind blows. The force was more than enough to rip the gate clean off its lower hinge so that it spun outwards at the very moment that Milo, still walking forward, planted his foot high up and kicked. The gate fell back flat on the ground and Milo continued marching forwards, straight into the camp.

Almost immediately, a figure appeared to the right and swung an axe at his head. As if in mild irritation, Milo growled 'Fuck off!' and jabbing his sword backwards like a dagger, drove it deep into his attacker's side. And still he walked on, not slackening his pace for one instant.

Then everyone froze. No other tribesmen attacked. The soldiers simply stopped and stared. Milo too. A scene of unimaginable squalor and brutality met their eyes.

Around the sides of the camp, the Attacotti had driven wooden stakes into the earth, and to these were tied a number of their prisoners. Some of them were dead, some of them still breathed. All had been mutilated. Arms had been hacked off at the shoulder. Eyes gouged out. Blood pooled on the ground.

And in the firelight sat the tribesmen. Eating. One of them, wearing the most elaborate head-dress, was in the very act of raising a roast of meat to his lips. It was a forearm.

A moment later the spell was broken. Milo started to walk towards them, and the startled tribesmen began to scramble to their feet and reach for their weapons. Milo strode straight across the orange embers of the fire, making a direct line for the tribesman in the fancy headgear. The tribesman was on his feet, and making a dash for his great two-handed axe that was propped up against the tottering clapboard fences at the back of the camp, when Milo planted a hobnailed boot firmly in the small of his back and sent him sprawling into the mud.

The fight was fierce but brief. The Arcanus had underestimated the number of tribesmen. There must have been more than a hundred. Some scrabbled away into corners, snickering like hyenas, and were butchered where they crouched. Some slipped out of the gates behind the soldiers' shield-line, and fled into the hills. And some lived up to their reputation and fought ferociously, heedless of any wound they received but the last. Finally all was still, and the weary soldiers stood around in the centre of the camp, eyeing each other, saying nothing.

Milo reappeared from the back of the camp, bloodied

sword in one hand, the other a bunched fist holding a tribes-man by the scruff of the neck and dragging him along in the dust behind him like a sack of dung. It was the tribesman in the gorgeous head-dress, now sadly bedraggled. At his waist, the soldiers now saw, he wore two severed human heads. He twisted and turned in Milo's grip, and gave out curious high-pitched screams. Finally Milo could stand no more. Glancing down at the wretched creature, he spat, 'Will you just *shut the fuck up*?' and at the same time, he dragged the tribesman up into a sitting position and slammed his head down with terrible force against his own raised knee.

The tribesman went silent.

Milo looked up and smiled with great satisfaction. 'We got us a chief,' he said.

'How can you tell?' asked Caelius.

'The fancy headgear,' said Milo. 'Chiefs of any tribe always overdress. Ours, if you think about it,' he added sardonically, 'are just the same.'

The men grinned, their teeth white in the firelight through the grime and sweat of their faces.

'OK,' said Milo looking round. Then he opened his fist and let the unconscious form of the chieftain slump to the ground. He walked over to the stakes where the prisoners were tied and went from one to another, putting his fingertips to their necks. Only one was still alive. He cut him down and laid him in the mud, and called two men over to see to him.

'See to him?' queried one of the men.

'Just keep him alive, at least,' said Milo. He came back and gave the order to clear up. 'Any casualties?'

There was nothing serious.

'I'm exhausted,' said Marcus.

'Battle-weary,' said Mus. 'It's not the same as tired. It's when you've seen so many die so quickly, even hairy great barbarians like this lot. It's a tiring thing to see. Leaves you empty.' He gave the boy a gentle cuff on the shoulder, which nearly knocked Marcus to his knees. 'Come on then, sunshine, help me hump these corpses outside.'

They cut down a couple of stunted hawthorns in the valley below, and piled loose planks and timbers from the camp on top, and then they piled the bodies of the dead prisoners on top again, a gruesome pyre. But the Attacotti dead, Milo ordered to be dragged outside and dumped in the ditch. 'Let the foxes have them,' he said. 'If they don't choke.'

When the bitter work was done, and fresh earth was scattered over the bloody arena of the camp, the men went down and washed their hands and faces in the icy water of the burn below. All of them longed to cleanse themselves of the blood they had spilled. Barbarian blood was crusted under their fingernails, and their clothes were stained with gore.

Many of the soldiers prayed as they washed themselves. Even Milo, Marcus saw, muttered softly to himself as he rinsed his hands and scooped a trail of water over his cropped head. What god or gods they prayed to, he didn't know. Mithras, or Christos, or Jupiter Optimus Maximus: some such gods. But all of them bent the knee to Fate. All soldiers honoured the goddess Fate.

Then Milo came over to the boy. 'And what god do you pray to, boy?'

'The gods of my fathers, Centurion.'

The answer of the unreflective, thought Milo. 'Mithras is the god for soldiers,' he said softly. 'One day you will learn that.' And he walked away before Marcus could ask more.

Afterwards, though they were still begrimed and filthy, the soldiers sat around the campfire chewing on strips of dried pork and hardtack, sluiced down with thin vinegary wine, and felt a little more at ease.

'Peace and quiet after fighting,' Mus philosophised. 'It's always a good feeling.'

'A strange kind of peace,' said Crito softly, 'that sits in the firelight with its clothes still drenched in blood.'

Mus grinned. 'You know what I'm talking about, Crito, and don't be such a smartarse.'

'Philosopher,' said Crito.

'Whatever,' said Mus. 'Name of Light, I wish we had some decent fuckin' booze.' He glanced at Marcus. 'Here, you want to get that seen to. You're still bleeding.'

'Oh, it's nothing,' said Marcus, 'really.'

'Don't be such a wanker,' grunted Mus, 'you'll wake up tomorrow morning with no more blood in you than a lemon.'

'Show,' said a voice. It was Milo, standing behind them. Marcus raised his right arm and showed him the wound. He was quite proud of it. It didn't hurt that much, and he had no idea how he had got it. In fact, he couldn't remember much about the fighting at all.

Milo looked down at the ragged cut along the back of the boy's forearm, a handspan or more and still oozing dark blood. 'Hm,' he said. 'First blood. Just a pity it's yours.'

Mus intervened. 'He clocked at least one of the bastards, I saw him do it.' He looked at Marcus. 'You did too. Right in the guts.'

Milo grunted with approval. He scrutinised Marcus' arm again. 'Bad enough, but not life-threatening. Unless the painted bastard had his dirk greased with poisoned fat before-hand.' At the expression on the boy's face, he relented. 'Only kidding,' he said, patting him on the shoulder. 'Here, Thales, you're Greek, you must know all about medicine and stuff. Get over here and bind this kid's arm up, will you?'

Grumbling to himself, Thales got up and came over and stared at the wound. Then he went to his pack to fetch a roll of linen.

'How d'you get it?' asked Mus.

'I honestly can't remember,' said Marcus. 'I can hardly remember much about the whole battle.'

'That's normal,' said Mus, settling back onto one elbow. 'Specially at first. It'll all come back to you when you sleep.' He belched. 'Then you'll wish it hadn't.'

☆ ☆ ☆

The men huddled down together around the fires and tried to sleep. They knew the Attacotti wouldn't return, but they still felt the horror of this place of butchery, and disliked having to pass the night here. They slept poorly, despite their exhaustion. They longed for greater numbers, more company. For women, wine. But in their few moments of snatched sleep, they had only their red nightmares for company.

Some time near dawn, neither asleep nor awake, Marcus felt someone shaking his shoulder, and a deep, throbbing ache in his forearm. He looked up. It was the Arcanus, crouching by his side.

'What?'

'Over here,' gestured the Arcanus, standing and moving over to a dark corner of the camp.

Puzzled and irritated, Marcus staggered to his feet and went over to him. The Arcanus turned and looked him steadily in the eye. 'My name is Branoc,' he said.

Even more irritated, Marcus mumbled back sarcastically, 'Pleased to meet you. My name is Marcus. Now if you don't mind, I'd really like to . . .' and began to turn away.

The Arcanus reached out and seized his arm – his left arm, fortunately. 'You do not understand. That is my name.'

'Yes, I'm sure it is.'

'It is a pact between us. No one else must know my name, except that I tell them. It is my power. None of my tribe tells their name to one from another tribe.'

'So why have you told me?'

The Arcanus – Branoc – smiled. 'Your modesty is manly,' he said.

Marcus wondered if he was dreaming. 'Look, I'm sorry, but what are you talking about?'

'The fight,' said Branoc. 'You saved my life. Now we are brothers.'

'I did *what*?'

Branoc frowned. 'You must remember. The axe of the

Attacot warrior was close to biting my belly wide open, when you came alongside and drove your sword straight into him. You killed him where he stood. He exhaled like a punctured bladder. We are brothers.'

Marcus laughed weakly, too tired to think straight. 'Honestly, I don't remember it at all. I *sort* of remember killing one of them, like Mus said . . .' He shrugged helplessly.

Branoc slipped a squat little knife from his belt and, in the same flowing movement, drew it sharply across his own right forearm. Then he turned his arm and pressed it against Marcus' own right arm, bandaged and seeping fresh blood. He fixed the boy steadily in the eye. 'We are brothers,' he said. 'The goddess has said it.'

Marcus nodded politely, and drew his arm away. 'Um, Branoc. Yes.' He wondered how not to offend him. 'It is good,' he added clumsily.

Branoc nodded. 'It is good,' he said.

Marcus went back to sleep by the fire.

An hour after dawn, the bedraggled little column was formed up outside the camp and ready to move off.

'OK!' roared Milo at their head. 'Mission accomplished. Move out.'

And the men, Milo's sarcasm stinging, followed on.

They knew his words were directed as much against himself as them. The mission was hopelessly *un*accomplished. They had survived: that was all. They had failed to bring back a single head of stolen cattle, and they had failed to police the frontier sufficiently. A whole gang of nomads had been slaughtered, barely a day's march from the Wall. And, most irritating of all, two more had died in the night: the mutilated prisoner, and the Attacot chieftain, by his own hand. It had been a cock-up of an expedition and Milo, though proud of his men, was not proud of himself.

He summoned the Arcanus up to ride with him and

questioned him more closely about the Attacotti.

'They teamed up with the other lot a few years back,' Milo began. 'A whole confederation of tribes, caused us no end of trouble. Our Divine Emperor Constans had to come up and sort them all out. Do they usually form alliances and such?'

The Arcanus shook his head. 'The Attacotti are detested by all the other tribes. But though they are cruel, they are not cowardly. And though they are barbarians, they are not stupid. Their power is spreading.'

'A tribe on the move?'

The Arcanus spoke distantly. 'All the tribes of the north are on the move,' he said.

So they were; and not only the tribes of the north. For all across the Empire, across Europe and Africa and Asia, tribes were moving and clashing and moving on. And still further to the east, beyond any world that Rome knew or imagined, across the vast, dry grasslands and steppes of Central Asia, the greatest movement of peoples the world has ever seen was beginning. Yet unknown tribes, with names like Huns, and Goths, and Vandals, were moving with the sun on their fast, shaggy little horses, oxhide bucklers on their backs and elegant bronze axes at their sides. Hungry for new land and easy wealth, and knowing that it could be found faraway to the west, where the great but weakening Roman Empire lay.

They were back at the fort on the Wall an hour after sundown. The other men there met them with a mixture of jeering and respect.

'Had a run-in with the Painted People, did we?'

'Just a few hundred of 'em,' they called back. 'Nothing serious.'

Marcus was ordered straight to the camp doctor. The doctor was the most lugubrious man Marcus had ever met. He treated men and horses equally, and had no confidence in either. He liked to recite with relish a kind of grim litany of the ailments and diseases that could afflict a horse. 'Mad staggers, sleepy staggers, the rot, the rising of the lights, red colic, glanders, farcy, lockjaw, stag evil, pissing evil, pole evil, gripes, fret, gullion, fistulous withers, thrush, strangles, clap in the back, fractures, windgall, bog spavin, hernia . . .' He would shake his head in quiet despair. 'Don't talk to me about *horses*.'

Now the lugubrious doctor peeled back the linen bandages around Marcus' arm and grimaced. The wound was healing well enough, and not badly infected, but it had been bound too tightly. The lips of the wound were pressed together, and would heal in a ridge of scar tissue. He bathed it with saltwater and laid a compress dipped in pitch on it and then bound it up again with fresh linen.

'Is it OK?'

The doctor nodded gloomily. 'You'll live. It was bound well enough, too tightly, if anything. You'll have a pretty scar. But you know what they say: all the ladies love a man with a good scar or two.' He laughed sourly.

Then Marcus, like all the other men, spent a long time in the baths, getting clean again.

All except Milo.

He hadn't slept for forty hours. But first things first. He had a report to make to the camp commandant.

It was good to have engaged already, and faced a man and bettered him. But it was the last engagement for some time. Marcus still rode out on sorties, but the tribes were peaceful again, and there was no further news of the Attacotti.

Life on the Wall was often tedious, and always cold, but the comradeship made it bearable. The others still teased him, called him 'boy', but nothing was meant by it now except affability. He still ate more than anyone else in camp, including Mus. And that, together with the daily grind of weapons training, route marching, hefting wood and stone, repair work on the Wall, and riding, meant it wasn't long before he began to put some meat on his bones. Sometimes he would sit crosslegged on the edge of his pallet and, when he thought no one was looking, spend quite some time admiring his own burgeoning pecs and biceps.

Winter dragged out long and hard up there, and when spring finally appeared it was enormously welcome. With the reappearance of the sun, came the reappearance of Branoc, standing patiently one morning, unannounced, in the main square of the camp. When he finally caught sight of Marcus, he walked straight over and embraced him warmly.

'My brother,' he said.

Marcus saluted him awkwardly.

'Now it is the hunting season,' said Branoc. 'We go hunting.'

'I'll have to ask permission,' said Marcus, and went to find Milo.

'Tell me about it,' said Milo.

So Marcus told his centurion about the blood brotherhood he had stumbled into with the Celtic Arcanus, that night in the marching camp, and how he couldn't tell him his name. Milo looked very grim. After Marcus had told him, he came over and pushed his face almost into the boy's.

'Now you tell me his real name, soldier,' he said softly, 'just as he told you. Or I will have you beaten and then chained up in the henhouse for a whole month.'

Marcus thought about it. Being chained in the henhouse was one of the worst punishments. You were so tightly crammed in that you couldn't move an arm or a leg. By the end of the first day, prisoners in there were whimpering ceaselessly with the pain. But he shook his head.

'I'm sorry, Centurion,' he said respectfully. 'But an oath's an oath. And this is a kind of oath, even with a barbarian.' He hoped desperately that his hunch was correct.

He breathed out. It was. Milo had only been testing him. He stood back and crossed his arms and grinned broadly. 'Good lad,' he said. 'I hate a man who breaks an oath. Even an oath with a barbarian. You never know, he might be a useful friend to have one day. Now fuck off hunting.'

So Branoc and Marcus rode out that morning onto the high moors, and it was the first day of many. Marcus took a single javelin. Branoc took a spear and bow and arrows.

Whooper swans flew over their heads, heading north for their summer breeding grounds, none knew where. They saw a pair of ravens too, high in the sky, male and female, courting. They flew side by side for a while, and then the male flipped over and flew on his back. Branoc smiled. 'The way of all the world,' he said. 'The boy showing off to his girl.' They saw a golden plover taking off from its nest, the sunlight brilliant on its feathers. Passing a rowan tree, most beautiful of all the trees of that high country, a few red berries still lingering from its autumn glory, Branoc reached out and touched it as they passed.

'*Rowan tree and red thread, hold the witches all in dread*,' he muttered.

Marcus wondered and said nothing. They rode on.

After a while they picked up a deertrail crossing a last thin patch of snow on a hill's sunless northeast face. Branoc reined up his horse and glanced down at it. 'Only ambling,' he said. 'See how the hind foot is set in the track of the forefoot?' A little later on he glanced down at some droppings beside the trail and pronounced it a stag.

He scolded Marcus for riding too close to the ridge and skylining himself. 'The deer is just the other side,' he murmured.

'How do you know *that*?' asked Marcus.

Branoc fingered his chin. 'Some signs you read. But some you just feel.' He shrugged. 'The goddess taps you on the shoulder.'

They dismounted and, holding their weapons in their hands, they crawled up to the ridge on their bellies. The wind was directly in their faces. And Branoc was right. Down in the valley below was a fine young stag, drinking delicately from a peat-brown moorland pool. Then came a slow process of inching closer to the stag each time it lowered its head to drink, and freezing every time it raised its head. At one point the stag moved away from the pool and it looked as if all their efforts had been in vain. But then the animal stopped again, only a few yards on, and began to browse. They resumed their stalking.

Marcus was just beginning to think that they were close enough now to have a potshot, when in a movement of lightning speed, Branoc notched an arrow to his bowstring and pulled back and let it go. The stag never knew what had happened. The arrow hit the animal with an audible thump, at a calculated angle, low in the chest, just behind the shoulder. When they had skinned and gralloched it, Marcus saw that Branoc's arrow had taken it straight through the heart.

And so it was for many days of the ensuing spring and summer. They went out hunting a lot. They ate a lot of venison.

One day, Marcus asked Branoc how old he was. He was flattered that someone so evidently about twice his age should be happy to spend so much time with him.

'I am twenty-six, my brother.'

'*Twenty-six*!' Marcus cried. 'You look at least ten years older.'

Branoc waved his hand. 'The wind, the sun,' he laughed. 'And the nagging of women. They all age a man.'

'But *twenty-six*,' Marcus said again.

'Twenty-six,' affirmed Branoc. 'Twenty-six seasons of the deer, twenty-six snowfalls, twenty-six midsummer suns. It is all One.'

Marcus regarded Branoc's lined, leathery face, and still wondered. 'Perhaps you have some different way of measuring it. You do look about forty, or thirty-five at least.'

Branoc smiled. 'Twenty-six is my age, little brother,' he said. 'Even in your Roman years, I am twenty-six. Some things cannot be tampered with. A horse has four legs. Holly is green. I am twenty-six.'

Marcus loved Branoc's brevity.

One day he began to tell him about the Lacedemonians.

'The Lac . . .' queried Branoc. 'I do not know this tribe.'

'OK, the Spartans. And there was a neighbouring tribe called the Macedonians, who had a great, warlike King called Philip. But the Spartans were also warlike. And they were famed for their brevity, for saying things really pithily and pointedly. So we call it *laconic*, after them.'

Branoc lowered a jaundiced eye on the boy. 'Do not speak to me as if I were a child, brother.'

'Oh no, sorry. So: there was the time a foreigner came to Sparta, and sniggered at how short the Spartans' swords were. "Yes," said one Spartan, "but they reach our enemies' hearts well enough." '

Branoc smiled. 'That is good. Tell me more.'

'OK. Philip of the Macedonians. One day he decided to invade Sparta, but first he invited them to surrender and save themselves the trouble, because the Macedonians were a far greater and more powerful tribe than they were. But the Spartans refused. So Philip sent another messenger, to say to the Spartans, "If I, Philip, conquer Sparta, I will enslave you all and raze your city to the ground." And the Spartans sent the messenger back, with a message of just one word. '*If.*'

Branoc smiled even more broadly. 'I do not know these Spartans, nor the country where they live. But I like the sound of them. Many words, many evils. But the language of truth is simple.'

'Aristotle said that!' exclaimed Marcus. 'Those very words! *The language of truth is simple.* How odd.'

'I do not know this Aristotle either,' said Branoc. 'Is he a man of your tribe?'

'Not exactly, no. In fact, he's dead now. But he was a very wise man.'

'There you are,' said Branoc. 'Aristotle the Iron Hat, and I,

Branoc. The thoughts of wise men the world over run together like raindrops on a shield.' Marcus glanced at him, and saw that the Celt's eyes were twinkling with mischief. Like raindrops on a shield.

After a hard day's hunt, it was good to sit and soak in the baths. Branoc scorned the idea, but to Marcus, as to the other soldiers, it was one of the rare luxuries of life on the Wall.

It was an afternoon when many of the soldiers were out on exercises, and Marcus found the baths almost deserted. He stripped off and stuffed all his clothes in a bundle into one of the arched niches in the walls, and went on into the hot room. It was filled with steam, but through the steam he could see Crito, stretching his limbs, touching the low ceiling. He turned when he heard Marcus come in, and nodded.

'Crito,' said Marcus.

'Been out hunting again?'

'Yes.'

Without further preamble, Crito asked, 'Are you and the Celt lovers?'

Marcus, about to sit down on the slatted wooden bench around the side of the steam-room, stopped and stared at Crito. The tall African just laughed.

'Don't play the coy virgin with me, soldier,' he said. 'Are you?'

'No, we're not,' said Marcus.

'Surprising,' said Crito, walking slowly over to where Marcus stood, strangely paralysed. 'You're a handsome boy.' He reached out and cupped Marcus' cock and balls in his open palm. Marcus couldn't move. Wanted to and didn't want to. Crito was stroking him and he was stiffening rapidly under his touch, in the hot steam. He looked down and drops of hot water dripped from his nose and fell on Crito's hand, moving rhythmically up and down. He opened his mouth for more air. It was all so . . . upfront. Sounds like a bawdy pun, he thought. But couldn't smile. He felt his buttocks tense, felt himself arching his groin forward, harder and harder against the

African's hand. Smiling victoriously, Crito laid his other hand on Marcus' shoulder and shoved him briskly back against the wall, knelt down in front of him, and took him in his mouth. Marcus closed his eyes, cradled Crito's head in his hands. He couldn't move. Wanted to and didn't want to. But didn't want to, mostly.

'So,' said Mus that evening as they were crawling under their blankets, 'Crito's had you too now, has he?'

Marcus couldn't decide whether to bury his head in shame or just give a brazen laugh. He did nothing.

Mus laughed for him, a low belly rumble. 'He has everyone in the fuckin' legion sooner or later, that one.'

It was some comfort to Marcus to realise that he was just one amongst many.

He learned soon enough that all the soldiers were more or less bisexual – although of course there was no such word for it. Certainly his rendezvous with Crito in the hot room became more and more frequent, to the African's wry amusement. It was a straightforward deal for a soldier, though. Young soldiers slept with other soldiers and whores; older soldiers, like Milo, tended to sleep more with whores than other soldiers; and when they retired from the army, they gave up the soldiers, and probably the whores as well, married some fecund young bint and fathered a whole brood of pinkfaced children.

What could be more natural?

One day Marcus and Branoc were out riding through the pinewoods, and challenged each other to a race. They hadn't galloped more than a hundred yards when they erupted into a glade and skidded to a halt, the ponies whinnying furiously, their rear hooves ploughing deep furrows into the black mud.

Five men sat around a campfire. They were on their feet

and surrounding the two immediately.

Their leader was a tall, skinny man, desperately trying to look more substantial by wearing a bearskin over his shoulders. He twirled a long, thin knife between his fingers with great dexterity and then said mildly, 'Hand us your weapons.'

Branoc looked stonily back at him. 'No,' he said. Then without further ado, he slid from his pony and, turning to Marcus, told him to do likewise.

'But ... *why*?' stammered Marcus, dismounting all the same. Surely being mounted was their only advantage? Perhaps it was some Celtic thing. Or perhaps it was the only way of avoiding a fight.

He was violently disabused of this theory when the fight started, about two seconds later. Branoc ducked under his pony's belly and, emerging unexpectedly on the other side, stuck his spear straight through the skinny leader of the pack. He and Marcus then resorted to their swords, and each wounded another of the gang, before the last two ran off, uninjured but yelping strangely, like frightened puppies.

'Bandits,' said Branoc contemptuously, cleaning his sword on the dead man's bearksin. 'Common thieves.'

'But why on earth did we dismount?'

Branoc looked at Marcus as if he was very dim indeed. 'It would be dishonourable to fight mounted against men on foot.'

'But Branoc, there were *five* of them! I think we might have been allowed *some* leeway.'

'It would be dishonourable,' Branoc repeated stubbornly. And Marcus knew it was no use arguing. There was no stubbornness in the world to match that of a Celt with honour on his mind.

He was just sheathing his sword when a figure, in eerie silence, rushed out of the woods and straight for Branoc's turned back. Marcus flung himself across the glade and hacked the figure down from behind. In the trees beyond, three further figures slunk away again into the forest gloom. Branoc turned and stared down at the fresh corpse at his feet.

'He was about to kill me?'

'Well,' said Marcus. 'I don't think he just wanted to shake hands with you.'

Branoc remounted his pony and then sat with his head bowed, looking unbelievably gloomy. So gloomy that his usual laconicism quite evaporated. 'This is a disaster,' he said. He raised his head again and gazed heavenwards. 'This is a storm, a tempest of my life, I am a shipwrecked man, I am ruined, I am as a butchered deer in the heather, I am buried under the snows of a mighty avalanche, and all my years on the green earth are ruined and in pieces under the sun.'

'I don't think it's *that* bad,' said Marcus, remounting his pony. 'I mean – '

'You do not understand,' said Branoc. 'Now you have saved my life not once but twice. And there is only one way in which such a thing can be repaid.'

Marcus stared at Branoc, and thought he could guess what Branoc meant. The Celt would have to die for him in turn now. 'Well,' he said, 'maybe it doesn't *have* to be – '

'But yes,' interrupted Branoc, 'the goddess demands it. It has to be.'

He turned his pony and rode on. Marcus followed behind, cursing the stubbornness of these cussed bloody Celts.

Another day he asked, 'Why aren't you married, Branoc?'

Branoc looked puzzled. 'But I am.'

'You are?' Marcus laughed. 'My apologies.'

Branoc nodded. 'She has given me two sons, one daughter, and no grief. I am a happy man.'

'It's just . . . you've never mentioned her.'

'What need?'

Marcus laughed again. Branoc the Spartan, he thought.

Some days out hunting, they could go from dawn to dusk and

not exchange a word – often of necessity, a single gesture having to suffice for a complex direction, so that the deer's keen ears would not twitch forward at their voices, and then it vanish across the nearest ridge or down into the woods below.

Marcus got to like that companionable silence very much. The plover's cry, the wind among the rocks, the ponies' legs brushing through the heather, and the air between them wordless and serene. Yes, he liked it very much. He thought of the chattering dinner parties of London. He thought of the politicking and the wrangling. He thought of Julia, too, and wondered what kind of girl she was becoming, in that world of gossip, and make-up, and flirtation. It was inevitable. He could not resent that.

But the deerhunt here, with Branoc, with his comrades. The bare hills. The silence. This was good.

And so the years passed.

CHAPTER THIRTEEN

Julia could never forget how upset she had been, how angry, when Marcus had just walked out of her life with a jaunty smile and barely a backward glance. And then his letters, so cursory and dry; and then none at all.

Life was so dull without him. Her stomach ached. She felt obscurely hungry, but not for food. The air in the villa curled up like a winter leaf.

She spent a lot of time in the temple of Isis. Before the candle flames upon the altar and arising from the six-foot candelabras, the smoky, perfumed air shimmered and twisted. And through her watering eyes she always saw the face of her mother, and afterwards she would walk slowly home with Bricca, who had waited patiently for her in her own place of worship, and say nothing but seem to feel everything. The thousand swirling conversations of the city. The voices and stories and dreams of everybody around her. Even the weak, reedy braying of a beaten donkey. She reached out and touched the donkey and it stopped its braying and looked slowly round at her in wide-eyed puzzlement. Bricca stared at the girl, the donkey, and then hurried on ahead without a word.

At home, within the villa's four silent, unbreathing walls, she lost herself in a world of books. Long hours and days spent in her uncle's library, curled up on the divan, reading of Dido, and Helen, Eurydice and Iphigenia. The failing light of a winter evening. Of love and life dreaming.

Suitors came and went, and with them her fifteenth and sixteenth birthdays. Her uncle gave up hope. There was something unmarriageable, unmanageable about her. She always found something to criticise in the men she met, and when she had voiced that criticism, Lucius was silently impressed to realise that she was right. One man talked about himself too much: that was obvious. But another man talked about himself *too little*. He was quietly arrogant and untrustworthy, and couldn't bear to be contradicted. Another man was charming. 'Too charming,' said Julia. 'With no real convictions, for fear that they might disagree with someone else's. He would make a good plebeian politician, but he'll not be my husband.' Some were more obvious in their imperfections. One man chewed fresh parsley the whole time because his breath was so bad. It didn't seem to help much. And another man quite clearly preferred boys to girls. 'And I do not,' Julia informed her uncle in her proudest tones, 'intend to spend my life as a *brood mare*!'

Lucius gave permission to a plump Greek merchant to propose to her. Valentinus, his steward, asked him if he thought this was wise. Lucius shrugged and smiled a strange little smile. Later, Valentinus asked his master how it had gone.

Lucius coughed. 'Hm. Our plump Greek friend was foolish enough not only to sicken her with flattery, but also to reach out an arm and touch her cheek.'

Valentinus looked worried. 'What did she do?'

'Not much. Just a few slaps and scratches; minor flesh wounds. But she also told him that if he ever dared to touch her again, she would tear his skin off in strips between her teeth and spit them back in his face.'

Valentinus nodded pensively. At last he said, 'So that was a "no", then?'

'I think we can assume as much, yes,' said Lucius. Inwardly he laughed, and despaired; and admired her more and more.

No one was safe from her acid tongue. One afternoon she

was accompanying her uncle into town, and walking across the forum, she looked up at the huge mounted bust of the Emperor Constantine that sat there.

'I mean, *look* at him!' she whispered, as if they had been talking about him already. 'He looks like a wrestler, or a ploughman or something. So *oafish*. How can you trust a man whose neck is wider than his head?'

Lucius glanced up and suppressed a smile. The thing about Julia's barbs was, that they always had an uncomfortable element of truth in them. 'It may be difficult to suppress such thoughts about our divine Emperors,' he murmured. 'But it is probably wiser not to voice them.'

Divine Emperors indeed! But she held back from saying it. Gods there were, she knew. But the Emperor of Rome, East or West, was no god.

She recalled a passage from her uncle's Epictetus: *'For can Caesar procure us peace from a fever? From a shipwreck? From a fire? From an earthquake? From a thunderstorm?'* And then, after all these natural disasters, he adds ironically, *'Nay, even from love?'*

Hermogenes stayed on, in some vague and unspecified capacity – as her director of reading, perhaps. It occasioned gossip among certain sections of London society, that Quintilianus should allow his niece to be locked up alone for such long hours with her Greek tutor – even if the man was about as attractive as Hephaestus. And then one day, Julia was quietly reading Apollonius, one of her favourites, when Hermogenes tried to persuade her into a discussion of the Moral Virtue of *sophrosyne*, meaning moderation, discretion, wisdom. (Hermogenes was very keen on his Moral Virtues.)

Julia laid down her book. 'Temperance, Fortitude, Justice, blah blah blah,' she sighed, somewhat irreverently. 'Yes I know. Except *sophrosyne* is unique, supposedly, in being an Intellectual Virtue as well as Moral Virtue. But it's all very boring. Life is much more complicated and muddled than that.'

Hermogenes wasn't interested in her opinions, however. 'An *Intellectual* Virtue, did you say? How so?'

201

'Well, at least according to Socrates – who must have looked a bit like you, come to think of it, Hermogenes. It's one of those supposedly "playful" etymologies of his, which are so wearisome. He derives *sophrosyne* from *sophia*, doesn't he? Moderation from Wisdom?'

'I don't recall that,' snapped Hermogenes, deeply put out.

'Xenophon, *Memorabilia*,' said Julia. 'Book Three, I think.'

After that she enjoyed several minutes peace, and no little self-satisfaction, while Hermogenes scurried around checking the reference. At last he laid down the scroll and asked quietly, 'Is your uncle at home today?'

Julia nodded, not raising her eyes from the book in front of her. Hermogenes left the room. A few minutes later he was back.

'Well, my lady,' he said, 'it seems my work here is done.'

Julia looked up in surprise.

'When the pupil can instruct the master on the etymologies employed by Socrates to analyse the true meanings of the Moral Virtues, I really do believe that the master is redundant.'

Julia got up and went over to him. She shook his hand and thanked him for all his instruction, and hoped that they would meet again, perhaps. Hermogenes wished her well. Under his thickly matted beard, she thought he might even have blushed.

And that was the end of Hermogenes.

One person who came to mean more and more to her was Cennla.

A deaf mute slaveboy could hardly be a suitable companion for a young lady of noble birth and distinctly haughty demeanour. At first, however, it was rather as if she was using Cennla to spite her suitors. Look! she was saying. The company of a mere slave is far more interesting than your bachelor burbling, and he can't even talk!

One day, however, she began to experiment on Cennla to see if he could be taught to read. She had just been studying

Plato's *The Meno*, in which it is demonstrated that an uneducated slave can be led into solving a problem of geometry simply by asking him the right leading questions. Intrigued by this idea, Julia started by showing Cennla chalk drawings on a slate, with the words for 'house', 'dog', 'cat', and so on, written underneath. His progress was astonishing. Within two weeks, he was able to write out at least one hundred proper nouns. (And he could draw better than she could too.) Teaching grammar was a little more tricky. 'I go into the house' demanded an elaborate charade that lasted for over an hour, and she was obliged to slap him fiercely across the face on several occasions to aid his understanding. Soon enough, however, he grasped the idea of verbs, pronouns, adjectives and the rest, and at the end of the first month, Julia presented him with his very own tablet and stylus. A few minutes later he came trotting over to where she was doing her wretched woollen work, and showed her his slate. It said: *You are verry kind*.

Normally she would have clouted him for the misspelling. But something stuck in her throat, and she just smiled, and then sent him off to the kitchens to clean out the ovens for the day.

Watching him go, she felt anxious for the first time. The attention with which he watched her. The intensity of his gaze.

At night, Cennla had begun to do something that would have earned him the most terrible beating, perhaps a branding if he had been caught. He would get up in the small hours of the morning, when all the household lay asleep, and creep across the atrium bathed in moonlight, and steal into his master's library. Once there, by the light of the moon – for he did not dare to use a candle – he would take down one of the scrolls at random, and try to read. In the mornings his eyes would be red-rimmed and bloodshot. But his mind felt full, as if it had dined well for the first time in his life.

And he watched the suitors come and go. He served them with wine and sweetmeats, and they talked and talked and quite evidently bored his lady almost to tears. Then he would go back to the kitchens, and in the evening he would take down his slate and write about her.

One evening he wrote, *They speak to you in smooth and silver words, as I cannot. But I love you in silence, and my love is golden.*

Soon after her sixteenth birthday, Lucius decided that his niece was old enough to accompany him to a dinner party, as long as it was of mixed company. He loathed such occasions usually, but it might be amusing to have Julia with him, and hear her views of the guests as they came home in the litter afterwards.

London society was not large, and the Palace of the Vicarius was never somewhere that Lucius could feel comfortable. However, there had recently been a new local governor appointed to the south eastern diocese, *Maxima Caesariensis*, of which London was the capital. His name was Flavius Martinus, and encountering him for the first time at the courts, Lucius took to him immediately, as an anxious and overworked man takes to a glass of fine wine. He was almost a mirror opposite of the Praepositus: ruddy-faced, sociable, Christian (nominally, at least), and with a strict rule about only working before noon. The afternoons were for baths and gossip. Lucius wasn't sure he was a man to command respect, but he liked him all the same. A dinner invitation soon followed.

It was a large dinner party by London standards. There was Flavius Martinus himself, and his charming and rather beautiful wife, Calpurnia. She looked serene and clever and amused all at the same time, and arched her eyebrows a lot. Clodius Albinus was there, inevitably, and Sulpicius too, but the dinner party was large enough for Lucius and Julia not to have to encounter them more than was strictly necessary. Sulpicius leered across at Julia in a way that disgusted her. He had still not married. Also present was a very fat and, gossip had it, extremely rich merchant called Lucius Solimarius Secundinus, whose *nomen* betrayed his eastern origins. He had a ridiculous little wife called Marcia, who twittered throughout dinner to no purpose whatsoever, and three daughters: the older two were Marcella and Livilla who, Julia immediately surmised, were every bit as dim as their mother. They had absolutely nothing to say for themselves, hid a lot behind their fans, and giggled every time a male of the company addressed them. They even seemed to be excited by the attentions of Sulpicius. Julia thought that either of them would make him a perfect wife. The younger daughter, however, a shy, pale-faced girl called Aelia, she liked more. Within minutes they found out that they both loved poetry.

'Of course, Father does not let me read whatever I like,' confided Aelia, 'for not all of it is suitable for a young lady. But he allows me to buy a certain number of books every week that are approved of.' Several books *a week*! Solimarius must be a very rich man indeed. Julia wondered if Aelia might also have wardrobes full of dresses that she didn't want any more . . .'What does your father allow you to read?' Aelia asked her.

'Uncle,' corrected Julia. 'Oh,' she said vaguely, 'mostly what I want. But nothing unsuitable, as you say.'

'Have you read Propertius and Tibullus?' asked Aelia.

Julia quoted some lines in response, and Aelia's eyes widened. 'How clever you are!' she murmured. Julia, only a little ashamed of herself, felt the golden glow of adoration in Aelia's gaze, and basked in it. Here, she decided, was a friend with whom she might get on very well.

A little later in the dinner, three more men arrived, with the mysterious glamour about them that they had only just come from Gaul. Julia and Aelia perked up immediately and fastened their eyes on them. They were quite a mixture.

Pamphilius, a Greek by birth, was unctuous and middle-aged and dressed in a long white robe that reached his ankles, caught around his feet, and trailed along the floor behind him in a way that looked positively dangerous. He was introduced simply as 'a Neo-Platonist'. Julia wondered what kind of day-to-day work this involved. The man who made this slightly mocking introduction was about thirty, with sad and gentle eyes and a rather ugly face, and Julia liked him immediately. His name was Ausonius, he lived in Gaul, and he was – Julia felt Aelia thrill with excitement by her side – a poet!

'Although, alas,' he added self-deprecatingly, 'poets' earnings being what they are, I also have to teach at a university.' And finally, he introduced a burly and grizzled man of about forty, with grey stubble and grey eyes, who looked determined but also honest. His name was Magnentius, and he was a general, no less, of the army in Gaul. A murmur of appreciation went round at this. Magnentius bowed his head with what looked like genuine modesty.

Both Ausonius and Magnentius seemed like interesting people, and Julia decided that she would like to talk to them. She was particularly vexed, therefore, to find herself separated from Aelia and trapped into conversation with Pamphilius, the celebrated Neo-Platonist.

If you could call it conversation. After Julia's first polite enquiry as to what Pamphilius believed, as a Neo-Platonist, it was pretty much a monologue.

Pamphilius explained to her, without looking at her once but fixing his eyes heavenwards, that he believed, with Plotinus, that there were three hypostases, which is to say, vulgarly speaking, realities. These could be called, in vulgar terms, Soul, Mind, and The One. The Soul is, in vulgar terms, discursive thought; Mind is Intuitive Thought; and The One is Pure Mystical Awareness.

'What about the world we see around us?' Julia managed to ask. It was a question that Pamphilius clearly regarded as intolerably vulgar, not to mention a very rude interruption of his train of thought. Nevertheless, he endeavoured to explain.

'Nature,' he said, 'is a quasi-hypostasis, emanating from the hierarchy of the three true hypostases. Mind,' he went on to explain, 'is Thought-Thinking-Itself. There are Thirty Aeons of Light, and Sophia, Pure Wisdom, is their daughter. Ultimately, all will be reunited, to put it vulgarly, in a final, restitutive Apocatastasis.'

'I hope you don't mind me asking,' Julia asked at this point, 'but how do you *know* all this?'

Pamphilius clearly regarded the question as too intolerably vulgar even to merit an answer. He continued to divagate upon the *scala perfectionis*, the Ladder of Perfection, whose higher rungs, so he believed in all humble sincerity, he himself was now approaching. He talked of the Intervention of the Gnosis, the Divine Pleroma, and the Illusory Nature of Pain, at least to Higher Initiates such as himself.

At this last observation, Julia had a strong desire to lean across and prick Pamphilius in his belly with a fruitknife, just to test his no-pain theory. Or at least, to see if he popped like an overripe plum. Fortunately, at this point, she felt the presence of Calpurnia behind her, who drew her aside to speak to Ausonius. Perhaps he would talk more sense. Certainly, the wisdom of the Neo-Platonist was no wisdom, or merely the wisdom of the timid rabbit that has never left its burrow to view the world in hard unblinking sunlight.

She felt the force of this image all the more, because she feared it applied to herself too.

The poet was diffident and modest, and even though still only thirty, had done things and travelled and seen places, and was amusing too. He had come to Britain on this occasion specifically to pay his respects at the grave of his Uncle Contemtus, who was buried at Richborough. Julia silently admired this piety. He charmed and flattered her, and did it in such a way that his flatteries were almost like a conspiracy between them. 'You know I don't really mean what I say,' he seemed to be hinting. 'But we both know that you like me to say it.'

He had a seductive melancholy to him as well – a common

affectation among poetasters – but in Ausonius, she felt, it was genuine. The son of a successful doctor, he was born in Bordeaux, 'my native nest', and now taught Rhetoric at the university there. At the age of only eighteen, he had been summoned to Constantinople to be tutor to the young sons of Constantine.

'What were they like?' asked Julia, fascinated.

'Just what you would expect future Emperors to be like, as boys,' said Ausonius. 'Brave, noble, honest, diligent, conscientious, obedient, pious . . .' He spoke with just enough irony to make his meaning quite clear. Julia laughed. 'Constantius, at least,' he added, 'was a fine horseman, and had the makings of a good soldier.'

'What was Constantinople like?' interrupted Julia.

'Oh, vast, grandiose, hugely impressive, very wealthy, populous . . . Give me Bordeaux any day.' He knocked back his wine. He liked his wine, Julia noticed. She sipped her water. Ladies did not drink wine. 'Then five years ago, I returned to Bordeaux, and married.'

'Oh?' said Julia.

'We had three children, my wife and I, though the first died in infancy. Little Ausonius. He was just two. We buried him in the same grave as his great-grandfather, so that he wouldn't be lonely.' Ausonius smiled such a gentle, melancholy smile that Julia wanted to reach out and touch him. 'And then my wife died too.' He spoke her full name, lingeringly. 'Althusia Lucana Sabina.' He wouldn't look up at her, his eyes rested on his winecup for a while. The last thing he was fishing for was pity or sympathy. Then a bullish voice called from the other end of the room. It was Albinus.

'Tell us your latest epigram, Ausonius, the one about Myron and Lais!'

Ausonius turned from Julia and drained his wine and set his empty glass down on the table. 'Myron and Lais: Lais rejected him on account of his old white hair. So Myron dyed his locks black with soot, and asked her again. "Fool!" said

Lais. "I have already said no to your father!" '

How everyone laughed. Julia, politely. Was she the only person in the entire Empire, she wondered, to find ordinary conversation so much more amusing than these strained epigrams?

A little later, beginning to slur now from rather too much wine, Ausonius launched into more scurrilous epigrams.

'Did you hear about the low-born, nouveau-riche Trimalchio who covered his villa with decorations of Romulus and Remus?' he cried. 'Makes sense. Like them, his father was unknown and his mother a bitch!'

Uproarious male laughter. And a nod from Calpurnia that it was time for the ladies to depart into the further room and leave the men to their wine and raucousness.

The ladies-only company was not, Julia felt, so interesting. But no doubt the all-male party next door was desperately dull too, in a different way. All red faces, drunkenness and vapid braggadocio. This division of the sexes was such a foolish idea.

Calpurnia, however, the wife of Flavius Martinus, took a great interest in her. 'So you are Quintilianus' niece? We have heard so much about you.' She saw Julia's puzzlement, and laughed. 'Nothing bad, I assure you. I trust you are now well-versed in the mysteries of Neo-Platonism?'

'So well versed,' said Julia, 'that I began to lose touch with vulgar reality even as I was listening to him. But,' she added, risking a witticism, 'perhaps I was just falling asleep.'

Calpurnia's laughter was rich and deep. 'We have heard correctly. You are a, ah . . . *sharp* one.'

'Am I?' Julia was genuinely pleased.

Calpurnia laid her hand over the girl's. 'No fool of an average husband for you, I can see, my dear. We are going to have to find you someone *very* special, aren't we?'

At last it was time to leave. Ausonius kissed her hand goodbye – and then, not to be outdone, so did Sulpicius. Ausonius said he thought he might write a poem about her. Julia flushed. Both Calpurnia and Aelia said that they hoped they would see her again soon. Calpurnia, childless, felt a tug as she watched the girl depart with her uncle, and knew exactly what it signified.

'So,' said her uncle in the quiet of the litter. 'You made the acquaintance of some interesting people?'

Julia enthused about both Calpurnia and Aelia.

'And Ausonius, the poet?' asked Lucius.

Julia turned her head away and smiled.

Another, far grander litter, passed that way in the small hours of the morning. Inside sat Albinus and Sulpicius. They, too, were talking of the dinner party, but in the curiously clipped, elliptical style which men of power use when they are on guard.

'So what do you think?' asked Sulpicius.

Albinus shifted his burly body. 'He is an utterly good man. Incorruptible. Steadfast. As indifferent to gold as a . . .' he waved his hands, 'a blind goat.' Sulpicius smiled. Albinus did not. He added sarcastically, 'He is our latterday Seneca.'

'Surely not *Seneca*, brother,' purred Sulpicius. 'Not the noble Stoic philosopher, who loaned money to the Britons at forty per cent – and when he called in his loan, so enraged the tribes that he precipitated the Revolt of Boudica.'

Albinus laughed. He always appreciated the way his brother was such a mine of malicious information, and could dish the dirt on anyone, even Stoic philosophers. It kept people in their place. There were no heroes in Sulpicius' world. 'And I thought the Boudican thing was a war of *honour*. I thought it was a war of revenge against those who had whipped the bitch and raped her daughters.'

'Mere folk memory,' Sulpicius assured his brother, 'retrospective aggrandisement. Money lies at the root of everything. Everyone has a price tag on them.'

'Except *him*,' sighed Albinus. 'And people like *him* can be terrible obstacles in the path of an ambitious man.'

Sulpicius raised his finger to his lips and smiled. 'Impatience is a far worse stumbling-block for an ambitious man,' he counselled. 'Watch and wait, brother. Watch and wait.'

As the seasons passed, there were many more half-amusing dinner parties for Julia, interspersed with the tense boredom of waiting for something that never came. Half the eligible men in London, so her uncle said, wanted to marry her, yet not one commanded her respect. Several positively disgusted her.

'And you, Uncle,' she asked cheekily one day. 'Why have you never married?'

Lucius smiled the saddest smile, and absentmindedly touched the fine silver signet ring that he wore on the little finger of his left hand. Clearly it meant something to him. 'There was a girl, once, a long time ago,' he said. 'So long ago that I was actually young then. But . . . well, I do not blame her. Why should she marry a dull, gloomy fellow like me when she could marry a party-giving millionaire like – like the one she *did* marry, soon enough.' He looked up, still smiling sadly. 'But there were never any others to match her.'

How alike we are, she thought, my uncle and I. Choosy, difficult individuals. She had half a mind to throw her arms around him and kiss him then. But such things were not done. So instead she smiled at him and tried to say everything with her eyes.

Along with the dinner parties came the gossip, the small-minded provincial twittering. Julia enjoyed her new friendship with Calpurnia, for she at least talked sense. And there was Aelia, sweet and pale-faced and always desperate to please her. Julia was honest enough to admit to herself that her pleasure in Aelia's adoring company might not be entirely healthy. But it passed the time. As for her two ridiculous older sisters, both Marcella and Livilla were married off in quick succession, to husbands so idiotic that Julia felt quite sure no woman could possibly love them – not even women themselves so idiotic as

Marcella and Livilla. But perhaps they were marriages made in Heaven. Certainly, their doting mother Marcia wept floods of tears at both weddings, much to Julia's ill-suppressed amusement.

Sometimes she thought of the funny, ugly poet, Ausonius, as sad-eyed as a lotus-eater, there in his lotus country of Bordeaux, with his vineyards and his poetry. Sometimes she thought – only a little guiltily – of what it might feel like to be taken in the strong arms of the soldier, General Magnentius, and crushed under his hard, irresistible weight. And sometimes she thought of that boy, Marcus, her one-time playmate, and saw him as clearly as the day he left, sauntering out of the courtyard gates with nothing for her but a backward, boyish grin. Years ago now. What had become of him? Occasionally her uncle still received letters, formal, dry as dust, detailing army movements. But nothing more.

In the summer, she and Aelia were taken by Calpurnia to the sacred waters of Sulis Minerva, in Bath, where they rented an elegant town-house and spent a great deal of time avoiding drinking the water, and commenting on the many foibles of those they met there. Aelia's admiration of Julia's witticisms knew no bounds.

But Julia also felt that this was a holy place, despite the unholy taste of its waters. In the baths, those waters bubbled and seethed, green and opaque, and words of comfort and longing were carried through the thin veil of mortality on the vaporous air. She knew that this was a gate to the Underworld, and that her parents were waiting for her just beyond, hands outstretched, smiling.

She went often to the Temple of Isis there.

At the end of the summer, with the skies greying into autumn, they rode back to London, and then, oh! The dullness of life there!

Sometimes she felt so cloudy and sleepy that she came out of the dining room and stood in the darkened hallway and shook her head as if to clear it of the tangled sheep's wool of vapid tittle-tattle and gossip. Her life was wasting away. She was nearly twenty now, and still unmarried, still scornful of what suitors came her way. Where was he? The One.

Not Pamphilius' One either, not some abstract Greek absurdity. The One with strong arms and an easy smile, but a determined mouth and jaw, thick black hair, and whose dark, feeling eyes fixed on hers and felt no need to move, whose lips had no need to speak. The flesh-and-blood, mortal, imperfect, sublunary One, who was the only one for her.

Such were her daydreams and dreams. Life was elsewhere, love was elsewhere. Waiting for her, somewhere, faraway.

The books in her uncle's library became ever more precious to her, each one a world in itself, which she knew better with each passing year.

One of the books in his library was a great yellowing scroll, edged in goldleaf and very precious, which she would take down with utmost care and unroll across the wide shale table in the centre of the room. She could feel the papyrus absorb her into itself, drown her, and she drowned willingly.

It was a map.

One evening Lucius came in and found her there, poring over it, and smiled a flickering smile. How beautiful, how feminine she is, he thought, with her dark coiled hair and dark liquid eyes, there in the lamplight. But what a fierce, masculine mind! He hoped that her husband, whoever he might be, would have a thick skin.

He told her that women did not read maps. Maps were for men. If women did read maps, they didn't understand them. Julia smiled and said nothing. She supposed that he was right, for the most part. She couldn't imagine Marcella and Livilla ever having looked at a map in their thin, dim lives. If they did, they wouldn't understand a thing about it. But to Julia, a map was a kind of poetry.

The coasts were painstakingly edged in blue ink, and the

mountains evoked by numerous little angular squiggles. And the *names* ... She read out the names to herself, from all around the Mediterranean and beyond, and each one called to mind a picture or a story, and left her faraway-eyed in dull provincial London, sad and silent and longing.

There were names she knew of old, like Cordova, which stirred memories of the banks of the Guadalquivir thick with flowers in springtime, and the mountains of the Sierrra Nevada to the south, topped with snow. Or those African provinces that her father knew, where lions came from: Numidia, with its yellow marble, and Cyrenaica; or the great, bustling, argumentative city of Alexandria, by Lake Mareotis, all pink Egyptian granite under the white sun, with its powerful Jews, and quarrelsome Christians, its camels and bazaars, its huge lighthouse, and its half-ruined library that Caesar had burned, once the wonder of the world.

She dreamed of what it must be like to sail past Constantinople, with its hundreds of temples and palaces, and its porphyry columns and mosaic pavements, and on into the Black Sea, past the shores of Bithynia and Pontus to far Colchis where Jason once sailed, to find a golden fleece hanging from an oak tree in a sacred, haunted grove.

Or the desert beyond. For surely it must be sad and marvellous to sit in the green shade of the date palms of Palmyra, and watch the Arab caravans come and go and pass on into the shimmering heat of Syrian desert, their cameltrains laden with goatskin flagons filled with date wine, and rolls of Chinese silks, and tiny, precious bags of gum of Frankincense, worth more than their weight in gold. Or to stand by the docksides of Tyre – she could smell the odour of damp seaweed as she dreamed – and see the Phoenician sailors hauling in the creaking creels of shellfish for their purple dye, so precious that men had fought and died in wars because of it.

Or names still further off and vaguer, like the Kingdom of the Nabataeans, by the shores of the Red Sea, beyond even the furthest reaches of the Roman Empire. Or mighty Babylon of the Euphrates, with its one hundred gates of bronze, and its walls of burnt brick four hundred feet high. Did they still stand? And within, every woman, slave or free, must once in her lifetime go and sit in the precincts of the temple of the Babylonian Goddess of Love, whom they called Ishtar, and offer herself to any stranger for a single silver coin. She could refuse no man. Julia touched her hand to her throat.

She dreamed of travelling the endless dust roads of the Persian Empire, across the great Salt Desert, to visit the fabulous city of Persepolis, which legend said was made of glass; or ride on through wild Hyrcania with its terrible tigers, bigger than elephants. Further still, into the sun, to the banks of rivers like the Jaxartes and the Oxus, and the rolling Indus itself, where Alexander finally stopped and sighed. Or south to the shores of the sounding sea, and the cities of Barbaricum or Barygaza, their harbours filled with Roman ships bringing wine and copper, dates and gold, and shipping back turquoise and diamonds, spikenard and indigo, tortoiseshell, silk, and pearls the size of a man's fist. The map blurred before her.

Life is elsewhere.

Oh when will it happen? When?

CHAPTER FOURTEEN

One morning, the order came that Marcus had been dreading. They were to return to London. 'But,' added Milo mysteriously, 'we may not be there for long. And on top of that, I've lost my bloody optio.'

'Oh?' said Marcus.

'Caelius smashed his kneecap last night. The surgeon's hacking away at him right now. If you listen hard, you can hear the screams. He might never walk again – and he'll certainly never manage twenty-five miles a day in full kit. Wasn't in exactly heroic circumstances, either. Fell down some steps whilst drunk, being chased by a jealous husband. A blacksmith.'

Marcus grinned. 'Have you got a replacement?'

'Of sorts.' Milo looked up. 'You.'

It took a while for his centurion's words to sink in. When at last he realised – he, an optio! a lieutenant, second-in-command to Milo, in charge of eighty men! – Marcus could have kissed Milo where he stood, and danced out of the room for joy.

But he thought better of it.

It was drizzling with soft May rain as Marcus crossed the cobbled courtyard to the Legate's lavish quarters in the heart of the legionary fortress at York. As he approached the doors, they opened and a figure slipped out into the dusk. Marcus made to go on in, when he was stopped in his tracks. He stared at his feet, and then looked around again. The figure had vanished. But he could have sworn . . .

He shook his head. He could have sworn that was Sulpicius. Sulpicius of the Baths, the Vicarius' shitweasel of a little brother. But what on earth would a metropolitan playboy like Sulpicius be doing up here in York?

Marcus went on in. The ceremony was brief and informal. The Legate asked him a few questions about his career, told him that he had known his father and that he was a good soldier. He asked him about his 'esteemed guardian' back in London. Then he touched him on the shoulder with his drawn sword, had him swear a fresh oath of allegiance to the Emperor, declared him an optio, and finally poured him a glass of wine. It was good wine. After some minutes of chatting, Marcus asked casually, 'I don't suppose you get many visitors from London up here, do you?'

The Legate laughed. 'None at all, to be exact.'

Marcus laughed too.

Back in the barracks, clearing out his stuff to move over to the officers' quarters, Marcus expected some keen-edged ragging from the men. But it didn't happen. He was an officer now, and when they saw him, they all – Mus, Crito, Britus and the rest – stood respectfully to attention. He ordered them at ease, gathered his kit together, nodded, and was gone.

That evening, he underwent another ceremony. In the greatest secrecy, in the darkness of a temple, where every other worshipper wore an animal mask to hide his true identity, he was bound naked in a pit, with an iron grid covering it. He shivered in freezing water, he swore to do good, to be honourable, and always to keep the secrecy of the faith. Finally, the water was drained away and a young white bullock was sacrificed over his head, laid out on the grid; its blood rained down upon him and its warmth revived his frozen flesh and he was reborn, a worshipper of the dying and rising god named Mithras.

☆ ☆ ☆

The march to London was brisk and easy in the May sunshine, the verges of the roads thick with cow parsley and the air thick with summer insects. Marcus thought back to that first march north, and how it had exhausted him. Now he marched back with full pack, weapons – like Milo, he disdained to ride an officer's horse – and barely noticed the twenty miles a day.

Eight days from York and they were passing back through the gates of the Southwark camp, where he was given his new officer's quarters. He couldn't believe how comfortable they were.

'But remember, Optio,' said Milo, 'we all still shit the same.'

'What, even the Emperor?'

'All *except* the Emperor,' conceded Milo. 'The Emperor shits turds of purest gold.'

The following afternoon Marcus was given a surprising four months' back pay, plus the first month of an optio's. The weight in his purse felt good.

After taking first command of his men in the morning, and putting them through drill with satisfactory results, he spent the afternoon soaking in the bathhouse. Then he dressed in a clean linen tunic and leather belt, with a light woollen cloak over his shoulders. He pondered for a moment whether to wear the leather armbands – too ostentatiously soldierly? But then he decided he would, to cover up the ugly pink scar on his forearm, if nothing else.

He went out into the town, to the finest barber's he knew. The man beside him was having his hair curled with heated curling-tongs, and then smeared with a paste of cassia and cinnamon. Stank like a Syrian brothel. Marcus opted for a neat trim of hair and beard, and was done and out in half an hour.

Finally he came to a side door in a villa wall beside Walbrook Stream, and knocked. After a while it was opened.

'Young master!' cried Bricca, breaking into instant and copious tears. 'Why, such a handsome young man you've

218

grown! And look at your beard! I hope you made offerings of your first shave, like you ought? Oh master, oh mistress, do come and see!'

Managing finally to detach himself from Bricca's rather forward embrace – not the sort of behaviour one would expect from a slave, even in a household as enlightened as this – Marcus looked up and saw a young woman standing under the colonnade. She wore her dark hair piled up on her head, and her equally dark eyes were fixed on him. She wore a long dress, high-waisted, saffron yellow, and a pair of small ruby earrings. No other jewellery, no make-up. When she stepped out from the colonnade into the sunlight, Marcus was speechless to see how beautiful she was. He hadn't really considered what she might look like. He knew she would be older, of course. Nineteen now, almost twenty. Older, though still three years his junior. But he hadn't anticipated that she should be so . . . changed. Nor that he would, in consequence, be so abjectly tongue-tied.

'Well, I must go and get the master,' said Bricca, and bustled away, wiping the tears from her eyes with her apron.

She came over to him, moving with the steady grace of a lady who has spent many hours cultivating such a gait, walking about the garden with a plate of cherries on her head and feeling utterly ridiculous.

She held her hand out to him. 'Marcus,' she said.

He kissed it. 'Julia.'

'So,' she said, turning away almost immediately, 'No word of warning, no advance letter. You just turn up on our doorstep like that – after nearly seven years!' She looked back and saw that he was struggling hopelessly. 'But I don't suppose manners are the first thing you are taught in the army.'

'No, indeed, I . . .'

Marcus was saved from further laceration by the sudden appearance of Lucius, bursting from the doors at the end of the atrium and hurrying towards him. It was so out of character for Lucius to hurry anywhere that Marcus wanted to laugh.

The next thing he knew, his guardian had thrown his arms around him and hugged him so lovingly that the young man's bubbling laughter vanished and he felt instead a lump in his throat. Lucius stood back again after a while and, holding both Marcus' hands in his, gazed at him with tears of pride.

Julia stood aside, twitching with jealousy.

'My son,' said Lucius.

'Father,' said Marcus.

They stared speechlessly at each other for a while. At last Lucius said, 'I hear you are made an optio.'

'I . . . yes.'

Lucius nodded and beamed and could say no more.

Men, thought Julia. No matter how nobly-born and educated they may be, it takes only the slightest flutter of real feeling to reduce their articulacy to the level of boars. She also thought, as she had begun to think more and more often nowadays, of another amusing thing: that her uncle, for all his Stoicism and dispassion, was in reality the most deeply *passionate* of men. This perception never failed to please her.

Entering the diningroom that evening, Marcus was astonished to see Julia helping the slave, the youth called Cennla, set out the dishes on the low table. Indeed, they seemed to be giggling together at something. They stopped when they sensed him standing there, and Cennla scuttled out of the room and back to the kitchens. Marcus stared at Julia without expression.

'I taught him to read,' said Julia, continuing to arrange the dishes and studiously ignoring his moral indignation. 'Now we can communicate by signs and expressions as well.'

Marcus said nothing. He had never felt jealousy before. Then he held out a little wooden box in the palm of his hand. 'This is for you,' he said.

Julia took it and opened it. Inside, the box was carefully padded with the finest red silk, and nestling in among the folds were a variety of hair rings, pins, a bracelet, a necklace and a pair of earrings, all made from the finest, darkly gleaming Whitby jet. She couldn't look up.

'I . . . I bought it in the north, from a little shop in York,' he said. 'It comes from the east coast. I . . . I thought it would suit your colour and that.'

Now she looked up, entirely composed. 'Thank you,' she smiled. 'They are very beautiful.' She looked back at the table behind them. 'Dinner will be ready in a quarter of an hour or so. I must just go and put these in my room.'

Marcus knocked on the door to his guardian's study and went in. 'I have something for you, Father,' he said. 'A gift.'

Lucius unwrapped the gift – a kind of stone – and regarded it gravely.

'Is it not unusual?' asked Marcus.

Lucius traced the strange patterns under his fingertips. 'It is indeed,' he said.

'I found it just near the Wall. I thought you might like to place it somewhere in the garden.'

Lucius considered. 'It is remarkable,' he said. 'I think I will keep it in here.' He looked up and smiled. 'Thank you, my dear son.'

Marcus bowed out of the room. His guardian looked sad and burdened still, he thought. But somehow he had mellowed, too. Was this just old age?

Once the door was shut, Lucius reached forward and placed the large ammonite fossil at the corner of his desk. *Wonders are many*, he thought, contemplating the strange stone and quoting the celebrated line of Sophocles. And then, completing the quote, looking up towards the door where his son had just vanished: *But none is more wonderful than man.*

Marcus found the dinner that evening both strangely formal and yet deeply touching. He was touched most of all by the discreet way in which Julia had vanished up to her bedroom, to reappear in a crimson dress, and the jet jewellery that he had brought her: bracelet, necklace and earrings, all shining brilliantly in the lamplight of the dining room. Black would not have gone so well with the yellow dress, so she had changed it specially, saying nothing. Against the red, the black jet looked quite beautiful.

There were moments, too, during dinner, when Marcus again felt a twinge of jealousy. But he forced himself to be philosophical about it, and accept the simple truth. He must recognise that Julia and Lucius were deeply attached to each other, with an indissoluble bond. They even teased each other nowadays. Their affection went far deeper than familial duty. It was clear to him that Lucius truly was Julia's father, in all but the literal sense; while to Marcus he was and would always be his much revered and respected guardian.

Lucius enquired searchingly about life in the army, and then in turn told Marcus that things in the Western Empire were not good. In the Eastern Empire, too, Constantius was in the thick of a brutal war with Persia, 'which neither side,' added Lucius bitterly, 'can possibly win. How large do they think an Empire can grow before it breaks?' But at least Constantius had the respect of his men, commanded reasonably well, and retained his dignity. Constans, on the other hand, with his close circle of handsome German boys . . .

Marcus raised an eyebrow, at his guardian teetering on the very brink of treacherous talk. 'Let us just say,' Lucius concluded, 'that Constans does not have the support of his men as much as he should. The army, in particular, is . . . wayward.'

'What does Magnentius say?' asked Julia.

Both Marcus and Lucius shot a look across the table. It was unorthodox, to say the least, for a woman to enter into military and political discussions. But then, this *was* Julia.

'Magnentius,' Lucius explained to Marcus, 'is a general in Gaul, who has dined with us on occasion. I believe he is anxious, too, about the condition of the Western Empire.'

Marcus remembered what he had seen, or thought he had seen, at York. He told Lucius. The older man listened and looked grave.

'The Legate there is a Christian, as you know,' he said. 'Sulpicius may have gone to see him there, though for what reason, I cannot think. You recall the visit of the Emperor Constans, when he rode north to suppress the Picts? There were strange rumours around then, that some factions were using the Picts, paying them even, to foment disorder and even to attack the province as a whole, in order to wrest power for themselves. Of course, they were roundly defeated. But nevertheless, it is disturbing to think that there might be alliances made between Romans and such barbarians.'

It was good to be home again, thought Marcus. But news from the Empire was grim. How he hated it all now: the politics and backstabbing, the grubbing for power. Rats in a panic, scrabbling over each other's backs to reach the corn.

Towards the end of the meal, Lucius insisted on going to retrieve his strange stone from his study to show to Julia. As he left, Julia extended her right arm towards Marcus and showed off the new bracelet around her slender wrist.

'It suits me very well, does it not?' she asked.

He nodded. And then something caught his eye, which shook him to the core. He pointed at the back of Julia's right arm. 'What's that?' he said.

She glanced down. 'Oh that,' she laughed. 'It's just a catscratch. I tried to take a chicken wing off Ahenobarbus one day, and he made his displeasure keenly felt.' She ran her fingertips over the thin scar. 'Unfortunately it got infected, and I'm left with this. Is it so terrible a blemish on a young lady?'

'No, it's not that,' said Marcus, his voice distant with bewilderment. Then he unlaced the leather armband that he wore on his right arm to cover his own, much uglier scar. Much uglier, but ... He twisted round and held his arm alongside Julia's, feeling her soft skin against his. They both looked down in stunned silence. The pattern of the two scars was exactly the same.

Julia asked, 'What date did it happen?'

'Don't even ask,' snapped Marcus. He didn't want to know. Neither, on reflection, did she.

Marcus sat back again and laced up his armband. 'It was a while ago, in a skirmish with some tribesmen called Attacotti.' But he knew Julia wasn't listening. Her eyes were fixed on him. He looked at her, and neither of them could speak. They both knew they were linked now by something greater than them, chainlike, unbreakable, and neither was quite sure they liked the feeling.

Finally, Julia broke the heavy silence with a lighthearted joke. 'Still, at least the ladies will be full of admiration for *your* scar. More than the men will admire mine.'

'You don't really admire men with scars, do you?' he demanded, quite fiercely.

'No, in fact I don't,' she said.

He laid his head back again and relaxed. 'That's good,' he said. 'I hate women who admire men for their scars. Such brainless . . . excuse me, but *tarts*.'

Julia thought of Marcella and Livilla, lately married but not averse, rumour already had it, to taking lovers, to relieve the ennui of having no brain to speak of. Now *they* would love a soldier with a scar. 'I'm sure I could introduce you to a couple,' she said.

'Please don't,' he said.

They were laughing when Lucius returned.

That night they both dreamed of scars. They both dreamed that an owl flew down at them and scratched them both at the same moment, one talon rasping at each right arm. They clasped arms, and the blood flowed together. Then they stood together in a boat, and a hooded boatman took them across a dark river, all the world around them silent but full of expectation.

They never shared their dreams with each other.

☆ ☆ ☆

Early the following morning, Julia was just about to issue her orders to the slaves for the day when there came a terrific hammering on the door.

'What on earth . . .?' muttered Bricca, shuffling over and flinging it open.

A red-faced, sweating messenger stood in the doorway. 'An urgent message from Southwark camp, to the Praepositus, and –' he glanced down, 'the Lady Julia.'

Julia swept up behind Bricca and snatched the message from the slave's startled hand. She read:

> *To my dear father and Lady Julia, greetings,*
>
> *And in haste, for we have only been informed this last hour, to proceed straight to the harbourside and embark for Antioch. It seems we are being transferred with some urgency to the Persian Front and the direct generalship of the Emperor Constantius himself. Apologies again for much haste, remember me in your prayers as I remember you,*
>
> *Marcus*

If Marcus had been there in person, she would have struck him with all her might. Instead she thrust the message into Bricca's hands and ordered her to take it to her uncle forthwith. Then she pushed past the waiting slave in the doorway and ran, in a most unladylike fashion, all the way to the harbourside below London Bridge.

The harbourside was a chaos of porters and lightermen lading up the ships with casks of water and amphorae of wine and dried meat and biscuits; and bawling soldiers, cramming themselves onto the two small but sturdy square-sail ships that were drawn up alongside the crowded wharves. Julia pushed her way through determinedly, trying to blink her eyes clear enough to see. One of the ships was already laden, the gangplanks were being hauled in, the sail was being let down to harsh cries in a language she did not even recognise. *Syria*!

It was the other side of the world. And life expectancy on the Persian Front, fighting Rome's most ancient and implacable enemy, was somewhat lower than in the garrisons of the Wall.

At last she thought she saw him, leaning back nonchalantly against the taffrail in the midst of a crowd of laughing soldiers, nodding, smiling. *Smiling.* How dare he!

She called out his name but he did not hear. The air was filled with voices and shouting, and hers was one among many and not the strongest. The bow and stern ropes were uncoiled from the harbourside capstans and hauled in. The ship drifted out very slowly from the harbourside, then caught the force of the downstream current tumbling through the great arches of London Bridge, and began to take speed.

She called again and again. He did not look back. She watched for a long while, until the ship, intermittently obscured now by the second ship that followed on behind, finally rounded the bend in the river where it curved northwards again through the marshlands of Wapping and Rotherhithe, and passed from view.

At last she left the harbourside. She wiped her tears angrily away, slapped a slave even more angrily for blocking her path. She would never see him again. And even if he came back in five years' time, begging to see her, she would refuse. She would refuse ever to see him again as long as she lived.

CHAPTER FIFTEEN

The Channel run was long and arduous, tacking doggedly into a westerly wind all the way. The Bay of Biscay was its usual lively self, and Marcus, along with a large proportion of the other men, was violently sick for days. Milo liked to position himself alongside them at the taffrail, munching on a hunk of dry bread liberally dipped in the strongest smelling fish sauce. He evidently found it all highly amusing.

At its worst, the ship was rolling through a full ninety degrees, and one young idiot managed to slip straight off the deck and into the drink. Trying to bring the ship around and hold her steady while a longboat was lowered – the ship now sail-less and wallowing dangerously, rolling through more like a hundred degrees – took them the best part of the day. But the young idiot was saved. As he was dragged up onto the deck and dumped like a drowned puppy, Milo turned to Marcus.

'A decent officer doesn't lose a single man if he can help it. Remember that.' He turned back to the drowned puppy. 'Right, get him below and give him twenty-four lashes.'

It was a severe punishment. Eighty lashes could kill a man. But at least he would live.

The sea was calmer as they rounded Cape St Vincent and weighed anchor at Cadiz for fresh water and provisions. Thereafter a bracing but welcome north-westerly drove them rapidly through the Pillars of Hercules and into the Mediterranean. Looking north, Marcus saw the high peaks of the

Sierra Nevada, and thought of how Julia had lived there once, in the heartlands of Spain, near the banks of the Guadalquivir.

The air of the Mediterranean smelled different almost immediately, denser and saltier, and Marcus longed to see Rome again. Instead he saw Syracuse with its Great Harbour five miles or more in circumference, where they took on fresh provisions again. They were due to stop at Crete as well, but the wind took them on so fast and the fresh water was holding out, so Milo decided to make straight for Antioch.

Antioch: few of the soldiers on board had ever dreamed of going to Antioch. After Alexandria and Rome herself, she was the third greatest of the Empire's three great cities. Standing on the left bank of the beautiful valley of the Orontes, Antioch was famous for its date wine, for its fanatical and disputatious Christians, and for the excellence of its whores.

'I'm too old for that lark,' grumbled Milo, who made much of being angry at this transfer to the east, so late in his career. But Marcus didn't believe a word of it. He knew Milo was relishing this last chance for a crack at Rome's deadliest enemy. As for the other soldiers, already red-nosed and blister-lipped from the unaccustomed sun and the saltwater, they were keen to taste the delights of Antioch. Now, after the long sea voyage, they had almost a week to lie up in the barracks of the town before the march east to the great fort of Dura Europus, and then on to the Persian Front.

Marcus had never in his life seen anything like Antioch.

He had no memories of Rome. He had been too young when his family left for Britain. The biggest city he had ever seen was the small provincial capital of London, a town of around five thousand people, ten thousand at the most on the busiest market days. But Antioch, they said, was home to more than half a million souls, although nobody really knew the exact number. Marcus couldn't even begin to comprehend the idea of half a million people. Then the Empire as a whole, comprised a *hundred million* people – all real human beings, like him, all with stories to tell, comedies and tragedies hopelessly mixed up together . . . It was too much to think about.

Unlike London, Antioch was densely packed, a maze of narrow winding lanes between tall buildings, shaded from the relentless Syrian sun, and filled with jostling crowds of many nations – Greeks, Jews, Armenians, Cypriots, Egyptians, Arabs . . . and donkeys heavily laden with firewood or water-panniers, and camels, malodorous and bad-tempered, flaring their nostrils discontentedly at the ignobleness of life.

Marcus passed the week in something of a daze. The city was overpowering, an assault on the senses. He saw a sheep being slaughtered in the street. He saw a leprous girl without legs pulling herself forward with her hands in the dust. He watched a whore walking by swinging her slender hips, and in the dust behind her as she walked on, her hobnailed sandals printed in Greek the words, 'Follow Me.' He listened to a Christian preacher haranguing a jeering crowd, who threw little copper coins at him, telling them that they were all going to perish, and soon. Marcus thought the preacher might just be right.

He learned that his older brothers, Titus and Sylvanus, were out at Dura Europus with the Fourth legion, where they themselves, with a motley crew of other remnants and odd cohorts from the west of the Empire, would soon be marching.

'Total bloody chaos,' said Milo grimly. 'Shapur is kicking our arses all over the place.'

Marcus agreed. Antioch was chaos, the army was chaos, the Persian campaign was chaos. Sometimes it felt like the whole civilised world was breaking down into chaos.

'Only one thing a soldier can do in times like these,' Milo told him. 'Keep your kit in order, oil your sword, and look to your comrades.'

It didn't seem like much reassurance, but it would have to do.

☆ ☆ ☆

After the long voyage, the soldiers quickly recuperated. In the mornings, they trained hard in the hills above Antioch, and spent long, lazy afternoons in the taverns of the town. They drank date wine under trellises of trailing vines, and Marcus found himself thinking that life was good in the east; it could sap away your will and your soul and you didn't mind. You could happily do nothing for the rest of your life.

On one occasion they got talking to a small, wiry man in the tavern, who moved his eyes restlessly about and never answered a question directly. His ears were pierced and gold-ringed, like the pushy freedman from the Euphrates in Juvenal's first satire. He introduced himself as Johurz. Marcus asked what nation he was from, but Johurz didn't reply. Instead he produced some dice and they played for an hour or so, and Johurz won all their money and then offered to buy them a drink in return. Mus belched sourly by way of gratitude.

'Let me tell you about my country,' Johurz said as the fresh jug arrived. 'You are from the west, you understand nothing.' He took a deep draught of wine and sighed theatrically.

'Johurz is sad and restless as a hart.'

It was the way they talked here, Marcus was beginning to realise. Someone had once said to him that Rome had only one true religion, the religion of pragmatism. But here in the east, they had no time for pragmatism. Everything was poetry. Everything shimmered insubstantially in the desert heat.

Johurz continued talking of himself in the third person, elliptical, wary, dramatising.

'He has stood in the front ranks of the army of the King – forgive me, yes, in my younger days and my foolish youth – and he has washed his sword in blood a thousand times. In the market-place there are beautiful girls who would willingly love Johurz. But he finds no joy in this. "My gold is as good as any man's," says Johurz. And finds no joy in this. "I will make myself allegories," says Johurz, "to comfort me."

' "I am as a cedar of Lebanon, strong and beloved of God. I am as a camel in the desert of life, protected of God." And Johurz finds his allegories are but frail mockeries, and does not believe that he is as a camel, and does not believe that he is protected of God. "I am as restless as a hart, as a rabbit," says Johurz. "My city is of gold, my temples of marble and my streets of most fine stone. And I am as poor as a desert fox!" And Johurz laughs even though he cries. For he knows that the world is finite, and his needs infinite.'

Then the strange man called Johurz set down his date wine and laughed. Tipped back his head and roared. When he stopped, he looked expressionlessly at the mystified Roman soldiers around him. He said, 'You are going into the desert. Well. There is truth in the desert. And,' he added, laughing again, 'there is also truth in the scorpion's sting!' Then he drained his wine and got up and left them without another word.

Marcus knew then that he was beyond the reach of Rome, wherever the borders of the Empire on the maps might lie. He was in the east now, where men talked about God as if He were their friend and walked beside them, and all seemed drunk on God, and were driven a little crazy by the loneliness and silence of the desert that lay beyond them and all around, beyond this small, huddled oasis of Antioch with its half a million lost and mystical souls.

He sipped more date wine and felt pleasantly woozy. He was learning, among other things, how to take his drink. You learned how to take your drink, he had discovered, by taking your drink. Regularly, and copiously. It wasn't too hard.

He smiled sleepily at the Armenian dancing girl in her red skirt and veils, her hair caught up in a fillet, swaying her flanks before them. What else was there to do? Everything was a mystery. She clicked her castanets and fixed Marcus with her lazy eyes, half-closed, lascivious, herself half-drunk, carmine-lipped. She sang in heavily accented Greek that he struggled to understand:

But what can slow the flying years?
When we are young, sweet it is to love,
Sweet it is to lie in the shade,
And feed on the scarlet lips of a pretty girl.
We will not be always young,
And O, alas! love will fly away with the years.

When she had finished her song, she reached up and pulled the fillet from her head and her thick black hair, glossy as a raven's wing, fell heavily around her shoulders. She lowered her head and looked through her eyelashes, and then tossed the fillet straight into Marcus' lap. He stared stupidly. Crito kicked him under the table.

'You won't regret it,' he teased. 'You know what they say about the girls of Blessed Antioch.'

Marcus got to his feet, and the girl reached out and took his hand, and they disappeared into a curtained room behind the tavern.

Marcus didn't regret it.

In fact, he was gone for over three hours.

Her name was Alina, and the week passed quickly in her arms. When he wasn't in her arms, he was often in the arms of Papia, a plump little Greek girl. He spent his last night alternating between the arms of both Papia and Alina, much to the two girls' amusement. He learned a lot that night.

He found the next day's march especially tiring.

They marched up the fertile valley of the Orontes where Marcus struggled to name the alien plants – hyssop, aloe, evil grey thorns – and glimpsed elegant cranes in the reeds. Then they cut up through the mountains and into the vast and trackless deserts of Syria, thornland and scrubland, thirst and hunger's kingdom: scuttling partridges in the dunes, wolves, scorpions, and the desert foxes with their huge, comical ears.

It was two hundred miles or more to the Euphrates, but it seemed further, far further. Each soldier carried two water panniers, supposed to last him all day. But for the first time in his life, Marcus felt what it might be like to die of thirst. Nevertheless, he still disdained an officer's horse, and marched with his men, half-blind with sweat and seared eyes. Milo marched before him.

They marched through dunes and desert and scrubland, cut across with dry wadis that wearied them still further, struggling out of them each time with the sand falling away beneath their scrambling feet and no purchase to be had anywhere. The sand lodged between the leather straps of their sandals and their flesh, and rubbed the skin raw. Some of them, old desert hands, stopped to bind their feet in strips of linen to save themselves from this new agony.

After many days' marching, they came in sight of the glitter of the wide river of the Euphrates, snaking its way across the wide Mesopotamian plains, and Marcus murmured to himself, '*Thalassa, thalassa*. Well, sort of.'

Mus wanted to know what on earth he was muttering about, so as they marched on down the valley of the Euphrates, Marcus beguiled the time by telling him the story of Xenophon's *Anabasis*, about the retreat of the battered Greek army across the high tablelands of Armenia, and how they had cried out with such joy when they caught sight of the sparkling waves beyond Trebizond, *Thalassa, thalassa!* The sea, the sea!

Mus pondered the story for a moment. Then he opined, 'Well, fuckin' Greeks, what do you expect? Fuckin' *nancies*, they are.'

Marcus couldn't help feeling that Mus had rather missed the point of the story.

Finally they saw up ahead of them the massive fort of Dura Europus, shimmering mirage-like through the heat haze. More of a city than a fort, it was set on a massive sandstone outcrop dominating the wide, lazy river. All around the walls and across the desert below stretched acres of tents of the camp followers: tradesmen, merchants, con artists, hucksters, whores.

They ascended the ramp up to the fort and, once inside, Marcus heard his name shouted out. He raised his hand in salute, and was almost immediately clapped on the back by two hearty young officers, a few years older than him. Titus and Sylvanus: his own brothers, whom he hardly knew.

They teased him relentlessly, and they all got drunk together, and his older brothers were clearly proud of him and his new optio status. And yet, when he finally crawled blearily into his bed, Marcus knew that they had been too long apart for feelings between them to run deep. If he had a family at all, he knew it was back in London: with a mournful, middle-aged Praepositus called Lucius, and a young woman called Julia.

Life at the fort was the same as soldiering life anywhere: ninety-nine per cent boredom, routine and drill, cut with the occasional thrill of terror and excitement at the rumour that they were on the march tomorrow to meet the Persians. But weeks went by and nothing happened.

And then one night there was a tumult that disturbed the soldiers in their sleep. They woke the next morning to hear that Constantius – the Emperor himself! – had arrived in the middle of the night, by barge down the Euphrates, and was now in command of the camp.

They would be marching soon.

Constantius had an unfortunate reputation for winning civil wars but losing foreign ones. He was also regarded as untrustworthy, like most Emperors, and quite ready to sacrifice his closest colleagues if it would win him some advantage. On the other hand, he was a good horseman, a decent soldier, and commanded a certain respect. What most soldiers found absurd was his fondness for theological disputation. A Christian, of sorts, Constantius currently favoured the Arian doctrine regarding the true nature of the Jewish god, Christos; which is to say, Christos was of similar but not the same substance as the Father. This was very important. But Constantius might change his mind at any moment. 'Inconstant Constantius,' he was known in some court circles.

For now, however, the Emperor had left such things far behind him in the poisonous courts of Constantinople, along with the sycophancy and the back-biting, the gold and malachite and porphyry, the brocades heavy with rubies and emeralds, and the mosaics glimpsed glowing through the clouds of frankincense. For now he was a soldier-emperor, fighting (yet again) his old enemy, Shapur II of Persia. And soldiers have little use for theology.

The war had been going ten years already, and had seen numerous battles, and yet there had been no result whatsoever, apart from the sands of Syria and Mesopotamia strewn with the bleached skeletons of many a Roman and Persian soldier, and a very healthy vulture population.

'One of the most pointless wars Rome has ever fought,' Lucius had told Marcus back in London. 'Neither side can possibly win, and the only territory in dispute is worthless desert. But you know Kings and Emperors.'

Shapur II was a magnificent figure, statuesque, black-bearded, with eyes of burning coal. He always took the field himself, he was as strategically cunning as he was bold, and his armies were as highly trained as the Roman ones. He was every inch a king, famously crowned in his mother's womb, his father having died two months before he was born. His mother was laid on her back on a table of marble and gold, her robes delicately parted, and a crown of pure gold placed by reverent, priestly hands upon the bare mound of her belly. The metal was cold. The baby kicked inside her.

He was Shapur the Great, the King of Kings, Brother of the Sun and the Moon, Lord of All Persia, the Terror of Rome. Rome had been no more than a huddle of huts beside the unbanked, unbridged Tiber when Persia was an Empire that stretched from the Aegean to the Indus. The Empire had lasted a thousand years, and would last a thousand more. Rome was a vulgar upstart, and he was the King of Kings.

How he loved fighting Rome.

Two days later, they marched.

Their army was some forty thousand strong, followed by a straggling train of camp followers of many thousands more. Somewhere in the midst of the great dustcloud marched Marcus. His brothers were up ahead, marching with the Fourth. And somewhere else in the column, in the Imperial purple, rode Constantius himself. Marcus hadn't even seen him yet.

They marched north, and camped each night out on the great stretches of plain between the Euphrates and the Tigris. Scouts rode many miles ahead and to the east, on the lookout for Shapur's approach. None came.

The logistics of building a camp were extraordinary, and Marcus marvelled at the efficiency with which it was done. The leather tents in serried rows, the thorn brakes, the immense surrounding ditch hand-dug to a depth of twelve feet and a width of twenty, the piquets and revetments, the terrible pits lined with fire-hardened stakes in a quincunx pattern, which could kill a horse, let alone a man. 'Lilies,' they called them: a soldierly joke.

An army that can organise itself this well, thought Marcus, can never be beaten.

Finally, as they set up one night at the foot of Jebel Sinjar, not far from the River Tigris, scouts came riding furiously back into camp to report a sighting. Marcus was emerging from the officers' barracks when he heard the rumour, and made for the square outside the Imperial quarters. He arrived just in time to see the scouts go in. A few minutes later, the scouts reappeared. There was no sign of Constantius.

Marcus collared one of the scouts as he remounted his horse.

'Well?'

The scout looked down at him. 'There's a dustcloud beyond the Tigris the size of a mountain,' he said. He rode out.

'What's he *doing*?' asked Marcus.

'He's taking it cool,' said Milo.

They were sitting in the officers' mess, digesting the news. It was clearly Shapur, on the march and heading straight for them. The scouts had estimated his army at up to one hundred thousand men. The obvious thing would have been to make a stand at the Tigris, the only natural barrier for miles. But Constantius did nothing.

The soldiers watched from the heights of Jebel Sinjar, astonished, straining their eyes uneasily to see. And they saw the vast army of Shapur encamped on the far side of the Tigris, and the King himself supervising events, resplendent in red and gold. The Persians built three great pontoons, as swiftly and efficiently as any Roman legion, and the huge horde began to cross the river. They were still crossing as dusk fell.

They were still crossing *at dawn*.

Constantius did nothing.

The Persian army moved into the village of Hilleh, some six or seven miles from the Roman camp, and began to fortify it. They dug trenches around it, and threw up ramparts topped with palisades. They secured a water supply and built vast cisterns to contain it. They settled in. The dustcloud the size of a mountain finally settled. The two armies faced each other across a hard, flat desert plain. And waited.

Then Shapur set archers and slingers on the heights overlooking the plain, and the Romans knew they couldn't attack. They would wait for Shapur to come to them. That evened the odds. A successful attacker needed to outnumber the defenders at least three to one. The Romans sharpened and oiled their swords. They felt confident.

And then one morning, news came that the Persian army

was preparing to move out. At last, the Emperor appeared from his quarters. Marcus saw him riding out on a white horse in full battle array, and was impressed by his haughty, upright figure. The Emperor watched with calm approval as the centurions set up the battle-line, and waited. And waited.

Strangely, it was after noon before the Persians launched their attack. Fighting west and into the sun. Constantius sat on his white horse and wondered. The horse shifted its hooves uneasily in the sand.

Marcus was in the front rank, Milo at his side, his century behind him. This was different from anything he had faced on the Wall. This was his first real battle. His mouth was dry, his hands wet with sweat. The shield weighed heavily on his shoulder. He felt tired already. He hoped he would live, or die a clean death. He prayed to the Lord Mithras that he would not come out alive but limbless.

Their left flank was covered by the line of mountains, and their right by their own cavalry. Shapur had the numbers to try to outflank them if he wanted, so the Roman cavalry must ensure he didn't. The Persian cavalry were good, fast, cruelly unpredictable. It might all depend upon the right flank.

Marcus heard the army approaching before he saw it. The dust began to rise again as they marched, but it was the blare of the brazen trumpets and the thumping of the drums that struck him first. And the trembling ground. Shapur had elephants. The Romans were delighted at this news. It was well known that elephants always did more damage to their own side than to the enemy. Shapur must be losing it if he thought he could win a battle with elephants.

Through the haze of dust, Marcus could now make out the advancing line. They marched grimly forward, helmeted and crested, their shields round. Most of them were blackbearded. The line paused briefly and discharged their javelins. As one man, the Roman line knelt and hefted their shields and took the evil rain as best they could. It was a poor volley, half-hearted somehow, and too distant to do much damage. There were one or two eerie, isolated screams from among the ranks, as the odd javelin punched hard through a shield and took a man down. But the damage was minimal. They had faced worse than this, a lot worse. The iron line stood again.

And then the front ranks of the Persians.

With a recklessness that was as much fear as courage, Marcus stood forward and was one of the first to take the Persian charge. He knocked a man down with his shield, and was going in for the kill when he was knocked down in turn by another Persian. Immediately his prostrate body was surrounded by his own men, Milo and Mus flanking him and fighting off the swarm of sword thrusts. The rest of the line edged forward behind them, and the Persian advance was halted. Hand-to-hand fighting ensued.

From the ground, Marcus tried to thank his comrades for saving his life. Milo and Mus glared down at him. They looked almost like they might hit him. Thanks were inappropriate, he realised. Saving his life was just their job. They assumed he would do the same for them. Gratitude was an insult.

Marcus stumbled groggily to his feet and shook the blood from his eyes. It was a bad start. He was drenched in a cold sweat, even his own blood felt strangely chilly on his skin, but his heart beat furiously now, with a panicky rapidity, and he launched himself into the fray with a dogged fury. He took another battering with a shield edge, which knocked the wind out of him for several minutes; but not a single sword thrust got through. And he put several down himself, knocking and jabbing until the enemy lay dazed in the sand and then dispatching him with a sharp, unthinking thrust of his sword to the torso, punching straight through to the spine.

Around him, the men fought with the same Roman dogged-ness, at close quarters – as close as a short sword's length, less than an arm's length. At that distance, you cannot kill without being spattered in blood. Soon enough, no man wore white.

The cavalry on the right waited for the outflanking manoeuvre that they knew must come – but it never did. And there was no sign of the elephants either, much to the Romans' disappointment. The infantry engagement lasted some time, but finally the sound of brazen trumpets bellowed from behind, and the Persians backed off in an orderly, fighting retreat. The afternoon was growing late. Over the desert behind them, beyond the great Euphrates, the sun was riding down the sky.

Then, at last, the Persian cavalry appeared, in a strange pincer movement, outflanking their own infantry and clearly aiming to break up the Roman line and stop it cutting down their own footsloggers in retreat. The flat, level plain favoured cavalry over infantry; and the Persian cavalry were universally feared, in their masks and helmets, their cuirasses of bronze and iron plates, and their long pikes mounted butt-end into a strap at their horses' haunches. The Roman infantry, however, already elated at so easy a victory, advanced without hesitation and fell against the Persian horsemen savagely. It was an equal contest. The Persians inflicted great damage, but so too did the Romans, pulling down each armoured cataphract from his horse and butchering him where he lay. In time further trumpet blasts were sounded, and the remaining cavalry drew off. And it was then that the Roman chain of command – that iron chain – somehow broke.

Constantius ordered against a pursuit. He well knew how parched and exhausted his men would be, for in the desert, a victory is as thirsty a business as a defeat. But the Roman infantry never acknowledged the order and began to pursue the Persian line back across the plains towards their camp, running the entire way, five miles or more, in full armour, blood pounding in their ears, insensible with blood lust and thirst. Water at their camp was strictly rationed, but at the Persian camp, their scouts had told them, there were immense water cisterns, and the cool Tigris beyond.

An officer, seeing his men pursuing against orders, is faced with a choice. Either he goes with them, against orders, or he abandons them. One is ill-disciplined, but the other is cowardly. Marcus went with them.

Night fell as they came to the Persian camp.

There then followed the most eerie episode in all the Persian Wars: the episode that became known as the Night Battle of Singara.

When they reached the camp, the Romans plunged on in, smashing down the defences with sheer brute force. Once inside the camp, in the darkness, underneath a brilliant starlit sky, they couldn't believe how easy and profitable their victory had been. Everything they had heard about the water cisterns was true, and they quickly set about slaking their desperate thirst. Any Persian soldiers they found were unceremoniously slaughtered. Then they found meat. They found wine. They also found a magnificently armoured young man, lying half-dead in a shadowy corner of the camp. They brought him out into the torchlight, and realised that he was Shapur's son.

The major part of the Persian army had retreated beyond the camp, back to their pontoon bridges across the Tigris. Shapur himself was with them, and he ordered men up on to the heights overlooking the plain. The Romans were puzzled, for the conduct of war requires daylight. But for Shapur, the battle was not finished yet. He himself was raised up on a shield borne by four soldiers, for an overview of the flat plain before him. And he saw his own son being dragged into the centre of the camp, and he watched as his own son, his own seed, the son of the King of Kings and Lord of All Persia, was bound in ropes, flogged, pierced, and finally executed by a drunken rabble of Roman soldiers. Shapur wept and rent his hair. His howling was heard in the heart of the sacked camp.

When he raised his head again, it was to give the order for his generals, his satraps to be brought to him. When they were brought, he had them thrown to the ground; large stones were placed in the crooks of their elbows and behind their knees, and then their arms and legs were forced tight back over them and broken. He let them lie in agony for a while, and when he tired of their screams, he had them beheaded. He then appointed a new batch of satraps, and ordered his Syrian archers onto the heights, to rain down arrows and flaming brands on Singara – his own camp, now filled with Romans. And so the killing rain came.

The silence was the most eerie thing. The night air seemed to blanket all sounds, and it was as if he were deaf that Marcus saw the first arrows falling out of the velvet starlit sky and fall thickly into the crowded, drunken, exhausted, disarmed Roman troops. Screams rang out in the darkness, and men began to fall. Fire-arrows fell in among the thorn brakes and the wooden enclosures and they sprung into flame. The entire camp, now fiercely illuminated in the darkness of the surrounding desert, and packed tightly with milling, disordered troops, became a perfect sitting target for the Persian arrows. The rain continued and the slaughter was terrible. Along with the other officers, Marcus began to cry out to extinguish the torches, and to retreat. He bellowed the words to a soldier standing right in front of him. The man turned with terrible slowness and Marcus saw that he had an arrow sunk deep in his throat. The man dropped to his knees in front of Marcus and held his hands up in supplication and drooled a little blood and then fell lopsided into the dust. Perhaps this was what the strange Johurz had meant, had foretold, back in the tavern in Antioch. *There is truth in the desert. There is truth, too, in the scorpion's sting.* Here was a kind of truth.

All around, men stumbled and cursed over the bodies of their comrades in their mad rush to escape. And still the arrows fell ceaselessly, briefly gleaming in the torchlight before finding their ends in the flesh of men.

On the heights above the camp, Shapur watched. His face was without expression but his black eyes burned. Now his son was with his fathers. But the Romans were processing, an endless, bloodstained column, into the gates of hell.

☆ ☆ ☆

It was a grim band of survivors that marched back to Dura
Europus, shattered both physically and mentally. Two days
after their return, Marcus got drunk again with his brothers,
but this time they chattered very little, and got morose drunk,
not merry. Sylvanus got the most drunk. Lifting his goblet to
his mouth in a steady rhythm, in a desperate determination for
oblivion, he drank his wine unwatered. He raised his goblet
with his left hand. His right hand was gone. His right arm was
gone, under the surgeon's knife, severed just below the shoulder. A Persian arrowhead had struck him there and festered
rapidly in the heat. 'At least you're still alive,' some of his
comrades had tried to reassure him. But he knew it was worse.
Better to have died back there, in the nightmare of the Night
Battle of Singara. Many wounds were terrible, but to lose a
right arm . . . It was the end. And so Sylvanus got very, very
drunk.

The year was AD 348. It was eleven centuries since the
founding of the city of Rome, and should have been a year of
proud rejoicing. A hundred years earlier, AD 248, the celebra-
tions for the millennium had been lavish in the extreme, cost
many millions, lasted for weeks. But the passing of eleven
hundred years *ab urbe condita* passed virtually unnoticed, as if
its citizens and soldiery knew it was the last centenary Rome
would ever see, and were embarrassed to be of those last,
losing generations.

There followed desultory days and weeks back at Dura
Europus while the army waited for further orders, and Inconstant Constantius dithered. The summer campaigning season
was drawing to a close anyway, and everything was uncer-
tainty. Rumours abounded. Shapur had gone south into the
Arabian peninsula, his old campaigning grounds. More troops
were being sent for – more frontier armies being withdrawn to
feed the east. On the Northern Wall, and the Rhine, and the
Danube, the front-line was thinning.

Meanwhile in the silent forests and out on the plains beyond, the tribes watched and waited: the Sarmatians in their ox-drawn covered wagons, their cuirasses made of slices of horses' hooves, their spears with heads of fishbone, tipped in viper venom and human blood; the Huns in their round caps and goatskin leggings, eaters of raw meat, which they merely warmed a little between their thighs and the backs of their horses; the Attacotti with their faces scored with needletracks and dyed blue-black, mounted on their mountain ponies, their bridles hung with human heads.

The tribes watched and waited as the Empire tore itself apart.

CHAPTER SIXTEEN

The following winter, a birthday banquet was held in the town of Autun, in Burgundy. It was 18 January, AD 350, and a banquet in honour of the son of a certain Marcellinus, who was a senior officer in the army of the west, and in addition, Constans' own Master of the Imperial Household. Constans himself was absent from the festivities; he was out hunting that day in the Montagnes du Morvan, in some of the finest boar-hunting country in all of Gaul. He had a wonderful day out.

Some time during the banquet, one of the guests there, a very senior general much respected throughout the army, excused himself from the room. A few minutes later he reappeared in the doorway. He was wearing the Imperial purple. His name was Magnentius – the same Magnentius who, two years earlier, had dined in London, and whose modesty and grit had made such a favourable impression on the guests there.

When Constans heard of the coup, he fled south towards the Mediterranean coast. His German boyfriends abandoned him without hesitation. Only one junior officer remained loyal to him. Constans was finally caught at Elne, close to the Spanish border, in the very shadow of the Pyrenees. He was butchered with much the same briskness and lack of ceremony with which he himself had butchered his own brother, Constantine II, only a few years earlier. The loyal junior officer was also killed. His name is lost to history.

For a while, petty princelings popped up all over the place, declaring that *they* were the true Emperor. But unfortunately for their cause, few had the necessary military power to assist them in making their case really convincing. Some dim and distant cousin of Constantine's tried it on in Rome for a few days, before being bloodily silenced by a unit of crack cavalry sent down there by Magnentius. And one Vetranio, with a modest army behind him in Illyrica, decked himself in Imperial purple for a week or so, until a message came from the east by Imperial cursus, strongly suggesting that the choice before him lay between acknowledging Constantius or enjoying a short boat trip with Charon. Whereupon, as if by heavenly revelation, he suddenly realised that Constantius *was* the true and divinely-appointed Emperor after all.

Magnentius, however, stayed in firm possession of his new domains, declared himself the Emperor of the West, and had almost complete support from where it mattered most: the army. He also had considerable support from the patrician and land-owning classes. Although nominally Christian, Magnentius was perfectly prepared to tolerate the continuance of pagan worship in his provinces, unlike the zealous sons of Great Constantine.

In the east, Constantius could only gnash his teeth in fury at this unConstantinian usurpation of Imperial power. But he was heavily committed to a seemingly endless war with Persia, the great power in the east. And much as he would have liked to ride west at once and put down this shameful revolt, what could he do? Shapur engaged all his forces. Moreover, there would be no more reinforcements to draw on from the west. The Empire was now in a state of undeclared civil war.

For some, the coup had rather more personal repercussions. For a certain provincial Praepositus and his niece, for instance, in the city of London, it meant that a member of their family was now fighting, technically, on the opposing side to them.

Such are the little ironies of history.

☆ ☆ ☆

'What are we going to do?'

Lucius leaned forward and poured wine into his bulbous goblet, inscribed, appropriately enough he thought, *usque ad mortem bibendum*: let us drink until death!

'We continue to work, to serve the Empire.'

'*Which* empire?' persisted Julia.

'There is only one true Empire. Emperors come and go, but the Empire remains. Although if any man can save what is left to us, it would be a man like Magnentius, not . . . the other one. A good soldier, with a head unclouded by religious fanaticism and divisiveness.'

'That sounds dangerously like treason.'

Lucius sipped his wine slowly. He had the look of a man who didn't care much any more if what he said sounded dangerously like treason. He would always tell it like he saw it. Come what may.

As summer came round again, so did news that Shapur was once more on the move.

After some inconclusive skirmishes in the Arabian peninsula, he had retreated into the Persian heartlands to grieve for the loss of his beloved son, and then to raise the biggest, most highly-trained army that he had ever fielded in his long and illustrious military career. In May, he marched. As he neared the Tigris, the furthest Roman look-outs rode back to report that he had been sighted.

Shapur was riding west, making slow and ineluctable progress towards the great walled city of Nisibis, the bulwark of the east, some miles deeper into Syria than the old, fateful battleground of Singara. Nisibis dominated the northern reaches of the Euphrates, and if Shapur should raze it and pass on, he would be in striking distance of Palmyra, Antioch, and all of Asia Minor beyond.

The good news for Shapur's enemies was that Nisibis had

been besieged by the Persians twice before in this long and repetitively inconclusive war, and had not fallen. No doubt it would withstand a further assault. But Constantius, sending orders from Antioch, made it clear that he wanted it reinforced all the same. He commanded all the available horses at Dura Europus to be rounded up, and then a mounted detachment to ride as fast as they could for Nisibis. Marcus' cohort was one of the detachment.

The detachment comprised around four hundred and eighty men. It didn't seem very much, to defend a city against an army of a hundred thousand. But Constantius had no troops to spare, and didn't want to leave Dura Europus poorly defended, in case Shapur should swing south. Nisibis would have to fight as best it could.

Nisibis was a magnificently fortified city on the River Mygdonius, at the foot of Mount Masius in the heart of the fertile plain between the Tigris and the Euphrates. It was girdled around by baked brick walls, forty feet in height, and then a deep ditch. Not for nothing was it known to Rome as the Bulwark of the East.

Marcus and his detachment came to the city an hour after dawn one morning, riding across the flatlands with the mist veiling the rice fields and then vanishing in the sun. The golden walls of the city seemed to float on a sea of mist above the earth.

They were greeted by the Vicarius of the city himself, Lucilianus, a tough-looking customer, and the Bishop of Nisibis, heavily bearded, beetle-browed – an even tougher-looking customer, if anything.

'You are the reinforcements?' asked Lucilianus without introduction, surveying the two hundred or so mounted men.

'At your command,' said Milo graciously. Marcus suppressed a smile.

Lucilianus grunted and turned back into the city. They followed him in.

Within, they found a city of narrow, winding streets of cool ochre shadows, and then sudden, blinding squares only partially shaded by date palms. Marcus accompanied Milo on a tour of inspection round the city walls. The centurion was impressed.

'I don't care if Shapur has a million men,' he growled. 'You could hold this city with a century.'

The water supply was secure and considered impossible to interfere with. Rice and grain stores were estimated to be enough to keep the city's population fed for, at a conservative estimate, three years. Every smithy in the city was furiously turning out fresh armour, arrowheads, ballista bolts, huge grappling irons and lengths of chain. The mood was grimly confident.

The people of the city had immense faith in their Governor, Marcus quickly realised. He was amused to discover that they also had immense faith in their Bishop. One night he sat in one of the paved squares of the city and watched the people strolling by in the cool of the evening, as he sipped his wine and talked to a local merchant.

'During the last two sieges,' said the merchant, 'it was as much as we could do to stop His Grace, the Bishop, from flinging open the city gates and riding out on horseback to attack the Persians single-handed. He talked a lot of Gideon, and David and Goliath.' He rubbed his beard. 'I think he's mellowed a bit now he's reached his ninth decade.'

'Name of Light,' said Marcus.

There followed days of tense and anxious waiting, every hour they expected the arrival of a breathless outrider with news that Shapur had crossed the Tigris. But none came. The soldiers settled in. By day they dug horsepits out on the plain, and covered them over with thin reeds; they widened and deepened the ditch around the city, and they carried bales of new-slain hides up onto the walls and laid them down beside huge 120-gallon barrels of water. When the attack came, these would be soaked and hung over the walls to kill the Persian fire-arrows.

By night they drank in the taverns and bedded the whores. Nisibis was a strongly Christian city, but every city must have its whores. For the citizens, it seemed a lesser evil than having several hundred lusty legionaries chasing after their daughters.

There was one girl in particular who caught Marcus' attention. She worked in a tavern that he and Milo frequented. Once, when a drunken soldier tried it on with her, she smashed a clay beaker over his skull. This was no ordinary whore; or no whore at all. She reminded him of someone, some other girl . . . Marcus knew exactly who, in fact, but tried to avoid the thought. He couldn't take his eyes off her. Sometimes she returned his stares, her dark liquid eyes fixing on his and not flinching. It was a whore's look; but she was no whore. When she looked at him he felt like he was drowning.

She was just a serving-maid in a tavern, in a remote and threatened city far out east. She and Marcus never exchanged a word.

He grew to love the mood of Nisibis: the air heavy with expectation, danger, camaraderie. At night they would sit in the squares, get gently drunk by firelight, and listen to the tales of the storytellers who had travelled the length of the Silk Road to the Empire of China, and had seen six-legged camels and men with the heads of voles.

'*Voles*?' queried Marcus, slurring a little. 'Are you *sure*?'

'Quite sure, my friend.'

On the edge of the Empire, at the limits of reason's jurisdiction with only Oriental despotism lying beyond, anything was possible, of course, he mused. But *voles* . . .

Later, two dancing-girls came out and swayed in the orange light, their flanks a satin sheen. A man produced a crude musical instrument, a gourd strung with catgut, and began to sing. The gourd was not so good, but the singer's voice was faraway with longing. He sang in Greek, but his subject was not Greek. Marcus listened to him and thought of the girl in the tavern.

> *From the mountains of Elam I have come*
> *With the sun in the west*
> *And my shadow behind*
> *Now my head lies heavy on my lover's breast*
> *And I do not find what I would find*
> *And I do not find rest*

It was late one afternoon when the message came that they had been waiting for. A scout on a small, fast pony came skittering to a halt outside the eastern gate and demanded to talk to Lucilianus. A few minutes later, Lucilianus himself – with the Bishop standing at his side, and visibly twitching to get on with the fight – appeared on the steps outside his palace, already armoured, and announced that Shapur and his forces had been seen crossing the Tigris near Peshkhabur. They would be here in two days.

The following night, Marcus sought out the singer with his gut-strung gourd, and heard him sing a different song.

> *A pearl of joy I saw*
> *Pendent from my lover's ear*
> *She whispered of our bed and the long night*
> *Come here, my love, come here*
>
> *But my heart burns for war, O my lover*
> *My love and I apart*
> *My treacherous heart, why do you not break?*
> *Why do you not break, O my heart?*
>
> *For I am sick of war*
> *Sick with desire for my lover in jewels*

But hard is the gods' will
My sorrows but increase
And I must weep, my lover
That wars will never cease

When they looked out from the walls the following morning, the desert beyond the rice fields had turned red. Red with the red cloaks and the plumed and nodding helmets of a hundred thousand men.

Shapur sent small parties of fast-riding cavalry up against the walls of the city, firing arrows ineffectually over the battlements and testing the firepower of the defenders. Lucilianus ordered them not to return fire. Instead he asked for the Persian arrowheads to be collected up and taken down to the smithies for smelting. Milo smiled. This was going to be one tough nut to crack.

Shapur saw it too, and smiled a different smile. *Those stubborn Christians . . .*

He waited for his outriders to return, and others from further afield. One of the last parties to return had ridden to the banks of the Mygdonius and then followed it north into the foothills. Now they came back and reported their findings to Shapur. The river was torrential with snowmelt from the mountains of Armenia. There would be no shortage of water.

Fools, thought Shapur. 'Tell me,' he said. 'How many city walls do you know, however great and strong, that can withstand the force of a river in full spate?'

The outriders' eyes grew round.

Milo was standing on the northern walls with Lucilianus and Marcus, watching the Persian sappers work. They were digging great trenches cutting east-west, to drain the surrounding land and lower the water table. Sooner or later, the wells of Nisibis would run dry.

But something wasn't right.

252

'Shapur knows very well that the wells of Nisibis are inexhaustible,' murmured Lucilianus, squinting out over the plain.

'So why is he going to all the trouble with the trenches?'

'I wish I knew.'

They knew soon enough, when the siege engines began to be brought up to the northern wall of Nisibis.

'On to the north wall and fast!' Milo ordered his troops.

Marcus began to command the archers there, hunkered down behind the battlements. They kept up a steady fire against the approaching monsters rumbling over the stony ground on their wooden wheels higher than a man. It made no difference. Soon enough the siege engines were despatching their own fire, while approaching ever closer to the walls. Then they stopped. Marcus stared. Something really wasn't right.

'What's up?' It was Milo at his side.

'Something,' said Marcus. 'I don't know what.'

'The Vicarius says the same,' said Milo. 'I hate surprises. Every soldier's worst nightmare.' He clenched his fists and laid them on the top of the wall. 'Think. Shapur has been here twice before, and got nowhere. He knows siege engines aren't enough. He should be attacking from the east, not the north – it only stretches out his line and exposes his flank if more of our lot arrive; which they won't, but he doesn't know that. And now his siege engines have stopped short. They're not going to do much damage from that distance. And what's with the sappers?'

'They're not intended to do much damage,' said Marcus slowly. 'The siege engines.'

'What do you mean?'

'They're just for cover. They're to hide what the sappers are doing behind them. Look.'

Almost half a mile away, a party of sappers, working furiously, had dug a trench that now reached almost to the banks of the Mygdonius itself. Now, standing safely out of the trench, they began to break down the last of the mud bank that lay between the water and the new water-course . . .

'He's turning the river,' said Marcus. 'He's draining it off and turning it against us.'

The two men watched, stunned. How much difference could it make?

The mud bank gave way with a muffled splash, and the cold river water began to flow into the rough trenches that the Persians had dug. Only a few moments later, around the sides of the nearest siege engine flowed a wide, shallow slick of water, oozing towards the walls of the city and turning the sands of the desert a mud-brown as it passed.

'What happens to walls that are built on sand,' asked Marcus softly, 'when that sand turns to mud?'

As Shapur watched the water's progress from a little man-made hillock back to the east, he folded his brawny, black-haired arms across his chest and smiled. The walls of his enemies would fall like walls of paper. Great were the gods, and great was Shapur, the King of Kings, Brother of the Sun and the Moon. And when this accursed city finally fell, he would show no mercy. Twice he had come here and called for its pigheaded citizens to acknowledge him and surrender. And twice they had turned him away, in contempt. They would not turn him away a third time. Already he could hear the sounds of those walls crumbling. Already he could see his men sacking and raping long into the night, and well they deserved it. Already he could see the streets of the city gleaming in the torchlight, black with Christian blood, and see the infants plucked from their mothers' breasts and dashed in pieces at the head of the streets, and hear the sound of ten thousand nights like that night, and knew that those ten thousand nights of Nisibis were nights of horror . . .

For a time, panic set in. Flights of arrows, and the rumble of siege engines, and the earth-shaking battering ram at the gates were all very well. These were things of substance, which you could fight against. But the soft, insidious flow of water, silently dissolving the very foundations of the city and seeping into the citizens' souls, chill as mountain meltwater – that was different.

The following morning, however, things did not look quite as expected. The full force of the Mygdonius had not been turned against a single point in Nisibis' walls, or it must certainly have breached it and drowned half the populace with it. Instead, because the Persian sappers had done their work so hurriedly, the river had simply flooded out onto the wide plain, and now Nisibis stood, like some haughty island, in the middle of a vast lake of inch-deep water and foot-deep mud.

Shapur considered. It was a help, but it was not a final solution. The walls' foundations, however, must have been weakened. He called his forces back to the plains east of the city, regrouped, and waited another day. The following dawn, he ordered his artillery up to the edge of the man-made lake, and no further. The city was perhaps two hundred yards' distance. But since some of his biggest machines, his onagers – so called because they kicked like a mule – could throw a hundred-pound missile over four hundred yards or more, this was fine. He called on his artillery to load up. While they did so, he surveyed the east wall. Surely, somewhere, the foundations were sinking. The very bricks were sweating, and straining, and losing hold.

He stared at the central tower. There was the greatest weight. And there, around the foundations, the soft mud oozed, the killing water eddied. So, they should hit the brickwork beneath the tower – just above ground level, if possible. The onager teams shifted their machines accordingly, each lining it up with the point in the wall which their commander had indicated.

The artillerymen worked furiously, drenched in sweat, cloths bound around their foreheads to keep the salt from their eyes. On the walls of Nisibis, archers were lining up to rain down arrows. Here and there an artilleryman took an arrow in the chest or in the gut. But Shapur never flinched. There were plenty more where they came from.

The artillerymen hefted the great stones into their slings, and then began to crank up the terrific tension needed to hurl them up to a quarter of a mile or more. Two men heaved on the ratchet handle, biceps bulging, drawing back the windlass, the two mighty coils of rope in the coilchambers creaking with pent-up power. Finally the leader of each onager team dropped a fat iron pin into its socket and the windlass was stayed. They awaited orders. Shapur surveyed the city before him one last time, and then nodded.

The leader of each team raised a two handed mallet and hurled it down onto the head of the iron pin. The pin shot out, the huge beam flew up into the air with extraordinary force, hit the cross beam with a deafening bang, and the missile flew. Once the stone had gone, the whole machine reared up, just like a kicking mule, bucking under its own momentum, before the back wheels crashed down in an explosion of dust.

Six of Shapur's biggest machines had fired. Every missile hit the wall but one, which crashed short and sent up a shower of mud and water. Two hit the target dead centre, almost in unison. The report of their hit came back to Shapur's ears a moment later. Straining his eyes, he thought he could see – and then, yes, he definitely could see – a rift running from top to bottom of the city wall, just to the left of the tower.

He bent his head and prayed to the gods.

Then he raised his head and gazed at the cracked wall ahead of him and smiled like a desert wolf.

'Hit them again,' he said.

By the time evening fell, the breach in the eastern wall was a hundred and fifty feet wide, and the citizens and paltry soldiery of Nisibis could be seen milling around inside like panicked ants in a ruptured nest.

Since noon, Shapur's satraps had been trying to persuade

him that the gap really was wide enough now to force an entry into the city, and they really ought to get on and do so before nightfall. But Shapur ignored them. He liked the noise the missiles made as they hit the wall, and he liked the plumes of brickdust that erupted at the shock. He even liked it when the missiles missed their target and fell short. He liked the big, noisy splash they made. So, after each fresh volley, he smiled with great satisfaction, and then said, 'Hit them again.'

'But your Sacred Majesty,' said one of his more senior satraps, unable to prevent a twinge of impatience from entering his voice, 'if we leave it until nightfall, the Christians might use the night to build up the wall again.'

What a ridiculous suggestion. It would take more than a single night to build up *that* wall again. Shapur ignored him.

'Hit them again,' he said.

When night finally fell and the monstrous fire from the Persian onagers stopped, Lucilianus, Milo and Marcus took a tour of the wreckage. Behind them stumbled the crookbacked, ferocious figure of the octogenarian Bishop.

Even Lucilianus looked despairing. An entire section of wall was reduced to rubble. The rubble might slow a cavalry attack, admittedly. But you would need five hundred men, three ranks deep, even to contemplate defending such a breach.

'We might have sued for peace,' said Lucilianus softly. 'But not any more. Surrender is not an option with Shapur.'

Milo nodded. He turned and surveyed the rubble field that was once a forty foot wall. Then he turned back to the Governor.

'Call up as many able-bodied men as you have.'

'But they're no soldiers,' said Lucilianus. 'It'll be butchery.'

'We don't need soldiers,' said Milo. 'We need bricklayers.'

The populace, cowering in their houses with crucifixes clasped to their breasts, praying to their Christian god and

257

loudly lamenting and reciting what snatches of the psalms they could remember in their panic, were reluctant to emerge. But when the first of them did so and saw the hard-bitten centurion from Dura Europus taking charge, apparently quite unperturbed by the disastrous breach in their walls, they took heart and began to line up for their orders.

And so, by uncertain torchlight, they stretched out along the breach and started to build up the wall by hand. Milo ordered them to leave as much rubble in the foreground as possible, but to make sure they had a height of at least four cubits – six feet – before them. Behind the wall, he wanted a platform of brick rubble, on which they could stand and fire down at their attackers, who would surely come at first light tomorrow.

'And the mud?' asked Marcus. 'The water? Shouldn't we try to drain that off somehow so we're not weakened any more?'

Milo smiled in the darkness and shook his head. 'The water's on our side now,' he said.

They came at first light, as Milo had predicted. Unfortunately, their appearance nearly caused a full-scale desertion from the city, for Shapur was sending in his elephants. And a six-foot wall of rubble is a poor defence against elephants. Even Milo looked a little dismayed.

They came trumpeting across the plain with swirls of dust up to their bellies, topped by archers in iron towers, and with a crouching mahout on their shoulders. Each mahout carried a long, two-handed dagger bound to his wrist with a leather thong. If the beast beneath him should take a bad wound and start to run amok, the mahout would loosen the dagger from his wrist and drive it straight downwards into the elephant's brain, killing it with a single thrust. He would then do his best not to be lying underneath it as the animal fell.

Marcus stood behind the low rubble wall, the hilt of his

sword gripped tightly in his fist. His skin was caked in brickdust and sweat, he had had less than two hours sleep, but felt anything but tired. The ground beneath his feet was trembling and feverish. It was matched by a fluttering deep within him, leaflike and feminine, and he was ashamed. He longed for the fighting to begin. The only cure for cowardice was to face danger down and kill it.

And so it was Marcus who responded first, with the necessary foolhardiness to mount a serious defence. He sheathed his sword, seized a javelin, leaped up on top of the rubble wall and hurled it at the nearest elephant. He was greeted by a return shower of arrows from the mounted archers, and dropped back down again. But his example had done some good to morale. Behind him, the line of archers let their arrows fly. They curved up into the blue air and fell upon the advancing line. By great good fortune – for the people of Nisibis, not for the poor animal in question – an arrow stuck fast in that most sensitive part of an elephant's anatomy, its trunk. With a bellow of rage it curled round on itself, raising its injured trunk up high and splitting the air with a shrieking bellow. The mahout could be seen unlacing his dagger immediately, and then wavering, uncertain whether this merited outright termination. The elephant was wheeling round and round, and as it wheeled, the mud and water about its feet grew thicker and thicker, and its maddened bellows halted the other elephants in their tracks. Finally the mahout could bear no more and despatched the poor beast, which crashed to the ground almost where it stood.

A mere thirty yards separated the fallen animal from the rubble wall, and without thinking Marcus ordered his squad to draw their swords and follow him. Leaping over the wall, he sprinted across the rubble, thinking that the worst that could befall him just at this moment would be a broken ankle.

As the Persian archers emerged from their iron towers and dropped to the ground, they were startled to find themselves under lightning attack by a mere five or six Roman soldiers, who cut them down in a trice and then disappeared.

The rest of the elephant attack, meanwhile, had stalled around the fallen animal. Something else was becoming clear. The lake of mud that surrounded that city was the worst possible ground to cross with an elephant.

Marcus scrambled back over the wall, Britus and Caelius following close behind.

'Good work,' said Milo

'The water's on our side,' gasped Marcus. 'I see what you mean.'

If Shapur had sent in his heavy infantry that day, he would have surely triumphed. Instead, he sent in everything else. First his elephants, which churned up the man-made lake into a quagmire. Then his cavalry, which fared even worse. Finally, for reasons that no one could understand, he decided to attempt to open up another breach in the walls to the south, and went to vastly complicated lengths to mount a grappling tower on a wooden raft and float it across the lake that he himself had made, and which was now proving such an obstacle. Floating as it was, the tower was unstable anyway, and the defenders had little difficulty in throwing out a grappling iron of their own and toppling the tower sidelong into the mud.

In fact, the entire Persian offensive was foundering in mud. And the more forces Shapur threw in, the worse it got. When he finally committed his elephants again, in a white fury, the beasts tripped over the corpses of elephants that had gone before. They lay there, trumpeting softly, their huge eyes registering the nightmare of their slaughtered fellows around them and not understanding, their trunks snuffling up the viscous odour of blood blindly, in their brains a cloud of dim regretfulness. And then they were massacred where they lay, their blood flowing out and mingling with that of the broken bodies of men and horses, and with the wreckage of siege

engines and fallen missiles that choked the man-made quagmire.

The heart of the battle still lay, however, at the breach in
the walls where the six-foot rubble wall had been hastily
substituted. Here Marcus slogged it out for the whole day,
urging his men on, positioning himself at the very centre of the
wall and using a javelin, rather than his sword, to thrust and
stab into wave after wave of Persian attackers. It was a modest
and hasty line of defence – but it was enough. The occasional
Persian soldier crested the wall and leaped down inside, only
to be quickly despatched by the second line of defence behind.
A mere one hundred Roman soldiers kept the breach: it was a
stretch, but it was enough. Another hundred manned the
walls. And behind them, the citizens of Nisibis kept their
defenders armed and watered. Occasionally, Marcus scanned
the faces behind him for a sight of the girl from the tavern. It
would be good to take a drink of water from a flagon held in
her hand. But there was no sign of her.

Though really, he thought to himself, turning back, he
shouldn't be thinking of that stuff just now. Not just – battering a big, bearded Persian in the face with his shield-boss – not
just at this moment.

Shapur returned to the attack the next day, and for four more
days thereafter. And each day he was thrown back. Each
night, the exhausted, stumbling soldiers and citizens of Nisibis
built up their improvised wall once again. The land around the
city began to look more and more as if a great wind had blown
down from the mountains of Armenia and simply bowled
everything over, knocking men, horses, elephants and siege
engines to the ground with equal, godlike indifference. Each
day, the Persian approach to the city walls became more like
an obstacle course, took longer, exposed them to greater and
more concentrated fire from the battlements above. Soon, they
lost heart.

The people of Nisibis, on the other hand, only seemed to gain in strength and resolution. This was not least on account of the great tirades delivered by their octogenarian Bishop, standing upon the city walls, shaking a claw-like, liver-spotted fist over the battlements at the pagan hordes below.

'O woe unto you, Nineveh, and unto you, O Babylon! For you that were puffed up with pride and haughtiness, a stiff-necked people, are brought low, yea, and the axe is laid to the trunk and you are hewn at the root! For you were mighty in your day, like unto a cedar of Lebanon, like unto Tyre and Sidon! But where now is Tyre, and where is Sidon? For you regarded not the Lord God of Israel, who shall scatter His enemies like chaff before the threshing, for the Lord of Hosts, the Lord God of Israel, has declared His wrath upon you, O proud Persia, and your days are numbered in the counting. Your mighty men and your men of war shall be slain in the high places, your women and children driven away in chains into captivity, and your cities made utterly desolate! The winds of the desert shall blow through them, where once were your palaces and temples, and the owls and foxes and coneys and the wild beasts of the desert shall have their dwelling there! For the Lord God has declared it, and His people shall prevail! You have regarded not Goliath of Gath, who was laid low by the boy David and utterly destroyed; nor have you feared the fate of Moab, nor of Edom, nor of Midian, nor of Amalek; nor of that day in which Samuel, the chosen one of the Lord, slew Agag and hewed him in little pieces before the Lord in Gilgal! So shall it be with you, O Persia! And you shall be like unto the footstool of the Lord, as Moab was His washpot!'

There was more, much more, in the same vein, and even Marcus began to grow a little irritable by the end of each day. But the people of Nisibis seemed to derive great comfort from it, and dearly loved their Bishop.

The situation might have dragged on for weeks like this, for Shapur had the manpower, and no lack of will. But then a messenger came from his own kingdom, to report an attack by a great horde of Massagetae – Scythians, from the plains of Central Asia – upon the eastern border of the Persian Empire.

Shapur was furious. But there was only one thing to do.

Or, rather – two things to do.

The first was to summon all his satraps and have them beheaded. He ordered them to be tortured for a short while beforehand, but this soon became boring.

The second was to turn and ride home.

Nisibis would have to wait for another year.

When they realised that it was not a trick, and that Shapur had indeed turned round and ridden away, the soldiers threw down their swords and wept. They were too tired to sleep; and even if they had tried to, the clangour of the bells all night long in the cathedral – the Bishop, again – would have prevented them. Instead, they got very, very drunk.

For the next few days, they helped the people of Nisibis clear up. They erected wooden scaffolding to a height of fifty feet, and set up slings and winches, and rebuilt the broken wall to the height of its former glory. Out on the plains beyond, they constructed enormous pyres, for men, and horses, and even elephants. The pillars of oily black smoke could be seen for many miles around. When the people saw that, in his retreat, Shapur had deliberately trampled across their rice-fields and destroyed the entire year's harvest, they were momentarily downhearted. But the Bishop rallied them, saying that they had grain and rice in store, and would simply have to plant again.

Finally, the day came when Milo decided they had done as much good as they could, and were now more of a hindrance than a help. It was time to leave the civilians to it.

They rode out of the southern gate along streets lined with cheering people throwing rose petals over their heads and laying palm leaves beneath their horses' hooves. It was no great and ostentatious triumph in the Roman style, with chariots of gold and hecatombs of bulls, panniers fronded with damp seaweed and filled with Baian oysters for the troops to gorge themselves upon, and donatives of gilded prostitutes, also for them to gorge themselves. But, thought Marcus, it felt good all the same. It felt as if they were heroes. He could get to like it.

It felt even better when a girl stepped forward from the crowd and held out a single red rose for him. He stopped and leaned out to take it, and realised that it was the girl from the tavern. The girl with the eyes you could drown in. She reached up and threw her slim arms around his neck and kissed him full on the lips. The soldiers and the crowd round about whistled and cheered, but Marcus heard nothing. Finally the girl released him and stepped back into the crowd and the soldiers behind him pushed him on again and he lost her. He had never spoken a single word to her.

He wondered if he would ever come back to Nisibis.

It was with his heart already full and half in love that Marcus rode out with the tired but victorious column, back across the plains to Dura Europus. And riding out, he saw as if for the first time, or in a different, less pragmatic light, heart-full and sensitised, the blackened heaps of timber and burned flesh, the clinkered remnants of the battle's corpses, and could think of no words to say. There were no words. He could have wept again.

The wreckage, the trophies of the carnage, stretched far away across the plain: still uncollected corpses crowned now with rag-winged carrion birds, the earth churned to mud, dead flyblown horses, chariots and baggage wagons overturned, isolated javelins still stuck fast in the earth as if they had grown there, roots cruelly barbed. And the stench, not of death, but of the breeding of new life after death. For a dizzy moment it seemed to Marcus as if it had all been no more than a game, a vast entertainment, the scene much as it would be after a particularly splendid five-day spectacle in the Colosseum, staged by Shapur and Constantius for their own glorification, and he glanced back at the heights beyond the city, half-expecting to see there a huge crowd of serried spectators cheering the blood-boltered victors as they quit the arena.

He was brought back to the hard world by Milo trotting at his side.

'That was quite a kiss you got back there.'

Marcus stirred and smiled.

'Lump in your throat?'

Marcus still said nothing.

'Well, whatever,' said Milo. 'But no soldier of *mine* rides around with a fucking flower in his hat.' And he reached across and snatched the red rose from where it perched under Marcus' cap. Marcus thought he was going to drop it in the dust, but Milo relented, and instead handed it back to him. 'Keep it under your cloak, soldier,' he said. And he galloped back to the head of the column.

To whom did he owe loyalty now?

He had a lot of time to brood back at Dura Europus. The aftermath of battle was brief elation and then long boredom.

For the first time, the consequences of Magnentius' revolt sank in. He was now of the eastern army, and there was another in the west. With any luck, Magnentius would see sense and surrender to Constantius. The only alternative was bloody civil war.

He talked to Milo. The centurion clenched his jaw.

'The whole thing's fucked up,' he said. 'There can only be one rightful Emperor in the west, and Magnentius has no claim whatsoever. Constantius is the only surviving son of Constantine, his son and heir.'

Marcus could hear the lack of conviction in Milo's voice. He knew that if he'd still been in Britain, he'd be finding reasons to support the usurper.

'And Magnentius has his Frankish and Saxon legions,' said Marcus. 'The best in the world.'

'Like I said, the whole thing's fucked up.'

Marcus felt he no longer knew anything. What love was, who he served, who to pray to . . . Was the Lord Mithras really there, in the heart of the battle? Had he survived, and other men died, because he was under his Lord's protection, and they were not? Was it all pre-ordained, or brute luck? And what of the endless suffering, there on the plains of Nisibis? The limbless men ebbing gore into the crusted sand, the elephants' groans, the screams of white-eyed, disembowelled horses. Who was there to protect them?

More and more, Marcus began to feel that the only true god or gods were unknown and unknowable, beyond good and evil. They were indifferent to mortal suffering. Or – even more terrifying – they were both good *and* evil. Animal-headed, barbaric, serenely smiling, inhuman, eternal. They took as much delight in creating a pretty girl as they did a poisonous snake. They enjoyed the sound of a plucked harp and a sweet night-time song no more and no less than they enjoyed the bewildered bellowing of a wounded and slowly dying elephant. The world was their arena, and everything in it pleased and entertained them equally.

How could one honour or pray to such gods?

He had lost hold of his religion, his culture, his identity. His loyalties had shrunk down and down, his public world had tottered and died, all that was left to him was the private: his comrades, and the two people back in London he had once known and called his family.

Rome was just a madman's dream – who had said that? The Emperors were squabbling boys. A battle won was as heartbreaking as a battle lost. Love was a mystery not worth the unravelling. You could bed a different whore every night, and then fall in love with a girl who merely kisses you and gives you a rose, about whom you know nothing, not even her name. Love was about as tough and long-lived as a rag of mist over a rice-field at dawn. The gods were indifferent. By the standards of human morality, they were immoral! What else to do but hunker down with a bottle of wine in the tavern, play dice, love the whores, and curse tomorrow? *Vivite, ait mors. Venio.*

Live, says Death. I am coming.

It was with such disordered thoughts on his mind, that Marcus heard of the arrival at Dura Europus of the Emperor Constantine himself.

The very next day, an Imperial herald came and knocked on the door of the officers' mess and requested the presence of Optio Marcus Flavius Aquila in person.

Marcus came to the door, unshaven and hungover, and stared. The Imperial messenger looked utterly out of place in the camp. He wore a long, embroidered dalmatic of pale cream linen, and on his feet were what appeared to be slippers with curled toes. A prize specimen straight from the perfumed and incensed courts of Constantinople. How he must *hate* being out here at Dura! thought Marcus, somewhat cheered by the idea.

The Imperial messenger wrinkled his nose at the sight of this unkempt soldier. Don't you wrinkle your nose at me, you perfumed ponce, thought Marcus. My men have died to keep parasites like you fed and watered and perfumed in your fancy fucking gold embroidered slippers.

But he said nothing.

'His Excellent and Divine Majesty, the Emperor Constantius, commands your presence.'

Marcus looked startled.

'Marcus Flavius Aquila,' confirmed the messenger. 'Immediately.'

Shit, thought Marcus.

Constantius sat on a plain wooden chair on a stone podium. Marcus bowed and looked up again.

The middle, and now the only surviving, son of Constantine the Great was an impressive figure at first glance. In his late thirties or early forties, he had the same strong nose and cleft chin of his father, broad shoulders, and penetrating eyes. But they were too penetrating. He needed to know everything. It is those who trust nothing who feel the need to know everything. His eyes were eager, greedy and devouring. And he himself was closed off. His voice, when he spoke, was more sinuous than commanding.

'So, you are the optio who served so bravely at Nisibis, I hear. Marcus Flavius Aquila?'

'That is my name, Excellency.'

Constantius twitched. 'You did *not* serve bravely?'

Already His Divine Majesty felt he was being contradicted. Name of Light. Marcus stammered, 'You are very kind to say so, Excellency.'

'Not I, I assure you.' He turned and picked up a small gold medallion on a strip of rawhide that lay on the table beside him. Marcus knelt before him and the Emperor looped it over his head. Marcus stood again.

'I am honoured, Excellency.'

'Indeed you are,' murmured Constantius with a wispy smile. 'So.' Having flattered the man, now it was time to milk him. 'You are, I believe, in the invidious position of having as your guardian the Praepositus of London, one Lucius Fabius Quintilianus. Am I right?'

'You are, Excellency.'

'An awkward position, is it not? Although not unique, in these divided and unnatural times. Where do the allegiances of . . . London lie, I wonder?'

It was an impossible situation. 'With Rome, I am sure, excellency.'

Constantius smiled. The optio was not going to get off that easily. 'And is Rome ruled by myself, or . . . Magnentius?'

Marcus was silent for a moment, staring at the floor. Constantius let him squirm. Then a figure stepped forward from the shadows beyond. Marcus looked up.

The man was in a plain white robe to his ankles. His head was completely shaven, and he was beardless but for a little black tuft on his chin. He seemed ageless. His eyes were fixed on Marcus. Around his neck was a chain, and from it hung a big silver Chi-Rho symbol.

'Ah, Paulus,' said Constantius. 'My good and faithful servant.' He smiled. Paulus did not smile. He in turn began to question Marcus, who was surprised that he did not ask the Emperor's permission first in order to do so.

'Your uncle is not a Christian?' he asked.

'My uncle is loyal to the religion of his forefathers – the religion of Caesar Augustus, of Trajan, of Severus . . .'

Paulus held his hand up and Marcus fell silent. It would do no good at all to get angry in the snakepit. The snakes would bite faster than he could hit.

'Magnentius has a lot of support in Britain, I believe. Many of his troops are British.'

Marcus gave no answer, since none was required. Silence was a friend who would never betray, and much the best friend here.

Constantius said, 'I am fond of Britain. My father was first declared Emperor there, of course. At York.' There was a long pause. Marcus thought he could hear the drip, drip of his own scared sweat.

'Despite the treachery of this *Magnentius*,' said the Emperor, 'an iron curtain, as it were, has not fallen across our Empire. Merchant ships still sail from the ports of the Levant to furthest fogbound Britain and back. All is, alas, confusion. We have our own loyal army in the east, and there is a wretched, mobile field army in the west, commanded by the usurper, and apparently ready to face us in battle. Of course, our heart most sincerely longs for peace. But we are afraid that the road to peace will be bloody. Is that not an irony?'

Again, Marcus said nothing. Constantius looked down and twiddled the numerous rings on his fingers and then looked up again.

'Despite his adherence to false gods, I hear nothing but good of your guardian. He is reputed to be an honest man.'

'He is indeed, Excellency. Honest and loyal.'

'Please do not interrupt me. I am not an unreasonable man, and pagans, as you know, continue to occupy positions of influence throughout our Empire. However, I need to know more about the situation in Britain. You will write out a full report of what you know about the situation there. I must know every detail. In time, when Magnentius has been put to death, you will return there and be our representative. There will be much to do, to – *clean things up*. And in all the excitement and hubbub, there is always a danger that the innocent and loyal, such as your beloved guardian, Quintilianus, and his niece – he has a niece, I believe? – might be caught up in trouble. Unless they have someone to look out for them and their best interests.'

Marcus bowed his head again. The Emperor took it for a sign of obedience, concurrence. But really it was just defeat. He would have to accept, it seemed, that most disgusting of roles: a spy.

When he got outside, he took a deep breath. It felt like the first breath he had taken for a long time.

Constantius rested his chin in the palm of his hand and drawled to his secretary. 'A letter, Paulus. *To Clodius Albinus, Vicarius, at London. Greetings in Christ.*'

Paulus, Constantius' most faithful servant, was known as a zealous Christian. However, his full name was not Paulus the Zealot. It was Paulus Catena – *the Chain*. He was the most feared interrogator in the eastern empire. After only a handful of questions, his victims felt like his words, and indeed their own words, were wrapping them round in iron and unbreakable bonds. Marcus had experienced a taste of it just now. No one was ever found innocent after interrogation by Catena; their guilt was always exposed. Catena was a great believer in guilt. He called it *original sin*.

He had become acquainted with sin early in life. His family were Christians in Spain, during the persecutions of Diocletian. The Vicarius of Spain at the time was called Datianus, and he was a great persecutor of Christians. One day, when still a boy, Paulus was up in the hills with a rod and a bent pin and a pouch of maggots. He had caught nothing all day and didn't care. The sun was hot and life was good. Down below in the valley, his family were in church, but Paulus had feigned illness, stealing a handful of white flour from the kitchens and rubbing it into his cheeks, dabbing his forehead with cold water. His mother had tutted and left him there in bed, in the care of the slaves, while she went with the rest of the family to worship the Christian god, down in the valley below. As soon as they were gone, Paulus was up and out of the window.

Sleepily now, Paulus heard shouts and cries down in the valley. He stood and peered curiously over a rock.

The village was milling with soldiers, and a man on horseback commanded them. Paulus watched as they dragged women out of the church and stripped them naked. He saw his mother and one of his sisters among them. They were stripped naked and suspended by one ankle from the lintel of a barn. They were whipped, and then questioned. When they refused to give in to the soldiers' demands that they should worship and make sacrifices to the Emperor Diocletian, they were whipped again. Paulus watched as they were lashed with whips dipped in vinegar and salt. Their cries carried up to his ears on the wind. A man who had been dragged from the church was suspended like the women, and a lighted brazier set under his head. After a while his hair began to smoke. Other Christians from the church were exquisitely tortured with pointed reeds driven under their fingernails, or blistered and burned with boiling lead. They did not fight back. It was against their creed. Their holy books were bundled onto a fire in the middle of the village square. More of them were beaten.

A man with an axe began to behead them one by one, but

there were too many, and it was too hot, and soon the blade of his axe grew blunted and chipped, and it was taking him three or four clumsy strokes to every cussed neck. Finally, the man on horseback ordered him to stop, and had all the surviving Christians led or dragged insensate back into the church, where the rest of them were still held captive. They herded them inside and nailed up the doors and then bundled brushwood against them and set them alight. The church burned well, the flames roared up. But over the roar of the flames, Paulus on the hillside, still clutching his fishing rod in one hand and his pouch of maggots in the other, open-mouthed, could hear the rising screams of the villagers. A single, infernal wail blended together, comprising among the many other screams, the screams of his grandfather and his mother and his father and his aunt and his two brothers and his sister and also his baby sister. And as his mother felt the smoke enter her lungs and begin to suffocate her she clasped her baby daughter tightly to her and suffocated her baby against her own breast.

Paulus Catena was a great believer in guilt. He was a great believer in *original sin*.

CHAPTER SEVENTEEN

There was one more battle to come. It was the battle against Magnentius, who had not sued for peace, as everyone had hoped. Even his own troops had hoped for it. But history turned out differently.

In May 351, a miraculous cross of light was seen over the Holy City of Jerusalem – at least, according to the Bishop there. Constantius took this as a good omen, and sailed his troops from Antioch to the Balkans, where they disembarked at Spalato and marched upcountry. Magnentius and his legions meanwhile marched east.

Constantius marched into the plains of Lower Pannonia and encamped at a place called Cibalis. He fortified his position heavily. Magnentius came down from the north, hurrying because the summer campaigning season was coming to a close and the bitter Balkan winter was not far off. He tried to tempt Constantius from his advantageous position, but the Emperor of the East wasn't going to be fooled by that tired trick. A Frankish general called Sylvanus deserted to Constantius' side.

Magnentius turned away and besieged the town of Mursa. The gates of the city were aflame and his men were scaling the walls when news came of Constantius' approach. They turned and battle was joined, on the level and merciless plains beside the River Drave. Constantius himself retired to the nearby church to pray, in the company of Valens, the Arian

Bishop of Mursa. Valens assured him of victory.

It was 28 September AD 351. The legions, accustomed to meeting with flailing hordes of barbarian tribesmen easily broken, met each other, their mirror opposites, like two wrecking balls colliding with a shock that shivered them to pieces: legion against legion, iron line against iron line, shield against shield. The soldiers fought all day, baffled and embattled. Mus swung his sword at men who spoke the same Saxon as he did. Marcus killed men whom he might have commanded back in Britain. Britus died. Caelius died. Crito died. Milo lost an eye. Marcus lost two fingers. He remembered a saying of Lucius': 'All men are brothers. They just don't know it yet.' But this was even more terrible. They knew they were brothers – and were still fated to treat each other as enemies, to be cut down without mercy or quarter given.

The unarmoured Saxons suffered heavy losses from Constantius' deadly Syrian archers. But Magnentius used his own cavalry to bloody effect on Constantius' right flank. Finally, however, it was Constantius' own heavy mailed cavalry that broke the line of the western legions and drove them into confusion.

It was a terrible battle – one of the most destructive battles of the ancient world. At Mursa, each side lost as many as thirty thousand men. Sixty thousand in one day.

It was not the weight of the dead but the wreck of the line that gave Constantius victory – if you could call it victory. It achieved absolutely nothing, and so history has forgotten it.

Marcus did not forget it.

Singara, Nisibis, Mursa: three titanic battles, one a defeat, one a victory, one a disaster. It was enough. It was enough for Marcus now to call himself a full-blooded soldier.

Magnentius fled from the field with a handful of light cavalry; Constantius followed him for a while, and then delayed. There was no hurry. The self-declared Emperor's brief reign was broken. Constantius was now *de facto* ruler of the entire Empire, from the Scottish border to the banks of the Euphrates.

There followed one more minor battle, at Mons Seleucis in Gaul, where Magnentius' power was finally wiped out completely. He committed suicide in August 353, at Lugdunum.

Wintering lavishly at Arles, Constantius ordered a victory banquet. The severed head of Magnentius, presented to him on a golden platter, was the high point of the evening's festivities.

The Emperor confided a great deal in his secretary, Paulus, and always listened to his advice. He began to sign himself 'My Eternity'. And he began to grow very suspicious. When he had had the real threat of Magnentius to deal with, he was happy. But now it seemed to him that the threat had not vanished so much as metamorphosed into something less distinct. It was all around. He had tremendous responsibilities, great power, ordained of God; and all around him there were schemers and conspirators and pagans plotting to cast him down and restore their own vile gods and abominations. Britain, especially, seemed to him to be in need of correction.

He sent a small force over to London. Among its number were the useful young optio whose guardian was Praepositus over there, and his faithful Paulus – the Chain.

Marcus himself was happy to go back. Or at least eager, concerned. The night before he received his orders, he had a dream. He and Julia were comparing scars again, and then her scar began to bleed afresh, and somehow it was his fault. She was very ill, in danger. There was also a letter from Lucius in his dream, begging him to return, for it could not be long now . . . He was puzzled and upset by the dream. He must go back to London.

Five years had passed since Marcus was last in London; it felt like much longer. He found a city huddled and half-empty, sullen and oppressed, and already shivering under a thin layer of snow on its tiled and thatched rooftops. Winter had come early this year.

Julia answered the door to find a man standing there in the uniform of an officer. She knew it was Marcus – but so changed. She stared at him. He was twenty-seven now, but looked much older. The wind and the sun of the desert had aged him, left him with lined and leather skin. He had fine laughter lines around his eyes, and those eyes still had plenty of life. But the set of his jaw was grim, and behind the laughter in his eyes was a sadness.

Marcus saw before him a young woman of twenty-three. He looked at her searchingly, still haunted by his dream in which she had fallen so ill. But she was less changed than he. She was still very beautiful, still perfectly poised. She still wore no ring on her finger. Her eyes were large and dark, reminding him of the eyes of another girl, many thousands of miles away in a desert city: liquid eyes that you could drown in. But her expression was not so simple or so languid. Her eyes flickered as if she was often bored. There was even a hint of sourness around her mouth. A woman whose eyes roved over the men available to her as husbands, and found not one worth resting on. And so moved on. But now her eyes rested, on a grown man with a lined and world-weary face. A man, no longer a boy.

She took him into the covered atrium and ordered Cennla to bring him a glass of wine.

When it came, Marcus did not touch it. He twisted his fingers together and tried to answer her questions. But there was so much distance between them. The more they each realised this, the politer they became. At last Marcus snatched up the wine in front of him and drained it in a single gulp. When he set his goblet down again, Julia reached out and took his hand. Instead of coolness and politeness, suddenly an echo of her former self came back again.

She looked him in the eyes, and smiled, and said, 'It's good to have you back.'

Hardly knowing what he was doing, he hugged her close to him. There was so much to tell and not to tell. So many tales, wonders, horrors. He clenched his eyes tight.

Finally he sat back. He wanted to tell her about Mursa.

When he had finished, there was a long silence. Finally he looked up and gazed at her, still not sure if she had understood, wanting her to understand. He said, 'I saw Rome go down in flames that day.'

She said nothing. He thought she understood. She called for more wine. Then she reached out and took his hand again – the other hand, his right hand, with the great scar and the missing fingers. She smiled.

'It seems this arm has all the bad luck.'

He smiled too, though he had never felt so much like crying. 'Your sword arm always gets it. My fault for driving my bare fist into the other man's sword-edge. Fingers never come off too well against hard steel.'

'Looks to me like they come off very easily,' she said.

At that they managed to laugh.

Marcus drank more wine and Julia sipped water and then they had dinner together. There were long silences and lingering looks, but they became less awkward as time wore on.

'Five years,' murmured Julia wonderingly.

'Five long years,' said Marcus. 'Ahenobarbus . . .?'

'Became very fat and sedate, at last, and died at a dignified old age, and enjoyed a handsome burial in the garden.'

He nodded. 'And you still not married?'

She scowled – a flash of the old, splendid temper. 'If there were one of them worthy of me!' she said. 'I cannot tell you how I despise them. Oh Marcus, I have nearly gone out of my mind with boredom. But I suppose I shouldn't complain, if the alternative to boredom is . . . Mursa.'

Marcus said nothing to this. Instead he commented, 'But at least you have the company of your beloved uncle.'

'Not lately I haven't.'

Marcus looked puzzled.

'He's up in York, or even on the Wall.'

'Lucius! On the Wall!' Marcus was both amused and alarmed. 'I assumed he was just at a late session at the courts.'

Julia shook her head. 'You have no idea – I'm sorry, I know your troubles have been far worse, but there have been troubles here too. There is no money to pay the troops. The conditions on the Wall are near mutiny. There's even talk of the soldiers doing secret deals with the tribes. It's a terrible mess up there.'

'And Lucius has gone to sort it out? As Paymaster-General?'

'He took some silver – under heavy escort. The roads have never been so lawless. But really, I'm not sure what Lucius' aim is. He never trusted the Legate at York. And that snake, Sulpicius – you remember? – has been up and down Ermine Street for heaven knows what reason.'

'You still see Clodius Albinus?'

'As little as possible.'

Marcus looked grim. 'There is a new secretary in town, Constantius' own interrogator. He is here to suppress any remaining support for Magnentius' revolt.'

'But Magnentius is dead!' Julia almost laughed.

'It is a little bizarre,' agreed Marcus. 'But Constantius sees treachery everywhere nowadays. Even from the dead.'

'Careful,' said Julia. 'That sounds treacherous for a start.'

'Not to worry,' said Marcus. 'His Eternity approves of me for some reason. I'm supposed to be his eyes and ears in London. But bugger that. I'm here to make sure you're all right. You and Lucius.'

Julia touched him on the shoulder. 'Such a big, brave soldier,' she said.

They were laughing when Cennla came in with a fresh basket of bread. He saw them laughing together, so close. They ignored him; he was invisible. Suddenly, he who had been her closest confidant, it seemed, for five years, was once more just another slave. His heart burned.

When Julia laid down her head to sleep that night, she felt more *occupied*, more *interested* in life in general, than she had for a long, long time. He had come back – unannounced, as usual. Coolly knocking at the door. But he had come back, sunburned, leanly muscled, world-ravaged, sad and laughing-eyed, hair close cropped and soldierly, eyes so kind, jaw so firm. She knew she could not really understand what he had been through, but it showed on his face. Twenty-seven, but looking much older. She liked that. She liked a man who looked a bit – she smiled – battered. But she mustn't smile. This wasn't cosmetic battering for her appreciation. This was horror unimaginable. He had seen his friends die in his arms, heard screams he would never in his life be deaf to. Everything was closing in. But it was all right, she thought, because he was here, with his strong arms, his kind eyes. It was all right because of him. Rome would go down in flames and they would escape to live in peace and quiet somewhere, far away, in the woods or the hills, some unknown valley somewhere, there to live unseen, like Horace in his sunlit Sabine vale . . .

Like when they were still children. That night sitting on the quayside staring out across the starlit river, munching pilfered bread and cheese. Their hands in each other's. Their children's dreams.

And now he was back. After Singara, Nisibis, Mursa – those barbaric names! – he was back, grown up and sorrowfully wise. No longer the cocksure boy nor the young braggart of a soldier who boasted of the whores he had bedded (she swallowed hard). Not that he ever was that sort of animal. But whatever flaws he did have had been burned away under the hard sun and what was left was just a man. A man that she could very well . . .

Well. She smiled and laid back her head to sleep.

But she did not sleep.

In the morning – the strangest thing – Cennla tried to kiss her! Cennla!

She slapped him so hard that he fell back across the table and then crashed to the floor. He held his hand to his inflamed cheek and stared at her as if she had gone mad. Of course, she then gave him the most terrible beating. But the expression on his face puzzled her. It seemed as if he was at first baffled that she should be beating him at all, and then rather angry about it. His eyes positively glimmered with fury. It was a little worrying – but rather funny!

They were invited to dinner parties as brother and sister. Marcus thought these rather a chore, but Julia found some new pleasure in London society, not least on account of having such a handsome soldier on her arm.

Marcus was always questioned closely about his army experiences. Julia often tried to make sure in advance that they did not ask him about Mursa. One evening he was forced to reveal his heroism at Nisibis – only because it would have been impolite not to do so, since his hostess had heard about it from another source. Julia was both cross with him and amused that he had so modestly kept this episode from her. On the way home in the litter she gave him a kiss on the cheek, and compared him to Diomedes, to Hector, nay, to great Achilles himself!

Marcus touched his cheek where she had kissed him and murmured, almost shyly, 'Don't be daft.'

Another dinner party left him fuming. It had been an evening spent in the company of, among others, the rich merchant, Solimarius Secundinus (now richer and fatter than ever), his ridiculous little wife Marcia, their equally ridiculous daughters, Marcella and Livilla, and their two downtrodden husbands, so disheartened by the serial infidelities of their respective wives that they had long since ceased to say anything at all.

Marcus, of course, was an object of great fascination to Marcella and Livilla. They positively pawed at his scarred arm, and caressed his de-fingered hand with something approaching awe. Julia felt no jealousy. They were too ridiculous for that. But she felt unhappy for Marcus, who was obviously hating every second of their attentions.

Once in the litter on the way home, he erupted.

'By all the gods, how I hate those twittering society ladies! Sitting forward fat-arsed on the edge of their cushioned couches, gazing up at me damp-eyed, lips apart, beseeching, hands palmed across their breasts (Marcus here affected a squawking falsetto) – *No! But how terrible! You mean you saw your friend's head sliced CLEAN OFF? Ghastly! Oh you are so brave! Brave but terrible! Oh do go on* . . . I could choke. I would grab those fat, twittering bitches by the arm and set them on the front line against the German tribes and then let them see those two-handed axes falling on flesh and the blood steaming and grown men, twenty-year veterans, limbless on the forest floor, writhing in their own guts and gore, screaming out like birds, like beardless boys, crying out for their mothers, for their gods, for someone, anyone, to kill them . . . and then see what those lipsticked bitches think of the *nobility and heroism of war*.' He spat. 'They know *nothing*. Bitches on heat at the thought of men out there on the frontiers, shedding blood for them. Oh, so heroic! Such Homeric heroes! They're sick to their souls. As long as women are dumb enough to worship the blood-stained conquering hero, men will fight. Men may fight the wars but women fuel them.'

Julia let him breathe easy awhile. Then she said, 'I'm sorry.'

He turned to her. 'You're all right. You're no scar-worshipper.'

She smiled. 'Well, only a bit.'

He looked at her for a long time. Then he sighed and smiled.

On another occasion, however, he was driven beyond endurance, and erupted at the dinner party itself. It was a dinner party held by Flavius Martinus and Calpurnia. One of the women present had actually said that she found the idea of all those wild, hairy tribes beyond the eastern frontier '*really rather exciting*'.

'And so here you sit,' said Marcus, setting down his wine, 'in your dim, cushioned, provincial capital, with your hot baths and your Rhenish wine, and you think it is all safe and lovely here, and yet you live on a knife edge. You have no idea what is out there, beyond the frontiers. What horrors. Or perhaps you think they are there for your entertainment, your thrilled, spine-tingling delectation, on winter nights around the brazier. Madam, there is nothing thrilling about such savagery. It is a tale of nothing but sadness and gloom and men descended to the level of beasts, and lower. How can you even imagine that barbarism and cruelty could be exciting, could be anything but a tedious, endless repetition of spilled blood and victims' cries?'

The dinner guests stirred uneasily. What on earth had got into the man?

Marcus continued more evenly, more resignedly. 'But I see the belief is gone from Rome. The walls may still stand a while longer, but the belief in them is gone. The People Who Lost their Soul. Who Forgot Their History. Who Misunderstood the Nature of the World.' He shook his head. 'There is an east wind blowing and you don't feel it. We can feel it. Every soldier who stands on the eastern frontier can feel it, and it cuts through his mail and chills him to the bone. And the fire that thaws him will not be the fire he sought.'

It was no good. The guests were utterly baffled, and his angry words were wasted. When he had gone, they said among themselves, 'Poor fellow, head quite turned. I can't think *what* came over him . . .'

As they were about to enter their litter for home, however, Calpurnia slipped out to talk to them.

'That woman is, I'm afraid, quite the dimmest in London,' she said, taking Marcus soothingly by the arm. 'My husband thinks you did a very good job back there. And so do I.'

Marcus nodded. 'I do apologise for such an outburst.'

Calpurnia shook her head. 'I have never been on the frontier myself, obviously. But I know when a man speaks the truth.' She turned and smiled at Julia. 'My dear, he's nearly as hot-tempered as you are.'

'Not usually,' said Julia. 'I'm usually *far* worse than he is.'

Calpurnia turned back to Marcus, her eyebrows arched enquiringly. 'Well?'

'It's quite true,' affirmed Marcus. 'She has the foulest temper of anyone I've ever met.' Julia slapped him hard. 'You see?'

Calpurnia was greatly amused. Strangely, she also felt that she was intruding. Julia was always going to need someone very special. But here, perhaps . . . She bade them goodnight and went back inside to soothe the ruffled feathers of the dimmest woman in London.

But Julia was very proud of Marcus that evening.

In the Temple of Isis she prayed for him.

She even went into the Christian chapel nowadays with Bricca, and prayed for him there. Can't do any harm, she reasoned.

She still found most Christians stupidly intolerant – spiritually tone-deaf, as it were. But the chapel had a mood that she liked. The little circle of presbyters sang '*Salve, salve, Virgine*' to the mother of their god, the slow, sad, unaccompanied voices chanting in the Phrygian mode.

All gods are one, she now believed, and the mother of their god is the mother of all the gods. The immemorial, nameless mother of us all . . . She blinked tears from her eyes. The gold of the sanctuary dimmed, blurred, and in that blurring of the eye, in her much-moved blindness, everything became clear. Blinded by tears of love, she could finally see.

CHAPTER EIGHTEEN

Paulus Catena stayed in rooms at the Vicarius' Palace. He had met Clodius Albinus before, in Gaul. He and the Vicarius, and his brother Sulpicius, got on well together. They were all Christians, and they were all loyal to the His Eternity, the Emperor Constantius. They saw eye to eye on many things. They agreed on the necessity for strong government, tough measures, the grim work of rooting out and destroying sedition. The tribes were massing on the borders of the Empire, and internal dissension would only weaken it the more.

They found that there were certain – *obstacles*, to the security of this particular province of Britain. Already, some of these obstacles were being removed. That sybaritic wastrel, Lucianus Septimius, for instance, the Governor of Britannia Prima, had been far too lax in enforcing Christian standards in his province. He was known to have dined with Magnentius, the usurper, on more than one occasion. And, like Magnentius, he seemed to think it didn't matter much either way if people worshipped the True God or the pagan gods. But now he was being persuaded of his error. He was down in the cells beneath the Vicarius' Palace at this very moment. Catena would be questioning him further this afternoon, once the guards had managed to bring him round again.

If he did not survive his stint in the cells – and with a rather weak, flabby individual like Septimius, that was certainly possible – then naturally his considerable wealth, his fine villa in the Cotswolds, and as many as one thousand acres of prime sheep country in the hills around Cirencester would fall into the possession of the state, to be administered, for the good of the people, by the financial offices of Clodius Albinus himself. This was a regrettable but wholly necessary by-product of the firm enforcement of Imperial, Christian order in the province. There could be no room for loose-tongued, Falernian-quaffing, women-chasing, louche, laughing subversives like Lucianus Septimius in the new Britain.

Indeed, there could really be no room for pseudo-Christians or pagan-tolerators at all; and certainly none for out-and-out pagans, in positions of power and influence. One could never know where their true loyalties might lie. The Praepositus, for instance. Now he was a difficult customer.

'The People's Friend,' murmured Sulpicius.

Catena and Albinus nodded at his little sarcasm. They understood exactly what he meant. This one needed careful handling.

For, astonishing as it might seem, Lucius Fabius Quintilianus – the paymaster, the tax-gatherer! – was a man *deeply beloved* by the mob. Was there anything so extraordinary? He must be the only example of a popular tax-gatherer in the entire Empire. Even though he was known for a pagan and an unbeliever, a defender of freedom of worship in a city increasingly Christian and disinclined to tolerate anything but Christianity, apparently, he was almost a hero of the masses. A People's Friend, indeed. The amusing thing was that Quintilianus himself seemed to have no idea that this was so. Even if he had, it would have meant nothing to him.

So high-minded. So *noble*.

For one thing, the populace and the merchant-classes of London seemed to believe – and awkwardly, all Catena's prying and spying had only proved them right – that Quintilianus had never pilfered a single copper for himself, in all his years as Praepositus. It was regarded in most provinces as a simple perk of the job: every Praepositus became wealthy as a result of his office. There wasn't much else going for it, frankly. But here was Quintilianus, still living as modestly as he had always done, in a villa in town with his niece and only a handful of slaves. He didn't even own a country property. In the summer, he would rent, or stay with friends, such as poor old Lucianus Septimius – reason enough for suspecting his loyalties, surely?

And for another thing, there was this ridiculous, senti-mental story, popularly known as the Tale of the Pork Butcher, doing the rounds of every tavern in the city. Apparently what had happened, if vulgar tittle-tattle was to be believed, was that one day last summer, Quintilianus had been in session as a magistrate at the courts, when a dodgy pork butcher had appeared before him. The pork butcher had been warned by town council officials before about the state of his stall but had rebuffed them with considerable insolence, and told them to mind their own business. Then, one hot summer's day, as many as forty people had fallen violently ill of some kind of food poisoning, and one or two had almost died. The source of the poisoning was traced back to the pork butcher, and more particularly to a batch of pork and garlic sausages he was selling, which should have been consigned to the rubbish dumps a week ago. The fellow narrowly escaped a lynching, and was dragged into the magistrate's court.

He might even have been sentenced to a dozen lashes in the forum, but the magistrate hearing the case disapproved of physical punishment as a public spectacle. Instead he imposed a massive fine on the pork butcher, demanding full and immediate payment. The poor man, already genuinely mortified at the outbreak of poisoning for which he was responsible, broke down and wept. He said that such a fine would utterly destroy his business. He would have to sell his house, everything he owned. He had a wife and three small children, but they would be turned out into the gutter to starve. They might even have to sell themselves into slavery to pay the fine; such a thing was not unknown. He begged the magistrate to take a more lenient view of this, his first ever offence, and reduce the fine. The magistrate listened, stony-faced. And when the butcher had finally stopped his pleading and his sobbing, Quintilianus simply repeated, utterly unmoved, that the fine should be paid, by sundown tomorrow, in full, at the council offices. Then he left the court.

The butcher's curses rained down on his head.

However, as he lay outside in the dust of the forum, where he had been thrown by the court guards and left to sob his heart out, a slave came and tapped him on the shoulder. The pork butcher did not look up, so the slave shrugged and tossed a little leather bag down beside him. After a while, the butcher raised his head and peered inside the bag. He found it contained a handful of gold solidi, exactly enough, no more, no less, to pay his fine.

Quintilianus had tried to make absolutely sure that no one would ever know about it. But evidently the slave blabbed. Soon it was known throughout the city that the Praepositus had imposed a heavy fine on the dodgy pork butcher, in strict accordance with the law – and *then paid the fine himself*.

What nobility!

And besides all these sentimental folk tales about him, there was nothing against him. Absolutely nothing: no dishonesty, no pilfering, no seditious talk. Just a huge undercurrent of popular support here in London. It was all very awkward. Any attempt to arrest him, let alone take him down to the cells for a little gentle persuasion – suspended by his wrists over hot coals, for instance, with the confession that would release him from his agony just inches away from his nose – any such attempt, and there was every likelihood that the news would get out, and you would have a full-scale riot on your hands.

It was all very awkward. And yet there was no doubt that

Lucius was a serious obstacle, and that if he *could* somehow be removed, with the minimum of fuss and attention, then the responsibility for tax-gathering, and all the concomitant responsibilities and, ah – benefits, would fall, for the time being, within the remit of the Vicarius himself.

'You know that he is up on the Wall at the moment?' said Sulpicius. 'I do wonder if I might not have a word with some of my . . . acquaintances up there.'

Albinus looked interested.

'Ensuring, in one way or another,' said Sulpicius, 'that he spends a very long time up there on the Wall. Or even beyond it.'

Albinus looked across at Catena, and then back at his ingenious young brother. He smiled.

'And then,' Catena put in, 'his equally noble-spirited young ward, the optio Marcus Flavius, might be persuaded to go after him, and meet with a similar disappearance.'

This was almost too duplicitous for Albinus to comprehend. 'But I thought you had hired the ward as your ears and eyes in London, when you had an audience with him before the Emperor in Syria?'

Catena purred, stroked the Chi-Rho around his neck. 'It was a test of sorts. But, like his guardian, I fear that optio is just too high-minded for his own good. We shall see. But it is my humble opinion that he would prove to be every bit as much of an obstacle, as Quintilianus himself. In which case . . .' And he waved his hand vaguely, as if to signify disappearance, vanishment into airy nothing.

Things moved fast.

'What do they mean, Lucius has disappeared?'

Julia looked up at Marcus, and then down again at the letter she held in her hand. 'I don't know,' she said. 'It just says that he was out riding with a small party beyond the Wall – hunting or something, although that doesn't sound like Lucius

– and they evidently met unexpectedly with a war party from one of the tribes, and . . .' She struggled to maintain her composure, had a brief, harsh fit of coughing. 'They have not been seen again.'

Marcus held the back of his hand to his mouth and paced to and fro. 'What kind of chaos *is* it up there? I know the tribes have always been beyond our jurisdiction, but for them to be able to kidnap or, or . . . whatever, a senior official, and get off apparently scot-free.' He scowled at Julia. 'If you'll forgive the pun.'

She didn't smile. 'What are we going to do?'

'We?' He was already walking towards the stairs. '*I* am going to sail for Wallsend on the evening tide. I should be able to have my men released from Southwark camp as well.'

Julia stood. 'I'm coming with you.'

'Don't be ridiculous,' he said, still walking.

'Cennla!' she called. 'Bricca!'

Now he stopped, and turned. 'You are not coming with me.'

'Then I'll go under my own sail,' Julia retorted. She wanted to remind him that Lucius was *her* blood relative, not his – but she swallowed down her sudden spite. It wasn't his fault. Instead she added, 'I have sailed before, you know. It's further from London to Spain than it is to the Wall. I am coming.'

'You are not coming, and my word is final. And in Lucius' absence, I am your legal master.' He scowled at her ferociously. He was wasting time, and was already tired of arguing. She bristled at him, her mouth set hard. Would he have to order her to be forcibly restrained? She had no idea what life was like beyond the Wall. The thought of a female up there was preposterous.

'Never,' he said to her slowly and carefully, 'have I met such stubborn, mule-headed wilfulness in a woman. Allied,' he went on, lest she should take this observation as some kind of compliment, as well she might, knowing her, 'to such a complete and utter ignorance of the true harshness of the world.'

'And what would *you* know about the true harshness of the world, soldier?' she spat back, knowing it was a stupid riposte.

'More than you, my lady,' he replied, bowing out of the room with utmost formality. 'More than you.'

She slammed her small, hard fists against the table-top. How infuriating the truth could be. And was it her fault, that she had been kept so much from the world and all its harshness?

The commander of Southwark camp sighed and released his men without the slightest glimmer of interest.

In the square, Marcus was accosted by Milo, fully uniformed. 'I heard about Quintilianus. I knew you'd be sailing.'

Marcus laughed resignedly. 'You are taking command of my little outing?'

Milo shook his head. 'Only technically. I'm not bothered.'

'Then why are you coming?'

Milo looked around, surveying with his one eye the frosty, gritty streets of the fort, the drill-square, the soldiers huddled round the charcoal braziers waxing their boots. An aura of safe, camp-apathy settling over the place like fine, smothering snow. He looked back at Marcus.

'Boredom,' he said. 'I like the north.'

'Even in winter?'

'Especially in winter.'

As soon as Marcus, Milo, Mus and the rest had marched out of camp for the docks, the commander dictated a message. *To Clodius Albinus, Vicarius.*

Albinus read the message and then dropped it in the brazier.

In the old days, the Vicarius could simply have forbidden them to go. In the old days, the Vicarius was supreme civil *and* military power. But since the separation of powers, under the reforms of Diocletian, he had no way of stopping them.

But Albinus, and Sulpicius and Catena with him, were not unduly concerned. Beyond the Wall was a big place. They would never find Lucius.

Later that day, it was Catena's turn to receive a message, saying that there was someone asking to see him – a slave! Not only that, but a deaf and dumb slave! What was he going to do, *blink* at him? Catena was so amused by the idea that he called him in.

The slave couldn't talk but oddly, he could write. And what he had to write was very interesting. Catena read what he had written, and then wrote his reply at the bottom of the paper, pushed it back to the slave, and dismissed him.

Well, you never knew. It might help. It might be a neat solution to all their problems in one fell swoop. He sat back and smiled.

The merchantman they requisitioned was small and bulbous, but it would do the job. The ship's captain was less than happy about it, though. He was fully laden and all ready to sail for the mouth of the Rhine with a cargo of wool and a chain-gang of Welsh slaves. He started to kick up quite a fuss. But Milo took him aside and had a quiet word with him, and he seemed much happier about things after that.

The wool and the Welsh slaves were shoved back into the warehouse, and the soldiers marched on board. They sailed, as Marcus had said, on the evening tide.

The wind was a favourable southwesterly, and only two days later they sailed up the Tyne and stepped ashore at Wallsend.

They returned to the camp where they had been stationed five or six years ago. It was from here that Lucius had ridden out with a small troop of cavalry, making for the next fort west.

'He was a good man,' the camp commander told Marcus. 'His concern about the troops' back-pay was genuine. But . . .' He raised his hands. What could he do? Not even Lucius could summon gold out of thin air. On the way north, he had levied back-taxes on various potteries, ironworks and mines that were behind with their payments, but it was not enough. It was never enough.

The apathy here was even more pronounced than in London. The camp's wooden palisade walls seemed in a state of dangerous neglect, but there were no efforts being made to repair them. The soldiers drank a lot. Most of their rations came from what they could glean or hunt. They were hated now by the local populace, for their lightning raids on precious winter stores. People even dreamed of when they might be called back to the south. The signs of decay were everywhere.

'There's work to be done here,' said Milo.

'But a war-party to be hunted down first,' said Marcus.

They would ride out at dawn tomorrow.

In the night, in a pelting rainstorm, two visitors arrived at the camp.

One was a stocky male slave, seemingly too sodden even to talk. The other, ludicrously out of place up here on the Wall, was a young woman who might have been elegantly dressed when she set out, but now looked more like a whore who had been caught cheating and dropped in a ducking-pond. However, she was clearly a lady, and the commander ordered her to be shown into his quarters and offered a change of clothes.

A few minutes later, a tired-looking young optio stepped into the commander's quarters. He stared wordlessly at the woman for a while, now wrapped in a large white blanket. Her hair was wringing wet and gleamed in the lamplight. She ignored him. Finally he said, 'I cannot *believe* you have come all this way on your own.'

She started to speak but then broke into a fit of violent coughing. When she had regained her composure, she said, 'I didn't come on my own. Cennla escorted me.'

'Oh well, that's all right then,' he snorted. 'Name of Light, *anything* could have happened!'

'Anything didn't happen. Here we are, safe and sound.' She gave another rasping cough, but he refrained from pointing out the obvious.

'How did you get here?'

'By sea, the same way as you. We even had your ship in our sights for a while, but you were faster than us.' She began to dry her hair.

'You're not coming any further, anyway. That's certain.'

She looked at him, wide-eyed. 'But you can't leave me here, alone, with all these rough soldiers! *Anything* could happen.'

He smiled without mirth. 'This time I mean it. You stop here. Any rough soldiers try anything with you, and they'll come off much worse from it, I have no doubt at all.'

She held out a linen cloth. 'Would you dry my hair for me, please? I'm awfully tired.'

He hesitated a while, and then went over to her. Here he was, a trained soldier, an officer, with an award for bravery from the Emperor himself, awakened in the middle of the night by this importunate, infuriating young madam, and made to *dry her hair for her*. He must be a mug.

But her hair smelled sweet. As it dried, it filled out, became ticklish to the touch. The silence was like a secret between them. The oil lamp flickered. The white woollen blanket slipped a little from her shoulders, and in the lamplight, her white skin gleamed.

They rode out at dawn, as planned, with Milo and Marcus at

the head. Behind them rode a column of some sixty mounted infantrymen, Mus among them, straddling a pony which, to scale, looked about the size of a dog. In the heart of the column, to the ribald surprise of the troops, rode an elegant young woman in a fine woollen cloak. Marcus sometimes glanced back at her, there in the heart of the column. Where all the most precious *baggage* goes, he thought, tugging hard at his reins with a considerable confusion of emotions.

They had only been riding for an hour or so when the first tribesman was seen, skylined on a ridge not a quarter of a mile to their left.

'Could be an outrider from a party,' Marcus muttered. Milo gave no opinion. It wasn't his command. Marcus halted the column and ordered the men to draw swords. He looked back. The outrider was a pretty useless one, sitting skylined and unmoving like that. Then he pulled his horse round and cantered down the hill towards them. Marcus waited until he drew close. Finally, the rider reined in with a flourish and a caracole, directly in front of them, and nodded his head.

'My brother,' said Branoc.

'Branoc,' said Marcus.

'Ah, how sweet,' said Milo.

News travelled fast along the frontier. Branoc, sitting back in his village one evening, heard that a group of Romans, including a mighty man among them, had been surrounded and taken prisoner by a war-party from another tribe, and ridden off north. It made little sense, which excited much interest locally, although Branoc was indifferent. It was not his tribe.

Then he heard that the mighty man's son had come to the Wall, and was riding after him to bring him back and kill his enemies. This was of more interest, but still not his tribe. And then, as he was riding by the camp only yesterday, he happened to see a man outside inspecting the hooves of his horse, and recognised him of old. But Branoc never entered the camp of the Iron Hats if he could help it. So he had waited until today, when they rode out, and followed them – the Iron Hats never noticed him, they had as much sense of the land as a fish – and then he outflanked them and rode up onto the ridge so that they would see him, and his appearance before them should be as suitably dramatic as he thought fit. It would have been shameful to have come hobbling up behind them like some old woman.

Now it seemed he had been misinformed, but gossip was ever thus. His brother, the Iron Hat Marcus, was not the son of the mighty man who had been taken, but his *ward*. They did not even share blood. So how could they be of concern to one another? Not for the first time in his life, Branoc reflected that the ways of the Iron Hats were strange. Almost as strange as the ways of women.

Marcus was delighted but tried not to show it. Secretly, he had not until now had much faith that they would really be able to track down Lucius and rescue him. Secretly, he believed him long dead. Why should the tribes want to keep him alive? And even if, for some peculiar reason, he *was* still alive, he had been taken nearly two weeks ago now. How could they ever find him?

Branoc looked the same as ever. Except that he now had two sons and three calamities. They rode alongside each other.

'Calamities?'

'Daughters,' explained Branoc. 'But my wife is still good. And you, you are not yet married?'

'Not yet.'

'You have a woman in your party. She is not your woman?'

'No.'

'Then you are mad.'

Marcus laughed. 'What, not to have married her?'

'No, to have brought her along.' Branoc looked forward again. 'Not married, and how old?'

'Twenty-seven.'

Branoc glanced at him. 'You look a lot older.'

Revenge, at last. They laughed. Then it was time to be more serious.

'Do you know where Lucius has been taken? Or who took him?'

Branoc looked grim. 'He is probably dead. But I will ride with you. We can track the party. I know which tribe took him.' He shook his head. 'They were working as slaves, not as warriors.'

'What do you mean?'

Branoc stared far ahead of him, at where the contemptible slaves had gone. 'Gold crossed their palms.'

Marcus considered this in silence and they rode on.

They rode on up the wide valley and then out onto the bleak moorland where the wind cut across the skeletal winter bracken and chafed their skins raw.

The second day the wind dropped, and for the few hours while the sun was up, just above the rim of the horizon, the land was beautiful. The recent dusting of snow melted away on the south-facing slopes and the land beneath was still the golden brown of autumn. They stopped and watched a great flock of snow buntings fly overhead, as many as five hundred, heading east for the feeding grounds of the coast. A little later, they saw a merlin winging in straight out of the sun and stooping down on them. The merlin caught its prey with ease and then was gone.

They rode down another long wide valley that was snow-dusted and the shadows among the rocks were blue on the snow and the sedge was thick and coarse and the ground beneath was sodden with water and crusted here and there with ice that cracked beneath their horses' hooves. Then they rode up again, and had the first hint of the high country ahead, the granite outcrops scabbed with orange lichen, the gathering clouds on the distant peaks.

The weather worsened.

They wrapped their cloaks around themselves and lowered their hoods. Marcus turned back to ride alongside Julia. Her face was bowed into the stinging sleet, and when she raised it she was pale and drawn. He thought of saying to her that she should not have come – but what good would it do? She said nothing to him.

'Branoc – our guide, who I knew before when I was here – he will track the war-party for us. He believes Lucius is still alive.'

'Of course he is still alive,' said Julia. 'I haven't come all this way just to take him home in a coffin.'

Each evening, after so little daylight, they dismounted some time before sundown and built a marching camp: a rough ditch, a thorn brake, leather tents within. Julia needed a tent of her own, which she hadn't brought, so the rest of the men had to squeeze into one less. They didn't grumble, but secretly they thought it was mad to have brought a woman. When they learned that she was the niece of the kidnapped Praepositus, they admired her more.

A dozen men were posted on each watch throughout the night. Cennla slept across the entrance to his mistress's tent, like a dog. Now that *was* mad. He awoke each morning with frost sparkling on his blankets.

In her tent each night, Julia prayed to the goddess Isis to keep them all safe from harm. She fingered the amulet around her neck and squeezed her eyes tight shut. They would need all the help they could get.

'We have been riding five days, and no sign,' said Milo. 'I don't suppose a Roman patrol has been this far north for centuries.' He meant, how much further are we going to go? And, are you sure you trust your scout? But he didn't need to say it.

'We will find them,' said Marcus, not looking at him,

staring ahead to where Branoc sat his horse on a snowcrested ridge. 'Not much further, and we will find them. Branoc is good. I trust him with my life.'

The land became harsher, bleaker. The rolling moorland with its russet softness was giving way to more rock and ridge, black peaks rising, land of crag and corrie, scaur and scaup. Crossing a wide scree slope, one of the ponies stumbled and then regained its footing, sending a glidder of stones to the valley bottom. Marcus cautioned his men to take it steady. The very next day, the same thing happened. This time, the pony fell back heavily on its hind leg, and within minutes was lame. Marcus stopped and examined it, and shook his head. They roped the animal down and butchered it, and ate it that evening in the marching camp. Its rider got none, and had to walk thereafter.

A day later, they saw a huddle of naked corpses in a ravine below them. Branoc cantered off, and came back looking grim.

'The trail has changed,' he said. He sat his horse and pondered awhile. At last he said, 'We will go another way. There is a village I know.'

They came at evening to a village in a deep, narrow valley, shadowed perpetually by the ring of mountains that encircled it. They barely recognised it as a village, for it was no more than a huddle of mud-daubed huts crouched within a thorn hedge and ditch. Like a huddle of herd animals, crouched and passively waiting for the hot stench of the predator passing by. Prowling with dripping flews, out there beyond the brake. And then his silent pounce.

Branoc indicated to them to stop, and then rode on in. A few minutes later he rode back.

'I know where your father is,' he said. He couldn't even bear to use the word 'guardian'.

'He's alive?'

'Yes, he is.'

'Well, that's good, isn't it?'

'No,' said Branoc. 'It is not good.'

'What do you mean?'

Branoc's horse whinnied under him. He looked down, and then up at Marcus again. 'We stay here the night. You will hear.'

CHAPTER NINETEEN

Marcus sat in the largest hut in the centre of the village. The equivalent, he thought sourly, of the Roman Basilica. Here was where village politics took place. A peat fire smouldered in the middle of the hut and the smoke ebbed slowly through a ragged hole in the roof. But not as fast as the peat fire smouldered. The hut was thick with smoke.

With Marcus sat Julia, Milo, Branoc, and an aged man with long, straggly grey hair, naked to the waist, writhled dugs, his belly a little sagging mound over his leather breeches. In the shadows beyond, a woman stirred a steaming vat of fermented barley broth and handed them bowls of it at regular intervals. It tasted quite disgusting but it warmed their bones.

Branoc translated as the old man spoke.

'Young men from a village only some valleys away from here,' said the old man, 'they took the Iron Hat and his party. Other Iron Hats had given them gold to do that thing. They were working as slaves for the Iron Hats. Now they are dead.' The old man smiled. His teeth were yellow and wolvish. Julia thought he looked quite horrible, but his eyes had a gleam that held her attention.

'What happened?' urged Marcus. The old man was in no hurry. He picked at his fingernails, sipped his bowl of barley broth, smacked his lips. Eventually he resumed the story.

'The young men from this other village, some Iron Hats

gave them gold to raid these other Iron Hats, among them your father. They told them to take them well away and then kill them. But as they rode away, over the mountains, full of glee that they were rich and had pockets full of gold, they had the misfortune to be set upon in their turn, by a war-party from quite another tribe.'

Marcus held his breath. He remembered the scene of carnage, all those years ago, in a place called Bran's Cauldron. The old man nodded at Marcus. He seemed to sense what he was thinking. 'Yes,' he said softly. 'That tribe whose name we do not even care to mention, that tribe from the Black Hills and the Western Islands, they have come back. They kill our sheep, our horses, they kill anything. They kill the red deer for pleasure, and leave a herd rotting on the hillside. They kill as a wildcat kills the baby birds in the nest, for the sheer joy of killing. They killed all the young men from the other tribe who had taken gold from the Iron Hats.' He spat. 'That was a good riddance. They had sold themselves as slaves, not warriors, and they deserved to die. Besides, they were not of our tribe.' He paused. 'But the mighty man whom they had kidnapped – his body was not among the corpses. That tribe – the Attacotti if they must be mentioned, the goddess cleanse my tongue – they have taken him alive.'

'Why would they do that?' It was Julia who asked.

The old man glowered at her briefly, angered that a woman should speak to him. But then the ways of the Iron Hats were strange. He sighed, and deigned to reply to her. She was young and beautiful, after all.

When the old man had finished speaking, Marcus put his hand out to stop Branoc from translating. His heart felt like lead. Something was terribly wrong. All the evil in the world was concentrated in this hut, like the peatsmoke, a miasma you could not see through or shine a light through or fight against . . . Human evil was infinite, and human strength to fight it pitifully weak. He beckoned Branoc to follow him outside. Milo went with them. Julia rose to go too, but

Marcus turned and said harshly to her, 'No, you stay here.'

Julia sank back down on the ground. She wanted to hear and not to hear. How she hated this country already. How she longed for . . . But no. Lucius was all that mattered. They would bring him back alive or die in the attempt.

A little while later, Branoc came back alone.

He shook his head and knelt down beside the girl. He felt his heart might break, for it was her blood relation, not his brother Marcus'. The man who had been taken by the Attacotti, Lucius he was called – he was her mother's brother. He was her blood. He felt heavy with pity for the girl. How could you tell a girl?

Tonight they would sleep in the village, and tomorrow they would ride back. The pursuit was at an end.

The old man from the village hummed a low song to himself. He closed his eyes and flew into the air and looked down from a great height. He saw many strange things. He hummed his spirit song to himself and rocked gently back and forth and felt the warm glow of the barley broth in his belly and he looked down and saw many wonders and strange things, like an eagle looking down from the air and seeing its own land of wonders beneath it.

He saw two ponies, tied together with a golden chain around their necks, and they slipped and skidded on a scree slope and then both tumbled down in a glidder of stones together to the bottom of the valley and died there, both still linked by that golden chain. But when he flew down closer to them, it seemed as though they had died not of their fall, but of some terrible disease, some fever, for they were both drenched in sweat. And then he saw that, nestled right between them, alive but weeping, crouched a little girl who was hugging a tiny ginger kitten to her breast. And he knew that it was the girl who sat with him now in the hut, the girl who had so insolently spoken to him. And yet his heart went out to her.

He also knew she had the gift. He saw her in another place,

by a small stand of trees in a sunlit valley, reach out and touch her fingertips to a riven treetrunk that was weeping amber resin and the tree shivered and sighed beneath her touch and the wound closed and was healed.

And he saw other signs and wonders, and they made his heart ache and he could not interpret them: he saw blood-red berries withered on the thorn; he saw a white bird in a dark sky; and then a much greater, darker bird, flying low over a forlorn and desolate country, stooping on some terrified creature, and then caught outstretched in a thorn tree, barbed there, wings outstretched, like a criminal. He saw great buildings of stone aflame and he saw crowds panicked and fleeing and he saw multitudes driven like autumn leaves before the wind.

He tried to see the girl again, whom his heart went out to now. But he could not see her. He could not see what lay ahead of her or where she was going.

He opened his eyes.

Julia sat shaking with fear, her hands cupped around the warm bowl of broth, the warmth alcoholic and alien inside her. She wanted to close her eyes too, perhaps hum a song, a lullaby her mother used to sing to her. But the old man, the shaman, kept his eyes open now and fixed on hers and she could not turn away from them. With his eyes fixed on hers, the shaman spoke in his own language to Branoc.

'The man who has been kidnapped by the . . . animals. He is her father?'

'He is her mother's brother,' said Branoc.

The shaman nodded very slowly. 'Then I am very sorry for her.'

There was a long silence filled with meaning. Julia had the strangest feeling that the shaman was somehow communicating with her in the smoky silence of the hut, or reading her mind. It did not feel intrusive. It did not feel like anything at all. But with the warm glow inside her, she gradually began to feel that she did not hate this barbaric country so much after all. Here was strangeness, wildness, yes. But here was adventure too. Here was her adventure, that she had always longed for, read about. Here was something to believe in: to bring Lucius back alive. Suddenly she felt an absolute confidence that they could do so.

The shaman stirred at last and said to Branoc, 'Translate my words to her.'

Branoc nodded.

'It is the Attacotti that now have your mother's brother,' said the shaman. 'I weep for you.'

Julia wanted to interrupt desperately, at first. But she knew that she must not.

The shaman looked into the dim firelight. He said that the Attacotti were not human beings. They were animals in the shape of men.

'We believed that we were the whole human race, my people. There were no others. And when we first encountered others, crossing the great sea, we believed they were animals, not like us. Now we know we were wrong. But about the Attacotti, we were not wrong. They are still not human beings. The Great Mother on the day she made that tribe, she dropped her clay in a bed of evil flowers: nightshade and ivy ... Bracken to a horse. That is what the Attacotti are made of. Poison runs in their veins, snakes nest in their hair. Their nails are claws. They are the neglected offspring, the evil children of the Great Mother. And it delights them to be so. For evil is like a potent drink, and when you drink it at first, you are sickened; but after a while, you desire more. And your appetite for it waxes, and you need more, and then more ...

'And we ourselves, we tribe of Human Beings, we ourselves are afflicted now with the curse of the Attacotti. And the Great Mother has visited us in anger and we do not know how or why and the children and women bewail it nightly. But we grow stronger under it. This is strange.

'There was a man' – the shaman stopped and stirred the fire

at his feet for a while – 'there was a man who rode out one morning on his pony, his young son at his back, his little arms too short still to reach right around his father's waist. The father was taking the boy out to hunt in the hills in the deer-coloured heather in the autumn time. The mother, his wife, had said, "Be careful, be careful of our son, he is our firstborn and our only child." And the man said he would be careful. He had no fear then.

'They had good hunting. They hunted hare and partridge and down by the loch they hunted waterfowl and had a sackful of good meat. On their return they saw and slew a lone deer, and the man dismounted and showed his young son how to bind up the dead deer by its hooves and haul it up by rope over the branches of a pine so that the wolves should not come by it. They could return in a day or two days with a fresh pony and bring it back to the village.

'And when they had done this they remounted as before and turned to ride away, at which the man heard the whistle of an arrow in the air and was afraid, very afraid. He rode away fast but as he rode a second arrow flew and it struck his young son straight in the middle of his back. It struck his young son so hard and straight that it passed through his body and entered into the man's back, and he could do no other but gallop on, blind in his horror, to escape those children of evil who now came out of the forest to shoot at him. And as he rode he felt his dead son pinned to his own back by a single arrow, his son's little head lolling loose like the head of a slain animal bound across a pony's back, and knocking against him as he rode.

'Such horrors you never awaken from.

'When the man had ridden free, he had to twist and thrust his right hand down between his back and his little son's belly and find the arrow shaft and pull the head from his own back and staunch the flow of blood with wool and tight binding. Then he broke the arrow in two and pulled each end from his son's body with a touch as gentle as a mother's. He bound his son's body up in cloth and laid it across his knees and rode on. And he thought his heart would break.

'But when he came into the village, and his wife came running to him, her eyes glad to see him again, and she saw with her own eyes the bundle that lay across that man's lap . . . then.

'Then his heart did break.'

The shaman bowed his head and there was a long silence. Finally he shifted and turned himself around on the dirt floor of the hut. There in the dull firelight, beside his bony white spine, could be seen the ragged edge of an old arrow wound. He turned back to the fire and drank from his bowl. He set it down. His eyes were watery in the dim light.

'Surely grief is great in this world,' he said at last. 'And yet are we to rail at the gods, to blame them? For they made the Attacotti as they are, and we cannot know why. Our eyes are shut to their ways. So should we blame the gods, for making us out of the suffering clay and setting us upon the suffering earth, knowing what our destinies will bring each of us? Are we to wail like children and be forever hating the gods and cursing and bewailing our destinies like children? For does not a mother bring forth her child in a welter of blood, both of them weeping, and she knowing full well what griefs and sufferings and finally death that her child born will have to endure in its life? And so she is, as it were, bestowing these things upon her child? And yet do we say wrong when we say that that mother *loves* her child? Would *die* for it, if she could?'

The shaman nodded into the fire again.

'There was a man who taught me much when I was young. One day we walked out and we came to a young hare pinioned by a younger eagle, who had stooped on it and caught it and now stood staring at it as if stupid, not yet knowing how to kill. The first hare it had ever caught, perhaps. And so the hare was not killed cleanly, as a full-grown eagle would do, but was in agony, stuck to the earth by the eagle's claws, and it screamed. It *screamed*. And I, still a boy then, I turned to the man I was with and asked why the Great Mother did not come and save the poor hare. How could She let the hare suffer so? And the man turned to me and touched my head, and he said that the Great Mother was not in some far distant heaven watching over all. She was here, now. She was with us, suffering. She was in the hare. She was *in the hare's scream.*'

The shaman nodded.

Julia nodded. She no longer thought the shaman looked horrible. She thought that a handful of words from the shaman were worth all the great books in her uncle's library. Worth more, even. There was wisdom here. But it was not Roman wisdom.

He said, or rather sang, in an old, cracked voice,

> *I have been a multitude, a dewdrop in the grass,*
> *I have been a warrior, an eagle on its nest,*
> *I have been a maiden, I have been a fool,*
> *And a thousand thousand heads have lain upon my breast.*

He smiled and said, 'All of us are stories. And when the tale of the world is done and the book of the world is rolled up end to end and burned in the fire of the last days, then each of us will live on for all eternity as a story. You will live in other people's lives, and other people will live in yours.'

She wanted to speak to him, somehow, to tell him . . . but she was tongue-tied. But there was no need. The shaman saw her eyes shining with something unexpressed, and reached out and grasped her wrist and said to her softly, 'Few words and simple are ever needed. And often, none at all.' He smiled. 'You have listened well.' And then he sprang to his feet with astonishing agility, and was gone.

She could never have explained why but Julia slept well that night. She felt comfortable, at last, with the idea that her uncle had always taught her: Providence. What would happen would happen, and nobody could change it. It was for the best. It was a mystery, but what was destined was right. Whatever was wrong would come right, and all would come round again. Metempsychosis, that was what the shaman's song had intimated: the same as the Pythagoreans believed. All had been and all would come again. Nothing endured except change. But all would be well.

Marcus did not sleep well. He dreamed of a bleeding bird. He awoke in a sweat, colder under his blankets than he had felt all day in the saddle in the cutting wind. All that Branoc had told him came back to him. The reasons for Lucius' capture. What lay ahead for him – if it had not happened already. The Rite of Blood Eagle.

They would take him, the just man, the baffled, bewildered victim. The noble, the incorruptible. They would take him and lay him out naked upon a stone, and slice him open from between the ribs down to his groin, and they would take out his intestines and lay them outspread upon the stone at his sides, so that he looked like a great red outstretched bird. When at last he died – and it could take a full day for a man to die this way – they would eat him. He was a mighty man of the tribe of the Iron Hats, and eating him would bestow power.

Marcus prayed that it had happened already. When they came back to London, they would set up the finest memorial to Lucius that money could buy. Then he would find out who had plotted his guardian's kidnap by the allied tribes, and kill them.

It was not until they crested the ridge south of the village and had begun to head back down the slope to the valley beyond, that Julia broke from the column and galloped to the front where Milo, Marcus and Branoc rode three abreast.

'Where are we going?' she asked.

Marcus raised his hand and the column ground to a halt.

'Back to the Wall,' he said.

'What do you mean?'

'What I say. The pursuit is over. I thought you understood that. When we arrive back in London, we will – '

'When we arrive back in London, we will have Lucius riding with us!' cried Julia, suddenly furious. She steadied herself with her fists on her horse's back, sitting high, her cheeks hectic, livid. She coughed harshly, buried her head, coughed again, said, 'I do not understand, no. You said you know where they are headed. You know the tribe and everything.'

Marcus shook his head wearily. 'You have understood nothing. Lucius is almost certainly dead already. The tribe will have taken him many miles north, days riding away, into territory that we know nothing of. Perhaps even beyond the old Wall of Antoninus, or west to the islands. We would have no chance. And *don't* starting shrieking about cowardice either,' he said, growing angry himself now. 'I am not marching a column of sixty good legionaries into dangerous alien territory to look for anyone, without a hope of finding them.'

'We will find him,' said Julia. She spoke more quietly.

'Not even Branoc could track them,' said Marcus. 'How would we find them?'

'Branoc,' said Julia. 'Could you track them?'

Branoc shrugged. 'Depends on the weather,' he said. 'And if we pick up their trail.'

'Well,' said Julia, looking back at Marcus again. 'We can try, can't we?'

Marcus ignored her. 'Ride on!' he called.

Julia stood in their way, wrenching her horse furiously to left and to right. 'We are not riding on anywhere until we have rescued Lucius! How dare you think of anything else!'

'I am the commander of this column, and I shall think what

310

I like. You have no idea what it will be like further into this wilderness, in the depths of winter. Look around you! Our mission is at an end. Now get back in line.'

Julia lowered her voice and said softly to him, 'Somewhere out there, Marcus, my uncle – *your guardian* – is still alive. And he is going to be killed. He who took you in and cared for you and raised you as his own son – you are going to abandon him. What kind of a son are you?'

At last she had hit home. Marcus lowered his head and gritted his teeth. God *damn* her. He could feel Milo looking at him too. He glanced sideways at him and looked questioningly. Milo shrugged. 'We could go on,' he growled. 'The weather will only get worse, and there aren't enough of us even to make a century. But we could go on.'

Marcus turned his horse round and considered. And then he did a most unusual thing. Unprecedented, possibly, in the annals of Roman military history. He rode back along the column and asked his men. He told them the situation, and said that there was every chance they would be butchered on some desolate hillside, dying unknown and unmourned by any relative. Or they might just find the Praepositus, and come back alive.

Mus spoke up from near the van. 'I'm coming back alive,' he said. 'But I'll teach those barbarians a lesson first.'

And that was the general consensus. The men weren't exactly relaxed about the prospect of heading further north, but for the time being, they could live with it. They would go on a while longer.

Marcus rode back to the head of the column and ordered it around. They rode north.

Julia returned to her place in the centre.

They rode on into the vast, empty, bone-chilling Caledonian wilderness.

They came one day to a rolling moorland crossed with the

311

remains of a turf dyke. Marcus rode up onto it and looked back.

'The Wall of Antoninus,' he said. 'What's left of it.'

He rode on down the other side, and they followed him. It crossed the minds of some of them that one day, the great Northern Wall of Hadrian might also be no more than a turf mound, and people would ride across it and barely notice that it was there. Empires, like people, are mortal.

Once, and once only, the Roman army had marched beyond this northern outpost. Back in the first century AD, an army had marched up the east coast and defeated a Caledonian alliance at a place called Mons Graupius. But that was long ago. The land was different now. The tribes were different. Roman ambitions were different. Everything was different.

And then Branoc called out. 'Here they are!'

Marcus spurred over to him. Branoc indicated a churned patch of ground at the foot of the dyke. 'This is the trail?' he said, with rising excitement.

Branoc nodded.

'How do you know?'

'The speed they are going, how long ago, the shape of them, the number of them.'

Marcus was baffled. 'And how many are there?'

'Perhaps a hundred or more. Riding ragged, the way they do.'

Marcus nodded grimly. 'God be with us,' he said. 'Ride on.'

The news spread back through the column that they were on the trail.

Julia felt her heart burning. Now they were quite beyond the reach of law and reason, into the wilderness, the barren lands. No sombre magistrate would come here and distinguish the just from the unjust, award punishments, stripes, death . . . Here was no rule of Rome. Here was only self-reliance, the self stripped bare, exhilarating, dangerous. She had never felt such exhilaration. Her heart burned. Her lungs burned. Her cheeks flushed red. She would prove herself the equal of any of them. She knew that she could.

They came to a dark pine forest that lay thickly across the valley ahead of them. Marcus held up his hand and hesitated.

'Never hesitate, Optio,' said Milo at his side.

But Marcus did hesitate, and turned in his saddle and scanned the high peaks all around. It was a hard one. The wind and the sleet driving in from the north-west would be bitter up on the peaks, and the traverse much longer. On the other hand, it was wide open country. The dark forest ahead, on the other hand, put Marcus uncomfortably in mind of Varus and his three legions, ambushed and massacred to a man in the mist and darkness of the German forests.

But Milo was right. A commander should never hesitate.

He raised his hand. 'Ride on,' he said.

The forest was as dark as he had imagined. The troops hated it, huddled close, kept their left hands whiteknuckled on the reins, their right hands on the hilts of their swords. They prayed to their gods or whatever gods might be. They muttered mantras of protection. They rode fast. But the forest was endless, the track heavy with mud beneath the thin scattering of pine needles, and their progress was slow. The forest watched them silently as they passed. No birds sang. Only the shuck and sigh of their ponies' hooves in the glutinous black mud.

It was Mus who heard them first, riding in the van. But glancing back, he realised he should have heard them earlier. The two last outriders at the back of the column behind him, raw recruits, redfaced boys, were gone. He called out and the column halted. Marcus turned and rode back past the column to Mus, the low dry branches of the pines whipping his bent face as he passed.

'Two men down, sir,' was all Mus said.

Together they scanned the forest, the dark pines and the darker emptiness between. The stillness was terrifying.

Marcus wanted to shout out a challenge, to hear his own voice echoing among the trees, to break the killing silence, to bring life, anything. Rather than this watching, waiting death. But there was nothing.

He called another man back to ride with Mus at the rear. 'And if you see anything, hear anything,' he said, 'scream like a woman.'

He rode back up the column and took his place beside Milo. Milo said nothing. They rode on.

They were nearly out of the forest, he was sure. He thought he could see light ahead. But maybe it was only a mirage. The cool waters appearing on the desert horizon to the man dying of thirst. They should have taken the heights. Marcus speeded them up. The sooner they were out of this accursed forest . . .

At first he thought the sound was the whistling of an arrow and flinched downward. Then he realised it was the whipping of a rope. Riding along the track, they had cut a thin tripline without noticing it, and now something came crashing down through the trees just in front of them. The needles showered around them like dry rain, then slowed and stopped. They blinked their eyes. In front of them, suspended just above the ground by their ankles, hung two naked bodies. The two lost soldiers, he knew, even though their heads were gone. Their bellies had been ripped open and their intestines hung about them in grey and glistening coils.

'Do not hesitate now, Optio,' hissed Milo so that no one else could hear.

With a great effort of will, Marcus shook the horror from him and rode forward. He slashed through the ropes from which the two obscene and headless corpses hung. They slumped into the mud. Marcus dismounted and walked over to them. There was every chance that this was more than mere mockery, that this was a trap, and dismounting to pay their respects was just what the tribesmen wanted. But strangely, Marcus felt that he didn't care. Let them come. He would kill them and then be killed. He was resigned to whatever might come.

He hauled the two bodies to the side of the track and rolled them over into the ditch. He took a handful of pine needles and scattered them over the two white bodies, their damp skin like the skin of mushrooms in the dark forest. Their necks gaping and obscene. And then he spoke loudly, so that all the column could hear, and without a hint of hesitation. He blessed the souls of the two soldiers and prayed that their journey to the Otherworld was safe. Then he remounted and raised his hand.

They rode on.

At last they emerged from the horror of the forest. It was past noon and the day was already darkening. They rode out into a wide plain that led up to a high plateau. They needed cover before nightfall, so Marcus ordered them into a rapid trot. They must find somewhere that was sheltered and defensible.

Julia broke from the column and cantered forward to ride alongside Marcus.

He spoke before she could. 'You are not to blame,' he said rapidly. 'They were soldiers. It goes with the job. If anything, it will spur the rest of the men on. Revenge is as good as the promise of gold to a soldier.'

'But they were already dead, weren't they? I mean, before they did – *that* to them?'

Marcus realised that she was close to tears, stricken with guilt, and no doubt as afraid as the rest of them. He couldn't help himself. He looked at her almost with hatred, and was unable to reply. Then she knew. She bent her head. When she looked up again he was ignoring her, looking straight in front of him. Now there was something obsessive, relentless, cruel in his determination to pursue the war-party. She knew there was nothing more she could say. She rode back and joined the column.

After they had been riding some time, they came to the head of a deep, narrow valley. Halfway down there was a steep scree slope and above it, what looked like caves carved out of the granite sides. They began to make their way down.

Branoc said, 'Everything that the Attacotti do, they do for their own enjoyment.'

'What do you mean?'

'They will do nothing unless it amuses them. It depends on how they feel. This is why they are so dangerous. It is impossible to say or to know if they will fight bravely or not. Sometimes they are more cowardly than sheep, they run off wailing like girls. Sometimes they will fight in open battle, and seem to be utterly heedless of death. In general, they will not fight us in open battle unless they are many more. If they are only a hundred, I do not think they will attack us. They will rather pick us off in the darkness of the night or the forest. You must not fear them. They are neither cowards nor brave, but they are madmen.'

The valley was a good place, with two large caves set into the cliffs and the steep scree making sudden attack impossible. They dragged brushwood up to the mouths of the caves and lit fires and cooked meat and made barley broth. It was the first hot food they had had for three days. The caves warmed well and the soldiers slept huddled together. A dozen stayed on watch, looking over the ponies without which they would be lost indeed.

Julia had a little recess of her own, screened by a horse-blanket. 'Fit for a princess,' said Marcus.

He sat at the fire with Branoc and Milo and Mus.

'How much further will we need to ride?' asked Marcus.

'As far as they want us to,' Branoc shrugged. 'They are setting us a deliberate trail, for their own amusement. But they will come to regret it. They will come to fear us, if we show no fear. They are sheep.'

'Sheep with big fuckin' teeth,' rumbled Mus.

They almost laughed.

Mus and Branoc turned in to sleep. Marcus and Milo sat late. Their eyelids were dropping but they could not sleep.

'What do you think, Milo?' Marcus asked him. 'Is the Lord Mithras with us?'

He meant it jovially but Milo did not take it that way. He stared into the fire for a long time and when at last he spoke, it was not with words that Marcus had expected.

He said that in truth, he knew nothing of the Lord Mithras, or whether he was alive or dead. He said that in all his life, he had only known Heaven to be deaf or capricious, to be feared or worshipped, but that a man would find no love or safety there. There is no love in the universe, he said.

'The gods are harsh and harsh is the gods' will, their realm is power, not love, and in the end it is death and destruction for us all. And I say yes to it. If that is how it is, then I say yes. I am true to my creed and my comrades, and that is all. And when at last the world goes down in flames, as it surely will, as all men and all worlds must, then I will stand with my comrades shoulder to shoulder against that evil day and fight until my strength is gone. And then I shall die knowing I have been true to myself, and to the hard world that made me.'

He set down his bowl. 'There,' he said. 'Now I can sleep.'

Marcus sat late, his eyelids dropping, and could not sleep.

A while later, he was aware of another presence beside him. Perhaps he had been asleep after all. It was Julia. He realised how his head ached.

'Tired, soldier?' she whispered.

'A little weary, yes.'

'You should get some sleep.'

'I should.'

There was a silence between them, but there was nothing awkward in it. The fire crackled and their wind-burned faces glowed.

'He is still alive,' she said. 'I know he is.'

Marcus nodded. 'I know it too. They are using him as bait.'

Another long silence. Finally she said, 'Do you remember, when we were young—'

He interrupted her. 'I remember it all.' He looked at her.

'The sun shone a lot then. In fact, it shone all the time, as I recall. When we were together.'

'It didn't shine the day Lucius beat us.' She frowned. 'I can't remember if it shone the day you went away.'

'It didn't,' he said.

After a while she said, 'Do you remember the night we sneaked out and sat on the harbourside down at the port, and talked about all the places we would go when we were older?'

Suddenly he looked animated, his eyes shone. 'Yes,' he said. 'And the time we climbed right up on the roof of that temple, on the wooden scaffolding. Lucius would have *killed* us if he'd ever discovered that!'

'And the time . . .'

They remembered so many days, so many childhood years. Escapades in the bustling streets of London, night adventures, the sundrenched meadows of the Cotswolds, Bricca's unintentional jokes, snuffling, bearded Hermogenes, Julia's first pony, Ahenobarbus, lying all one afternoon by the little river that lay below the villa in the country, their cool feet trailing in the clear water.

'When this is over,' Marcus said at last, 'I think we deserve a long time doing nothing in the Cotswolds.'

'Hm,' she said dreamily. 'Sunshine. *Food*.'

'Lucius pacing about,' he said.

'That's it exactly,' she said. 'Lucius pacing about. *Worrying*.'

They talked a lot more. Often they started saying, 'When this is over . . .' There was much to do and enjoy, when this was over. This nightmare.

Finally she stood and said she must go back to her bed. 'Well, my clump of heather and my blanket, anyway.' She stooped and kissed him just as he turned his head, so she kissed him first on the forehead, and then fleetingly on the lips. Then she was gone.

His lips tingled. He smiled softly to himself. His headache eased.

He sat a while longer in a strange reverie, thinking only of her. Then he heard a noise close behind him. He looked around and there was the deaf and dumb slave, Cennla, on all four knees and crawling towards him. Marcus stared at him and said nothing. When he knew that he had been seen, Cennla stopped and grinned and then turned and crawled slowly back into his corner. Not a word or a sign passed between them.

Marcus turned back to the fire and pulled his blanket tighter around him.

CHAPTER TWENTY

The first thing they saw the next day when they rode out, was two tribesmen sitting their ponies on a distant ridge, spears held above their heads in defiance. Then they turned their ponies and vanished down the far side of the ridge.

A few miles later, they came to a stunted hawthorn in a gully, the last haws dark red now and rotten on the thorn. Impaled on the thorns and among the tattered branches were human hands, raggedly severed at the wrist. They stopped and stared, unable to comprehend this new atrocity. Finally, Marcus spurred forward and examined the hands. Marmoreal white, unreal, a ragged ribbon of blood and skin around each wrist. Then he saw the hand in the centre of the collection, and turned away, and ordered his column to ride on without delay.

He kept it to himself. He could not tell her. He could not tell her that the hand at the centre of the mandala of severed hands wore a fine silver signet ring on its little finger.

She did not see the hand. But she saw the determination in his face, and loved him for it. She had loved him before, but now she admitted it to herself. She loved him, and first acknowledged it. Not so much his power, his command, his pensive, world-weary features so much older than his years. Not so much his deep sorrow or his abiding courage, though these she loved as well. What she loved was not his strong, soldierly single-mindedness, but something more complex. It was that his mind was torn. It was the sense of his inner battle, between his loyalty to his men, and to Lucius, and to her. The struggle in his soul. It was not his scars that she loved. It was the moral struggle within him, and his resolution in spite of it, that she loved above all.

They were crossing a high plateau when, through watery eyes, Marcus thought he could see a circle of figures up ahead, in the mist. He stopped and Milo reined beside him.

'Camp there?'

Marcus then realised what he meant. They were not men, but stones. One of those eerie stone circles that the Celts or their forefathers had built long since, high in the mountains, to worship whatever gods they worshipped.

He led his men into the circle, and ordered them to dismount. The ponies stamped and champed their bits and steamed gently in the low sunlight. The sun was riding down the sky and bleeding red light into the hazy winter horizon. There might be an hour of daylight left, no more. This would be the place for tonight.

The men brought up bundles of thorn and stacked them between the stones to a height of six feet. They added what defences they had outside the circle – caltrops, a bundle of sharpened stakes. Though if it came to it, the best defence was the same as always, the Empire over: a strong right arm, and stab, don't slash.

They heard them first. A low, animal howl from beyond the red horizon. At first Marcus thought of desert jackals, but he knew at once what it foreboded. The Attacotti were coming. He set the men around the perimeter of the circle, and ordered Julia to take cover among the tethered ponies. He wanted so much to stay with her, to make her survival his one duty, but his command was needed. He set four men to guard her with their lives.

The animal music grew louder and then yowling, whooping, screaming, they came riding out of the mist and across the plain. They erupted in a thunder of hooves and drums, spears held aloft over their heads, arrows already notched to bowstrings. They wore next to nothing, and what they wore was purely decorative: scars and weals of blue paint, feathers and furs, the severed heads of their enemies, or anyone else they had happened upon.

The Iron Hats had taken up residence in the sacrificial circle, which amused them no end. They could already feel their victims' warm blood spilling over the backs of their hands, its rich metallic tang on their tongues.

Marcus waited until the horde was within thirty yards. One of the galloping ponies hit a caltrop and went down screaming but the rest came on. The first volley of Roman javelins struck them hard, and the second volley, at no more than ten yards distance, struck them harder still. When they came to the thorn and stone barrier, they were more puzzled than anything. They were unaccustomed to fighting against a force in fixed defence. Some of them began to gallop round the circle, letting off arrows as they rode. Others tried to jump the wall but their ponies were poor jumpers. One tribesman managed to straddle his mount halfway across a heap of thorn, and was rolling into the circle when he was promptly beheaded by a single blow from Mus.

Without archers, the Romans could do little but defend their boundary. However, any tribesman foolhardy enough to dismount and try to breach the wall was promptly skewered by the regimented thrusting of hard swords. If any gaps appeared in the wall, they were filled by a shield and a legionary, immovable as a stone. Finally the Attacotti drew off, howling with rage and frustration, and vanished as quickly as they had come over the horizon.

Marcus wanted to say, 'That wasn't so bad,' but restrained himself.

Sensing too much elation, Branoc said, 'They'll be back.'

☆ ☆ ☆

They were back sooner than expected, and with far more strategy.

Riding out of the camp the next day with outriders posted well ahead and to the sides, the column left the high plateau and came to mountain country again.

They were riding up a narrow valley, a mere gully, through thick snow, the column orderly and watchful, when, rounding a narrow defile between two high rocks, passing only two abreast, Marcus saw the sprawled, headless bodies of two of his outriders in the snow. Up ahead sat the Attacot war-party, not three hundred yards away, closing the gully, sitting their horses, waiting patiently. Marcus realised his mistake immediately.

'Hell,' breathed Milo at his side.

The tribesmen were on higher ground. The ground between them was hard and fast. And there were more than a hundred of them. More like two hundred. They bristled with spears, ready and waiting. When they saw the first Iron Hats appear round the corner, some of them grinned and hallooed.

Marcus and Milo reined in.

'Hell,' agreed Marcus. He wondered if Lucius was there in the party somewhere, roped to a pony, a prize trophy. But he could see nothing.

There was an eerie stand-off.

There were two choices: to mount a charge, uphill, over two hundred yards, against a party two, perhaps three times their size; or to turn and retreat downhill, backs bare and vulnerable.

Either choice stank.

The only other option was to sit and fight here – a choice rapidly lost to them when they saw Attacot bowmen crawling up on the heights above the gully.

'Allow me?' said Milo.

Marcus shrugged.

Milo turned and called out for Mus. Mus came trotting up to the front.

'You and me, soldier,' he said. 'Hold this little gap no trouble, eh?'

Mus just grinned.

'That's not a choice,' snapped Marcus, just as an arrow clattered into the bare rock above his head and fell.

'It's the only choice,' said Milo. 'We hold them while you turn tail and fuck off as fast as you can. As soon as you're out on the plateau, we'll join you.'

'And how will you mange that, pray?' said Marcus with angry sarcasm.

Another arrow winged its way past them, missing Mus by inches. He reined his pony sideways and muttered, 'Fuck a duck.'

'It really is time to decide quite quickly,' said Milo.

'Damn you.' Marcus wheeled his pony. 'Damn you, Centurion.'

Milo grinned and hefted his shield high on his shoulder.

Marcus ordered the rest of the column to turn and retreat out of the gully.

The moment they were moving, the Attacotti charged.

Milo and Mus squeezed two abreast, just ahead of the narrowest part of the defile, and swung their swords in readiness.

'Well, Centurion,' said Mus affably.

'Well, soldier,' said Milo. 'We've got about a hundred each, I should say.'

'I should say so too,' agreed Mus. 'Piece of piss.'

A well-aimed arrow slammed into Milo's shield and lodged there. Mus reached up and snapped off the haft for him.

'Not counting the archers, of course,' added Milo.

'Archers,' snorted Mus. 'Fuckin' nancies, archers are.'

Milo grinned.

Here they come now.

Come on then, you hairy Celtic bastards.
'Fuckin' *barbarians*!' roared Mus.

Marcus galloped his men up out of the valley and onto the plateau, and they cut down every archer they found at full gallop, not slowing for an instant. Then they rode to the lip of the valley where they dismounted and hurled their javelins down into the thick of the Attacot pack. The instant the tribesmen knew they had lost the high ground, they lost heart, and they turned and fled in a confused mêlée. Many of them lay dead or wounded across the floor of the valley. They piled up thickly at the narrow defile. They piled up thickly where two bloodied Roman soldiers still stood, battered but unbowed, their horses killed beneath them.

Marcus called down to them. They looked up and grinned. They looked quite tired.

Julia bandaged Milo's arm for him in thick linen bandaging. He looked down at her handiwork and was impressed. 'Maybe it wasn't such a damn fool idea to bring you after all,' he muttered. He lifted his arm. 'Feels OK, that does.'

Julia smiled. Praise indeed.

They had had to abandon some of the baggage to free up two ponies for Milo and Mus to ride on. This second skirmish had emboldened the column still further. They felt they had the tribesmen on the run now. Running scared.

For a while they gave chase, but the Attacotti knew the country and outpaced them. At evening they came to a lakeside and set up camp there. Julia bathed Milo and Mus' wounds again and the two soldiers were startled to feel their wounds healing already.

The next morning they rode on, deeper into the mountain wilderness and the barren wasteland. The world had grown weird around them, the landscape alien and beyond all imagining. They ascended mountain ranges and traversed saddles and came down scree slopes, or padded softly through the blanket bogs of the sodden valleys, Branoc's eyes on the trail with ceaseless vigilance. One of the hundred and fifty or so of the Attacotti's ponies was riding lame, favouring its left foreleg and barely imprinting the right in the soft ground. He could distinguish this from all the other hoofprints and follow it as clearly as a red thread or a trail of rowanberries in the snow. And there were other signs too: dropped feathers, tufts of horsehair caught on thorns, a spatter of blood on a pale grey rock, haunting and inexplicable. They came to where a deer lay recently slain beside the trail, part butchered but left with good meat still on its shoulders, a little ragged from the beaks of birds but substantial nevertheless.

'Seems a shame to waste it,' said Marcus.

Branoc grinned and shook his head. 'The Attacotti don't leave gifts for their enemies,' he said. 'Eat that and you'll soon be as dead as the deer.'

'Ah.' Marcus nodded, and they rode on.

They rode across a high moorland valley surrounded by ominous mountains as black as basalt, louring over them and watching their progress with ancient indifference. The rain swept across the moor almost horizontal and penetrated through their layers of leather and wool and chilled them to the bone with a chill like fear. Then the wind chilled further and within seconds they were riding through a blizzard and the need for shelter was desperate. Marcus turned back and rode to Julia's windward side, and told her, shouting, that they would soon find shelter. She kept her head down and did not reply.

He sent outriders to scour the terrain for shelter, for caves or a rockfall affording a windbreak, anything. They searched for half an hour but found nothing but mountains massive and unriven, and no shelter from the storm. Marcus rode closer to Julia and they rode on.

By evening the wind had dropped and the snow fell softly from the darkening sky. They dropped down from the high valley and there beside a highland stream they found shelter of sorts in among a stand of downy birch trees, interspersed with the occasional rowan. Branoc was particularly happy to sleep beneath a rowan. The magical tree that in his language they called witchwood. He knew in his bones then that they were safe from attack here. No tribesman would attack them in the heart of a witches' wood.

But he had not reckoned on attack from within the camp.

Near to dawn, Cennla crept out from under his blankets, took his knife and clamped it between his teeth and began the long serpent crawl through the camp to the tent where his enemy slept. Soft snow was still falling. The guards on watch saw nothing, their attention all turned outwards. He came to the officers' tent, unlaced the leather flap and peered inside. Milo and Marcus both slept. He leaned forward, placed his left hand firmly on the ground, and raised his right hand high to his shoulder to punch it down and drive the blade of the knife deep into his enemy's throat. But as it descended, something stopped him. Iron fingers clamped around his fingers and squeezed so tightly that he dropped the dagger. Milo sat up abruptly, laid his other hand across the back of Cennla's elbow, snapped his forearm back against it and broke his arm. It was Cennla's silent writhings that awoke Marcus.

'Wha' happen?' he mumbled.

'We have a traitor in our midst,' said Milo.

Milo was all for hanging Cennla from the nearest tree at first light. Marcus stared at the silent slave, now bound up and motionless in thick rope, his right arm dangling and useless. He agreed.

Julia, however, emerging from her tent hectic-eyed, would have none of it.

327

'Lady, with all respect, he just tried to kill our commanding officer,' said Milo.

Julia looked baffled. Cennla avoided her eye. She wondered about him and tried to avoid thinking back to the time he had tried to kiss her. The look he had given her, and once or twice, to her amusement, the looks he had given Marcus. Was it possible? She shook her head. 'Untie him.' No one moved. 'Untie him! He is *my* slave, *my* property!'

Marcus sighed. 'Untie him.'

They spun Cennla round like an unwound bobbin, ripping the rope from around him. As the tail of the rope flicked free, something else followed. A scrap of paper fell from his tunic. Marcus scooped it up and read it. 'Ah,' he said. He handed it to Julia.

She read the paper. There were two people's handwriting on it, the first of which she recognised as Cennla's. Writing that she herself had taught him. She read, *'I will go north with my mistress Julia and the soldier. I will kill the soldier Marcus if I can. He is my enemy.'* Another hand had written, *'A hundred solidi if you succeed. A beating if you fail.'* Julia looked up.

'A hundred solidi?' mused Marcus. 'I'm worth at least a thousand.'

'Who was paying you?' demanded Milo. Cennla said nothing. Milo stepped forward and dealt him a ferocious backhander across his bowed face.

'Enough!' said Julia. She added acidly, 'It is a little pointless questioning a dumb slave, don't you think?' She made Cennla raise his head and then signalled to him for some time. There was a long pause, and then Cennla signalled back with his left hand. Julia thought about this for a while, and then turned.

'He says someone called Paulus Catena was paying him.'

Milo snorted. 'Does a bronze horse fart? Does a slave tell the truth?'

'This one does.'

'I know Catena,' said Marcus. 'I came across him in Syria: the Emperor's enforcer. He's in London now. He's not a good man.'

Milo was not giving up on Cennla. 'He's just tried to kill our commanding officer in his bed, and you're telling me he's trustworthy?'

'I am.' Julia stowed it in the folds of her dress. 'You can let him go.'

'But why would Catena want me dead?' Marcus was wondering aloud. 'I mean, I'm very flattered and all that, but – '

'There's some wider conspiracy going on,' said Julia.

'It seems to me,' said Branoc, stepping up behind them, 'that someone is trying to wipe out your family entirely. The other tribe that first took your father, they were paid to do so. Gold crossed their palms. Now this slave is paid more gold to kill you. It is the same thing.'

Marcus nodded slowly. 'This won't be over when we get back to London,' he said. 'It'll just be beginning.' He looked again at Cennla, feeling suddenly weary. 'Let him go.'

Milo objected violently, but he said nothing. Julia made some more signs to Cennla. She wondered fleetingly if it wasn't crueller to send him off into the snow, alone and unarmed, than let him be executed here. But she could not allow that. It was her only choice. Cennla gazed at her awhile, and Marcus realised with a sudden stab of feeling what that gaze said. Then he made three brief signs to her. Then he bowed his head and walked away up beside the mountain stream with his right arm hanging loose at his side, with a light flurry of snow falling again, and thickening as he ascended higher up the valley and above the treeline, the snow drawing in and closing around him like a drawn veil and his footfalls muffled and silent in the deepening snow, as silent as his world had always been.

They watched until he had gone and then they decamped and mounted up and rode on.

☆ ☆ ☆

They crossed a desolate plain where the heavy grey sky over their heads suddenly came alive with a skein of wild geese. Later, standing alone and miles from its herd, like a creature from heraldry, like a statue, they saw a great white auroch amid a pile of broken rocks on a mountainside, with an arrow buried deep in its withers. Deranged with the pain and yet motionless, no blood staining its fine white pelt, the auroch stood bellowing with rage at the cold mountains around, at cold Heaven itself, and Heaven echoed back its bellowing of pain and nothing changed.

It occurred to Marcus that here was good meat to have. But Branoc shook his head.

'Disregard it,' he said. 'It is not any more in nature.'

Branoc's words made no sense, but they were enough. They passed the dying auroch and rode on with its bellowing still sounding in their ears.

The sky overhead was a darkening grey, a beaten iron shield, but along the horizon was a seam of silver light that seemed to seep in from an enchanted world beyond, as if they rode under a giant lid, claustrophobic, shut off from grace. Their fear grew continually, and their courage grew to meet it. All of them were quite prepared to die, half-expected it now. But they would go down fighting, in this half-hell.

In the centre of the valley they saw a single stunted hawthorn tree. Everything was alone here, solitude's own domain. Everything stood alone under the cold Heaven, and it was only alone that you could learn to survive. You survived inside.

They dreaded coming to the thorn and finding fresh tokens of cruelty, more severed hands or human remains half-eaten or worse. But instead there was a barbaric beauty to the buzzard that hung there, long since dead, its wings outstretched. They guessed that it must have stooped upon an animal or a small bird, and crashed with wings outstretched into the thorn and impaled itself there, crucified like a criminal of the wilderness.

330

If not an emblem of the bird's own self-destroying speed then it must be a tribal totem, a ferocious forebear of the Christians' own crucified god. They did not and could not know. Ignorance and fear preyed on them.

At nighttime in the caves or in the rare stands of trees in the steep valleys, by the white waterfalls, by firelight, they shared out their ignorance and fear among themselves, and diluted them with comradeship. If they died, they would die together, shoulder to shoulder. Marcus and Julia sat together long into the night and said little. They remembered their childhood together, always sunlit as Marcus said, and they thought that their childhood had been lived out not just in another place than this, but in another world entirely. In a world of grace. That enchanted world beyond the glowering horizon, from where the silver light came.

They said little, and what they said was always prefaced with, 'When this is over . . .'

At last they felt the land descending from the mountain country to the sea, and they could smell the salt and taste it on their chapped and stinging lips. They knew they were nearly there now and there would be no more baffling atrocities, no more slaughtered villages that marked the long, tormenting retreat of the Attacotti back to their own country. They were nearly upon the killers.

They rode down and emerged suddenly onto a sandy shore where the light was hard and silver and the sky vast and the seabirds cried and rode the wind with delirious freedom. They rode along the shoreline for some way and at last they saw up ahead of them, on a windy hill above the shore, a great circle of wooden palisades, smoke rising from within, and knew their journey was nearly done.

On a high dune sat a single warrior on a skewbald pony, waiting for them. When he saw them he rode down and came easily towards them. He wore leather breeches and a strip of bearskin around his shoulders and carried a spear. His bare flesh was blue with cold, as blue as the ink-dyed weals across his cheeks, and curling and whorled across his chest and back. He did not feel the cold.

He stopped in front of them and nodded. He spoke, and Branoc translated.

'You can only have your father back at a great price.'

Marcus smiled. 'Lead us to him,' he said.

A track led through the marram grass to the gate of the Attacotti camp. It was lined with stakes, and on each stake was impaled a human head. Crows and gulls were eating from them. Everywhere there were totems of witchcraft, crucified birds nailed to crosses, figurines of feather and fur, eyes hollowed out from wooden masks, mouths agape and crying out in silent horror. Branoc eyed the totems and sucked in his breath through clenched teeth. Such evil would not wash away for generations.

Marcus stayed his men at the gate to the camp and rode on in with Milo and Branoc close behind him.

On a raised platform sat the Attacotti chieftain. He was old but powerfully built. He nodded to the three men and ordered them to dismount. They did so. He stood and came towards them. His eyes were red-rimmed and bloodshot, and he carried a hobnailed club. He stopped in front of them.

'So you are the Iron Hats who have followed us for so long. You value your mighty man highly?'

'We do,' said Marcus.

'So do we,' spat back the chieftain. He turned and called out for two of his warriors, Sky-in-Tatters and Bloody Midnight, to bring the mighty man. Marcus had a terrible vision of Lucius being dragged out through the mud laden with chains, beaten and bruised, and where his eyes had been, two scabbed sockets. But when he came, he came as serenely as Marcus had ever seen him. He stood tall in his filthy long tunic, his feet bare, his gaze distant and unperturbed. His left arm was tucked neatly into the folds of his tunic. Marcus then thought he might have gone mad with his suffering, taking refuge, as men sometimes must, from the howling of the world's pain inside the quiet cave of his own mind. But Lucius levelled his gaze upon him and said softly, 'Marcus.'

Marcus did not know what to say. Suddenly there was a cry and a shape flurried past. The surrounding tribesmen hefted their spears in readiness, and the shape fell upon Lucius. It was Julia. She flung her arms around him and wept. Lucius reached out and put his right arm around her and bowed his face and kissed the top of her head and murmured to her words that no one else could hear. Her inner tumult was so great that she broke into a fit of fierce coughing and held her sleeve up to her mouth. Lucius patted her on the back.

The chieftain scowled at the female and ordered her to be pulled off. Julia had the wisdom not to fight back, and was held between two tribesmen like a slave. Her eyes sparkled and shone, she could not tear her gaze from her uncle. She seemed indifferent to anything else around her, quite unaware of any danger.

The chieftain grinned. His teeth were filed to sharp points.

'Here is your deal,' he said. 'You take the mighty man, we keep the female. Has she given birth?'

Marcus grinned back. 'No deal,' he said.

The chieftain lost his temper with remarkable rapidity. He chomped his mouth and then hissed, 'You are in no position to bargain with me, you are half-dead already. You will do as we tell you or we will kill you all.'

'And you are a disgusting old cannibal,' replied Marcus, 'with ridiculous pointy teeth and the most terrible halitosis. And no, *we* will kill *you* all.'

Behind his back, fighting down a powerful urge to laugh, Milo signalled to the men at the gate to get their hands on the hilts of their swords.

Branoc took a deep breath and, already reaching for his knife, translated Marcus' last words.

'Kill them!' screamed the chieftain.

☆ ☆ ☆

Afterwards, Marcus knew that he had really had no choice but to fight a pitched battle with them. But it was a terrible battle, and if he had known the consequences . . . Two hours later, the Attacot women and children had fled into the hills, with only a handful of their warriors left. The rest lay dead in and around their camp, as many as two hundred of them. Among them lay the bodies of his slain soldiers. Of the sixty that had ridden out with him, fewer than forty would be riding back. But he knew that they regarded that as a fair deal. They had won. They had got back the prisoner. Those who had survived had survived. It was a fair deal for any soldier.

Among the wounded was Milo. He was slumped, half-sitting, half-lying, in the dust in the corner of the camp. Marcus went over to him and Milo grinned up at him.

'On your feet, soldier.' He kicked him gently.

'Just a few more minutes, officer,' whispered Milo.

The grin was fine – the grin was pure Milo. But the whisper wasn't right. His voice had lost all its force. The roots of Marcus' hair felt cold and damp. He knelt in the dust beside him. The centurion's arms were clamped across his chest, and blood was welling from under them. Marcus understood.

Milo saw the look in Marcus' eyes. The understanding. It was all right. Milo felt strangely content.

Milo suddenly remembered some line of poetry from his boyhood. *Farewell, warm time. Hail, cold eternity.*

Never would he have that good farmland in the south country, or that pretty, plump little wife. Or the gout, or the palsy, or take slow and stumbling steps to his cold grave. He'd die like a soldier, sword at his side.

Ah well.

Into your hands, O gods – whoever you are – I commend my soul.

Julia was suddenly kneeling beside him. She reached out her hand and touched Milo's arm and then quickly withdrew it, as if stung. As if she had touched ice.

Milo eyed her. 'Lady.' He struggled for breath. 'Save your energy.'

Marcus wanted to tell him to hold on, that he would make it, that they would get him back in one piece. But there comes a time when such urgings are merely undignified. Instead he stretched out his hand and laid it on Milo's shoulder.

'Pleasure working with you, soldier,' whispered Milo, his voice almost inaudible. 'You did the right thing. *Mostly.*' He saw his optio's glistening eyes. 'You big nancy,' he whispered. He closed his eyes.

Julia had blood on her sleeve too. Marcus pointed to it. 'You hurt?'

She shook her head.

'Well, what is it?'

She couldn't say. She shook her head again, her cheeks livid with something suppressed, censored. Then she burst into another fit of coughing, holding her sleeve. When she drew it away, there was fresh blood on it. Marcus stared at it stupidly.

'It's what I believe the doctors call,' she said gently, 'a *pulmonary phthisis.*'

The words sank in: the dry Greek, Julia's own dry, unself-pitying, sweet, soft voice. He felt furious with her more than anything else. That she should come with them here, in winter, knowing that she had ... Marcus backed away and then whirled around and bawled into the air above him, 'Fire the camp and then move out!'

They dragged the bodies of the slain tribesmen inside the camp and uprooted the vile stakes along the pathway and tossed them in too. Then they closed the gates and piled up brush-wood and driftwood against them and set the whole thing alight.

After that they dug into a nearby dune and buried their own dead. Marcus ordered his men to find a flat stone and write on it the names of the dead and set it into the sand. He himself found another flat stone, a good size, and carved some words on it and then rode inland a little way and set it firmly in the earth. It read simply,

Near this place died Decius Milo
Soldier

He rode back to the shore and formed his men up in a column. They moved out.

He rode at the head with Branoc. Behind them rode Lucius and Julia. They said little to each other; Lucius, in fact, barely spoke at all. But the silence between them seemed full of words, full of communication and feeling. They rode so close that Marcus felt almost jealous, but he stamped on the unworthy feeling. He prayed for them both: his beloved guardian, riding serenely, as if no longer quite of this world, his left arm always tucked into his tunic so that no one should know of his suffering; and the woman he loved – the woman they both loved – riding with sparkling eyes, and hectic cheeks, and a racking cough, flushed and happy and for once needing nothing more than what she had beside her.

CHAPTER TWENTY-ONE

The ride back was long and arduous, and took many days, but at last they came to the Wall and re-entered the Empire of Rome. The doctor at the camp shook his head when he examined Julia and said that she must rest, but it would be best for her to go south, best of all to be back at home in London with the fine city doctors to care for her. Marcus wondered whether to send her back by sea, but the wind was all wrong and seemed set in for days. They would have to travel overland.

They travelled with a much larger train of men, Julia now lying in a baggage wagon, her breath laboured, wanting Lucius with her often. Marcus prayed for her every waking hour. He slept little.

At the end of the first day's ride beyond the Wall, Branoc took his leave.

'I must return to my wife and my sons and my calamities,' he said. 'I will petition the goddess for the health of your wife.'

'She's not my wife,' said Marcus.

Branoc gave a slight, quick smile. Then he looked grave again. 'The ways of the goddess are very strange. I should have died in the camp, not the soldier Milo. He was a good man, and it was I who should have died in place of him, to pay you back for the two times that you saved my life. But instead here I am, still alive, and Milo lies dead.'

'Maybe,' said Marcus slowly, 'maybe the goddess looked

down, and saw that though Milo was a good man, he had no wife or children. Whereas you have a wife and two sons and three . . . calamities. Maybe,' he added, 'maybe to the goddess, daughters are not such calamities.'

Branoc thought for a moment and then grinned widely. 'And maybe you're not so stupid after all, for an Iron Hat!' He thumped Marcus hard on the back. 'Brother, we will meet again, and then get very drunk!' And with that he galloped furiously away across the moor and was gone.

They were coming down through Hertfordshire when the weather turned atrocious, cutting in from the east and freezing the dew on the axles of the wagons. Marcus looked anxiously over Julia, terrified that she might be unable to breathe the glacial air at all. Lucius read his mind, and told him that one of the villas of Flavius Martinus, the governor, was not far from the road a few miles on. They rode fast and arrived there at nightfall. The slaves showed them into the covered hallway. After a few minutes, Calpurnia herself appeared. She was wearing mourning. There was no time for her to explain. They carried Julia inside and laid her down in a warm room with a charcoal brazier and soft blankets.

'My poor child,' Calpurnia kept saying, kneeling beside her bed and resting her cool hand on Julia's clammy forehead, 'my poor darling. Oh God be with you, my poor child.' Her eyes brimmed with tears. 'She must stay here.'

'She needs the London doctors,' said Marcus.

Calpurnia did not look up at him, but continued to gaze down on the sick girl, willing her to live. 'The doctors can come out to her here,' she murmured. 'Offer them all the gold I have. But make them come now. She must rest here.'

Lucius took her hand and raised her to her feet. Despite her grief, Calpurnia was startled at his touch. Quintilianus was not a man who usually took ladies' hands. But something had changed in him. Everything had changed. In his eyes were both serenity and horror. There was no time to tell all, though, and he might not tell all anyway, even in time. She knew that he had vanished north of the Wall – and now here he was again.

'My husband,' she said, waving her hand over her mourning robes, 'my beloved Martinus – he killed himself.'

Lucius didn't understand.

'London is a nest of vipers,' she said. 'At the heart of the nest is the Imperial Secretary, Paulus Catena. The Chain. He has done nothing but accuse innocent men of treachery, of being supporters of the usurper Magnentius – and when they have denied it, he has taken them and put them to the most terrible tortures. When they die, he seizes their wealth and land. Oh Lucius,' she wept, 'it is a new barbarism.'

Lucius thought for a while. Then he said, 'Martinus stood accused?'

She shook her head. 'My husband was so outraged at the turn events were taking that he tried to intervene.' She smiled in spite of herself. 'Dear Martinus was never much of a politician. His idea of intervening was simply to go blundering into the cells beneath the Vicarius' Palace, alone, sword at his side, and challenge Catena to stop what he was doing or die. Catena ridiculed him, and when Martinus attacked him, Catena simply had him thrown into a cell. Apparently he told my husband that he would be back tomorrow to put him to the torture. I think the man is a little mad, as well as evil. I think for him, the spectacle of human suffering is like an afternoon at the arena.' Calpurnia held her breath and stifled her sobs. She touched a handkerchief to the corners of her eyes. 'When they came back the next day, they found that – like the noblest Romans – Martinus had fallen on his sword.'

Lucius held Calpurnia's hand in his own, more tightly. 'He died well,' he said. 'He was a good man. As for Catena – there is no knowing what drives men to such evil. Perhaps he has suffered evil himself before. Some who suffer evil, become noble under it. Others become evil themselves. There is no knowing.'

'What are you going to do now?' she asked after a while. 'You can't go back to London.'

'We must,' said Lucius. 'We must go now. To bring justice to bear on that nest of vipers. And to get doctors for . . .' He could not even bring himself to say her name now. So fragile that it might break with saying.

Calpurnia raised his hand to her lips. Quintilianus kept his left hand concealed in his robes – she wondered why. But she raised his right hand to her lips and kissed it and let him go.

Julia's sleep was fitful and feverish and Calpurnia watched over her. She tossed and turned under her sheets, eyes half-closed, perspiring. Calpurnia bent over her and cooled her brow with a damp cloth. When Julia looked up at her and murmured, 'Mother,' Calpurnia thought her heart would break.

Later, it seemed she had fallen asleep, and Calpurnia snuffed out the lamps and closed the door behind her. But Julia's sleep was worse than her waking; it was nightmare-ridden. Troubled dreams of her whole life condensed into a single day's journey, with a sea-crossing from Spain in the morning, a long, lazy afternoon in a London garden, and then a darkening evening riding over high mountains under a louring sky. She dreamed they came at last to a thorn tree in the middle of a desolate moor, and there was Marcus impaled upon it, crucified like a common criminal, and she awoke with a start. She knew then that he was in terrible danger. He and her uncle both. They had gone to London, into the vipers' nest, and they would suffer the worst.

In a last, consumptive burst of febrile energy, Julia made her way to the stables. Everyone else was asleep. The chilling wind had died down now and out of the sky fell soft snow. She found a fine grey mare and, with trembling hands, laid a

saddle-cloth across her back, and fitted a bridle and reins.
Then, with a head as light and fizzing as a shower of sparks,
she walked the mare out of the stableyard on to the muffled
white road and mounted up and galloped for London.

In the main audience chamber of the Vicarius' Palace sat three
men. A fourth one stood uneasily. The man on the high dais
was broad-shouldered, with a cleft chin and dark, searching,
restless eyes. To his right sat a burly, blond-haired man, and by
his side another thinner man with sloping shoulders and pale,
watery eyes. Around the room paced the fourth man, in a long
white tunic and with a big silver Chi-Rho symbol on his chest.

'And so Martinus was never put to any questioning?' asked
the man on the high dais. His voice was smooth and utterly
commanding.

'No, Your Eternity,' said Paulus Catena. 'That, of course,
would have been the natural thing to do the following day. But
by the time we returned to his cell, he had already killed
himself in a shameful act of self-slaughter, against all the tenets
of the Christian religion.'

Constantius waved his hand impatiently at this. Theology,
for once, was not his primary concern. 'And Septimius? And
Gallus? And all the rest?'

'Everywhere we looked, Your Eternity, we found more and
more evidence of sedition, of lingering support for the revolt of
Magnentius.'

'So you continually tell me. And the wealth that was
sequestrated from these – seditionists? What has become of
that?'

Albinus shifted in his seat and looked a little to the right of
the Emperor. 'It is all safely reserved under the auspices of a
specially created office of the vicarial jurisidiction, Your Eternity.'

Constantius gave a thin smile. 'What an amusingly elaborate way you have of describing your own pocket, Albinus.'

The Vicarius flinched visibly.

Constantius' smile vanished. He was not here to be amused. He did not have time to come over from Gaul to this decaying little corner of his Empire, to sort out the incompetence and malpractices of his officials. But it seemed that he must. He had heard that his hitherto trusty, if sometimes over-zealous servant, Paulus Catena, was wreaking havoc in London. And the people of London were an awkward, pig-headed bunch, always complaining and revolting about something or other. It was bad policy to antagonise them needlessly. 'The whole thing is a mess. You have done nothing but increase local hostility to Our Person. I despatched you to Britain, Catena, entrusted with the delicate mission of obtaining information regarding any remaining opposition to Our Rule, especially from pagan quarters. Instead, together with these two shifty-looking brothers – appointees of my own poor, departed brother, alas – you have done more damage in this benighted diocese than Magnentius himself.' He considered. 'Finish off whoever remains in your custody and dispose of them discreetly, and then there are to be *no more* arrests. Who does remain in your custody?'

Catena spoke calmly, despite his inner fury at the Emperor's criticisms. 'In the cells at the moment, Your Eternity, we have Quintilianus, the erstwhile Praepositus, and by all accounts – against the reports that we had received previously – a deeply dishonest man who has done nothing but line his pockets since the day he began his post. He is a follower of Greek philosophy, too, rather than the True Religion, and given to a number of unorthodox pronouncements. He is also inexplicably popular with the common people in this city. We suspect he may have been peculating from the Imperial coffers, and then using the money to buy popular favour. Casting his gold before swine.' Catena waited for the Emperor to smile at his little joke. Constantius remained impassive. Catena clenched his fists and went on. 'We also have his ward, the young soldier called Marcus Flavius Aquila. We spoke to him at the camp in Syria –'

'I remember,' cut in the Emperor. 'Do you think me so old and forgetful, Catena?'

Catena swallowed. 'Quintilianus and Aquila were north of the Wall recently, perhaps fomenting disorder among the tribes – questioning so far has revealed nothing, they are as stubborn as mules. They came storming back to London, all ready to accuse *us* of injustice and treachery –'

The Emperor held up his hand. He thought for a while, his eyes fixed on Catena. At last he said, 'How strange your account is, my good and faithful servant. As you know, I have long heard reports of this Quintilianus, and although I was perturbed about his beliefs, I had – *have* – no reason to doubt his loyalty. His ward, too, this Aquila, I liked when we had audience. I cannot help thinking how unlikely your account is, my dear Paulus.' Now the Emperor smiled. Catena wished he hadn't. His smile was worse. 'Nevertheless, you leave us in an awkward position. For the public good and common weal, it may well be better now to despatch these two men in secret. For surely, after having been "questioned" by you, they will be very bitter against us.'

There was no time to say more. There was a sudden hubbub outside, and seconds later the doors were flung open and in marched a diminutive female figure in a soaking wet riding cloak. She marched straight up to the high dais and stopped before the Emperor. She threw her hood back and bowed briefly. Her face was very pale but her eyes were bright with passion. Against all the rules of court etiquette, she began to speak.

She spoke in a ceaseless torrent of eloquence. She told the Emperor all that had happened. She flattered him cunningly, by saying how relieved she was to find him in Britain, come to set his diocese aright. And she impressed him genuinely with her fervour and her seeming loyalty to her own line. Quintilianus and Aquila were both good men, she said. There had been treachery, but it was not from them. It was from another quarter. She turned and shot Catena such a look of hatred that he felt as if he couldn't breathe. He felt momentarily that he had been buried alive.

Loyalty to one's own was something that Constantius had always admired. Finally, the girl produced a letter from the folds of her dress. It was damp but legible. Constantius read it, and then looked up and stared very hard at Catena. He tutted and shook his head. He then turned and dropped the letter in the brazier by his side and watched it smoulder briefly and then burst into flames.

'Call up the prisoners.'

When Lucius and Marcus finally stood before him, Constantius thought he had never seen two men look so tired.

'We had every good reason to believe that you were guilty of the gravest sedition,' he declared to the two bewildered and blinking men. 'Your loyalty was seriously in question. However, thanks to this lady here, your niece, I believe, Quintilianus? Thanks to her, a letter has come to our attention which we cannot disregard. I recognise the second hand on it myself.' He looked across at Catena. The secretary seemed uncomfortable, but Constantius knew of old that this was not the same thing as remorseful. Catena knew as much about remorse as a horse knows about Plato.

'We are granting a general amnesty to all remaining prisoners. You, Paulus, will sail for Gaul on the evening tide. You, Albinus, and you, ah . . .

'Sulpicius, Your Eternity.'

'Sulpicius, yes, of course.' In truth, Constantius knew it very well, but he had long since learned that there was no better way to make someone feel inferior than persistently to forget their name. 'You and your brother will sail for Gaul with him. In Trier we will find you each a bureaucratic position – an extremely modest position – more suited to your talents.'

Albinus' shoulders slumped. Catena headed for the door. Constantius ordered him to wait. He turned to Lucius.

344

'Praepositus,' he said. 'The release of yourself and your ward is conditional upon you both keeping silent about the circumstances of your arrest and questioning. It would not do to have the common people get all – *excited* about it. Do I have your word?'

Lucius nodded, so slowly that it seemed as if his head was made of lead. 'You have my word.'

'So: how would the position of Vicarius of Britain suit you?' He knew he would say no, so it was a safe offer.

Lucius smiled. He had never felt so tired. 'I thank Your Eternity, but I regret to say I am too old for such a demanding position. I would happily return to my old position as Praepositus.'

Constantius hummed. 'And I understand that there has never been a more honest and respected Praepositus in the province. However – the answer is no. You are to retire. You have done enough.'

Lucius felt the weight lift off his shoulders for the first time in thirty years. The burden was gone, the journey was over. He bowed his head and dreamed of sleep.

'And you, Optio?'

'I would . . . I would request to quit the military life, Your Eternity.'

Constantius raised his eyebrows. 'Oh? When the Empire is so short of good men and officers? Including intelligence officers?'

Marcus looked him steadily in the eye. 'I would no longer be a good officer, Your Eternity. And I was never a good intelligence officer.'

Constantius thought for a while, not pleased. But at last he snapped, 'Very well. Your commission is at an end. Make good use of it, whatever it is you find so necessary to do.'

He turned finally to Julia and merely waited. She tried to speak but she could not find the words. The words sounded distantly in her head, but she could not let them out. This is how Cennla must feel, she was thinking. The room spun about her, and her head was light and cold and haloed with frosty air. The ceiling was spinning, and the walls . . .

'Look to the lady,' said the Emperor.

She lay in a darkened room – her old room, the room she had slept in since childhood, in the house of her uncle beside Walbrook Stream. She lay on her back with her eyes closed. A single lamp burned in the corner of the room, on a three-legged lamp-stand. Lucius sat to one side of her in a basket-chair. To the other side knelt Marcus, touching a cooling cloth to her forehead.

The doctors came, and pronounced a pulmonary phthisis, just as Julia had foretold. They came and stood over her, and frowned, and tutted, and then suggested that she inhale thrice daily from a steaming bowl of water infused with sage and coriander. And then they quoted Hippocrates, and Galen, and Celsus, and they sighed, and said that it was in the lap of the gods, and through her fevered haze she begged them to go away. Which, with pompous and injured tread, they did.

Late into the night, Marcus looked up and saw that Lucius had fallen asleep in his chair. Julia herself was still awake. He said to her, 'What on earth made you come back from Hertfordshire when you did?'

'I knew you were in danger,' she said. He looked blank. She said, 'Sometimes you just know. And I had Cennla's letter. I knew I had to be here.'

'You always have to be there,' he teased her. 'You had to be there north of the Wall too.' And now look what it's done to you, he added to himself. But he couldn't say it. He couldn't be angry with her. She had known how ill she was, and what that journey would do to her, and still she had come. And now look what it had done to her. Now she was leaving him. But he couldn't be angry. She was what she was. He wouldn't have loved her different.

She whispered something to him. He couldn't hear her, and leaned closer. She said, 'You must marry again.'

He realised that, in her delirium, she believed they had already been married. He smiled. 'I will,' he lied.

'But,' she went on, strangely excited though as weak as a kitten, 'we shall meet again, beyond the river. I know we will. I can already see it.' She lay back, exhausted. Exhausted but triumphant. It was all as it was meant to be. The sorrow was left for the living, and for them she prayed. For the two men that she loved the most.

But she had lived and her life was done, and now she was on the last journey, back to her parents, with a head full of stories and a soul full of wisdom. And one day another two figures, the two men that she loved most, would come across that glittering river, that thin divide between the living and dead, nature and supernature, and they all would be reunited, never to be divided though the mountains melt in the sun.

She reached out and touched him. Her hand was as cold as death. And as she touched him, it was as if a bolt of pain passed over to him; but abstract pain, and also the power to take that pain away.

He leaned closer still to her, so that her soft black ringlets tickled his unshaven cheek. 'I love you, Julia,' he said.

'I love you too, Marcus Flavius Aquila,' she whispered back. 'Why have you got so many more names than me?' She laughed a little, and it turned into a cough, and a little spray of blood came from her mouth. He mopped it up with a cloth.

'Hold me up,' she said.

He slipped his right arm underneath her back and raised her up. He enfolded her in his arms and clasped her tightly and buried his face in her hair, and he felt that his heart was breaking. She reached up and laid her cold hand on his shoulder. They stayed like that for some time. And then her arm slipped from his shoulder and lay motionless at her side. He reached down and took her arm and laid it back across his shoulder so that it stayed there. They stayed like that for a long time.

At dawn, Lucius rose from his chair and kissed her cold cheek and touched Marcus on the shoulder. Then he went away to his rooms. He knew that his heart had broken, but it had not broken with a shattering pain. It was more like it had crumbled away into dust, with a resigned sigh, like an old manuscript no longer needed. There in his rooms, serenely, he lay down and folded his arms across his chest, the rolled book of his beloved Cicero's *Dream of Scipio* by his side, and slept forever.

They buried her alongside her uncle, in the finest plot beside Ermine Street on the road to York, just outside the city gate. Her uncle was buried in a fine mausoleum, and she in the ground beside him, with only the shaped lid of her sarcophagus left visible. They buried her among the dark yews and the resplendent tombs and mausolea where she and Cennla had once slept the night as runaway children, long ago, under a quartermoon. She wore her finest robes, of silk and wool shot through with golden thread; her hair was tied up and dressed, and her head laid down on a bed of fresh bay leaves. The coffin was of lead, decorated with moulded scallop shells, proudly pagan, to symbolise a safe passage to the afterlife. The coffin in turn was laid in a great sarcophagus of Barnack stone. Beside the stone sarcophagus, Marcus laid the gleaming black jewellery and hair decorations of Whitby jet that he had brought for her from the North, and that she had so loved. 'It matches my wonderful, lustrous eyes, does it not?' she had said, twirling around before him, laughing, showing off abominably. How he had loved her. Now he could barely see for blurring eyes as he laid the jet beside her.

Among the cortège, behind the official mourners, walked Marcus, with Mus following on behind him, red-eyed and snuffling. Then came Bricca, weeping softly, her shawl pulled over her head in mourning, and the other slaves of the household: Valentinus, Bonosius, Sannio, Silvanus, and Vertissa. And behind them, a snub-nosed, ageing little pedagogue called Hermogenes, who tried desperately to think lofty and consoling philosophical thoughts, and failed miserably. There also walked with them Calpurnia, who felt she had lost both a husband and a daughter of late. And further back in the crowd stood the wealthy merchant, Solimarius Secundinus and his wife, their two married daughters with their husbands, and also Aelia, who had so worshipped Julia as a girl.

As well as the imposing cortège, the streets of the city, and Ermine Street beyond, were lined with the citizens of London, much moved by the news of the death of their good, honest City Treasurer, the gentle, incorruptible old Roman, who had once imposed a fine upon a pork butcher; and then paid the fine himself. They were much moved, too, by the news of the death of his beautiful niece, who had died from a midnight ride in winter, to save the lives of the two men that she loved the most.

It was some weeks later, in the early Bordeaux spring, that a poet called Ausonius heard of the sad news of the death of Quintilianus, the Praepositus of London, and of his beautiful, fiery niece, whom the poet remembered dining with on one occasion, years ago, and finding so fascinating. He smiled sadly to himself, acknowledging that he had fallen a little in love with her. He guessed that every man who had ever met her had fallen a little in love with her.

Two days later he went walking through his fields, and a poem came into his head. Though it was hardly the time of year for elegies, with the spring bursting out beneath his feet and around his head as he walked, he realised that the poem was an elegy of sorts for the girl he had once met and never forgotten, and for her stern, good uncle.

They wander in deep woods, in mournful light,
Amid long reeds and drowsy headed poppies,
And lakes where no wave laps, and voiceless streams,
Upon whose banks in the dim light grow old
Flowers that were once bewailèd names of kings.

When he wrote the poem down and read it again, Ausonius felt that it was an epitaph not just for the beautiful girl from London and her uncle, but for the whole of the pagan world itself, to which they had so proudly belonged, and which was now paling and passing into history.

EPILOGUE

Some years later, on a summer's afternoon, a small boy was playing by the marshy banks of the River Lea, where his family lived. They were Danish immigrants. The boy's name was Hakon.

On an island in the middle of the river, there lived a hermit. The hermit frightened the little boy. He had only three fingers on one hand, and a cruel scar on his arm. Each day, the hermit walked all the way into London town. One day, Hakon followed the hermit without him noticing. On his way, the hermit stopped to pick wildflowers: red campion and white campion, herb robert, yellow archangel. Then he walked on to the great north road, Ermine Street, and he laid some of the flowers down on the grass beside a mausoleum, and some upon a buried sarcophagus. He knelt and seemed to pray for a while, and then he walked back to his island.

After that, Hakon often followed the hermit to the town, and one day the hermit stopped to talk to him, and told him that his two fingers had been bitten off by a dreadful dragon in the desert. Hakon thought he must be very brave, and so they became friends.

One day Hakon went to the hermit feeling very sad, because his father was ill and looked as if he was going to die, and his mother and sisters were all weeping and wailing and making a real noise. And so the hermit came to where his father lay and talked to him for a while, and then he laid his hand on his father's forehead a while longer, and then he went away. The next day, Hakon's father was better.

Hakon went with his father to say thank you, but the hermit didn't want to be thanked very much and talked about other things. Hakon asked the hermit why he hadn't cured himself, if he could cure people, and given himself back his two lost fingers? The hermit laughed and said the one person a healer couldn't heal was himself. Or herself. He said that he had known someone else once, who had the gift of healing, but she . . . And he stopped and looked sad.

Then the hermit said something to Hakon's father, something about how the dead still walk with us, and it is love that keeps us alive, both before death and after it. And his father nodded and looked very wise, like the hermit himself, but Hakon got bored and went off to look for eels instead.

But that was how the news of the hermit on the island spread. And that was how Hakon saw him ever after, as he grew older: sitting on his island and healing the people who came to him. Touching them lightly with his three-fingered hand, with the sun setting over distant London, and the ivy leaves touched with gold about his hut, and the sun brazen on the waters of the Lea. And him smiling, that young-old hermit, and the people coming to him, running to him, and him healing them, healing them, far beyond the sounds of walls and empires crumbling . . .

NOTES ON THE CHARACTERS

Decius Clodius Albinus
Is fictional, as is Sulpicius, I am delighted to say. But there was
certainly still a Vicarius of Britain at that time, and public and
official buildings which may have been his residence have been
discovered and thoroughly excavated, where they once stood
beside the Thames, and on the east bank of the Walbrook,
where Cannon Street Station now stands. The buildings
included a 115-foot pond and fountain, an 82-foot hall, and a
number of similarly vast staterooms.

The Attacotti
I regret to say were all too real, and practising cannibals to
boot. Had this information come from a Roman military
source, we might suspect propaganda. But the grisly details
come from no less an authority than Saint Jerome, who
records that the Attacotti tribes were marauding through Gaul
towards the end of the fourth century AD – and eating human
flesh.

Ausonius
Was a real, and mostly rather bad poet – but an endearing
character, all the same. I am particularly touched by the story
that, when his little son, also called Ausonius, died in infancy,
the mourning poet buried him in the same grave as his
great-grandfather, 'so that he should not be lonely', a story that

I mention in the novel. Ausonius wrote a great deal of poetry about the varieties of fish to be found in the River Moselle. He was nominally Christian, but didn't seem too exercised about it. He did indeed have an uncle, Contemtus, who was buried at Richborough, as he says at the dinner party with Julia. And after the events of this novel, he passed a happy retirement among his vineyards of Bordeaux, 'the nest of my old age', as he called it. Here he wrote a lot more bad poetry, and also his memoirs, which are still extant and have a gentle charm. The most beautiful translations of his best poems are to be found in Helen Waddell's superb anthology, *Medieval Latin Lyrics*. It is her translation of Ausonius' *The Fields of Sorrow* which appears at the end of Chapter 21. In this one brief poem, as Waddell puts it, Ausonius 'has created the twilight world of Western Europe'.

Branoc
Is fictional, but his name is not. I took it from the (Celtic) name of an excellent beer, Branoc Ale, which is only brewed at one of the finest pubs in England: The Fountainhead, Branscombe, in Devon. I have spent many happy evenings in Branoc's company.

Constans
Was a real character. All the details of his fondness for handsome German youths, his military incompetence, his rather farcical campaign in Britain and his ignominious end are correct. The standard source for him, and this entire period, is the entertaining and reasonably objective *History* of Ammianus Marcellinus; but for the best account of Constans, and his rather more effective (or ruthless) big brother, Constantius, see Gibbon's *Decline and Fall of the Roman Empire*.

Constantius
Continued to reign after the events of this book, in a state of ever-increasing paranoia, until his death at the age of forty-

five, in AD 361. His character, says Gibbon, was composed of 'pride and weakness, of superstition and cruelty', and he damns him finally in a typically Gibbonian put-down: 'The last of the sons of Constantine may be dismissed from the world with the remark, that he inherited the defects, without the abilities, of his father.'

Hakon

We know nothing about, except his name, and that he once lived by the marshy riverbanks of the River Lea in what is now East London. In time, etymologists tell us, Hakon raised a family on an island there, and it became known in Danish as 'Hakon's Ea' (*ea* being Danish for island). Nowadays the area is better known as Hackney.

Lucius

Is entirely fictional, although there must have been a Praepositus at the time of the story. However, certain of the details of his life are true. The temple of Mithras, for instance, really did stand on the east bank of the Walbrook, as I have described, on the site now occupied by Bucklersbury House. During the riots of the Christians, in Chapter 7, Sicilius is said to have buried the stone heads of Mithras and Serapis. In fact, the temple was excavated in 1954, and concealed heads of Mithras and Serapis were discovered, apparently having been buried in haste, some time during the fourth century, to prevent desecration. These can now be seen in the Museum of London, while the outline of the temple itself has been recreated on another part of the site in Queen Victoria Street.

Marcus

Is fictional, but I have deliberately taken his name from the work of Rosemary Sutcliff, as any readers of her brilliant books for children (and discerning adults), such as *Eagle of the Ninth*, will recognise. This borrowing is intended as tribute, not plagiarism.

Flavius Martinus

Was a real, and ultimately rather tragic character, though his wife, **Calpurnia**, is invented. Ammianus writes that Paulus Catena's treatment of Martinus was the 'one especial atrocity which has branded the time of Constantius with indelible infamy. Martinus,' continues Ammianus, 'who at that time governed these provinces as deputy, being greatly concerned for the sufferings inflicted on innocent men, and making frequent entreaties that those who were free from all guilt might be spared, when he found that he could not prevail, threatened to withdraw from the province . . . Paulus, thinking that this conduct of Martinus was a hindrance to his own zeal . . . attacked the deputy himself . . . Martinus, alarmed at this threat, and seeing the imminent danger in which his life was, drew his sword and attacked Paulus. But because from want of strength in his hand he was unable to give him a mortal wound, he then plunged his drawn sword into his own side. And by this unseemly kind of death that most just man departed from life . . .' He was arguably the first man in British history to die a martyr's death for the sake of, if not exactly democracy and human rights, then at least the rule of law. As Peter Salway writes in the *Oxford History of Roman Britain*, 'His name deserves to be remembered.'

Paulus Catena, 'The Chain'

Was, alas, all too real. Ammianus Marcellinus writes of him, 'Of this Court [i.e. Constantius'], a most conspicuous member was Paulus, the secretary, a native of Spain, a man keeping his aims concealed beneath a smooth countenance, and acute beyond all men in smelling out secret ways to bring others into danger. He, having been sent into Britain to arrest some military officers who had dared to favour the conspiracy of Magnentius, as they could not resist, licentiously exceeded his commands, and like a flood poured with sudden violence upon the fortunes of a great number of people, making his path through manifold slaughter and destruction, loading the bodies of free-born men with chains, and crushing some with fetters, while patching up all sorts of accusations far removed from the truth.'

We meet Catena again in Ammianus' history, in AD 359, in the East, where he is still 'skilful in all contrivances of cruelty, making gain and profit of tortures and executions, as a master of gladiators does of his fatal games. He did not abstain even from theft, and invented all kinds of causes for the destruction of innocent men.' But Catena met the end he deserved: in the novel, Julia's look of hatred makes him feel as if he can't breathe. And, sure enough, that was how he ended up. He was arrested for extortion and corruption under the pagan Emperor Julian in AD 361, and, as Ammianus says, 'It was only a deserved destiny which befell Apodemius . . . and also Paulus, the secretary, surnamed "the Chain", men who are never spoken of without general horror, and who were now sentenced to be buried alive.'

Shapur

'We must admire not only the fortune, but the genius, of Sapor [Shapur],' writes Gibbon. He was indeed one of the outstanding military leaders of his age, still campaigning long after the events of this book, and coming back to besiege Nisibis yet again in AD 360. He continued to war relentlessly with Rome until his death in AD 380, at the age of seventy. Peace between the two great powers followed soon after, with an exchange of gifts including gems, silk and Indian elephants.

Vidalius

Is fictional, although readers might discern that he bears more than a passing resemblance to a certain contemporary American novelist and essayist, whose opinions on Christianity and whose name are uncannily similar to that of Vidalius.

And last but not least –
Julia

Who is half-real, half-imagined. We do not even know her

name. The bare facts that can be discerned from her remains and her burial are these: she was in her early twenties when she died. She was about 5 feet 4 inches tall and her bones and teeth were in good condition. The fact that she was above average height for a woman of that time, as well as the lavishness of her burial, shows that she was a woman of wealthy family. From her teeth we know she may have spent her childhood in Spain. During formation of the tooth enamel, her teeth absorbed from the water she drank a certain kind of lead which is only found in Spain, Southern France and Italy.

The lead coffin, decorated with scallop shells, but conspicuously lacking any Christian symbols, shows that she lived and died a pagan. The scallop shell was a pagan symbol for the soul's safe journey to the underworld. It was later adopted by the Christians as a symbol of pilgrimage. The lead itself would have come from the mines in the Mendips, transported to London in the form of ingots. The sarcophagus was made of Barnack stone, a limestone quarried in the East Midlands, and it must have cost a great deal of money to transport it to London.

Her graveclothes were made of very expensive silk (brought from China and woven in Syria) and wool, shot through with pure gold thread. Her head was laid to rest on a pillow of fresh bay leaves, miraculously preserved in the bottom of the coffin. Around the sarcophagus were placed a beautiful and very rare glass phial for cosmetic oil, a long jet rod for extracting the oil, as well as a small circular box, a jet pin and a flat jet ring, probably used for binding up long coils of hair. These items may also have had magical properties. The Romans believed that jet would ward off evil spirits on the passage to the afterlife.

There were no signs of violence on her skeleton, so we must assume that she died of an infectious disease. Tuberculosis is a possibility as it rarely leaves any sign of damage to the bones. From her skeleton, also, we know that she never bore a child, which strongly suggests that she was never married. The grave objects buried with her date from the fourth century, so we know roughly when she lived. As the Museum of London sums it up, all we can really surmise of her is that 'she was the unmarried daughter of a rich Roman living in London around AD 350'.

But these are just the kind of details that drive the imagination: why wasn't she married? Why did she die in London when she was raised in Spain? What was it like to be of a prominent pagan family in a Christian (and increasingly intolerant) age? And so the story grew . . .

Now you have read it, and, if I have done my job properly, enjoyed it. And so, the next time you go in or out of Liverpool Street Station, crossing the pavement exactly where the people stood to watch her funeral cortège go by; or you walk up Shoreditch High Street, past the old Roman cemetery, where the dark yews once stood; or gaze out over the Thames, like she did; or pass by the NatWest Tower, just south of the old Roman gate where she knocked for admittance that night with Cennla, after fleeing from the wicked captain; the next time you cross Southwark Bridge, or pass by Cannon Street Station, beside which the Walbrook still flows underground, and the villa of the Praepositus once stood on the opposite bank to the Vicarius' Palace; or further afield, drive round the M25, and pass by Egham and Staines, south of Junction 13, where the old Roman road once crossed the Thames, and she rode out that summer's day for the first time, to the sunlit Cotswolds . . . Any time you pass by any of these places, remember her.

Because she was there too.

SUSAN VREELAND

Girl in Hyacinth Blue

Girl in Hyacinth Blue tells the story of an imaginary painting by Vermeer, and the aspirations and longings of those whose lives it illuminates, and darkens. From a proud father regretting his lost love to a compromised French noblewoman, from a hanged girl to Vermeer's own gifted daughter, Susan Vreeland's beautiful and luminous tales link to form an evocative masterpiece.

'A work of art' *Sunday Telegraph*

'Subtle and atmospheric . . . an impressive debut' *Publishers Weekly*

0 7472 6659 X

review

YVONNE ROBERTS

A History of Insects

It is early 1956 and the British Empire is crumbling. But for nine-year-old Ella, living with her parents at the British High Commission in Peshawar, Pakistan, the walls of class, snobbery and racism are still intact. Growing up is a lonely, painful exprience, and Ella withdraws, recording the hypocrisy of adult behaviour in her diary, *A History of Insects*, where she hides a secret that could shatter the lives of the people around her.

Written from the perspective of a young girl, and with all the charm of *Behind the Scenes at the Museum* and *The God of Small Things*, this is an illuminating and evocative account of the loss of innocence. It heralds a radical departure in Yvonne Roberts' writing, and has been critically acclaimed:

'Unputdownable . . . wonderful novel . . . A mesmerising tale of death and love and passion' *Times Educational Supplement*

'The intricacies of class and the social life of the British High Commission are beautifully observed, and Ella's confusion over race, politics and religion mirrors a society where nothing is quite what it seems' *Bookseller*

'Tells with charm and delicacy the story of a girl's unwitting collusion in her own loss of innocence' *Independent*

'Moving and intelligent' *Publishing News*

'The style is lucid, the plot absorbing and the characters engaging . . . an engrossing read' *Metro*

0 7472 6126 1

review

Now you can buy any of these other
Review titles from your bookshop or
direct from the publisher.

FREE P&P AND UK DELIVERY
(Overseas and Ireland £3.50 per book)

Hens Dancing	Raffaella Barker	£6.99
The Catastrophist	Ronan Bennett	£6.99
Horseman, Pass By	David Crackanthorpe	£6.99
Two Kinds of Wonderful	Isla Dewar	£6.99
Earth and Heaven	Sue Gee	£6.99
Sitting Among the Eskimos	Maggie Graham	£6.99
Tales of Passion, Tales of Woe	Sandra Gulland	£6.99
The Dancers Dancing	Éilís Ní Dhuibhne	£6.99
After You'd Gone	Maggie O'Farrell	£6.99
The Silver River	Ben Richards	£6.99
A History of Insects	Yvonne Roberts	£6.99
Girl in Hyacinth Blue	Susan Vreeland	£6.99
The Long Afternoon	Giles Waterfield	£6.99

TO ORDER SIMPLY CALL THIS NUMBER

01235 400 414

or e-mail orders@bookpoint.co.uk

Prices and availability subject to change without notice.